Scarlet Paths

An Alternate Universe Story

Melissa Plunkett

ISBN print: 979-8-9867536-4-5
ISBN ebook: 979-8-9867536-3-8

To anyone feeling like you're from a different world.

Maybe you are.

Other Titles

andor, the Kingdom of Elves

High Tower

White Star

Grita

Duncan's Village

Highland Road

The Shaking Tusk

Fort Khali

Castle Road

Ghostly Path

The Wildlands

Moren's Fane

Aegan

Mysogus

Legend

--- road
...... path
◇ goddess shrine

Storm Rock

N

1

Surnuna, did they take the right path? The one that didn't end in a mountain of bodies and the ravaging of their kingdom.

Cobble Road zig-zagged through rolling hills and dense forests on the southern edge of the elven kingdom, Eskandor. The path was named for the cobblestones the faithful placed on it from the trading port, Abrita Shores, to Fort Khali—the most eastern garrison of the kingdom. The faithful committed to such tasks to show their unbreakable devotion to the nine elven goddesses. Every stone was placed by hand with love and pride, blessed with the words of the goddesses spoken through the faithful. The trip from port-to-fort lasted two weeks in fair weather.

Gabriel Steel upturned his head to the falling rain. The shower had lasted days and showed no signs of slowing. Traveling in such weather was dreadful, especially for his men, but the ambassador braved the elements for his kingdom—even though it stood divided.

The Corrupted blight grew and the animosity between the crown and its people with it. The wails of those who had died by the Corrupted in the village Haven echoed through the kingdom. Their pain spread like wildfire, but those flames had not burned their king with outrage. Gabriel had not understood the inaction—the injustice of those murdered in Haven. Why had the king not sent reinforcements? Why were they not hunting down all the Corrupted to end this blight?

He shook his head. The blight never truly ended. High Elves, who let dark magics lead them astray, would always become the Corrupted. Gabriel knew this tragedy well. In the Forty-Second Battalion, he had killed many tainted

High Elves—some not even truly Corrupted but had progressed far enough for an order of execution.

The Forty-Second was not a battalion in the traditional sense. It had been a band of misfits recruited to do the dirty work of the crown. For the sake of records and salaries, they had been labeled a battalion. Gabriel had been the orator—the translator and negotiator. His linguistic skills had served him ill growing up in Abrita Shores, but as a vital member of the Forty-Second, he'd developed those skills to serve his brethren effectively. How many times had he talked them out of a fight or execution?

He lowered his gaze back to the road. Shiny white rocks illuminated the route. He wondered how long it took the faithful to place those stones. Had some died before completing this task? Had they given up family and a life to place rocks? Gabriel understood service, but even he had his limits.

The unanswered terror the Corrupted unleashed upon the kingdom weighed heavily on his mind. King Altamost, safe behind the walls of Casimere, the capital, claimed to his supporters all was well. They were making progress, but the ambassador had walked the kingdom alongside his countrymen. He knew the truth. If they continued to do nothing, there would be no kingdom left to save.

Though he had voiced his concerns to the king, such thoughts he kept to himself. Gabriel wouldn't give the king reason to reduce his role as ambassador. Generally, he would be abroad, in some other kingdom, voicing the crown's wishes to their neighbors, but the blight had sealed their borders. From the perspective of the crown, Gabriel's role was to gauge the loyalty of the lords and ladies of every major city, and to assure them the king had their best interests close to his chest. Gabriel knew differently. The king wanted to make sure he stayed in power, especially with the rebellion growing in numbers.

The fishermen, who had survived the attack on Haven, vowed vengeance. They would have nothing short of Altamost's head for the devastation of their people. Gabriel understood their pain, but he didn't believe killing one man, king or not, would help ease that pain. Destroying the Corrupted gave the kingdom a chance, but the rebels were blinded by their hatred to see that.

He exhaled. It had been a long year, but he didn't foresee things improving while the crown and rebels bickered over justice. Gabriel wondered briefly why he hadn't been sent to seek negotiations with the rebel leader, Kanaris, but he could only follow the orders of the king. So far, they hadn't included finding peace.

"Sir, we're here," one of his guards announced. Gabriel blinked at him, his blue cloak and tunic drenched. All his guards wore blue, like the king's guard. Although the ambassador was not royal—far from it—he was a respected envoy of the kingdom. One stationed high enough to fall on the rebel's eradication list.

Gabriel observed where his guard pointed, a tavern, swallowed by the forest around them, called the Crumble Crust. It was a large rectangular building that he knew would house them for the night. Inside, the smell of smoke, sweat, and baked pies greeted them. Gabriel ordered for the men to treat themselves to supper and drinks while he arranged for their rooms.

A plump woman behind the bar took his coin purse with a wide smile. She handed him a set of keys, each for a room down a narrow hall. Gabriel gave the keys to his captain, surveying the rest of the tavern. It was a lively night. Many of the patrons gambled at cards or darts. Men warmed their hands by the fireplace. A young woman plucked the strings of a harp lightly, singing a soft tune about Jana, the Goddess of Harvest, delivering them rain for the good of crops and family.

In the farthest corner from the main entrance, a Shade sat angled so he could see the entire room. Gabriel knew he was one by the black attire he wore. Shades fell under the sign of Wara, the Goddess of Strength and Courage.

Scripture claimed Wara disapproved of her sisters sharing their power with the elves, who she believed to be vulnerable creatures. Without the celestial power to properly harness magic, Wara knew it could poison the minds of weak elves. With this foresight, she had created the Shades. She made them perfect soldiers, purging any emotion that could distract them in battle, eventually creating empty vessels guided only by the goddess's order to protect the kingdom from the Corrupted.

It was strange to see a Shade alone. They generally traveled in units, but this lone wolf, the ambassador found remarkably familiar. A young, quick-tongued Gabriel had found his fair share of trouble when he'd joined ranks of the Forty-Second. He had only survived because he befriended the only other outcast in the battalion—one the others wouldn't dare challenge—the Shade named Vaiden Zarren.

The Forty-Second called them Sun and Moon, like the goddesses Surnuna and Moren. Build-wise they were both over six-foot in lean muscle. Although Vaiden was slightly taller with broader shoulders, Gabriel claimed to have bigger feet.

Vaiden was cold and empty as the night. Gabriel, by comparison, glowed with his sun-kissed skin and golden cloak. He removed his hood, running his fingers through feathery sand-blonde hair that fell past his chin in layers.

As the ambassador moved between tables, mindful of patrons' suspicious looks, the Shade watched him approach. Although Gabriel couldn't see his dark eyes in the shadow of his cowl, he knew Vaiden would never let harm become of his friend, like during their time in the Forty-Second.

"Cozy." Gabriel smiled at him in greeting. He tapped the back of the chair across from Vaiden with his fingers. "This seat taken?"

The Shade gestured at it with his hand dismissively. "How was your hometown of Abrita Shores?"

"Crowded." Gabriel took off his wet cloak and draped it over the back of the chair. The white gambeson appeared dingy from the rain, revealing his rank to the other patrons. He paid no mind, not with Vaiden watching his back. The Shade's eyes scanned the tavern, one hand resting on his hip, fingers playing with the pommel of his short sword strapped to his thigh.

Once Gabriel sat, one of his men brought him tea, soup, and a fresh slice of bread. The ambassador thanked the man, who flashed a wary look at Vaiden then shied away. The Shade ignored him, rolling himself a cigarette.

"What did you find out from the locals?" Gabriel asked, sipping his tea—bitter, but hot.

"Janette makes a wonderful apple pie." Vaiden motioned at the barkeep.

The ambassador frowned. "So, you found nothing at the duke's estate?"

"Say that louder, please. I don't think Opretta heard you."

Opretta, the Goddess of the Arts, was also known as the Bringer of Mystery, Joy, and *Curiosity*. Gabriel glanced over his shoulder, catching a few locals eyeing their table. The ambassador returned his gaze to Vaiden, frowning harder.

"You're right. Most of the trading port has aligned with the rebels," he said, "but did you find any evidence?"

"Nothing on paper." Vaiden lit his cigarette and took a puff. "If his allegiances have shifted, he's being careful not to announce it."

"To insinuate would only be met with outrage, even if it's true."

Vaiden nodded, taking a longer drag from his cigarette. He blew out the smoke slowly, his eyes scanning Gabriel's face. "What else did you learn in Abrita Shores?" he asked.

"Kanaris is in White Star."

"If he's smart, he'll stay there. White Star is a fortress and bloody hard to invade."

"Even by you?"

"It's easier for one person to do it than twenty." He shrugged. "But it's built into the shadow of the mountain. There's no back entrance."

"What about the mountain tunnels?"

Vaiden scowled. "Like I'd risk getting trapped in a small, secluded shaft never to be heard from again."

White Star was a fortress, not because of its size or walls, but because of the elements in the north. The journey up the mountain was enough to make enemies in the past rethink their strategies. It was the perfect place for the rebels to hold up for the winter, though it would not be comfortable living.

"So, I guess we have our next destination," Vaiden said, finishing his smoke.

Gabriel blinked at him.

"White Star."

"No, the king wants us to go to Fort Khali."

The Shade exhaled heavily; a look of disgust flashed across his face before he schooled his features. It was odd to see such emotion on Vaiden's face. Gabriel knew he'd learned to act, to conform around "normal" elves, but a general hollowness could be found in all Shades. Since he had returned from Earth, something about Vaiden had changed.

It had been fifty years since Vaiden first crossed through a door, a giant archway the elves had once believed to be passage to Aegan's banishing realm. There were several of these doors located inside Eskandor's borders. Though the charges had been unprecedented, Vaiden had been found guilty of treason and pushed through one of the doors.

It was the most helpless day of Gabriel's life. He'd begged King Altamost to reconsider. Vaiden had been a pivotal asset of the Forty-Second and a celebrated personal guard to King Rothnar the Daunting. He was a hero, but Altamost had ignored the ambassador's pleas.

Gabriel grieved the loss of his friend for decades, believing he'd found peace in Paradise. When they had learned the doors connected to another world called Earth, Vaiden's mother set out to find her son. After many years, she had sent Gabriel word of his survival.

Because Earth had no tolerance for Shades, claiming they would kill them on sight, Gabriel had been fighting to bring Vaiden home. Altamost had only allowed it because the rebels had managed to invade Casimere. Though he would never admit it, the siege scared the king. Gabriel would be personally responsible for Vaiden though. If anything went wrong—if Vaiden committed a crime—Gabriel would be the one who paid the price.

"For months, I have followed you around and around this godforsaken kingdom," Vaiden began. "Why won't you let me do what I do best? My purpose is to eliminate Kanaris, nothing else."

"I am following the king's orders."

"And the king doesn't want his enemy dead?" Vaiden leaned back in his chair, frowning. "Has Alty had a change of heart?"

Gabriel sipped his tea coolly, collecting his thoughts. "You think you can scale White Star and finish this war by killing Kanaris? It won't. I know that and, deep down, so do you," the ambassador explained. "It's gone too far. Too many have turned rebel. They won't be satisfied until the king is dead, no matter what happens to their leader."

"Then what am I doing here?" the Shade asked, hands spread wide.

Gabriel sighed, finally turning his attention to his food. His stomach ached, reminding him of his tiring journey from Abrita Shores. He picked up his spoon and scooped a healthy bite. It was a hearty soup, salty, but warm, much to his pleasure.

"You'll get your chance, but for now, we must trust in the king's plan," Gabriel answered.

"And what plan is that exactly?"

He shrugged, tearing a piece of bread and offering the rest to Vaiden. He waved it away while Gabriel sank his teeth into the fluffy, airy food. It was the best thing he'd eaten in months. Part of him was glad Vaiden had declined.

"I don't like being out of the loop." The Shade crossed his arms. "How can I be effective without all the information?"

"I don't even know the king's plan."

"Why?"

"I guess I'm not special enough."

"You're the ambassador, Gabe. You should know."

"I agree, but I must trust that, if the king wanted me to know, he'd let me know."

"You do remember this is the same person, who talked his way into being crowned by convincing everyone he was the long lost cousin of King Duncan after the tragic accident of King Chorlee."

"He fell from his horse."

"Yes, a seasoned soldier, who'd spent the majority of his life upon a horse, suddenly didn't know how to stay on one." Vaiden rolled his eyes. "Opretta knows the truth."

"Opretta knows." Gabriel nodded, growing serious. "You should watch your words, though, friend. That's close to treason."

"I've been convicted of that already."

They elapsed into a moment of silence while Gabriel ate his food. Vaiden's eyes scanned the tavern again, searching for anything suspicious. Perhaps Vaiden no longer worked as a personal guard, but old habits didn't die.

"What's in Fort Khali?" the Shade asked once Gabriel emptied his bowl.

"My embassy, unfortunately," he snorted. "I'd rather have it in Brevene than in the middle of a military fort."

"Brevene's nice, if you like pink."

"My wife likes the gardens and, yes, that means *those* trees too."

Vaiden frowned in response.

"We should get some sleep." Gabriel pushed away from the table, standing. "The journey is long to the fort, especially in this weather."

"Fine." The Shade climbed to his feet. "But, let it be known, I'm only going to see your hot ass wife."

Gabriel rolled his eyes, leading Vaiden toward their room. As the ambassador, Gabriel generally got his own room, but he'd share with Vaiden. One, to keep an eye on him, but also because he wanted the extra security. Although they didn't have proof in writing, Abrita Shores had turned rebel. Their list of allies thinned, but whilst they remained in the south, Gabriel would not leave his back unguarded.

Vaiden volunteered for the first watch. He sat in a chair, facing the only entrance, while Gabriel laid on the feather-stuffed mattress. He welcomed sleep. Although the journey from Abrita Shores had been long, the journey before them would be arduous. He trusted this new Vaiden would make it even harder.

Surnuna, help him.

2

Tatiana stepped through the metal detector and assumed the position. A female officer approached her with a frown, but otherwise said nothing as she conducted a pat down on Tatiana. She even ran her fingers through Tatiana's platinum blonde hair. It was overkill, she thought, but when it came to safety for both her client and the people of the Supernatural Detention Center, she didn't mind the thoroughness.

As a defense attorney for the preternatural, she was used to such formality—though, it didn't seem her colleagues in human law had to go through such vigorous precautions. In truth, it seemed silly. Why search for weapons when most of her clients had claws and razor-sharp teeth?

Still, she wouldn't give these officers a hard time. As the first line of defense, if they skipped protocol, something tragic could happen. People could get hurt or worse, then politicians would call for stricter protocols or eliminate visits altogether. The latter would be hard to achieve, considering preternatural citizens and immigrants from Arda had the same rights as humans in the United States of America, but Tatiana wouldn't doubt a congressman to try to chip away at her clients' rights.

Once the officer finished, she allowed Tatiana to move forward. She retrieved her briefcase and smartphone from the conveyor belt. They had been scanned through a CT for any possible weapons or suspicious materials. At least, they didn't make her remove her shoes, like at the airport.

From different angles in the room, five officers watched her throughout this process—more overkill, but no one had forgotten about the incident in Rhode Island, where a master vampire had posed as an attorney to free their lesser. Because both officers had been within the view of the master, he'd used glamour

9

to capture them before forcing them to shoot each other. In California, every supernatural facility required a minimum of five officers spread throughout the room to handle visitors.

An officer led her through a series of locked doors that someone from the control room had to unlock and let the mechanisms open and close the heavy, thick doors. They were said to withstand the strength of vampires, but Tatiana wondered if they had been tested against each kind of vampire (lesser, greater, and master). She couldn't believe a master incapable of damaging these doors, but perhaps the reason for them was to merely slow down the vampire rather than to truly contain it.

When they were free of security doors, they rode an elevator down to the basement level. The hallway they entered was brightly lit. The concrete floors needed a new wax, but otherwise appeared clean. The walls, also made of concrete, bore nothing, except the occasional sign that read *SHC*, which stood for Supernatural Holding Cells.

Remembrance of another concrete room flashed through her mind, except it was caked in dried blood and fingernail markings from ghosts of victims who'd died there. Heat clawed at her throat, like someone trying to strangle her. She rubbed down the column of her neck to soothe it, but the invisible hand squeezed. They were underground. There was only limited oxygen. Her lungs caved, begging for air. No, she shook her head. There was ventilation—plenty of air.

Finally, she took a breath and blew it out steadily. She would not panic. Not in front of this officer and not while a client needed her. In the back of her head, she could hear a siren. It willed her to the ground. It willed her submission. She took another deep breath, which made the officer glance at her.

"Are you alright?" he asked.

"Fine," she managed. "Sometimes I get claustrophobic."

"Me too, but you get used to these narrow halls after a while."

She wanted to say it wasn't her first rodeo, but instead she just nodded. He was being personable, something the officers in this facility rarely did. She knew they needed to remain objective. Any person entering the facility could be a threat, though the greater threats remained inside—or at least, that was what District Attorney Abraham Leanger would have citizens of California believe. Tatiana would argue she hadn't represented a guilty preternatural yet.

She glanced at the officer beside her. He was a fit man. Even in his security gear and weapons, she could tell he was someone who took his health seriously. The muscles in his biceps said weightlifter, but she bet he practiced hand-to-hand too. It was required of late for those in the special preternatural branches from PITF to the Marshals, the preternatural hit squad.

Focusing on the officer eased away the siren. He was under six-foot, but she wagered on his social media profiles he claimed he was six-feet tall. His skin was golden brown, but not the kind from outdoor labor, probably exercise. Maybe he was a runner, like her. He had the legs.

"Here." The officer gestured at a cell. "Your client is in there."

As she knew from her many trips to supernatural detention centers, there were four cells each level, with ten feet of reinforced concrete between them. The security guard led her to Cell Three. A man stood beyond the door in the hall. He was dressed in the same gear as the officer, but with different stripes on his shoulders.

"Sergeant." Tatiana flashed her best professional smile at him.

"Ms. Smith," he replied in a flat tone. Sergeant A.J. Pérez was in his forties, but in exceptional shape. His brown skin was a rich color that no amount of sun exposure could replicate. It came from genetics. He was shorter than her five-foot-seven, but he posed with his head held high and his shoulders squared. His commanding presence made him *feel* taller.

"The law commands me to state that the suspect in custody is of supernatural class. By submitting proper paperwork and following procedure, you are allowed entry by power of attorney. You do this at your own discretion," he explained, as if reading from a grocery list.

"It is my duty and my officer's duty to ensure the safety of you and the prisoner during this visit," he continued. "We will respect client-attorney privileges as requested by law, but if you fear for your life—or we fear for your life by the live feed available for us to monitor the prisoner." He pointed at the TV screen above the cell's control panel. "We will be forced to act in every way possible to ensure your and the public's safety." He paused. "Do you agree to the terms I have recited?"

"Yes," she answered.

"Do you have any questions for me before Officer Sampson opens the cell door?"

"The sound from the monitor will be off."

11

The sergeant gave her a measured look. It wasn't a question. It was a demand.

"Do I have to explain why the sound must be off?" she asked with a raised brow.

"No, Ms. Smith," he replied, but not like he was happy about it. "Officer Sampson, please turn off the sound."

He followed the sergeant's order without hesitation. If they would keep the sound off after she entered the cell was not under her control, but the fact that she had requested it bothered her. She would ask her fellow attorneys if they also had this problem. If she learned that the sound was left on, she would make a complaint.

"Do you have any other questions or *requests*?" the sergeant asked.

"As long as I have your full confidence, sir, we can proceed."

Pérez's eyes swept over her before he nodded at the other officer. He used a security card to unlock a keypad then entered a code, which he used his body to shield Tatiana from seeing. A yellow light flashed above Cell Three, communicating to the control room the door was authorized for entry. It buzzed before popping open.

It was slow movements, making Tatiana wonder if a client did attack her, how quickly could they extract her before the supernatural tore her apart? Not that she was afraid. Most clients could be guarded or suspicious of her, but none had tried to attack her.

Officer Sampson pulled the cell door open and moved so she could enter. He nodded at her but kept his eyes on the prisoner within. Tatiana walked into the cell and the door closed behind her. She did not look back, knowing from experience if she did, it made the client believe she was afraid of them.

"Hello, I am Tatiana Smith from Pearson and Associates. I am here to represent you as your defense attorney," she announced.

Across from her chained to a chair bolted to the concrete floor, sat a serpent. When most thought of the word "serpent," they pictured snakes, but her client seemed closer related to lizards or dragons than any snake.

Eyes of golden fire watched her enter, filled with age and experience. It wasn't his first time being locked up, she bet by his patient posture. She'd been around enough first timer anxiety to notice how calm her new client sat. His dark brown scales shimmered in the fluorescent lighting, making it appear silky despite the spikes protruding from his head. Like all serpents, he had a wide mouth with an overbite and side facing eyes.

"May I approach?" she asked.

He nodded.

Tatiana slid into the folding chair opposite her client, remaining poised. Serpents easily offended. It derived from their natural suspicious ways. They were also highly disciplined creatures. She recalled all the books and articles from serpent culture she had researched for a previous case.

It was the one that jump started her career—a difficult one for anyone, but especially for a rookie attorney straight out of law school. The prosecution was merciless. The media interfered with disinformation. The judge had a history of bias toward supernaturals. All these were expected in any high-profile case, but her client had been uncooperative from the start.

Part of it was her fault. She had not instilled confidence in her client, who withheld evidence that would have exonerated them of the charges because they did not trust her. A bad relationship with a client could sink a case as easily as testimony in court.

She had gotten lucky with that client, managing to recover their misunderstanding in time to provide evidence to the court of her client's innocence. History was made as the jury was the first to acquit a preternatural.

She placed her smartphone and notepad on the table parallel to each other. Although a small detail, she found clients responded well to organization. She generally kept her interviews with clients clean. No messy files spread across the table. No stacks of notebooks. No laptop, tablet, or other electronics. One notepad, one smartphone, and one pen.

The pen she kept in her hand, partly because she did not want to give her clients access to a weapon. Not that she thought they would hurt her, but to keep the trust between her and the officers outside and to make sure her clients did not use the object to injure themselves.

She doubted the serpent would try to hurt himself. Suicide was considered cowardice in their culture. If they killed themselves, it brought their soul great shame. They would be denied into Yanam, their culture's heaven and bound to wander the Morenlands deaf and blind.

Moren was the moon goddess of the elves as Tatiana had learned from her magical teacher and friend, Coastal. It was interesting that even though the serpents and elves had separate religions, parts of scripture intertwined. Of course, the same could be argued for some of Earth's religions too.

"Mr. Slaseezor, you have been accused of murder in the first degree." Tatiana opened her notepad. "As you are a member of the preternatural community who immigrated to Earth from Arda, it could mean deportation or execution." She rested her hands on the notepad. "It is my job to defend you against this charge and that depends on how we work together."

The serpent turned his head to the left, gazing at her with one of his dragon eyes. A muscle feathered in his cheek. She reminded herself, although these creatures appeared menacing, it was just their face. Like snakes and alligators, they could not help their intimidating features.

"What do you mean?" asked the serpent. "How do we work together?"

"I cannot help you unless you tell me everything."

"Did the police give you my file?"

"I want to hear it from you," she said. "Your statement says you killed another serpent during a blood ritual."

"It was an accident," he hissed. "I have performed this ceremony many times and have never killed anyone."

"What went wrong this time?"

The serpent turned his head, searching the room for answers. "The tools," he said. "The tools were not correct. We have two sets. One for decoration and one for the ceremony."

"What are the differences between them?"

"The decorations are real. They have been passed down through my family from our ancestors on Arda. The knives are sharp and were once used in sacrificial practices, but our kingdom outlawed sacrifice centuries ago. The knives were used only for show," he explained. "The ritual blades are, how do you say?" He spoke a foreign language for a moment. "Fake, like ones used in theaters here on Earth."

"A prop knife?"

"Yes, the blade is not real and goes into the handle when pressed down against someone."

Someone had switched the blades. Tatiana made a note. "How many handled the blades before the ceremony?"

"I do not know," he answered. "There are many who touched them as they are passed down the line to the altar. I cleaned them that morning."

"Before the ritual?"

He nodded. "It is custom to make sure everything is sanitary and polished."

Mr. Slaseezor seemed to be telling the truth, but as he looked away through his answers, she could not tell if it was because he was nervous, didn't trust her, or if he was holding something back. It was common for the preternatural, but especially for those who originated from Arda.

"Our strategy is to convince the jury this was a tragic accident," she explained. "May I have permission to enter your den?"

The serpent tilted his head at the attorney. His eyes flickered with amusement. Tatiana knew from her first high-profiled case that involved a serpent, she needed his permission to enter the den, not only because he was the leader of the faith, but because he was head of his household. If she spoke to the den without his permission, they would shun her. It was something she had not understood in that previous case and had caused great resentment and distrust between her and her former client and those of the client's family.

A little wiser, Tatiana asked permission to avoid conflict and to perhaps impress upon her clients that she did her research.

"Yes, you may enter the den," Mr. Slaseezor answered. "My wife will answer your questions."

"Is there anything else you would like to tell me now? Anything that may help your case? Anything the prosecutors will learn if they go through your personal accounts?"

"What would they hope to learn?"

"Cash deposits." She spread her hands wide. "The prosecution will be looking for motive and reward in their arguments."

"They will find nothing," he hissed. "My den is non-profit."

Tatiana jotted down some notes. Though he seemed to be telling her the truth, she would check all the background and financial documents of Mr. Slaseezor's personal accounts and the den. She'd been burned before by a client who had hidden accounts. The client was innocent of the crime, but the hidden accounts had made them appear guilty, especially since they had lied about them.

"I will talk to your wife," she said, standing. The serpent looked up at her curiously. "I will do everything I can to ensure you are released back to your family."

"If I lose, will they deport me back to Arda?"

She opened then closed her mouth. It was a loaded question. Most who immigrated to Earth did so for many reasons. One of the most common for serpents was the hostile government. It was harsh from what she had learned. One of her clients said if they returned, more than likely they would be put to death as a traitor for traveling to the "new world." Why that was offensive, Tatiana had no clue, but the serpent had been serious, so she did not doubt them.

"That is up to the judge," she answered.

"Do you think I am guilty?" he asked, his dragon eyes somehow soft.

"No, Mr. Slaseezor," she said. "I think you are a victim of a terrible tragedy, and I will work incredibly hard for your release."

"Thank you." The serpent bowed his head, a sign of thanks and respect.

Tatiana returned the favor, and then knocked on the door to let the officers know she was finished. Hopefully, she could live up to her words and return him safely to his den and family.

3

"**G**lades, a general? For which council member did he get down on his knees?"

"Vaiden," Gabriel warned. "He's served the crown well. You remember the Battle of Dae'ranarra. Without Glades, we would not have pushed back the vampires."

The Shade scoffed. "Yeah, and I'm super-agent man, James Bond."

Gabriel raised a brow at him.

"I'll explain later."

Once they had entered the flatlands, the rain stopped—much to Vaiden's pleasure. The journey through Eskandor had only made him miss the convenience of Earth, especially the vehicles. Riding by horse made places sore that hadn't been used in fifty years. He hated slow travel, but he hated walking more.

Months of riding, smelling of horse and sweat, while Altamost dicked them around city-to-city, kept Vaiden in a constant foul mood. He knew Gabriel had tried to make the best of it, but Vaiden was not the king's man. He wasn't technically a citizen of Arda. If only for Gabriel's sake, he'd returned to that place to kill Kanaris, the rebel leader. That was the king's orders. That was Vaiden's purpose, yet the king changed his mind week-to-week.

Vaiden didn't like it. For once, they knew the location of the rebel leader and instead, the king had sent them to Fort Khali. The Shade had it in his mind to defy orders and take the reins of this campaign himself. Altamost wanted Kanaris dead. Kanaris wanted Altamost dead. One had to die. There was no other ending to this civil war.

The Shade glanced at the ambassador, riding beside him. The hood of his golden cloak was pulled up to shield his identity. Why the rebels had targeted him, Vaiden couldn't understand. Maybe they didn't know Gabriel was the reason why the world wasn't ruled by vampires. He'd banded together the other kingdoms and had made the final decision that the vampires could not remain on Arda. They all had to be destroyed.

It was a little extreme for the ambassador, Vaiden admitted, but ultimately it was the right decision. Emperor Zerth and his vampires would have never stopped. They *had* to be destroyed.

Perhaps the rebels had forgotten Gabriel's heroics. It had been over half a century since the Last Vampire War.

"Sir," the captain of Gabriel's guards called. "Fort Khali is in sight."

Vaiden rolled his eyes. As if they could not see the garrison themselves.

Fort Khali was one of the elven cities fortunate enough to be built on flat land. It was shaped like an irregular pentagon with an impressive outer stone wall, fifteen feet thick, and around thirty feet tall. Between the outer and inner walls were a few houses, a tavern, blacksmiths, and stables. The garrison was a military fortress, nothing luxurious or attractive like Casimere or Brevene. The keep was massive, a fine stronghold. The walls were half as thick as the outer wall, but two times the height.

Many had tried to invade Fort Khali, but they had failed.

Gabriel sighed heavily beside Vaiden. "We'll report to the general first then—"

"Since when does he have authority over you?"

"He doesn't, but the fort is his."

"And that means you report to him?"

"No, I have questions."

"About what?" Vaiden arched a brow.

There was a tightness to Gabriel's face that he couldn't decipher. It had been months of interpreting looks and understanding feelings. It was confusing and annoying—and constantly had the Shade searching for answers in logic. Why did Gabriel's brows furrow? What did Vaiden say wrong? What did that face mean? It was exhausting. Vaiden suddenly missed being his old Shade-self, free of these pesky feelings. Damn bind.

"Just a few things that need clarity," Gabriel answered. "Glades will know."

Vaiden narrowed his eyes at his old friend. It was a non-answer statement and vague. What could Glades know that Gabriel didn't already?

The gates were open as they rode into the fort. Vaiden eyed the guards, who studied him with pinched faces—a common expression when someone realized he was a Shade. The soldiers wore brown tunics, like the mud thick and earthy underneath his horse's feet.

Citizens stared at the ambassador's party as they crossed them. Something in their frozen faces bothered Vaiden. Most were women and children—families of soldiers stationed at the fort. One mother grabbed her son from their path and clutched him to her skirts. She gazed at the Shade with round eyes, shiny with fear. Not of him, he didn't think. Something else—but what?

Vaiden turned to Gabriel, whose own expression appeared neutral, but his eyes studied the people too. Only his locked jaw, let Vaiden know the ambassador had noticed this odd behavior too.

They dismounted from their horses at the stables. Gabriel dismissed his men. They would report to the barracks for beds and supper, though a couple swapped desires to visit the tavern. Vaiden didn't blame them. A strong drink would help warm their bellies and soothe sore muscles. Though Vaiden would rather join them, he followed Gabriel.

The great stone walls with over high ceilings of the keep were made of brownstone, like the rest of the fort. It was a dull place visually, but it wasn't meant for travelers, only soldiers.

Banners of gold and crimson hung from the walls. Vaiden observed one of the golden leaves, caressing a shield with a mighty tree painted upon its face. The branches stretched wide across the gold-plated shield, its limbs forming lines and its leaves, soldiers. It was the insignia of Wara, Goddess of Strength and Courage—and the Shades' maker. Vaiden gazed at it hollowly. Bold were her banners—red for their enemies' blood to be spilled, gold for the shining victory they would win, yet she dressed her creations in black.

"This way," Gabriel whispered, gesturing up the staircase. They heard shouting halfway up the climb.

"I don't want to hear that again, captain!" Glades's voice shouted behind the wooden door. "How many were there? Where did they go?"

Gabriel and Vaiden exchanged looks.

"At least Glades is in a good mood," the Shade said.

A guard stood outside of the general's commanding office. He wore a simple tunic over chainmail, brown like the soldiers outside. When he saw the ambassador, he had the audacity to look surprised—or perhaps that wasn't the right word, Vaiden thought. Shocked? Stunned? He would get hold of these emotions one day.

"Ambassador, sir." The guard bowed slightly at the waist.

Gabriel waved his hand. "You don't have to do that," he said. "I'm not royalty."

"Of course, sir." He stood up straight, his eyes frantically glancing between the ambassador and Vaiden. "The general is busy, sir."

"I can hear that." Gabriel chuckled, easing the soldier. "I need a word though—"

"If you can't answer simple questions, then maybe I should throw your useless body over the wall!" Glades shouted.

The guard visually winced. Obviously, it wasn't the first time he'd witnessed an ass-chewing. "It's not a good time, ambassador, sir."

Vaiden scowled, pushing forward between the ambassador and guard. He threw open the door to find red-faced Glades towering over a young soldier. The general's head snapped at the intruder; his eyes blazed with rage.

"Get out!" he ordered.

"Like hell," Vaiden growled.

The general barreled his massive frame toward the Shade. Vaiden was over six-feet tall, but Glades easily dwarfed him with his bulging muscles and fists the size of the Shade's head. It was rumor the general's family had giant in their blood. Vaiden didn't know about that, but nothing was impossible.

Heat rolled off the general's body, like a boiler ready to explode. "I said—"

Gabriel stepped through the doorway, planting himself between the Shade and Glades. "General," he said with his shoulders squared and chin raised. His focus tore through the general the way claws did flesh.

Glades sobered quickly, fixing the collar of his red tunic. "Ambassador, when did you arrive?"

"Just now." Gabriel removed his riding gloves. "The king has ordered my presence here in Fort Khali. Do you dispute this order?"

"The king's order is heard and accepted," Glades returned with a flat tone.

"Good." The ambassador smiled, one of his professional smiles—fake, but with just a touch of something soothing that forced the general to relax. His coloring returned to its normal golden-brown, but his dark, beady eyes filled with impatience.

"I have some questions..." Gabriel's voice trailed off as he spotted the soldier kneeling on the floor behind the general. "Who is this?"

Glades eyed him like someone might a pile of dog shit. "Rise," he ordered.

The captain rose, his hazel eyes sweeping over the occupants of the room wide and alert. Elves were eternal. They grew to a certain age and seemingly stopped aging. Vaiden knew it wasn't true. They aged extremely slowly. Even so, he had proven to be quite good at guessing other elves' ages. This *captain* appeared barely eighteen. How did he rise rank so quickly?

"Captain Alvez, ambassador, sir," the boy replied, looking athletic even presently in his chainmail and brown tunic. He had short dark hair, like most young soldiers. His brown skin appeared weathered from spending too much time under the sun.

Gabriel dipped his chin at the soldier, turning back to the general. "What seems to be the problem?" he asked.

"We had an attack on a supply cart."

"Rebels?"

"Corrupted," Glades replied. "Soldiers died and this—" Rage boiled with every word. "—*boy* cannot seem to answer simple questions."

Gabriel nodded as if they were talking about the weather. "I see," he said. "Allow me to try."

The general waved his hand dismissively.

"Alright, captain." Gabriel moved closer to him, his hands clasped behind his back. "Were you there at the attack?"

"Yes, sir." Alvez looked away, something pained in his eyes. "There were eleven of us, escorting the cart. It was my charge."

"What route did this attack happen on? We didn't happen upon it on Cobble Road."

"The Ghostly Path."

"To the Wildlands?" Vaiden shot Glades a look. "Why would you be accepting goods from the south?"

"It's the quickest route to the continental trading city in Norreach," Glades explained.

"The borders are supposed to be sealed," Vaiden returned. "Can't very well be that, if you are sending soldiers back and forth through it."

"We have permission from the crown."

"It's still irresponsible to send soldiers down that path."

"What do you care, *Shade*?"

"Why don't *you* care?" Vaiden shot. "That path cuts through the Wildlands. The closer you get to Aegan's statue, the more Corrupted you'll find. That's common sense!"

The general waved it away. It made Vaiden's blood boil. His hands closed into fists. How could Glades, a supposed general, be so careless with his soldiers' lives? How could he not take a Corrupted blight seriously? Perhaps he didn't because their king seemed not to? What were wrong with these people?

Gabriel grabbed Vaiden's arm, forcing him to look at his friend. His face remained unreadable, but his eyes dipped to where Vaiden's fingers encircled a dagger. The Shade let it go and so did the ambassador.

"You were saying, captain," Gabriel said calmly. "About the attack?"

"I don't know how many there were, sir." Alvez's foot played with an invisible rock.

"Of the Corrupted?"

He nodded, not trusting his voice.

"How far from the fort did the attack occur?" Vaiden asked.

"A few miles."

"A *few*?" Gabriel did not hold back the alarm in his voice. "Are you sure?"

Alvez nodded again, something haunted in his eyes. "We were almost home."

"One more question, captain," the ambassador said. "After the attack, where did the Corrupted go?"

"What do you mean, sir?" he asked, finally lifting his gaze. "The only place they could—the woods."

"North, east, south, west?" Vaiden inquired.

Alvez blinked at him. "North, I think."

"You *think*?"

"Vaiden." Gabriel held up his hand. "The boy's been through enough."

The Shade cocked a brow at his friend before studying the captain. His tunic appeared clean, no blood or dirt that Vaiden could see. He wore gloves, though worn from use, they didn't appear to be dirty either. A fight with the Corrupted, especially a swarm of them, was messy. Something was off.

"Your sword, captain," Vaiden ordered, holding out his hand.

Gabriel shot him an inquiring look. Whatever he saw on the Shade's face, forced him to reconsider. "If you would be so kind," he said to Alvez.

The captain looked between them then to his commanding officer. Glades had been quiet, but he waved his hand, again dismissively. Vaiden didn't know why, but every time the general did that, he wanted to punch him. Damn bind.

Alvez unsheathed his sword and handed it to Vaiden hilt first. The Shade took it, observing the short sword. It was heavier than he'd preferred, but balanced. The grip was brown leather, not as worn as the captain's gloves, but used. The blade was sharp and in excellent condition. His eyes caressed the cross-guard and the tiny grooves someone had spent too much time creating. It wasn't a custom soldier's sword, more than likely a family weapon or a gift. Vaiden hated weapons with intricate design. It made them difficult to clean.

"This blade was not used in combat today," he announced.

"What does mean?" Alvez asked.

The Shade grabbed the blade and handed it back to him as it had been handed to him. The captain took it and quickly sheathed his weapon. "You didn't fight against the Corrupted."

"Of course, I did! My men were—"

"You are clean," Vaiden interrupted. "I've been in countless fights with the Corrupted. Never once did I come back looking like you. Beyond that, unless you had time to take your blade to the cleaners and not come directly to your commanding officer with news of the attack, then that blade is *remarkably* clean."

The captain paled, eyes wide and shiny with fear.

"Did you abandon your men?" Glades asked, already angry.

Alvez's whole body snapped toward the general with his arms up, as if surrendering. "No, sir, absolutely not, sir!"

"Then explain the Shade's findings," the general growled. Vaiden could feel him at his back, heat steaming like a physical aura.

"I-I-I..." Alvez took an unintentional step backward. "I...I didn't know what to do and it happened so fast. They were killing everyone. *Everything*. I just..." He sank to the floor, covering his face with both hands. "I didn't know what to do."

"Stand up!" Glades shouted. "You are a soldier! A *captain*. You were responsible for those men."

"Stop!" Gabriel hissed, kneeling beside the young captain. "He's been through enough."

"He abandoned his unit," Vaiden said.

"I didn't!" Alvez snapped, tears sliding down his cheeks. "I tried to get them to retreat, but we were surrounded."

"How did you escape?" the Shade asked.

"The-the wagon." He covered his face again. "The sounds! Surnuna, I can still hear the sounds."

They elapsed into a moment of silence as Gabriel consoled the sobbing boy. Vaiden didn't truly blame the captain for hiding or for running—whatever was the truth. He was one person—not a Shade. He didn't have a chance against a swarm big enough to take out a unit so effortlessly.

"Where was this attack again?" Vaiden asked.

"Why?" Glades arched a brow at him.

"I want to see it."

"Why?" he repeated.

"A swarm that close to this fort, and you're not a little concerned?" Vaiden crossed his arms.

"We've had many altercations with the Corrupted over the last year."

"And you're not curious if they've built a nest in your backyard?"

The general seemed to think about it. "Is that why you're here?" he asked. "To investigate a possible nest?"

"No, I'm just along for the ride," Vaiden answered. "But why would you think that?"

"The Shades have been recalled to Kiji."

"Recalled?"

"What do you mean?" Gabriel asked, standing.

"It's the king's order." He picked up a scroll from his desk. "All Shades are to report to Kiji Village."

Gabriel took the scroll, quickly unraveling it and reading the king's orders. Vaiden would let him study it. He didn't care to decipher political jargon.

"Does that mean I'm defying some order?" Vaiden questioned. "I'm supposed to stay with you."

"I know," Gabriel answered without looking up from the scroll. "I gather you are an exception to the rule."

"It does say *all* Shades," Glades said, smiling slightly.

"Does this amuse you?" the Shade asked.

"Well, technically, you are breaking the king's orders."

"It's the first I'm hearing of such an order."

"Doesn't make it untrue."

Vaiden rolled his eyes. "I'm not splitting hairs with you, Glades. My purpose is different from the rest of my kind."

"So, you *still* think you are special." The general chuckled. "You haven't changed, even from those days in the Forty-Second, but I suppose that's not surprising. Shades are all the same."

Vaiden's hands balled into fists as he stared up at the general, letting his eyes go dead as he found that vast empty void inside him. Glades's smirk slipped, replaced by an uneasiness that forced him to avert his gaze. Yeah, bind or not, Vaiden could still make the big man squirm.

"This doesn't make sense," Gabriel said, making them look at him. "Why would the king send the Shades to isolation during a Corrupted blight?"

Vaiden scoffed. "When has Alty made sense during this entire blight?"

The ambassador finally looked up from the scroll. Something alarming shined in his eyes, but he quickly schooled his features and handed the scroll back to its owner. Glades dropped it on the desk, forgotten like his other papers.

"I'll write to him," Gabriel announced. "I need to understand this new development."

"Don't expect much in return." Glades shrugged. "I already asked and haven't received a reply from the king or anyone in Casimere."

"What is—" Gabriel cut himself off. "It won't hurt to send another letter. Perhaps with my seal, the king will find it more urgent to reply."

Glades shifted on his feet, resting his hand on the hilt of his sword. He frowned, clearly annoyed by the ambassador's implication he was more important. Vaiden agreed. Gabriel was more important—not just by station, but as a person. Of course, the Shade might be biased.

"Will you grant the captain leave to show me the place where the Corrupted attacked the wagon?" Vaiden asked the general.

Glades blinked at him, as if he'd forgotten about it. He eyed the captain, still on the floor, but at least he wasn't crying anymore. His round eyes looked at the general, slightly pleading—for what Vaiden didn't know.

"Well, he's useless," Glades huffed, "but maybe you can get something out of him."

"I'll report back my findings." Vaiden left the office, turning back on his heel to snap his fingers at the captain. "If you didn't get the clue, you're with me."

Alvez climbed to his feet, dusting off his tunic. "I know that!"

"Well, make it snappy. We don't have all day," the Shade growled.

The captain shot him an unfriendly look. If Vaiden didn't think he was a coward, he might put the boy in his place, but he didn't want to break Alvez. They needed him to find the Corrupted swarm. Hopefully, Alvez wouldn't take them on a wild goose chase. There was only so much daylight left and Vaiden would never be caught in the Wildlands at night.

4

As she descended the steps from the Supernatural Detention Center, Tatiana wished she had brought security along for the ride. Pearson and Associates had given her a few bodyguards during high-profiled cases in the past, especially when protesters threatened her. She grew accustomed to lockdowns during those days. Bomb threats and riots had become routine at the courthouse, but as time passed and Tatiana gathered victories in court and in the media, the public's interests faded.

People hate what they do not understand, her father used to say. It became her mantra all throughout college and when she had begun her career. She could never understand the crowd's hate for her and her clients—not until Harvey Dellawood intervened in her life—not until she had witnessed firsthand the violence within the preternatural community.

She took a deep breath. What happened six months ago did not define the preternatural community, but it did allow her a new perspective in the reality her clients lived—and the fear those who lived outside of it shared.

There were no crowds surrounding the steps of the detention center that day, but there lingered a vulture—George Zeilberg, a prized journalist for the *Streaming Enquirer*. He gazed at her with a blinding grin, waving at her from the bottom steps, too lazy to attempt the climb in his brown sports coat and checkered shirt. In his youth, he might have been fit, but Tatiana could not imagine it. She pictured the same man, young and soft bellied with a round pleasant face—a nice man, harmless, but a guise meant to relax her. Tatiana knew better, or she had more recently.

"What a fine day it is," George Zeilberg said, wiping his face with a handkerchief.

"Mr. Zeilberg." Tatiana marched off the concrete steps never changing pace. She walked past him, not even making eye contact. "I'm in a hurry."

Somehow his short legs managed to keep up with her long strides. "It won't take but a moment of your time."

She grimaced, but said nothing in reply. She knew what he wanted—what he had wanted since she had given her statement to the police, when the public had learned she had been recovered from the cabin in the woods.

"It's been six months, Tatiana," he wheezed. "Don't you think it's about time you shared your side of what happened?"

Images of that dark cell flashed through her mind—the dried blood and nail scratches, scarring the concrete. The siren rang deep in her ears.

Tatiana stopped dead in her tracks, making the red faced journalist stumble. His breathing labored while hope glinted in his eyes.

"You have my statement." She managed to sound bored, despite the rage boiling deep in her core. "And that of witnesses."

"Statements made to the police and regurgitated to the press." He patted beads of sweat on his balding head with his handkerchief again. It was hot in the sun. Sweat slid down her back beneath the blue blazer. She wanted to take it off. The dark material would continue absorbing the heat the longer she stood there.

"There's nothing else to say," she said, continuing to the parking lot right of the building. She spotted her Chevy Cruze at the far end. Why did she park so far away?

"We both know that's not true." George hurried beside her.

"What exactly are you speculating, Mr. Zeilberg?" She emphasized his surname on purpose. Once they had been friendly. George was the only fair journalist who had given her a shot at the beginning of her career, which allowed him exclusive access to her cases and personal life. She hated that she'd trusted him in the past, allowing him to take advantage of naivety. He was a scavenger—an opportunist. Despite his friendly visage, he was a vulture.

"Tatiana." He pouted. "I think it would be beneficial for you to tell your side—to let it stop weighing you down."

"If I wanted to do that, I would speak to a therapist, not a reporter."

"Are you in therapy?"

She turned on him again. "You just don't stop," she gritted.

"I am asking as your friend." He placed his hand flat against his chest. His eyes softened, blinking up at her through his thick framed glasses.

"We're *not* friends." She frowned. "There's no story here. Move on. The news cycle has. Why haven't you?"

"I know there's more to tell."

She frowned harder at him and his kind face, pleading for her to relax, to submit—just like the siren. "No, what upsets you is, instead of drawing out a long tireless case, Gary pled guilty." She paused. "That has left you mystified on what to concentrate on next."

"That's not—"

"I don't have time for this," she snapped, rushing to her car. He did not follow this time.

"I'm here whenever you're ready," he called after her.

When she was safely behind the wheel of her car, George was nowhere to be seen. How did he move around so quickly, she wondered. How did he even know she would be interviewing a client?

He had said before he had friends in the police. Maybe one of them passed on the information about her client and he assumed she would visit to the SDC. Then again, she hadn't known she would be meeting a new client until early that morning.

She sat there speculating for a moment before finally letting it go. It didn't matter. George wasn't interested in helping her, no matter how he framed his words. He wanted a story. He wanted to pry into her careful mask and learn everything that had happened six months ago. She couldn't let that happen.

The drive back to the office took her downtown. She thought about going around the interstate but knew that lunch rush could not be avoided. Her stomach ached, reminding her to eat. The idea of something hearty and meaty made her mouth water, but there were few burger joints in downtown. It was more posh cafes and hot spots where everything was tasteless.

She hated fads, especially in food. Experimenting with cooking was necessary to expand the palate, but she didn't understand people who paid eighteen dollars for a garden salad filled with lawn grass and tree leaves with a side of flatbread that was like gnawing on straight cardboard. Did people really believe it made them part of the fad? Like a club? Like they were special to eat bad food? She pitied them and their bland taste buds.

Before she had returned to work four months ago, all she did was cook and bake. She had baked enough cakes and pies friends and neighbors had declined to take them. She brought them to shelters and handed them out to the homeless. Then came the casseroles, chicken dinners, and smoked salmon. She cooked and baked until an empty kitchen remained.

More food could be bought, but she'd exhausted her drive to make anything more, so she began cleaning. Her mid-century home hadn't been touched during the events six months ago. Blood had soaked and stained the living room carpet so thoroughly, she'd spent a week trying to clean it to no avail, so she removed it—the entire living room's floor—and had a new one installed.

The rest of the house seemed dirty compared to the new carpet, but it wasn't the carpet she knew. It was her old life. It needed to be washed away with the dust and grime from leaving the house uninhabited. She scrubbed until the tile floors sparkled, the marble countertops glossed, and the wood furnishings appeared brand new.

A month into her recovery, baking and cleaning, she had decided to sell the house. She couldn't live with the ghosts of her past—of the memories of Gary everywhere she turned—of that night when vampires had broken into her home and changed her life forever.

The house had sold quickly—too quickly—leaving her with too much time to think. She had lived to work and without her work...

The charity helped. Helping others was something her father preached often. But even the less fortunate had looked at her with pity obvious in their eyes, like a stiff breeze could knock her over. That was when she had started to exercise, to build muscle, get into shape, and run. Running had helped.

She exhaled into the silence of her car, her stomach growling, harassing her to eat something. She begrudgingly put her prejudices aside after spotting a sandwich shop. Though the prices made her nauseous, she did not have time to run to the other side of the city for something cheaper.

She took her expensive sandwich and ate it in the silence of her car. Traffic crawled forward through stop lights. Other drivers expressed their frustrations with honks as traffic from the interstate merged onto the avenue. It was a never-ending nightmare of cars pouring into the heart of the city. They all knew driving to the center would cause a jam, but they did it regardless.

Tatiana propped her head on her hand against the car door. It was the definition of insanity, but what could she do? It made her miss the rural community she grew up in as a teenager. Cornwork was a small town of five hundred or so people. Her parents still lived there. Her father, the primary doctor, ran a clinic. Her mother managed the park grounds and specifically the courthouse gardens. They were greatly admired by the people of Cornwork, though they did not know the truth about the doctor and gardener.

They were sorcerers—Tatiana too. She wondered what their neighbors would think of that, knowing the answer. The people of Cornwork lived in a bubble and didn't want anything to burst their simple lives, even people from a completely different world. They opposed Tatiana's politics, blasting her through their local paper for defending "monsters," but to her face, they were polite, ridiculously helpful even. It was jarring, but Tatiana knew theater when she saw it.

Though she hadn't seen it with Gary...

Her jaw clenched, tossing the sandwich wrapper into the recyclable bag hooked to her gear shifter. Tears stung her eyes, but she looked out her driver's side window, staring into the clear blue sky, willing them back.

George Zeilberg wanted to know the truth about the events of six months ago—when Tatiana's fiancé had played her and planned to give her to his monster lover. Jen had wanted her soul—her power and lifeforce to grow stronger. She hadn't won. She was dead and Gary was in prison. He'd pled guilty. The public knew a story—not the whole truth, but enough that the important facts shined through. A knot twisted in Tatiana's middle. Maybe not everyone believed Tatiana's version of events. George was evidence of this. He sought the truth only she knew, but she couldn't tell him. Some people could be hurt or worse if the real truth was revealed. She couldn't let that happen.

"Now, now, kitty," whispered through her mind, soft as a lover's breath, beckoning her for—

A honk startled her. She gazed at the greenlight and pressed the gas gently, finally driving through the intersection. Her heart hammered against her chest, forcing her to take deep breaths, willing peace, calm, and to forget everything about six months ago.

God, she wished it would be over. Gary had pled guilty. The circus was over, but she knew deep down, it would never end.

5

"I can't leave without seeing my wife," Gabriel announced.

Vaiden opened his mouth to say the ambassador didn't need to join them to hunt the Corrupted, but he quickly closed it and instead marched toward his home.

"You don't have to come with me," Gabriel said.

"I haven't seen Caroline in fifty years," the Shade returned. "I have to know if her ass still looks that good."

He frowned, quickening his pace. "Now I don't want you to come."

"Too bad." Vaiden grinned.

The Steel family lived at the embassy across the bailey from the keep. It didn't appear to be anything special, just another home, which was good camouflage if an enemy force somehow invaded the fort's walls. Guards let them through the iron swing gate.

"Stay here," Vaiden ordered Alvez.

He frowned, his eyes studying the grass that managed to spurt from the muddy earth. The Shade didn't like the captain's round lost eyes or the way his shoulders slumped. Being a coward was one thing, but being pathetic, he wouldn't tolerate. It was a problem for later, he decided, following Gabriel up the side staircase to the Steel family's personal apartment.

"Gabe!" the familiar voice of Caroline Steel shrieked when he opened the door. She was five-five and curvy with the softest pink skin. Green eyes dominated her round face and brightened with a wide smile. She threw her arms around his neck and pulled him down for a hungry kiss.

Something tugged at Vaiden's heart, watching his friends embrace. He didn't quite know what it meant, but standing alone with no one desperately clinging to him after a long journey—he longed for it.

Caroline moved back enough to see her husband's face. "I prayed to Surnuna every night for your safe return," she said.

"I'm here." He cupped her face with his hands, pressing his lips against her forehead. She sighed against his touch, a grin spreading on her lips.

Vaiden cleared his throat, startling them both.

Caroline gaped at him. Her long ears protruded horizontally from the side of her head. Most had their children's ears fixed when they were little, but Caroline's parents had let their daughter grow with the disfigurement. Not that she would ever believe her ears were such a thing—Gabriel either. He loved her wholly.

"Hey, Caro," Vaiden said, stepping closer. Her surprise quickly shifted into a fierce grin as she left the safety of her husband's arms, skipping into Vaiden's. He laughed against her dark brown hair, inhaling her sweet jasmine smell. She held him tightly, her breath warm against his chest.

"No funny business," Gabriel growled as Vaiden's hands dipped down her back. He raised his head, smirking at the ambassador.

"Oh?" the Shade dared, sinking his hands lower.

Caroline stepped back, fanning her blazed face. "He didn't tell me you were back. How are you? When did you arrive?"

"You didn't tell her?"

Gabriel raked a hand through his hair, looking positively innocent—charming as ever. "I wanted it to be a surprise."

Caroline whirled on him, untying her apron and smacking him with it. "You should have told me! What if something happened and you two were never able to come here?"

"That would be impossible," Vaiden said. "Even a king and his ambassador cannot keep me away from you."

She gazed at the Shade, a teasing smile playing with her lips, but it dropped quickly. Her brows scrunched together as her eyes swept over him. "You're different," she said.

Vaiden shrugged. "I let my hair grow out. Can you blame me?"

"What happened on Earth?" she asked, motioning to the kitchen table and chairs. "I want to hear everything."

Sun and Moon exchanged knowing glances. She—and no other elf—could know about Earth, but Vaiden held his stare for another reason. They had other business to attend before they could get all cozy.

"Darling." Gabriel wet his lips. "There's something else—"

"What?" Caroline's near-glowing face dropped into a glare that would have stopped running bulls in their tracks.

"I'm sure you have heard word about the Corrupted attack on the supply cart," Vaiden said.

She nodded. "Captain Windel mentioned it, but none of the Corrupted followed back the remaining soldiers to the fort."

"*Soldier*," Vaiden corrected.

"There was only one survivor?"

"Vaiden wants to see where the attack took place," Gabriel explained. "He'll be able to determine if this swarm of Corrupted is a threat to the fort."

"And, of course, you must go with him." Her tone was not friendly.

"He's in my charge."

She pulled out a chair and sat with a sigh. Her face fell into something sad and tired as she gazed at her husband. He kneeled in front of her, taking her hands, placing a small kiss upon them.

"I promise we won't be long," he said gently, like his words were made of glass. "It's just a few miles there and back."

She pulled her hands from his. "It's always a few miles!" Vaiden stepped back, surprised by the venom laced in her words. "The king says this. The king wants that. I understand you are bound by duty, but I pray one day you will come home and stay."

Gabriel studied her tight expression. He stayed vigilant, allowing her time to calm. She took a deep breath, closing her eyes.

"Could you not do this in the morning?" she asked, her voice softer, almost pleading.

"It's best to see the scene as fresh as possible," Vaiden explained. "I want to make sure the Corrupted have turned back south."

"And if they have not?" She opened her eyes. They consumed him like flies stuck in honey.

"Then the fort should know Corrupted are outside these walls."

"Vaiden, they're always outside the walls."

"We can't let more people get hurt," Gabriel said, taking her hands again. Her lips pressed into a fine line, staring down at him. "Vaiden's here. He'll watch my back."

"I won't let anything happen to him," the Shade added.

"You better not." Caroline glared at him, but the ends of her lips twitched. "It would no sooner send us into another Dark Age, and we cannot have that."

Vaiden raised a brow at her, perplexed what they had to do with the Dark Ages, millennia when Ardans lived without the sun. Most beings from that time were no more, only stories of the perpetual blackness that engulfed the world remained, but Vaiden knew someone who had lived through it.

"A moon without a sun," she said, grasping her husband's chin and lifting it higher. "I like the sunshine."

Gabriel beamed at his wife, kissing her hands again before standing. "Don't worry. It's just a scouting trip. Likely the Corrupted have moved on."

Vaiden opened his mouth to correct Gabriel. They couldn't know what the Corrupted would do, but he saw how Gabriel's words eased his wife. Vaiden wouldn't upset Caroline further. It'd only delay them leaving and he didn't want to be on the edge of the Wildlands at night.

"Let's go," he said instead, allowing his words to sound slightly impatient. Caroline gave him a look. *Yes*, he thought. *Let her be upset with me.* Then she rolled her eyes.

"Surnuna knows no one can stop you men and your missions," she huffed. "Go and be careful."

Gabriel kissed his wife once more before they finally left the safety of his home. Alvez waited by the gate, speaking with the posted guard.

"Shake a leg, captain. We've got Corrupted to kill."

Alvez's face twisted in confusion as he looked at his leg. He shook it, forcing a laugh from Vaiden.

"What?" the captain asked.

"Nothing. Not. A. Thing."

6

Pearson and Associates was officially named Pearson, Cobb, Johnson, and Blane, but everyone (excluding the named partners) called it Pearson and Associates. Tatiana's own business card had it in parenthesis underneath the official name because so many of her clients had referred to the law firm as such.

The building was in downtown near banks, other firms, and a ton of coffee shops, who supplied overworked employees with caffeine through their long workdays. The firm was a few blocks from the courthouse and police headquarters. Tatiana used the back entrance attached to the parking garage for employees to avoid another run-in with whatever journalist who might be hanging around front.

As she approached the elevators, a familiar face greeted her.

"Ana, why are you coming in so late?" Caden Pearson asked, threading his fingers through his almost black hair. He was nearly six-foot tall with slender shoulders and a narrow waist. Despite his last name and being a partner's son, he received no special treatment from seasoned attorneys or his fellow associates. If anything, they expected more from him.

Tatiana had met Caden and his wife, Josie, during college—back when they were all bright-eyed for the future and for changing society. Even though Tatiana had been the first licensed preternatural lawyer in the region and the first attorney to represent an Ardan acquitted for murder, she wasn't sure if her younger self would have been impressed, given their big dreams. Like Tatiana, Caden specialized in criminal law. He mostly took cases for non-violate offenders.

"I was meeting a new client," she answered, climbing into the elevator alongside him. She let him select their level, the second floor.

"Oh? What's this one about?" he asked with cool green eyes that appeared brighter against his dark complexion, as was the scar from his nose down to his upper lip. He was born with a cleft palate, something she knew he had struggled with growing up from medical operations and insecurities. Tatiana hadn't even noticed it when they had first met, only when he'd brought it up. She had thought he was the most handsome man she had ever met.

"A serpent has been charged with murder," she explained.

"How do you feel about it?"

"You know how finicky serpents can be."

He nodded. Tatiana wasn't the only one who had screwed up when they first took a case with the supernatural. Caden had his fair share of difficulty establishing trust with clients.

"Well, I know something that will cheer you up," he announced.

"What?" she asked as the elevator doors opened.

"Logan." He grinned mischievously. "Has he told you the good news?"

Tatiana followed him through the hall, trying her best to keep up with his long stride. "What news?" she demanded as they approached the central secretariat station. They playfully called it Command Central. Nothing came or went without one of the fine administrators at Command Central's assistance.

Caden leaned against the counter, checking out his list of appointments.

"Did you tell her?" one of the secretaries asked, handing him a clipboard.

He eyed the document. "What's this, Darling?"

"Delivery." Darling Brea tapped the box on the counter with her manicured fingernails. "More discovery for Cobb's case, I believe. He sent an email that you're responsible for this batch."

Caden made a face then signed the document as proof he had received the box. "Mr. Cobb seems to think because my father says no one is to coddle me, I'm his personal work horse."

Darling took back the clipboard. "As long as it is out of my hair, I don't care, pony."

"What did you want to tell me about Logan?" Tatiana asked firmly.

"Miss Brea, why don't you tell Ana the good news?"

Darling pivoted back to her computer screen, assaulting the keyboard with heavy clicks, answering dryly, "Mr. Reece took the bar."

"OK." Tatiana raised a brow at Caden. "That's commonplace for paralegals."

"And he's not just *any* paralegal," he said, heading down the hall with his box toward his office. Tatiana watched him go, wondering why he was grinning like a fool. Logan had taken the bar. What did it matter?

When she turned back to Darling, meeting her dark eyes, it hit her.

"That was a long time ago," Tatiana gritted.

"Well, you are the one who told him that you two couldn't date because technically you are his boss," the secretary explained. "Now that he's taken the bar—"

"He has to pass it first to become an associate."

"That boy is as smart as a whip." Darling's southern accent thickened when she was excited, angry, or wanted to emphasize a point. She was originally from Texas, but had lived most of her adult life on the west coast, first in Los Angeles for college then to Misplaced Stream where she was offered a position at the firm.

"That doesn't mean he will pass," Tatiana scoffed. "I took it twice. Most of everyone I know has, except Caden."

"He passed on the first try?"

"Third."

Darling suppressed a smile, pivoting back to her computer screen. "You have a meeting with PR at two-thirty."

"Great," Tatiana exhaled. Just what she needed. Another meeting with people who wanted her to work talk shows for exclusives about her experience with Jennifer Verniski, exploiting her trauma to promote the firm. She wasn't against promoting the firm, but she was tired of these media moochers wanting to discuss something she would rather forget. It was no one's business what had happened six months ago. It was over—she *wanted* it to be over.

A distant siren called to her toward a dark cell in her mind. She took a deep breath and shook herself. The pull alleviated, but only slightly. It would always be there—that siren, that cell. When would she ever leave it?

She shook her head. She had left. Jennifer Verniski was dead and Gary...

"Hey." Darling's warm hand squeezed Tatiana's arm, snapping her out of that cell and back to reality. Darling's black coils framed a round dark face with a short wide nose and full lips. Her makeup generally looked natural or only helped highlight her good genetics.

Darling had helped Tatiana through insecurities in the past, especially about her body. Lately things had changed. Every time Darling offered to listen, Tatiana couldn't find the courage to talk. She wasn't trying to avoid her, but Darling couldn't know the whole truth of what transpired at Jen's cabin. Like Caden, the authorities, and the public, they could only know the story Tatiana had given the police. Anything else could unravel their perfectly sculpted script and put good people in danger. Tatiana couldn't do that. She couldn't let other people—people who had helped her—get hurt.

She smiled slightly at Darling then took her hand back. Darling let her, the offering to talk shining in her eyes. She would listen. Tatiana wished they could talk.

"When Logan gets back, let him know I'm in my office," she said instead.

"Should I remind him about your deal as well?"

She scowled but didn't reply as she hurried to her office. It was nothing fancy. No corner office that overlooked the city with a big wooden desk or shelves filled with her endless awards. No. Tatiana's somewhat small office had enough space for her cheap desk, basic office chair, and two semi-comfortable armchairs for clients.

The built-in shelves on the wall sharing her office door was filled with books about California law, the supernatural, and reference case files. She set her bag down beside the desk. On it, sat her company laptop, case files, legal pads, and writing utensils. The only personal adornments in the room were copies of her diplomas, signifying her qualifications to clients. Once she had pictures of her and Gary Martin, but those had been thrown in the garbage where they belonged—where he belonged.

It was her second office. The first one she had set on fire with her power to escape a guard, who had worked for Jen. She missed that office with its private bathroom. Rotating offices was normal procedure though.

She sat in her chair and leaned back, closing her eyes—allowing herself a moment to breathe. Gary was in prison. He had been charged with a hefty list that had begun with murder and ended with conspiracy, to which he'd pled guilty in front of a judge and a gallery full of journalists. There was no lengthy, dramatic trial that the media thirst for every day since the Misplaced Stream Police Department had first reported his arrest. They had wanted a circus, but Gary had disappointed them all.

Tatiana didn't understand why the media and public wanted a lengthy trial. Had they want her to take the stand and explain all the horrible things Jen had done—the siren, the cold dark cell, how all she had wanted was for Gary to be alive again and when she had learned he was alive, he had betrayed her. He'd faked his death. He had never loved her. He had only loved Jen and wanted to feed Tatiana to her.

A shaky breath escaped her lips. She opened her eyes, staring at the ceiling. Everything had happened so fast between the cabin, hospital, police, and the press. She had read her script, something she had never imagined she would ever do. The truth had always been important to her, but—as she learned—nothing in life had been true. Everything was a lie—her family, her way of reality—even the love of her life—all lies, all theater. She didn't know what was true anymore.

"Here kitty, kitty," whispered through her ears. She shot up—her heart racing as the door opened.

"Good afternoon." A man just over six-foot tall stepped inside. He wore a gray suit jacket over a white button-up. His single knot tie, shoes, and slacks were black. The tailored ensemble made his long frame appear less lanky and his shoulders broader.

"Logan." She swallowed hard, drinking in his beachy hair and golden tan.

"You wanted to see me?" he asked, a bright smile on his lips. It was reminiscent of the smile he wore when his friends had empowered him to ask her out for a drink. She'd declined, stating she was his superior. It would be an inappropriate abuse of power—something in which his friends had teased him profusely. It wasn't long after that night that she had met Gary...

"How'd it go with the new client?" Logan asked, adjusting the clipboard and files in his arms.

"As well as can be expected from a serpent," she answered, her pulse finally calming. "We need to talk to the family. I have permission to enter the den, but I need you to start digging through financials and research about this religious practice the serpents perform."

"What's it called?"

She read the name the best she could from her notes. "It's a blood pack to join the den."

He fished a pen from his inside jacket pocket and jotted down the spelling. "I'll see what I can find."

"And I'll need to contact the prosecution or the lead investigator to get the case file."

"Oh, I have them here." Logan plopped down the hefty files from his arms. "As soon as they learned you were taking the case, they sent them over."

"Well, that's odd." She took the files. "Usually I have to spend hours on the phone arguing for them."

"I guess they want to try this case as quickly as possible."

Tatiana flipped through the file, spying the crime scene pictures. The siren hummed happily. She quickly closed it and gazed at Logan's teasing smile.

"What?" she asked.

"Did anyone tell you I took the bar?"

She leaned back in her chair, folding her arms under her chest. "Yeah, how did it go?"

He shrugged nonchalantly. Vague, she clicked her tongue, but Logan was quite intelligent. It was why she had poached him from the mailroom.

"I'm sure you did well, but the bar is hard," she said. "If you fail the first time, you are human after all."

"Hoping I do?" He raised a brow at her, a teasing smile slowly spreading on his lips.

"No, but if you do, the next test is in February," she explained, voice painfully neutral. "There is no limit on the number of times you can take it here in California."

He leaned on her desk. "Only around twelve weeks until I find out." *Until we can have that drink*, his bright hazel-blue eyes added through the silence.

She pushed another stack of files toward him. "I need you to file these for me."

He scooped them up. "On it," he said, slipping away before she could pile any more cases into his arms. She quickly closed the door behind him, slumping against it with a sigh. There was a time when she wanted nothing more than the attention of a handsome guy, like Logan. Lately, all she wanted was the drink and to forget about the past year.

Returning to her desk, she poured her attention into Mr. Slaseezor's case file, studying everything the investigators had learned, taking notes of what they might have missed while ignoring the siren wailing between her ears as she stared at the crime scene photos.

God, she wanted that drink.

7

A skeleton remained of the oxen feet away from the ravaged supply cart. No trace of Alvez's unit could be found in the grassy areas surrounding the cart. If someone had happened upon the dead oxen, they would have thought it had died weeks ago and the owners had left the cart abandoned.

A breeze played with Vaiden's hair as he studied the scene, the bones, the blood sprayed upon the cart, and the footprints scattered in the dirt path. The attack had been quick, lethal, and messy. The Shade squatted next to the ruins, observing a blood trail and where a body had laid. It hadn't been dragged away, not by the footprints Vaiden observed in the dirt. The body had walked away—into the woods left of the incident.

"Tell me what happened," Vaiden said, standing.

"I have already explained the attack." Alvez's voice shook, but he stood vigilantly beside Gabriel, though his hand white-knuckled around the pommel of his sword.

"Where did you grow up?" Vaiden countered.

The captain blinked at the Shade, like he hadn't heard him correctly. "What?"

"Where did you grow up?"

"Why?"

Gabriel sighed. "Just tell him."

The captain gave him a look before replying to the Shade. "In Casimere—my father's estate is in the second ring."

"Between the rags and the riches." Vaiden observed. "What does your father do for work?"

"He's part of the king's council."

Gabriel eyed the captain with surprise. "What's his name?"

"Callum Kazquer."

"Aw, yes, one of the few who dared challenge his majesty about the Corrupted crisis."

It made sense why Alvez had risen in rank so quickly. His father had influence in the capital—to the king, no less. Corruption, even in its simplest form, continually punished others. Alvez's unit deserved better than to be led by some baby face, whose Daddy bought him a place in authority. Such inexperience had consequences. They didn't deserve to be dead. Neither did Alvez, but whoever appointed him captain did. The blood of his unit was on their hands.

Vaiden studied the young man beside Gabriel. He tried to see him as more than a sniveling coward. He was young—too young to be giving orders. He was tossed into this mess, the same as his men. While he deserved criticism for a teaching moment, Vaiden wasn't a teacher, and he wouldn't coddle him.

"What happened?"

"We were distracted by a flock of birds," Alvez began. "They shot out of the fields, like-like they were afraid."

"Birds?" Gabriel raised a brow at the captain then glanced at Vaiden.

"Nothing lives in the Wildlands," the Shade returned.

"There were hundreds of them!" Alvez urged. "It was just so sudden and we were—we were overrun."

"Overrun how?" Vaiden asked.

"Ambushed."

"From where?"

"Everywhere."

"From the woods? From the fields? From behind?"

"*Everywhere*," Alvez stressed. "I didn't have time to issue any commands. They were on top of us, killing the men, and—and, oh-oh Surnuna, the *sounds...*"

The young captain stared at something unseen, his eyes wide and unfocused. It made him appear younger than he was. Gabriel patted his shoulder, whispering encouragement.

Vaiden focused on the open Wildlands behind them. The grassy fields spread for miles to the horizon, but Vaiden knew they eventually thinned, decayed until only the dry soil remained. A barren wasteland surrounded

Aegan's shrine, a few days' travel due south of Fort Khali. Life did not grow where evil thrived. No other goddess, but the Creator of Blood Magic, had the right to be called the Mistress of Evil.

Vaiden thought he'd met the closest evil to Aegan in Jen the Unfavorable. She'd fancied herself the true vessel of the goddess. Maybe she was right, but Vaiden wagered goddesses were immortal. They couldn't die, unlike Jen.

"Do you *feel* anything?" he asked aloud, mostly at Gabriel. "Any magic? A disturbance?"

The ambassador's eyes swept over the Shade, studying the woods behind him.

"Not really," Gabriel answered.

"Yes or no? 'Not really' isn't an answer."

"No then."

Vaiden exhaled, turning around to study the forest himself. Naturally he couldn't feel any magic. He was void of it. It couldn't hurt him. He couldn't harness it, but that had never been an issue in the past. He stared at the trees engulfed in shadow. Somewhere between them a swarm of Corrupted lived, hunting, eating, and creating monstrosities. Purposed swelled within him, adrenaline flooding his veins, preparing him for the fight.

"They're in there," he said, mostly to himself.

"We are not going in *there*." Alvez's voice trembled. "Are we?"

"Vaiden." Gabriel remained neutral, nudging the Shade for confirmation. He turned his head, casting a glance at the ambassador and the captain. Alvez's eyes darted between them, sweat sliding down his forehead. The sun dipped toward the horizon, painting the land in red and purple hues. They were running out of time. In full darkness, the Corrupted swarm within the woods would not be the only creatures hunting in the Wildlands.

The Shade faced the woods, purpose thudding with his heart. Instinct pulled him closer to the trees, to the shadows, whispering encouragement and commands. Find them, it said. End them. Nothing was stronger—more natural than a Shade in pursuit of the Corrupted—but he stood fast, a lone stone parting water. Vaiden took a deep breath. Eventually the stone would be eroded to dust, unless it allowed the current to carry it away.

"Let's go," Vaiden said, marching into the woods.

"Not me!" He heard Alvez protest. "They killed ten of my men like nothing. What can *we* do?"

"Come on," Gabriel urged.

The trees vanquished sunlight, wrapping them in thick darkness as they crept through the woods in a single file line. Vaiden's eyes quickly adjusted to his nocturnal sight, like adding a high contrast gray scale over his vision. It wasn't as good as vampire night vision but was better than other elves and humans.

"I can't see a thing," Alvez whined. "We should make a torch."

"No," Vaiden growled.

"Why?"

"Do you want to attract every predator to our location?" the Shade asked. "The Corrupted aren't the only monsters in these woods."

"Great, yeah, thanks for that," the young captain whimpered.

"It'll be alright," Gabriel whispered, clapping him on the back. "Vaiden's a Shade."

"Quiet," Vaiden demanded, glaring over his shoulder. Alvez swallowed hard, his eyes dancing at shadows. He looked pale, almost green in Vaiden's nocturnal sight. This boy shouldn't have had authority over a unit. He couldn't even stomach a walk in the woods.

The deeper into the woods they marched, a stench grew. Vaiden recognized it immediately, the smell of decay—of death, but in his vast experience, it didn't mean whatever had died wasn't walking around. He'd bet one of the Corrupted was a necromancer, generally one or two lived in a nest, but Alvez was vague on the size of the group that had attacked his men.

A nest, like the one living in Haven, was dozens of Corrupted. Swarms were smaller groups, ambushing travelers and remote cottages. Attacking armed guards seemed like something a larger group might do, but even that was odd and rare. The Corrupted were primarily scavengers, and at times, ambush predators. They didn't take on big game.

Perhaps, after Haven, everything had changed. It wasn't some remote cottage. It was a large fisherman village. Vaiden hadn't been there to see the wreckage, but he'd experienced enough battles, both magical and physical, to imagine it. A nest operated within the ruins of Haven. Why the crown hadn't sent the Shades to dismantle it was another thing entirely, but that nest wasn't Vaiden's priority.

Crinkling engulfed his expanded hearing, making him grimace. He shook his head, his eyes searching for the source of the sound. Limbs shook, making Alvez gasp, but it was only rodents scurrying through the trees.

"Vaiden," Gabriel whispered. "It's getting too dark."

The Shade opened his mouth to reply, remembering Gabriel didn't have his vision either, but an otherworldly scream sliced through his bones. Birds darted to the skies—a distraction—but Vaiden stayed on task, concentrating all his special abilities to the thick brush ahead of them. Movement—heavy footfalls thudded through his ears.

"What is that?" Alvez asked.

Vaiden didn't bother answering him, not as the monstrosity shot out of the darkness—the oxen morphed into something Vaiden's eyes could not quite decipher. A creature more than double the oxen's original size stood on two giant hooves. The Shade had observed many monstrosities the Corrupted created, but never one this big—or juicy.

A bile oozed from the open wounds where its grotesque appendages had been reshaped and forged together, albeit asymmetrically. Its jaw hung broken, black goo seeping down where a tongue once resided.

"By Surnuna's light!" Alvez gasped.

The familiar sliding of metal rang in Vaiden's ears, letting him know Gabriel had drawn his sword. "Steady," he commanded, mostly to the young captain.

The monstrosity didn't move. It stood there, staring glowing green eyes—the pronounced effect of necromancy—like it was waiting for something. An order, the Shade thought.

Insect buzzing overwhelmed Vaiden's expanded hearing until he realized it wasn't buzzing, but whispering, and not that of insects. Black hooded figures huddled in the shadows, but close enough his nocturnal sight registered their forms—the Corrupted. Vaiden quickly counted them, a dozen, maybe more—a nest—spread in a semi-circle around them.

"Slowly," Vaiden breathed between his teeth. "Retreat."

It was an order for which Alvez was made. He bolted like the wind couldn't catch him, but it only attracted the attention of the Corrupted, many of whom dissipated into the darkness, their whisperings wailing through Vaiden's ears. He shook his head, disengaging the expanded hearing.

The monstrosity snarled, rearing its head, and screamed like a banshee. Vaiden grimaced, fighting the instinct to cover his ears. It crumbled to all fours, black ooze pooling at its hooves, steam radiating from its contorted body. Another scream and it charged.

The Shade evaded, unsheathing the short sword strapped to his thigh. He turned to see Gabriel had also dodged its attack. The stupid creature rammed into a tree, splintering it, but that did not stop the monstrosity's rage. It busted through the tree into another one then another, slowly turning the monster back toward them.

A twig snapped behind Vaiden. He whirled, stabbing his sword through the chest of a hooded figure. Its hands were raised as if summoning magic. Vaiden stared into its diseased ashen face and the unnatural yellow irises with blackened whites of its eyes. The eyes were an easy sign of corruption—that and the blackening of fingernails. A pained expression quickly turned vacant as Vaiden withdrew his blade. It crumpled to the ground dead.

One down, the Shade thought.

"Vaiden!" Gabriel's voice drew his attention. His longsword sliced through soldiers—Alvez's unit, he presumed—overwhelming the ambassador from all sides. The monstrosity tangled in trees behind him while the Corrupted slowly crept forward. Vaiden unsheathed his other blade from his thigh, running into the chaos. The dead couldn't carry a blade, but they did have hands strong enough to tear through flesh.

End them, purpose pounded fiercely through the Shade's ears as loud as his pulse. His blades sank into flesh, cut through muscle and bone, cleanly lobbing a soldier's head from his shoulders. Cold blood sprayed Vaiden's face, but he continued to chop down the dead surrounding Gabriel, who'd cut down his fair share too.

A pool of carnage surrounded them while they stood back-to-back, catching their breaths. The monstrosity's scream pierced the air, alerting them of its attack. Hooves quaked the ground. Gabriel evaded again, but Vaiden ran toward it, blades tucked in until the massive abomination was upon him. The Shade sank to his knees, sliding underneath it. He raised his swords, allowing momentum and the power of the monstrosity to rip through its underside.

Vaiden lowered his arms, heavily drenched in black goo. The monstrosity stumbled, its insides spilling out, before finally collapsing to the ground.

Gabriel rolled his eyes. "Show off."

The only way to truly kill the beast was to burn it, but Vaiden didn't think the Corrupted surrounding them would give them time. The Shade would gladly kill them all, but a few had gone after Alvez. They needed to get to the young captain before the Corrupted did.

Hell, he was probably back at the fort by now, Vaiden thought, but he couldn't be sure. Not that the captain was important, but he was only borrowing the boy for this scouting mission. What was borrowed was expected to be returned. Not that Glades would miss him, but his father might. Vaiden was responsible for him and by charge that meant Gabriel was also responsible for him, and anything that might happen. Vaiden wouldn't want Gabriel to take the blame. It would be a political mess between the ambassador and the king's council.

The Corrupted did not advance. They held their positions in the shadows of the trees. Vaiden rejoined Gabriel, his back safely to the ambassador.

"What are they waiting for?" Gabriel asked.

One of them was a necromancer, Vaiden reminded himself. Maybe they needed time to prepare for the next nightmare, but Vaiden didn't know of Corrupted that planned attacks. Strategy was for the reasoning, and the Corrupted's brains were fried with dark magic. They didn't have the capacity for strategic thinking.

The Corrupted in front of Vaiden parted, giving room to another. It was robed in red, wearing a mask to conceal its face. He called it an "it" because he couldn't tell the gender under the thick robe. Not that it mattered to Vaiden. He would kill it no matter female, male, or other. He wasn't sexist.

The red robe was significant though. Plain Corrupted never wore color.

"Shit." His his fingers tightened around the grip of his swords through the slippery black goo. "Blood mage."

"Wara help us," Gabriel groaned at his back.

Vaiden nodded, a heaviness forming in his chest. He didn't like this. First a monstrosity, then a blood mage. What could be next? Aegan in the flesh?

The Corrupted all began as regular High Elves, praising whatever goddess with whom they sensed a connection. Most praised Grita, who created High Elves and blessed them with a tiny piece of the goddess's sorcery. Others praised Jana, The Mother, who created the elements, and gifted them with bountiful harvest. Then there were those who preferred Moren, the moon, Mother of Vampires, necromancy, and dark magic, which was not necessarily evil in its pure form.

But only the vile worshiped Aegan—only those looking for power and corruption. The blood mage standing before him was once one of those High Elves, but it had fallen as the Corrupted, transcended with Aegan's power, and second only to soul suckers.

Vaiden had killed the most powerful soul sucker in Eskandor's history many months prior. What was a blood mage?

With its hands raised high above its head, the gloved hands rolled around an invisible ball, but it quickly filled. Blood from the dead surrounding them snaked to the blood mage, igniting fire between its hands. Vaiden's jaw locked. It was no wonder why the Corrupted dipped their hands into blood magic. On the battlefield, blood was an endless fuel.

The blood mage threw its magic at them—a fiery ball of death, big enough to burn down all the woods. Vaiden took a step forward, the heat of the blast warming his face, but only for a second before it quickly dissipated around him.

The Corrupted turned to each other, hissing with alarm. Vaiden grinned at the blood mage, who tilted its head as one of the others whispered in its ear. Another one brought a staff forward and softly placed it in their apparent leader's outstretched hand.

Vaiden watched the exchange, the heaviness in his chest growing stronger. Something wasn't right. He studied the staff, knowing it wasn't any normal walking stick.

The blood mage raised it, shooting a beam of light into the sky. The Shade took a step backward, watching the light reach the clouds, disappearing into the atmosphere. His eyes fell back on the blood mage. There was no panic in it, even faced with a Shade. That was odd, especially for the Corrupted, even Jen the Unfavorable had recoiled when learning what he was.

The ground shook, forcing the elves to stumble.

"What the..." Vaiden fought to stay on his feet. "An earthquake?'

Gabriel grabbed his shoulder. "What's going on?"

"I don't know."

The blood mage stared at Vaiden with shielded eyes, studying his reaction. For what, Vaiden didn't know. Light rained from the sky, like a million tiny stars shooting through the trees, followed by meteors of fire.

"Fuck!" Vaiden grabbed Gabriel's arm. "Run!"

They ran, evading falling trees, and balls of fire. The magic wouldn't hurt Vaiden, but Gabriel did not have such power. Dirt and debris exploded with every meteor that slammed into the earth. It was a battlefield—a blast of pure magic—something Vaiden thought only the defense turrets in Casimere's wall or Mysogus's towers could replicate. What kind of staff was that? And where did this blood mage find it?

Vaiden put it at the back of his mind. He ran, keeping close to Gabriel. Their long strides made short work of the woods until it grew dark and quiet again, a field of dead grass before them. They'd made it back to the road.

Gabriel panted, hands braced against his knees. "What in Surnuna's grace was that?"

"I have no idea," Vaiden exhaled, resting his hands on his hips.

"We need to tell Glades." The ambassador started back toward the fort. "A blood mage with that kind of power. It could break through the wall."

If not level the whole fort, Vaiden thought, catching up. "Where are the damn horses?"

Further up the path, they found Alvez, wrangling the horses. Vaiden wanted to give him a taste of his mind for abandoning them like that, but Gabriel interceded, stating they needed to return to the garrison with haste. He wasn't wrong, but it didn't stop the Shade from glaring at the captain the entire ride back.

8

The PR meeting ran long. They didn't seem to understand or empathize that Tatiana didn't want to do a TV interview about her experiences six months ago. When they kept pushing, she asked for the meeting to resume at a later date. They were not happy, but she used her handy trump card—bringing in human resources—against them. A simple threat from HR made any department squirm. They agreed to return to the subject down the road.

She split the rest of her time at the office between updating other cases and making phone calls to experts she knew in the preternatural community. The blood ritual Mr. Slaseezor performed would be under great scrutiny. It sounded barbaric. Tatiana needed to find some way to soften its meaning.

Mr. Slaseezor had said the roots of this ritual dated back to his ancestors on Arda. People were interested in the foreign world and its cultures. Perhaps she could relate it to indigenous practices on Earth—something less alien to the public. She knew if Mr. Slaseezor sat on the stand, admitting that the practice was used for making sacrifices, it could make a jury see this was not some big secret. Everyone in the den knew the origins of the ceremony.

The prosecution could try to bend his words, meaning Mr. Slaseezor knew it was the perfect opportunity to use the ceremony to commit murder. He had access to the knives. He admitted to cleaning them before the ritual.

Her eyes fixated on the words "blood ritual," as if they had been printed in bold red letters, dripping off the page. A ceremony seemed harmless, but blood ritual? For any blood to be spilled, pain had to be involved. The prosecution would paint a picture of how these rituals were performed once upon a time on Arda and how Mr. Slaseezor had intimate knowledge about it, how no one else in his congregation had died during the ritual, but...

"Why this victim?" Tatiana asked aloud, glancing over the police report again. The victim was Earth-born, meaning he had never lived on Arda. He was new to their den and religion. Witness statements claimed the victim was a nice young man, helpful, and full of life and promise. Tatiana frowned. They would have probably said that even if he had been standoffish, but he had been tragically young.

She made a note to research the victim more thoroughly. They needed to work on any angles to prove that Mr. Slaseezor knew nothing about the knife swap or had ill will toward the victim. Why would he kill someone in front of an audience? She knew the prosecution would call it the perfect crime. No one would believe a religious man capable of such evil. Everyone would think it was some horrible accident, but it was a clever ploy to get away with murder.

They charged him with *murder* though, not manslaughter or involuntary manslaughter. The criteria for the others would have been easier to prove. They could probably convince a jury of involuntary manslaughter, that Mr. Slaseezor was careless with the ceremonial blades—that he accidentally picked up the wrong one, but the district attorney had chosen a mountain to climb with a murder charge.

When her eyes began to cross from concentrating too hard, she pushed away from her desk. The sun was setting. By the time she reached home, it would be dark.

Her apartment was located on the east side, close to downtown. She hated paying the inflated rent prices, but it felt safer to have neighbors, even if they were loud at times.

The gated parking lot was well lit. She parked in her designated spot and gathered the printed off research and updated files she needed for the new case. Her car needed a good cleaning, especially vacuuming. Crumbs littered the back floorboards. She needed to get ahead of it before ants invaded.

Inside the apartment complex, warm lighting guided her down tile flooring and off-white walls. Neighbors played loud bouncy music, and someone whined about their team not playing well. When she arrived at her apartment door, the files weighed down both her arms. She stared at the door, wishing it would magically pick up her card to scan as the front doors to the complex did. Unwilling to set the files down, she pinned them against the door and wrenched her hand free to search the bag for keys. She needed to clip them to her bag's strap for easier access, but paranoia that they would unclip or someone would swipe them, kept her from making things easier.

The apartment was dark when she entered, but she easily navigated to the catch-all table to the side of the entryway, heaving the files on top of it. A sigh escaped her lips, slipping off the bag, and flipping on a light switch. She closed the front door, locking it immediately.

Even after all these months, it didn't feel secure. A vampire could easily splinter the door—not that a human couldn't. They had been wrecking doors since such an invention had been made. The supernatural did it effortlessly though.

She took a deep breath. No one was kicking in her door. Jen was dead. Lizabeth LaBelle too. None of her enemies remained, besides the District Attorney Abraham Leanger. She briefly wondered if he would be trying Mr. Slaseezor's case or if he would appoint someone else since he had a losing record against her. They would have multiple people assigned to the case, especially if they knew she was representing the supernatural. It was custom of late.

She had Logan for the research. Sometimes a fresh-faced attorney would assist her with the more boring procedures of court, like admitting physical evidence. It was great practice for a rookie lawyer to find their footing in front of a judge and jury. The more times they presented a case, the more comfortable they would become.

She peeled off her blazer, strutting through the open concept living and dining rooms and kitchen. It wasn't as nice as her house, but at least ghosts of memories past didn't haunt her everywhere she turned. She discarded the blazer over her couch and jetted to the refrigerator for a bottle of wine.

A healthy glass of white wine would help relax her, but her magical teacher and friend, Coastal, would scold her for not eating. She opened the fridge, grabbing one of her prepared meals. It was a simple garlic butter chicken dinner with mashed potatoes and pan-fried green beans. She slid it into the microwave, pressing the reheat options.

While her dinner warmed, she moved the files to the living area. Logan managed to wrangle the den's financial reports while she was in the meeting with PR. Since the den was nonprofit and qualified for public exemptions, its reports had to be readily available to the public.

Tatiana knew some organizations managed not to publish all their records, but a simple subpoena could alleviate that issue—not that she believed Mr.

Slaseezor's den had anything to hide, but she would comb through the information to see if anything—even the smallest detail—appeared audacious. Before she would do that, she would ask the den for more records and Mr. Slaseezor's wife too. They needed access to their personal financials—anything to disprove incentive to the kill.

Pearson and Associates did have a private investigator to aid in criminal cases, but he was a little apprehensive to get involved with the preternatural community. Not that he was against the supernatural, but he claimed they were too difficult to work with. Caden had said his dad had talked to the partners about investing in more PIs for preternatural cases, but, as always, with anything pertaining to the supernatural, they were cautious.

Sometimes the divide between humans and the preternatural community frustrated her, but she understood too. The supernatural had a lot of reasons not to trust police and local agencies. It was why they relied heavily on the Underground to find some semblance for justice or revenge.

Six months ago, she had witnessed that operation from the underbelly of the preternatural community. Never in her life had she been so afraid, paranoid, and uncertain. Why would they want to use the Underground? It was dangerous, but then again, without Vaiden, what would Tatiana have done?

Vaiden—her heart fluttered thinking about him. She had tried not to during these long months since he'd returned to Arda. The kingdom recalled him to help fight in a civil war. She didn't know the intimate details, but Vaiden had told her he'd been charged with assassinating the rebel leader. She wondered if he was successful—not that she wanted to know if he carried out the plot. She just wanted him back home safe.

Technically, it was illegal for him to be on Earth. He was a Shade. They were the only race of elves banned from Earth because of their direct ties to the king's orders. They had to carry them out as protectors of the kingdom, which meant any Shade could be the elves' agent against Earth. Tatiana would argue any dedicated elf, serpent, or feline could be an agent of Arda, but she did understand Shades could be dangerous. Vaiden was.

She wouldn't deny he scared her when they had first met. He'd threatened her with harm and claimed he would kill her for the right price. Things had changed though. *He* had changed thanks to her accidental cast of a binding spell. She'd lassoed them together, unlocking emotions Vaiden did not before have. Coastal claimed the bind could be broken by a powerful enough practitioner, but Vaiden waved it away. He wanted to explore the bind's benefits.

Tatiana didn't know how to feel about it, being tied to someone, but when she had looked into Vaiden's eyes and found them filled with something new—not the void that had been previously there—her heart swelled with the idea he could be more than a Shade.

She didn't know if it was right or against nature, but Coastal claimed the bind didn't have any ill effects. Why not explore it?

Vaiden was a world away though, unreachable. Even with the bind, she couldn't feel him. She frowned, a siren growing louder in her ears.

"Kitty, kitty," whispered from behind her. She started, glancing around the room until her eyes landed on the microwave, beeping insistently that her food was done. Another sigh escaped her lips as she fetched it.

She sat at the bar, drinking her wine and eating dinner, wondering what next moves she must make in Mr. Slaseezor's case. She needed to visit the den and his family, get their side of the story, and permission for personal files. Mr. Slaseezor already gave his permission, but he was locked up. He had no rights currently, besides to an attorney and a fair trial.

Fair. Tatiana stabbed her chicken. Supernatural cases ran through expedient routes through all criminal courts. Caden's cases could take months, if not years, to try, but he worked non-violate crimes. Tatiana had a week at best, days at worst, to present cases to a judge. After opening arguments, the judge would decide if the case needed to go to trial or not, no need for a grand jury, pleas, or future scheduling. It was where her colleagues who only tried human violent crimes expressed their sympathy. They had ample time to prepare cases, months of digging up information and finding witnesses.

Sometimes Tatiana reveled in taking on two or three major criminal cases a month, but lately, she tired. She didn't know if it was burn out from all the pro bono work she'd taken on or from the trauma six months ago, or the fact the people who she chose to represent had wanted to kill her, but she needed something. Maybe that drink with Logan could help, but that was at least twelve weeks away, *if* he passed the bar.

A knock rapped on her door. She jumped off the sofa, staring inquiringly at it while it continued. Her heart pounded fiercely against her chest. This time of night she wasn't expecting anyone.

There were many who sought her out lately, not just journalists like George Zeilberg. Jen spoke of a magical organization who wanted to use Tatiana as a weapon. They were Mystic Crane. She had never met them personally, but Coastal had.

Slowly, she approached the door. She'd chosen to live in an apartment, hoping the presence of neighbors would keep people like Mystic Crane at bay. Maybe it was a silly thought. She could be endangering innocent people.

The familiar slide of heat snaked down her arms, letting her know magic glowed through her veins in electric blue. She leaned into the keyhole, a gasp escaping her lips.

Upon her doorstep, stood a vampire.

9

"We need to send word to Kiji Village," Vaiden urged.

Glades sat behind his wooden desk, his massive biceps bulging when he crossed his arms. "It won't help," the general said. "The king has ordered them to the village. That's where they'll stay."

"Then write the king. Change his mind. Tell him you need immediate assistance."

Gabriel was shocked by the alarm in Vaiden's voice, but they had barely escaped those woods. A blood mage capable of summoning meteors could flatten Fort Khali.

"What will that do? It would be weeks before the Shades even get here."

"It's better to have back up than none." Vaiden slammed his hands on the general's desk. "Why won't you help yourself? Think about your men."

"The king's orders are clear." Heat crawled into Glades's strong features. "We will get no help from Kiji. We must defend the fort ourselves."

Vaiden scowled, throwing his hands in the air.

"I'll write the king," Gabriel gently said. "Perhaps requesting assistance will give him the spark he needs to win this blight."

Glades shrugged, his color normalizing. "Do what you wish, ambassador, but know I've already written the king several times asking for Shade assistance. Each time, he's turned me down."

"For what reason?" Vaiden asked.

"He must have given one," Gabriel added.

"I'm afraid the king doesn't share his reasons with me," the general replied. "We must trust in his plans."

"Do you?" Vaiden asked. "Trust *Altamost*?"

Glades shot to his feet. "He is the king! You hold your tongue, Shade, or I will lock you in the dungeons myself."

"Some of your men have already died because of the king's incompetence," Vaiden argued. "When will you wake up and take action?"

The general bolted around his desk, but Gabriel planted himself in front of Vaiden, stopping him. He had his meaty hand wrapped around the hilt of his sword, ready to draw. The ambassador studied the general's bright red face, glaring a warning. Glades hated Vaiden—he had since their days in the Forty-Second. Then it was about glory, being the best at what they did. Times had changed. Glades was a general. Vaiden had been exiled; his reputation tarnished forever. Of what was there to be jealous? Perhaps it was because if Gabriel had let them fight, Glades wasn't guaranteed to win, even with his size advantage.

"Make preparations to protect the people of this fort, general," Gabriel said with his chin raised and shoulders squared. He was the highest ranking official in the fort. Glades would take orders from him. The general grimaced, his dark eyes stabbing through Gabriel at Vaiden.

"One day the ambassador won't be here to protect you, Shade."

"You think he's protecting me." Vaiden chuckled.

Glades stiffened, nostrils flaring, his fist tightening around the hilt of his sword.

"General, I gave you an order." Gabriel stood as tall as his frame would allow him. Glades dwarfed him, but when the general's eyes shifted to the ambassador, his anger faltered. "Be on your way."

He left them in a huff, barking orders to the guards stationed outside his office. Gabriel glared at Vaiden, who shrugged innocently.

"I don't know why you push him," the ambassador said. "He's our ally."

"Maybe he isn't." The Shade picked up a few trinkets on Glades's desk and put them back down. "Have you ever thought that?"

"Don't be foolish. We're all in the fight against the Corrupted."

"Then why is the crown doing nothing about it? Why send the Shades to Kiji?"

"Arguing with Glades will do nothing to protect this fort. We need to work together."

Vaiden rolled his eyes.

60

"I don't know what's going on with you, but you need to stop being a horse's ass. The Corrupted will come here. They will attack and we need everyone ready, including you."

"*Especially* me." Vaiden crossed his arms, giving the ambassador a measured expression. "I'm one Shade. I cannot fight all the Corrupted and with that staff—"

"Exactly why we need to work together." Gabriel pointed out. "If we take down that blood mage, the rest of the nest will be easy to destroy."

"They have a necromancer too."

The ambassador took a deep breath and exhaled. The Corrupted could be formable when they wanted to be. He recalled a time long ago when his own party had been ambushed by a swarm on his way to negotiations with Orcania. Those Corrupted were nowhere as dangerous as this nest, but they had managed to kill two of his men and injure several others. They needed to be eliminated.

Gabriel knew part of Vaiden's attitude had to be purpose surging through him. He needed to destroy the Corrupted and he had failed to do so in those woods. He'd get another shot. A Corrupted, with the kind of power the blood mage possessed, would not contain its power.

"I need to write the king," Gabriel said mostly to himself.

Vaiden raised a brow at him. "And probably take a bath too." He gestured with Glades's quill at the blood stains on Gabriel's clothes. Dirt, blood, and grime coated his skin, gluing his hair to his neck. Sometimes Gabriel thought shorter hair was more practical, especially after a fight, but he'd long been out of the military. Caroline liked his hair longer.

"You need one too. Surnuna knows what that black goo is."

The Shade wrinkled his nose, using the quill to pick at the sludge beneath his nails. "It smells worse than it looks."

"Well, Caroline will be upset if we don't check in with her, but just don't get mud all over her rugs."

"Do you think she'll bathe me personally?" Vaiden grinned darkly, tossing aside the quill and strutting for the door.

Gabriel snorted. "You're lucky if she lets you in the house."

"Oh, but she misses me. She'll be angry with you."

Gabriel followed him out, down the stone stairs to the base level. Soldiers scurried around the fort, completing tasks. A man asked about the stores in the cellar. If they managed to stop the blood mage, there was no guarantee they would beat the Corrupted on the battlefield. A powerful necromancer could revive an army of the undead. The fight could last days. They needed to be prepared.

Necromancers were harder to spot than blood mages, but their magic would betray them with a green glow. It wasn't the only green power, but it was the most common, especially among the Corrupted. The nest would protect their necromancer, especially if it had the ability to create monstrosities, like the one from the woods.

Despite the grime clinging to Gabriel's face or the blood sprayed upon his skin, Caroline kissed him with the same desperation she had when he'd first arrived. She quickly ushered him and Vaiden to the bathhouses, firing questions about the supply chart and the attack. She didn't bathe them, but she did supply them with ointments and potions that easily removed the grime. She helped Gabriel clean his hair, scrubbing it deeply. He let out a moan, maybe a little exaggerated to coax a whine from Vaiden.

The Shade remained quiet during his bath. His eyes focused on something unseen, lost in his thoughts. Gabriel let him be. Every soldier readied for battle differently. He had never given much thought to how Shades prepared themselves. They were made for war, especially against the Corrupted—their true purpose, the reason why Wara had created them.

"What is Earth like?" Caroline asked, making Vaiden blink at her.

"You know he's not allowed to say," Gabriel said, resting against the back of the tub while she combed his hair.

"We're all friends here," she replied. "I promise not to tell a soul."

"It's different," Vaiden said. "One of the strangest things in their history is long prejudice against people of different skin tones."

"What do you mean?" Gabriel asked. "If someone has fairer skin, they're ugly?"

"No, but yes, but no," the Shade exhaled. "Like I said, it's strange."

"Tell me something else," Caroline said. "Do they have beautiful places, like Brevene?"

Vaiden scrubbed his arms with a cloth. "They have a lot of pretty places on Earth. Some trees with pink leaves, but not bark. Magic there is different. It doesn't live in the plants like here. Some say there's old magic in untouched places, but I wouldn't know. I can't feel it."

Gabriel tilted back his head to spy his wife's lips purse. "What about faith? Do they—"

"Caroline," he warned. "Vaiden can't talk about those things."

"They have many different religions, just like Arda does," the Shade said, clearly ignoring Gabriel. "Ours is older though, but their history isn't as complete as ours. Humans aren't eternal."

His voice softened while he discussed humans. Maybe he had friends on Earth. It was odd for a Shade to want any, but Vaiden was changed. Life was precious, but elves could live for millennia. Human life was a blink to them, gone so quickly. Gabriel had never given much thought to humans. They had settlements east of Eskandor's border, but they were small in numbers, never rising a threat to their neighbors.

At one time they were citizens of the vampires' empire. Gabriel knew they were treated like cattle, given space in a pasture to grow, breed, and live peacefully until the time came for milking. Before the Empire, human villages fed a court of vampires in partnership for generations. The vampires protected them from trolls and other predators that would eat them.

After the formation of the empire, their relationship drastically changed. Vampires were their overlords, their gods. Gabriel once read reports about humans who worshipped the vampires as the goddesses. It was odd and truly an example of blasphemy, but the vampires had to create euphoria to control the humans.

With the vampires gone, the humans prospered peacefully, but Gabriel knew troll attacks happened from time-to-time. The serpents handled tragedies on their borders, but mostly the human settlements were a booming market for creatures across the continents to meet for trade. Gabriel hadn't been in years.

"Do you miss it?" Caroline asked gently. "Earth?"

The Shade exhaled sharply through his nose. "I miss the convenience of it."

"What does that mean?"

"You wouldn't believe me if I told you."

"Well, that only makes me more interested."

He looked away, his eyes staring at something unseen again. Maybe he was thinking about Earth, what he truly missed there, but Gabriel wouldn't push him. He patted his wife's arm, forcing her to look down at him.

Let him alone, his eyes said. She nodded, announcing she was going to prepare their dinner.

"You need to get her out of here," Vaiden quietly said while they dressed.

Gabriel pulled on a boot, arching a brow at his friend. "What do you mean?"

"We don't know what's going to happen with this nest," the Shade returned, his face serious. "Caroline and the villagers should get out of here while they can."

"The Corrupted could find them on the road."

"Send them east, not west."

"That's the opposite of help."

"There's villages to the west."

"Small ones."

"Remote and not worth the Corrupted's time."

Gabriel rested his elbows on his knees, staring up at the Shade dressed in black. There was something about the way he held himself, something unlike any Shade Gabriel had ever met. Confidence filled Shades' veins. They were void of fear, but then why did an uneasiness wash over Vaiden's features?

"We'll discuss it." Gabriel pulled on his other boot and climbed to his feet. "But she's not going to want to leave."

"I'll help convince her."

"Ambassador!" Alvez's panicked voice had them racing out of the bathhouse. "We've spotted movement due south. They're coming."

"Wara, protect us."

10

Tatiana slung the door open. "Zarah!"

The vampire raised a brow at her. "You're not ready?"

She opened her mouth to reply, but her eyes swept over the glittery gold dress that hugged Zarah's athletic shape like a glove.

"I forgot something, didn't I?"

Zarah folded her arms over the plunging neckline down her chest. "We've only been orchestrating this ladies night for several weeks."

"Five minutes!" Tatiana ran for her bedroom, leaving the door ajar for the vampire to enter at her discretion. Darling hadn't reminded her at the office, or she *had* and Tatiana hadn't been listening. Either could be true. She scrambled through her closet, searching for anything nice to wear. There were several dresses Darling forced her to buy that were on the sexy side, but she couldn't imagine wearing them out and being sure her ass wasn't showing.

She pushed them aside and grabbed the only other outfit that was both comfortable and clubbing approved, black skinnies with a peplum halter top. An inverted triangle had been cut out of the top, replaced with netting, that dipped into her cleavage. The metallic top was sleeveless, so she made sure her pits didn't need a shave before she applied deodorant.

"I'll do my makeup in the car," Tatiana announced, catching a glimpse of Zarah in the mirror. The vampire nodded, her hand gliding down the rows of dresses Tatiana decidedly pushed away.

"Why not one of these?" she asked.

Tatiana made a face, pulling her hair into a high ponytail. She grabbed her to-go makeup pouch and slipped her feet into a pair of simple flats. Something she could run in, if she needed to. Not that she believed anything would happen at the club, but she rather be prepared.

Zarah wore heels, making her closer to Tatiana's height than her actual five-foot-three. She was a vampire though, which meant supernatural speed. Not that it meant she could run in heels or fight in them, but Zarah was a trained warrior. She could handle herself.

The vampire tapped an invisible watch on her wrist, signaling their need to leave.

"Alright, just let me..." Tatiana snatched a clutch from the rack of purses hanging opposite of the dresses. It was small enough to fit in her pocket. It also had a strap to go around her wrist, so she didn't lose any of her important information or credit cards. She grabbed her office bag and transferred the needed materials to the clutch.

"Let's go," Zarah exhaled, leaning against the door.

"Just..." Tatiana looked around the room, searching for her phone. Where had she left it? She searched through her bag once more to no avail. She hadn't called anyone since she had arrived home, and she didn't remember using it at dinner. Her eyes landed on the blazer, laying absently across the back of the sofa. She retrieved it, finding the phone safely in the inside pocket.

"OK, ready!" Tatiana held up the phone in victory.

Zarah shook her head, the ends of lips curling.

Six months ago, Tatiana didn't know how to feel about Zarah. Her late husband, Harvey Dellawood, had drafted a reform to expel vampire courts. It had not gone well with his master. After he had asked Tatiana for aid in bringing down his master and promoting the reform (a deal that he ultimately withdrew), he'd put a target on her back. It was Zarah who had hired Vaiden to protect her.

Zarah had helped rescue Tatiana from Jen too, even after she'd lost her husband. Tatiana imagined it was difficult to set aside that pain for someone Zarah barely knew, but nevertheless, she was thankful for the vampire.

As they approached Zarah's BMW, she thought Zarah might be one of the few she could talk to about what happened six months ago. They hadn't spoken about it, except to go over the story they had orchestrated for how they met.

The story they developed claimed, after Harvey's death, Zarah had received a sizable inheritance. She decided the best way to explain their sudden friendship was that Tatiana had attended his funeral. They had met there and later discussed what to do with Zarah's inheritance. Tatiana had suggested donating it to charity and Zarah agreed, which she had ended up doing for the sake of records. A friendship had developed between Zarah's grief and Tatiana's trauma. That part, at least, was true.

While Zarah drove, Tatiana applied her makeup. She didn't normally wear anything heavy, just a simple frame, some liner, shadow, and mascara with a light gloss. Tonight, she decided to go with a smoky eye and red lipstick, which won Zarah's approval with a smile.

"You have gorgeous eyes," the vampire said. "You should accentuate them more often."

Tatiana scoffed, noting the wings sprouting from Zarah's eyes as if Cleopatra herself had applied them. Her golden tan skin, flawless and lean, somehow made her petite body appear stronger in the tight dress. Most would have mistaken her for Middle Eastern descent, but Zarah immigrated from Arda.

She was a beautiful woman—the kind with which other women compared themselves because they were jealous, intimidated, or they wholeheartedly respected and admired a confident, strong woman. Tatiana knew each kind of these women. She tried to be the one who admired women, but she found herself envious of Zarah's effortless beauty.

"Is Lewej coming?" she asked before applying her lipstick.

"She might." Zarah commanded the steering wheel, caramel-colored eyes studying traffic. "If she doesn't, it's because she's a brat. We will not coddle her or tolerate her complaints."

"How is she adjusting to her new job?"

"You would think a girl who keeps up with all things smartphone related, she would be good at selling them," Zarah exhaled. "Coastal has her hands full with that one."

"Will *she* be joining us?"

The vampire shook her head, brown waves rolling over her shoulders, dark and rich as chocolate. "Tonight is for worship."

"Oh, I forgot it's Friday."

"Clearly."

"Hey, I can't help that a new case dropped in my lap today."

"A likely story." A smile played with Zarah's lips. "What is this one about?"

"A serpent charged with murder." Tatiana wilted against her seat. "You'll hear about it on the news soon enough, but it's a case of ritual gone wrong."

"Serpents have many rituals," the vampire said. "Their kingdom is built on tradition and superstition."

"You don't have to tell me," Tatiana exhaled. "The last serpent I represented held back details from me because I didn't do the formalities correctly."

"They expect you to know the formalities without ever being told them." The car veered into a turning lane and waited in line with other vehicles for the light to turn. "I am glad I was assigned to the elves. I remember how our serpent ambassador complained about the many rules of their kingdom and how no one cared to share what they were."

Tatiana blinked at her friend, remembering she was the last vampire ambassador to the elves. It was a lifetime ago, Zarah would say, but Tatiana found it difficult to believe the woman sitting next to her was in her hundreds. She appeared around Tatiana's age, under thirty.

"State will argue how my client knew the ritual was originally designed to kill and how he intended to use that as the perfect scapegoat for an easy murder."

"There's no such thing as an easy murder." Zarah accelerated through the green light. "I suppose, unless you are a psychopath or a Shade."

A moment of silence befell the car. Tatiana thought Vaiden might agree with Zarah's assessment. Killing came easy to him. He'd hunted others since he was ten, as all Shade's were trained. The attorney's stomach churned thinking about the vampire she'd accidentally killed. She tried not to picture Bailyn Rosenhouse, a beautiful yet terrifying man, who had tried to drag her to Jen. The fear plastered over his face when he had questioned what she was, often haunted her dreams.

It was why she needed a new magical teacher. Coastal could only teach her so much as she didn't share the same magic as Tatiana. The High Elf, former High Priestess of Alumpius, was blessed with pure white magic for healing, creating defensive wards, and cleansing auras. Tatiana had quite the opposite—destructive magic for inflicting damage and burning down anything in her path. Bailyn's death was an accident. The blue fire had burst from her body, destroying everything in its wake. That couldn't happen again.

"Has Coastal received any word from Arda?" Tatiana asked gently.

"It's hard to communicate during war."

She nodded, looking out her window. Down this stretch of avenue, the crowds thickened around clubs and bars. On a Friday night, it might be difficult to get in, but Tatiana knew Darling had many friends, who happened to be bouncers at clubs.

Zarah pulled into the packed lot off Club Nerve. She paid at the toll booth and off they went searching for somewhere to park. Luckily, two rows in, someone was leaving the night early. Tatiana stored her makeup pouch in the glove box and grabbed her clutch, fastening the strap around her wrist.

As she followed Zarah through the lot to the long line stretching around the club, she wondered where Zarah stored her ID and money in that tight dress. She rarely carried anything that would hamper her hands. Perhaps something she'd picked up through training.

While they stood in line, Tatiana retrieved her phone, typing the beginnings of a message to Darling, when someone picked them out of the line. Zarah grabbed Tatiana's hand, ushering her toward the front where music bounced through the air. Inside, it hit them in blast waves. The foyer was dark, their vision only guided by strips of neon lights toward giant double doors.

Beyond it, the dance floor was packed with bodies writhing through the hypnotical beats. They scooted through a sea of onlookers, tightly squeezed in every inch of the club like sardines in a can. Zarah grasped Tatiana's hand firmly, voicing "excuse me" repeatedly throughout the crowd. Some people smiled down at the women, some with lustful eyes, others with drunken smiles. Tatiana didn't hold eye contact with any of them, in case they were vampires.

The crowd thinned around tables and seating areas where they found Darling, clustered with friends. Some of them Tatiana recognized as ladies from Darling's spin class, but she couldn't put faces to names; however, one natural redhead, downing a row of shots, she would never forget.

Josie Pearson raised her fists to the sky, a cheer of victory sounding from her pink lips, like a Viking who had single-handedly won a great battle. When she spotted Tatiana, Josie threw her arms around her neck, forcing her to stoop a little as Josie was closer to Zarah's height.

Under the mask of alcohol, the smell of fresh spring, floral and rich, filled Tatiana's nostrils. Josie held her tightly for a moment, then pushed back blinking eyes of sky blue at her. She beamed wildly, every bit the girl Tatiana had met in college.

"Drinks are on me!" Josie bounced in place. "Get anything you want." She pointed at a variety of shots and fruity cocktails on their table. Tatiana sipped one of the cocktails, pineapple flavored, eying Josie as she offered one to Zarah. The vampire waved her hand.

"Oh, I forgot!" Josie hit her forehead with the heel of her palm. "Sorry!"

"It's OK." Zarah said, faking a smile.

"They do have plasma fruit here, babe," Darling said over the music.

"Just put it on my tab!" Josie pointed at herself as she danced in place.

"You want me to go with you?" Tatiana asked Zarah. She shook her head and disappeared into the crowd surrounding the bar. Tatiana watched her go, her hand suddenly cold and alone without Zarah's. She studied the other girls. Her heart pounded in sync with the music. Darling's eyes swept over her outfit, an unimpressed expression frowning on her lips.

"What?" Tatiana dared.

"We went dress shopping a couple weeks ago." Darling leaned an elbow on the table. Her other hand pointed at Tatiana, gesturing up and down. "I know you have better options than this."

"What?" Tatiana pressed her fingers behind an ear, leaning forward. "I can't hear you over the music."

Darling rolled her eyes. "So much for showing off your summer body. What was the point of all that running?"

A siren wailed over the music, pounding between her ears. Tatiana swallowed hard, dipping her stare away from her friend. A few spin class friends whispered to each other, their eyes glancing her way.

"I'm just pulling your chain." Darling patted her hands then returned them around the stem of her glass. "It's good to see you enjoying yourself for a change."

"Thanks." She inhaled the rest of her drink. "Did Lewej make it?"

Darling pointed toward the dance floor. She squinted through the flashing lights until her eyes captured a young elf, grinding her bottom against the front of a man. Tatiana frowned. Lewej looked nineteen, but Tatiana didn't know exactly how old she was. She acted younger, perhaps because of her spoiled nature.

Something warm slithered around Tatiana's waist, making her jump. Josie's lithe frame cozied up against hers. Heat washed over Tatiana, but she forced it to cool, spying blue lines receding from her fingers. It was going to be a long night. Why didn't she wear sleeves?

"She wouldn't wait," Josie said. "Maybe we should join her?"

Tatiana opened her mouth to decline, but Josie grabbed her hands, bounding them toward the dance floor. For someone petite, Josie pulled her with the force of a mule, who'd spent their life transporting wagons through mountains. Darling and the other girls joined them, finding dancing partners quickly.

A guy asked Tatiana for her name, but she shook her head, turning back to her friends. Josie moved erratically, the living example of "dancing like no one's watching". Darling had rhythm, that smooth silky motion that reminded Tatiana of waves rolling ashore.

Club Nerve was preternatural friendly. She spotted felines, elves, and serpents mixed amongst the human-like faces. Vampires were among them, but unlike other creatures, they were harder to distinguish, unless they smiled widely to see fangs.

The hair on her neck stood up straight, ice sliding down her back. Eyes were watching her, but as she scanned the crowd, she found no one immediately looking at her. They were hidden then.

"Here kitty, kitty," purred in her ears. Josie hooked her arm in Tatiana's, whirling them around. Smiles and laughter filled her vision, bodies spasming against invisible forces, the stench of alcohol, sweat, and different perfumes overwhelming her senses. They kept spinning, impairing any sense of direction or focus on a landmark. Where were the exits? Where was Zarah? She was lost in the vast ocean of bodies on the dance floor.

Tatiana closed her eyes, taking deep breaths to steady herself. Josie's arms were around her waist, forcing her to sway with the jovial redhead. Tatiana leaned into her, welcoming the smell of freshly cut grass and blossoms. Everything else she breathed out of her head. It was only Josie's warmth at her back and the steady beat of her own heart, something stronger and everlasting than the music blasting through the club.

Her muscles relaxed against Josie, familiar and safe. It was ladies night—their night—to let loose and have fun. Nothing could stop them. The liquor warming her belly spread throughout her body, mixing with music wiggling through the air. Josie's grip loosened around her hips, letting Tatiana find her own rhythm.

"There you go!" Josie exclaimed over the music.

She forgot about everything, the new case, the blood ritual, the pact with Logan—everything. It was just this moment, this song. She let it play through her like she was the musician's favorite instrument. Their fingers were so familiar, plucking her strings, making her sing.

God, she missed Vaiden.

The thought of him—his strong arms wrapped around her sent heat clawing through her body. She spiraled out of Josie's arms, laughing breathlessly. Josie nodded at her, understanding she needed a break. Tatiana returned to their table, guarded by a few of Darling's spin class friends. She took a few deep breaths, glad for the space.

"Aren't you that lawyer?" one of the girls with curly hair asked. "The one who was missing for a few months?"

"Um, yeah." Tatiana's fingers played with the collar around her neck, unsticking it from her skin.

"I saw a story online about what happened." The girl managed to look sympathetic. "It's so terrible. Do you know how many paintings they removed from just one of those art galleries? It's unreal!"

"Completely." Bile climbed up Tatiana's throat, but she forced it down. The girl continued to talk, her hands animating wildly as she explained details about the story. Most of it, Tatiana lost through the music and a siren blaring through her ears.

"I even visited one of those galleries once." Her eyes were glazed in excitement. "I mean, it wasn't a horror show then. They actually served these really tasty appetizers. My friend, he's an artist—"

"Latisha." Darling's voice struck the girl quick and hard as a whip, tearing through flesh and muscle. The girl visually cringed. "Now, I know you're not bothering Tatiana with that garbage, especially after I told all you girls not to bring it up."

Latisha shied away, like a child being scolded by her parents. She returned to the other friends, who promptly suggested going to the bathroom.

Darling exhaled heavily beside Tatiana. "Sorry, babe," she said. "I know you don't know her. She's a good girl, just stupid sometimes."

"It's OK."

"No, it's not." Darling leaned her curvy frame against the table. "You shouldn't be subjugated to these weirdos obsessed with—that stuff."

"With Jen," Tatiana corrected. "She's not the first to fixate on an exotic serial killer."

"Still." Her brows furrowed into a worried arch. "I warned her and the rest of them not to bring it up."

Tatiana waved it away. If she made it a big deal, Darling would want to talk, or she would be compelled to talk to Darling. Tonight wasn't about her. It was about fun, living, and celebrating life as women. Tatiana wouldn't allow herself to become the focus.

"Let's get more drinks," she said, and a smile widened across Darling's face, but it didn't reach her eyes.

"Alright, babe, but you're taking shots this round."

Tatiana moved for the bar, her grin bright, but it quickly vanished from her face as she stared into the eyes of Jen the Unfavorable.

11

Green lights flashed in the distance, like a storm trapped in the woods. Vaiden peered through the spyglass Alvez had handed him, watching for that storm to break away from the trees. It remained, churning, growing in strength. What was the Corrupted planning?

"They're not moving yet," Vaiden said.

"How long until they do?" Glades asked from the other side of Gabriel to Vaiden's right.

"I don't know," he answered. "Hours, days, but sooner than later I would think, especially after that display of power in the woods."

"What are they doing?" Alvez questioned quietly.

"Growing monstrosities." Vaiden handed the spyglass to Gabriel. "A necromancer can raise the dead. Since we didn't burn your buddies or the monstrosity, they'll rise and fight us again."

"How do you know so much about this?" Alvez asked.

"He's a Shade," Glades huffed. "The Corrupted are their business."

The captain blinked at Vaiden, his brows furrowed together in the firelight. "You're not like any Shade I have ever met."

Gabriel chuckled at some unheard joke.

"I'm not part of the battalion," Vaiden returned. "But to answer your question, my father is a necromancer, and my mother was a High Priestess. Magic is deeply rooted in my family as is its education."

"And here I thought you spawned directly from the Aegan's realm," Glades scoffed.

"But that doesn't make sense, general," Alvez said. "Shades came from Wara, not Aegan."

"Quiet, captain."

Gabriel handed the spyglass to the general. "They're not attacking tonight."

"We'll watch them throughout the night," Glades said. "On the morrow, if they haven't attacked, I'll send soldiers into those woods."

"To do what?" Vaiden asked. "Be overrun by the undead, killed, and raised as more undead to attack the fort? Be smart. Let them come to us."

"I am the general here, not you, Shade," growled Glades.

Vaiden opened his mouth to argue more, but Gabriel grabbed his arm, dragging him away.

"Fighting him will not solve this," the ambassador whispered. "Let the general run his operation."

"His operation is going to get a lot of people killed."

Gabriel let him go, whirling around with his finger pointed at the Shade. He said nothing, only closed his eyes and inhaled deeply through his nose. When he opened his eyes, the calm ambassador the kingdom knew and loved shine through.

"The fort is his. The soldiers are his to command," he said, voice neutral. "They are not your responsibility."

"Killing the Corrupted is my responsibility. Giving the Corrupted more ammo is bad business."

Although his face was shielded by shadow, Vaiden could depict his raised eyebrow. "Ammo?"

"More weapons, bodies, *anything* to build their nest is bad for this fort."

"I agree."

"Then why are you arguing with me?"

"Because it is not our place to make such calls. You are a Shade. I am the ambassador. Glades is the general. He presides over the soldiers. They are his to command," Gabriel explained. "This would not normally bother you."

"I am the only Shade here." Vaiden's jaw locked. "I cannot fight all the Corrupted."

"Why do you *feel* it is on your shoulders to fight them all? The fort is filled with able-bodied soldiers." Gabriel crossed his arms. "This isn't like you, Vaiden. What is the matter?"

The Shade threw his hands in the air, pacing a short line in front of his friend. Purpose pulsed through his veins. It hadn't stopped since he'd approached that forest or lessened when he left it. The Corrupted were there.

Part of him wanted to join the soldiers Glades would send to the woods to finish the job. The other part of him—the smarter side—knew that would be stupid.

They were outgunned in the forest. At the fort with its high, thick walls, there was a strategic path to win. They had to be patient and hope the blood mage didn't pull out that meteor summoning staff from the beginning. Vaiden doubted it would. It would want to play—to show how powerful it was—a test for what was to come in this blight against the Corrupted.

"Vaiden." Gabriel's voice made him stop in place. "What happened to you on Earth? Why do you care?"

"I don't care," Vaiden replied immediately. When Gabriel didn't look convinced, his brain raced with reasons for his interest in keeping soldiers alive. "It's a poor strategy. Glades should listen to me. I am a Shade. I know more about the Corrupted than him."

"Again, I agree." Gabriel leaned on his hip, his hand resting on the hilt of his sword. "But why is it important that he listens to you?"

"What does that mean?"

"It normally would not bug you. Most of the time you wouldn't volunteer the information."

"But I did."

"Yes, you did. That's the problem."

Vaiden shook his head. "I'm done with this. Whatever point you are trying to make is lost on me."

"You're angry."

"I'm annoyed."

"How?"

"What?"

"How are you annoyed?" Gabriel stepped up to his friend, the suspicion on his face clearer in Vaiden's natural vision. "Shades don't get annoyed."

A knot twisted in Vaiden's middle. He'd wanted to tell Gabriel about the bind, but he didn't know how his friend would respond. A sorceress had managed to ensnare a Shade. He'd never heard of such a thing. He doubted Gabriel had. It would only create more questions and suspicions. Could Vaiden complete his mission? What else in him had changed? Vaiden didn't know and that would be a problem.

He hated the confusion in Gabriel's eyes and how that confusion confused Vaiden. He was still sorting out emotions and what they meant. It was slow and brutal, but a crash course on Arda would help him prepare for when he returned to Earth—to his life.

"Shade, sir," Alvez said.

"Vaiden," he automatically corrected, tearing his gaze from Gabriel. They would talk about this later—if they survived the night.

"You said your father was a necromancer," the captain began. "What else did he teach you about the Corrupted?"

"He taught me nothing," Vaiden replied. "His involvement in my creation was simply the act itself."

"But you know a lot about the Corrupted, about necromancy."

"Yes, but not from him."

"I don't understand." Alvez's shoulders drooped. "Does someone teach the Shades about necromancy then?"

"No, everything is a hands-on experience."

"Then how do you know? Did your mother teach you?"

"Some, yes, but most of my knowledge on that type of magic comes from a friend of mine."

"Who?"

"A vampire."

"Oh." The captain's complexion paled, or perhaps that was Vaiden's nocturnal sight turning on. He avoided focusing on the torches lighting the courtyard, but even from that distance it slightly burned his eyes.

"Is that vampire still alive?" Gabriel asked. "I think I know who you're talking about. You used to write letters to each other."

"Latimere Greenbrooke." Vaiden nodded. "Yes, he's still very much alive."

"Why does that name sound familiar?" Alvez asked.

"Because he owns High Tower," Gabriel explained. "It's the only property in the kingdom not owned by an elf."

"Is it still the vampire's if they can never return to Arda?" Alvez asked.

Vaiden turned to Gabriel with raised brows. "Well?"

"The agreement the vampire forged was with King Duncan, far before the Last Empire War. I'm not sure if the exile of vampire kind rescinds that agreement, but I doubt anyone would willingly go to High Tower to enforce it."

"So, the vampire could be living there." Alvez's eyes widened with shock.

Vaiden shook his head. "He lives on Earth."

"But he could come back here and stay at High Tower."

Gabriel replied, "He would do well to stay on Earth. If anyone finds him wandering Arda, he's dead."

"Speaking about death." The Shade eyed the ambassador. "We need to talk to your wife about evacuating."

He nodded, something crossing his mind. "She's making dinner. Captain, have you eaten?"

"No, sir."

"Come dine with us."

The smell of roasted meat and spice greeted the men when they entered the Steel's family home. Caroline bustled around the fireplace, stirring a big pot of stew. Warmth rippled through Vaiden's chest at the sight of one of his oldest friends. Her skirts whispered around the kitchen, whisking bowls to the table where fresh bread, a wedge of cheese, and berries sat. Gabriel hugged his wife, drawing her in for a quick kiss before letting her return to fetching stews then drinks.

"I told you we would return," Vaiden said. Caroline gave him a look—something he couldn't decipher—before her eyes landed on Alvez behind him.

"We have a guest," she announced.

"I don't count?" The Shade crossed his arms.

She batted his shoulder, offering a friendly smile to the young captain. "Welcome," she said. "I am Caroline, Gabriel's wife."

"Captain Alvez."

Realization arched with her brows. "The only survivor of the supply cart attack?"

"You have a beautiful home, Lady Steel." The captain straightened and smiled widely, his boyish charm shining with his white teeth. "Surnuna has blessed this evening."

Alvez stood taller, his shoulders more squared. His hand rested comfortably on the hilt of his sword, like any seasoned soldier. There was a confidence surging through his eyes while they stared down at Caroline, who blushed at his calling of her a lady. His smile widened at the reddening of her cheeks.

Vaiden eyed Gabriel, who also watched the exchange closely. "Sit, captain." The ambassador's voice remained neutral, but suspicion glittered in his eyes.

Alvez sat with his back to the fireplace. An interesting choice, Vaiden thought. Most wouldn't give their back to the room, but it would be warmer closer to the fireplace. Gabriel chose the head of the table, as any man of the house normally would, while Vaiden took the other head of the table, mostly because his back was to a wall, but also because he liked challenging Gabriel's authority, if only symbolically.

Caroline quickly added Alvez's table setting and a bowl filled with delicious stew. Vaiden picked up his spoon to taste, but Caroline batted it out of his hand. He cocked a brow at her.

"You know better." She shook a finger at him. "We recognize the goddesses first."

"Perhaps he's spent too much time with the humans on Earth," Gabriel offered. "He's forgotten his manners."

Vaiden crossed his arms. "I didn't hear you reciting any praises on the trail."

"I did too quietly for you to hear."

The Shade rolled his eyes.

"Captain, it would be our honor if you would start us off," Caroline said.

Alvez placed his arms shoulder width with his palms raised to the ceiling. "We thank the goddesses for their blessings. Surnuna, our light, gives us life," he recited. "Moren, our moon, gives us peace."

"Wara, our strength, gives us courage. Opretta, our wonder, gives us joy," Gabriel said. "Grita, our teacher, gives us magic."

"Jana, our nurturer, gives us harvest," Caroline continued. "Layetta, our heart, gives us love."

They all turned to Vaiden, waiting. He frowned at them. "Aegan." He clicked his tongue. "Our punishment, gives us obedience."

Alvez clapped his hands, picking up his fork, but Vaiden lifted a finger at him.

"*And* Alumpius, our voice, gives us wisdom."

The captain's nose wrinkled. "Alumpius is banned from worship."

"My mother was her last High Priestess." Vaiden picked up his spoon. "I would not dishonor her by not including her goddess, someone who Rothnar the Daunting only banned because he didn't want other people to have opinions. He was a tyrant."

"You shouldn't say things like that about a king, especially a hero like King Rothnar." Alvez sat taller in his seat, smugly eating a spoonful.

"I served as his personal guard for over thirty years," Vaiden countered. "I'll say what I like."

The captain opened his mouth to argue, but Gabriel interceded. "Rothnar did a lot of good for this kingdom, but deciding his word was more absolute than a goddess, perhaps was not a popular move and one still under great scrutiny to this day."

"If it was so bad then why haven't the kings following his passing reinstated Alumpius?" Alvez asked.

"Chorlee died quickly after being crowned." Caroline dipped bread into her stew. "And Altamost's reign has been met with divide, civil war, and a Corrupted blight. To say his priorities are elsewhere, would be an understatement."

"Where are his priorities, is the question," Vaiden murmured into his cup of wine.

"I'm sure the king knows much more than we do," Gabriel replied. "It all seems easy from our points of view."

"Please explain to me the angle of sending all the Shades to Kiji?" Vaiden challenged. "I certainly cannot think of a single reason why that's a good idea."

"The Shades are in Kiji?" Caroline looked at her husband, her eyes shining with alarm. "Why would Altamost send them there? They should be dismantling that nest in Haven."

Gabriel frowned at Vaiden, who leaned back in his chair happily eating his stew. "We don't know the king's plans, but we must trust the withdrawal of the Shades is for an important reason."

A diplomatic answer, Vaiden thought and effective as the others returned to their dinner. Alvez's eyes darted between the Shade and ambassador, but he added nothing more to the topic—Caroline either. She smiled at the captain, asking if he liked his food.

"Jana blesses you," he replied. "I haven't eaten a home cooked meal in ages."

"Your parents must be proud of you, for making captain so young."

"My father is proud." He beamed, but quickly it faded from his face. "My mother left for Paradise when I was little."

"She smiles down at you then," Caroline managed, her eyes clouding with something Vaiden couldn't define. She looked down for a moment, her hands sitting quietly on her lap, rubbing soothingly along her abdomen. A silent prayer quivered on her lips before she raised her head, her hand scooping up Gabriel's, squeezing it for a moment before letting go. He grinned at his wife, love shining brightly in his eyes.

Warmth spread through Vaiden's chest again, a small smile playing on his lips before he returned his attention to his food. The captain asked Gabriel where he'd grown up and the ambassador sprang into a tale about running a guild down in Abrita Shores. Alvez's mouth hanged agape, listening to the decorated ambassador—a good man—illustrate his days as the most wanted criminal in the trading port's history, the Nuisance.

Some of it was exaggerated, Vaiden knew, but for this moment, he enjoyed good food and the company of his friends, safe and distracted from the monstrosities crawling outside Fort Khali's walls.

12

Tatiana screamed, retreating until her back hit something hard. She sank to the marbled floor, her arms raised, fingers splayed in a stop motion. The club's lights dimmed, nearly dark. Her eyes frantically searched the crowd through the neon flashes before the lights brightened, nearly blindingly. Tatiana squinted, a figure approaching her.

"What happened?" Zarah's voice asked barely audible over the music and her pounding heart.

Tatiana blinked, her eyes quickly adjusting. Zarah kneeled beside her, clutching one of Tatiana's hands. She looked at their joined hands—solid and strong. Real, she thought. This was real. A shaky breath loosened from her lips. Jen was dead. Vaiden had killed her.

"Is she OK?" one of the spin class friends asked Darling, hovering over the women on the floor.

"Let's give her some air, ladies." Darling shooed them away, creating space. A few concerned onlookers off the dance floor shadowed Lewej, who frowned. Her green eyes narrowed, studying Tatiana and Zarah.

Josie crouched on Tatiana's right, opposite Zarah. "Are you alright?" she asked, alcohol thick on her breath.

"Take your time." Zarah's hand squeezed tighter. "Breathe."

Another shaky breath escaped Tatiana's lips, tearing her gaze from the crowd forming behind Lewej. They all stared, some even elevated smartphones, taking pictures and video. If anyone figured out who she was, they could sell that video to gossip magazines. Her eyes found Latisha, also with her phone raised.

"I want to leave." Tatiana's voice sounded quiet and foreign, even to her. Zarah nodded, taking her other hand from Josie, helping her stand. Darling helped Josie up, both moving to hug her, but Zarah put up her hand, stopping them.

"I'm fine," Tatiana laughed, trying her best to feign embarrassment. Her left hand shook in Zarah's, fingers tightly entwined while her eyes swept over the faces in the crowd, most of them returning to the dance floor or their tables. She hoped none of their videos would make it online, but she knew some would, followed by a caption, "drunk girl freaks out at nightclub."

"Are you sure you're OK?" Josie asked.

"Yes, I'm—" Tatiana let go of Zarah's hand long enough to hug Josie. "I'm going to go," she said. "It was a long day at work."

"Are you sure?" Josie's eyes searched hers when they parted. Her bright eyes glazed with drunkenness filled with worry.

Tatiana nodded, not trusting her voice. She hugged Darling too and waved at the spin class ladies. Latisha's phone was still raised—still filming. Tatiana turned away from the phone, taking Zarah's hand again.

The vampire led her away from the dance floor, out of the nightclub into the fresh warm air, despite the moon shining in the sky. A breeze played with Tatiana's hair, cooling the sweat sliding down her back. They walked in silence, ignoring the people standing in line down the sidewalk wrapped around the club.

Once in the safety of the car, Tatiana covered her face with both of her hands, panting. Zarah rubbed small soothing circles on her back, remaining quiet—letting her vent. Her shoulders shook with a sob, hot tears sliding down her cheeks. She moved back, remembering the makeup she'd applied. Zarah held a tissue out for her, and Tatiana grabbed it gently dabbing her cheeks.

"What happened?" the vampire asked again, her voice painfully soft. She should have been mad, Tatiana thought. They'd spent weeks coordinating that night. Everyone had busy schedules, but they finally had agreed that night would be right for everyone. Tatiana had made a scene and ruined everything.

She pulled down the sun visor, opening the little mirror inside. The lights turned on automatically, magnifying her red puffy eyes. Mascara lines ran down her cheeks. Her smoky eyes had smudged into those of raccoons, like a child had painted them. She wiped at them, realizing the tissue would do little to fix her situation. Zarah retrieved a pack of makeup remover wipes from the center console and handed them to her.

"Thank you." Tatiana sniffled.

"What happened?" she asked for a third time.

"I saw Jen."

"What do you mean?"

"I *thought* I saw her," Tatiana corrected. "It probably didn't help that I had to go to the detention center earlier today, down to the basement where the supernatural holding cells are."

"You went through a lot." Zarah brushed back a few strands of Tatiana's hair. "It takes time to deal with such trauma."

"I shouldn't have come and ruined everyone's fun."

"No one blames you," the vampire said. "And no one expects perfection from you either."

Tatiana stared at her hands, holding a dirty wipe filled with her makeup. "I know," she exhaled, though she didn't entirely believe it. Her bosses and clients all expected perfection—she strived for it. After all these years, climbing the career ladder, growing her ambition, and gaining recognition, she knew it would never be enough. She would never be enough.

"I'll take you home." Zarah turned the ignition and the car roared to life. "But you have to promise me to stop beating yourself up."

"OK."

Silence and streetlights filled the ride home. Tatiana stared out the passenger window, watching people celebrate a night out. Bars were packed, the sidewalks too. Everyone cheered loudly for whatever team won. It seemed foreign to Tatiana—this happiness bubbling from strangers.

Zarah said nothing during the drive. Her eyes stayed fixed on the road, navigating through traffic. She may be one of the few Tatiana could turn to about six months ago, but she found the words hard to form. Zarah had lost her husband and court. She was a lone wolf, roaming without a pack—not that Tatiana believed Lizabeth LaBelle's court was much of a family.

The bright lights of downtown dimmed the further they drove. Yellow street lights guided them toward her apartment complex. Zarah parked in a guest space—surprised no one had filled it. She followed Tatiana through the lobby and up the quiet elevator. Tatiana had to glance at her to make sure she was still there. Vampires didn't need to breathe. Sometimes it was unnerving.

From the clutch, she retrieve her keys, unlocking the door and immediately pushing it wide for Zarah to follow. The vampire closed it, locking it automatically. They were safe in the apartment where no one would judge them or take pictures.

Tatiana kicked off her shoes, pulling her hair from the high ponytail. She excused herself to the bathroom to further clean up, removing the clubbing outfit, and stuffing herself into sweatpants and a loose tee. She washed her face, scrubbing away the remnants of the night. A sigh escaped her lips, staring into the tired reflection of her face.

Zarah didn't want her to beat herself up, but Tatiana wondered when she would get over everything—when she'd move on or when it would leave her. Vaiden had told her to find a therapist, but how could she go through that process and not tell the truth? She couldn't tell anyone about Vaiden and Zarah's involvement that night, or that she was a sorceress.

She exhaled again. The latter wasn't true. She could tell people about her magic, but if they asked how she learned about it, the fact she'd killed a man might make them recoil. Why was she worried about how people may react? Supernatural abilities were rare in humans, but not impossible. Both of her parents were magical, though they also hid it from the public.

They had hidden it from her too—even her own magic. They had repressed it inside of her, caged and forgotten until that night at the cabin, where Bailyn Rosenhouse had tried to abduct her. Heat rippled through her chest, hot and intense. Her parents had lied to her—*still* lied to her. After confronting them with the fact she had destructive magic, they had refused to explain themselves for what they had done, claiming it was to protect her. From what? Mystic Crane?

Tatiana's jaw locked, her hands tightening around the sides of the sink. She'd killed someone. Even though her parents knew everything that had happened six months ago, they refused to tell her about their family lineage, magic, or what their real names might be. They admitted to changing names a few times to evade Mystic Crane. What good that did, she thought. Mystic Crane knew where she was. She wouldn't doubt they had followed her movements throughout the day.

Electric blue caught her attention in the mirror. She looked down at her arms, the blue fire filled her veins. She counted back from ten, breathing deeply until they faded. She needed to find a proper arcane magical teacher. Perhaps coming out as supernatural to the public would help her narrow down the search.

In the living area, Zarah leaned against the arm of the couch, tapping on her smartphone. Tatiana raised a brow, wondering where she had hidden it through the night. She left the vampire alone, skipping to the kitchen for a fresh glass of wine. From deep in the fridge, she grabbed another bottle, one with a graphic of vampire fangs sinking into fruit making it bleed.

"Do you want some?" Tatiana held the bottle out to Zarah. She nodded, turning her eyes back to the phone.

Tatiana poured the plasma fruit into a glass, the smell of blueberries engulfing her senses. She preferred her grapes, but she did admit the plasma fruit smelled better than traditional wine, less sour and an improvement from coppery blood. It was probably the greatest invention in modern science. Plasma fruit kept vampires from hunting humans for their blood. Not that they needed to hunt, she thought. A lot of humans would willingly let vampires feed from them. Some still did.

"Here you go." Tatiana offered Zarah the wine glass.

"Thank you." The vampire took it, immediately taking a sip. A small jingle sounded from her phone, catching her attention again.

"Updating Darling." Tatiana gestured at the phone, taking a seat on the sofa. Zarah joined her.

"It's just business."

"On a Friday night?"

"Business never sleeps." She smirked. "Much like us vampires."

Tatiana nodded, wondering what "business" could mean. Part of her didn't want to know, considering vampires conducted a lot of their business in the Underground. Zarah wasn't technically employed, but she had kept busy since her husband's death.

"I'm sorry for taking you away from the others." Tatiana threaded her fingers through her hair.

"It's fine." Zarah waved it away, tossing her phone aside. "But how are you? No longer seeing dead Corrupted?" A teasing grin vanished into the vampire's glass, sipping while her bright eyes watched Tatiana.

"I just had a moment."

The vampire licked her lips, studying her drink. "We all have them. If I think too long, I'll return to that night when LaBelle crushed my husband's heart in her hand."

"I'm sorry."

Zarah gave her a look, her full lips frowning. "You have no reason to apologize. You didn't kill him, and you certainly didn't ask for LaBelle to hunt you."

"No, but I understand what it's like to be alone with only your thoughts."

"We are always alone with our thoughts." Zarah patted her knee. "But you can share them with me. I won't judge you."

Before she could reply, Zarah continued. "Besides, I'm supposed to be looking out for you in Vaiden's stead. He would be very upset with me, when he returns, to find you rolled into a ball, hiding in a corner."

"I'm not hiding," Tatiana insisted. "I'm just busy."

"Busy with work, hiding from your problems, not letting yourself heal."

"I'm fine."

"You freaked out at a nightclub, thinking you saw a ghost."

Tatiana could tell her about Jen's voice in her ear or the siren, but she didn't want to sound crazy. God, was she crazy?

Zarah patted her knee again. "You're alone with your thoughts," she teased.

"I keep thinking about that room—that prison—Jen locked me in," Tatiana began. "She kept blaring this siren, not letting me sleep, not letting me feel around the room. She told me if I was good, she wouldn't do it, but she did it anyway repeatedly."

The vampire sat her glass on the coffee table, turning her whole body toward Tatiana. "She was a sadist. She got off on your pain, on making you suffer."

"I know, but—" She breathed in sharply. "I didn't want to give her the satisfaction of watching me squirm—but I did squirm."

"I watched LaBelle torture my husband, watched her slice through his skin with knives," Zarah said quietly, like the words were those knives and to utter a breath cut her deep inside. "I did nothing, said nothing, and hated every moment he wouldn't shut up. He made it worse by giving her what she wanted—his pain. She savored it more than any blood she'd ever drunk. If only he'd been quiet, like me, strong, like me—unmovable."

She exhaled, her eyes growing tired. "I paid the consequences by having my neck broken."

Tatiana winced, her hand immediately clutching her throat. "I'm—"

"Don't say you're sorry." Zarah pointed a finger at her. "I'm not. Being unmovable gave us enough time to escape—more time to each other before she finished it."

Finished *him*, she meant. Tatiana grabbed her hand and held it between their bodies on the sofa. "I wish he would have let me help him," she said. "Maybe we could have found a way to take down LaBelle without all the bloodshed."

"Jen would have gotten you though." Zarah's eyes searched hers, the brightness dimmed. "Gary would have brought you to her."

A knot twisted in her stomach. Gary Martin—someone she had wanted to marry once upon a time. Someone who had tricked her into a fantasy, knew how to manipulate her into loving him, and with whom she had truly believed she could have it all. Her heart pounded loudly in her ears—not from fear, but fury.

If she was honest and looked at their relationship, she could find holes in it where his mask had slipped, showing her the monster beneath it. She had chosen to ignore those times, had chosen to believe his lies, his apologies, and that he would change. Vaiden had told her Gary was the main reason she needed therapy. She could talk about that, if anything.

She let go of Zarah's hand, turning away. "He's in jail."

"I know. *We* put him in there." The vampire picked up her glass and took a healthy sip. "I didn't know my glamour would last so long. Perhaps it's better to know its limits."

She pursed her lips, lost in her own thoughts. Tatiana had wanted Gary to admit his crimes, but he wouldn't. Then there was the story they needed to tell, omitting Zarah and Vaiden from the record. Vampires had many powers, but one of the widely controversial ones was glamour, the ability to control and manipulate others. Zarah had implanted warped memories in Gary, forcing a confession of falsehood to the authorities.

With the glamour faded, Tatiana wondered which version of events he believed—the true one or the one Zarah had created. It didn't truly matter, not in the eyes of the law. He'd pleaded guilty, waiving any right to an appeal. Was that truly justice? Tatiana didn't know, but she thought it was fair—not just for her, but for the innumerable victims he had lured to Jen and had helped murder.

Tatiana drained her glass and asked Zarah if she wanted a refill. The vampire declined, but Tatiana wasn't done drinking. She wanted to feel numb to the world, to erase everything from six months ago. Alcohol wouldn't do that, but maybe for a night she could rest.

Zarah's phone dinged again as Tatiana returned to the sofa. "You don't have to stay," she said. "If it's important, go."

"You are more important," the vampire replied.

"I'm fine." Before Zarah could counter, Tatiana grabbed her hand. "I will be fine," she said, allowing a faint smile to play with her lips. "There's no reason for your night to stop here."

Zarah lifted a brow at her, those gorgeous eyes searching Tatiana's for the truth.

"I'm going to read over a case file and take notes, maybe even watch the news before I pass out," she explained. "If I start seeing the Ghost of Christmas Past again, I'll call you."

Zarah shot to her feet. "You promise?"

"Don't waste that dress here."

A smile crept on the vampire's face. "Next time you will wear one of those dresses hanging in your closet and you'll feel like a goddess."

"Or I'll roll into a ball and hide in the corner."

Zarah gave her a measured look. "You are beautiful. Why not embrace it?" Before Tatiana could reply, the vampire ran a hand of dainty, manicured fingers across her arm. "Have a goodnight and get some rest."

"You too," she returned automatically, turning her head to watch Zarah exit the apartment and close the door behind her. She exhaled heavily, turning to the case files spread across her coffee table, quietly singing the opening of "I'll Make a Man Out of You" under her breath.

13

Despite the late hour, Zarah found a middle-aged man sitting in his car outside of Tatiana's building. She'd seen him numerous times, a journalist who believed Tatiana owed him an exclusive over the incidents six months ago. The public knew little and that was how they wanted it to stay. The smaller the lie, the harder it was to disprove. Tatiana had held strong, but Zarah could see her breaking too.

She wanted Tatiana to confide in her, but she would only lower her shields so far. Zarah didn't know if she should push, but she was glad Tatiana had revealed her thoughts that night, however small. The vampire had promised Vaiden to look after her. Zarah would because she owed Vaiden a debt and because guilt crowded her mind.

Without breaking her stride, she approached the journalist's car and knocked on the window. He startled, fumbling to hide a notepad inside his jacket.

"Y-yes?" the man asked, rolling down his window.

"You don't belong here," she said.

He frowned at her, gesturing to the rest of the cars parallel parked along the sidewalk. "This is public parking."

"Perhaps." She clicked her tongue. "But you still don't belong here."

"Who are you?" The man's bushy brows furrowed, etching thick lines across his forehead. "What do you want?"

"I want you to leave Tatiana Smith alone," the vampire replied. "If you do not, there will be consequences."

"Is that a threat?" The man had the audacity to chuckle. "I am sitting in my car, hurting no one."

"Stalking is a crime."

"What proof do you have I'm stalking anyone?"

The vampire lifted the skirt of her dress, hiking it up far enough to retrieve the smartphone strapped to her thigh. She turned it on, navigating through the apps. When she showed the journalist the screen, his flushed face paled as she swiped through a gallery of photos with him sitting in his car or on the sidewalk, all clearly following Tatiana.

"And this one from this morning," she purred, showing him chasing Tatiana through the parking lot. "Or this one of you tailing her to a sandwich shop then to her work."

He reached in his jacket, slowly retrieving a laminated badge. "I work for the *Streaming Enquirer*. Tatiana is a figure of public interest."

"You have freedom of the press, but you do not have the right to stalk Ms. Smith. There's no story here."

"Why did she leave the club so early?" the journalist asked, his defensive mask dropping into something resembling concern. Zarah knew better. This parasite wanted information. "I worry she's not getting the help she needs."

"And *this* is helping her?"

"She needs to talk to someone."

"You mean, you want her to talk to you."

"That's not what I said."

"That's what you're implying." Zarah folded her arms over her chest. "If you do not stop following Tatiana around, she will file a restraining order and then how will you get your story?"

He scowled at her, his sympathetic ploy vanishing. "I want what's best for her."

"You don't know what that is."

"I know her!"

The vampire leaned down, losing the man to her cleavage for a moment before he willed himself to meet her stare. She thought about letting her eyes fill with glamour, fogging his mind and commanding him to drive himself into a tree. She had made Gary confess to killing Jennifer Verniski. She did it to protect Vaiden, someone she admired. Who was this journalist, but a cockroach that deserved to be crushed?

"Only Tatiana knows what she needs. You will get nothing from her," the vampire hissed. "Or I will report to your boss how you've been moonlighting, causing a woman, who's gone through terrible trauma, emotional stress. How do you think they will respond to an attorney, maybe one of the most popular in the country, filing a lawsuit against their paper?"

"Tatiana wouldn't sue," George said, but his quivering voice betrayed him. He swallowed hard, his bobbing Adam's apple catching her eye. She followed it, letting her eyes slowly crawl up the column of his thick throat.

Zarah smiled, letting her fangs shine under the streetlight. His pulse raced into a crescendo reverberating through her ears like a great orchestra, playing only for her. She patted his car door and straightened.

"Goodnight, Mr. Zeilberg," she purred. "I'll be watching."

He started the car, quickly peeling out of the parking space and sped away. Zarah watched him go, wiggling her fingers in a sensual wave until his car turned off the block, hopefully headed somewhere far away. She laughed to herself. What a ridiculous man.

Her phone dinged, forgotten in her hand—another message. She sighed, lifting it to her gaze.

You wanted this, read the message across the top of her screen. She clicked it, expanding the conversation to find an attachment. At the touch of her finger, it began downloading—a hefty file. It would take several minutes for the little bar at the bottom of her screen to fill.

She frowned, marching to her car. Inside, Tatiana's minty perfume lingered. She was a beautiful woman, riddled with insecurities and fear. When would she learn her power? Not the blue fire, but her true power, the magnetism she held in that ocean-filled gaze, how everyone couldn't take their eyes off her. Zarah admired her intelligence and poise, but Tatiana had more to offer herself. Self-worth for starters, Zarah thought, turning the key and igniting the engine.

She steered the car back through the streets to the main avenue that would lead her to the lit interstate. Not that it would matter if the road had lights or not. As a vampire, her sight bested any night vision goggles humans had developed. The ride was boring without Tatiana's lovely pulse bouncing in her ears. Her fingers pushed the controls on the steering wheel, turning on the radio. A man's silky voice filled the car, beckoning listeners to pay attention.

"What would you give for immortality?" he asked. "It's just a small fee and a little pain, but not too much. You will hardly feel it."

Her thumb pressed another button, changing the station. He wasn't the only hustler seducing people into joining his flock. Master vampires were the only kind who could turn people. They had special venom in their fangs that would flood a person's veins with unfathomable pain and sickness until their body writhed, expelling their humanity and leaving them with a new hunger that would never fully quench.

Zarah frowned. Harvey's reform would have abolished courts, but it wouldn't have stopped hustlers like that man from capturing naïve people, wanting supernatural abilities. Earth had romanticized what being a vampire meant with their stories—much of them created far before the *Discovery*, when humans had learned of Arda.

She didn't understand the religious symbols used as weapons against vampires. Was it some recruiting method to ward off demon spawn? It only worked if a person was a true believer after all. Of course, the most ridiculous weapon against vampires was the sun. Zarah tried to wrap her head around how a star millions of miles away could hurt her kind. They could heal almost any wound, except a blow to the heart. Or perhaps she judged too harshly. There were those who believed vampires were allergic to garlic, or they had to be invited in a home to enter it.

Since the *Discovery*, humans had learned these so-called "weaknesses" of vampire kind to be false. It didn't stop writers from spreading misinformation in their stories though. To each their own, Zarah decided. She'd read many fantasies filled with inaccuracies that she had enjoyed.

A ramp took her off the interstate to an industrial section. She slowed her speed to traffic, patiently waiting for lights to turn. Eventually, she turned into a lot where an abandoned computer manufacturer sat—or at least it appeared that way. The magic shimmered, its spell waning to reveal a simple ranch-style house where the building once stood. A thick covering protected a car, parked in front of it. Vaiden had left his special car in her possession too. She kept it covered, unwilling to be responsible for any injury to it. She parked, jumping out of her own vehicle to breathe in the heavy air. It would rain in the next few days, bringing relief from the hot weather.

Beyond the magical perimeter, the night shift bustled. Trucks delivered and picked up materials. Forklift drivers assisted moving product. A car honked in the distance. She watched workers taking their break outside, sharing conversation and a smoke. None of them would notice the vampire staring at them or know anyone who worked at the computer manufacturer next door. Perhaps they believed it to be vacant.

She unlocked the front door, shutting it soundly behind her and switching on the lights. The burnt umber wallpaper greeted her as the same eye sore. Ripping it off the wall would bring her joy, but she didn't think Vaiden would appreciate it. The open space concept between the kitchen and living area was divided by a wall where a heavy walnut desk sat. She sank into the chair at the computer, plugging a cable from it to her phone. The interface alerted her of the connection and asked her for next steps. She selected to access the phone and opened the attachment she had downloaded from earlier.

A flood of text and images erupted on the screen. She studied it, eying the snapshots of George Zeilberg, interviewing members of the Underground—mostly felines. Most of them were too high and suspicious to answer his questions. He had been poking around though and that concerned the Underground. Agents would take it upon themselves to stop the journalist. Zarah had no illusions of what that meant, but she knew George searched for information about Jen the Unfavorable and Tatiana. He would go to any lengths to find the truth—or whatever Tatiana was hiding. Zarah couldn't let that happen. Too many people counted on her to keep their secrets safe.

She rubbed her wedding ring between her right thumb and ring finger. The truth about Harvey's death would be unveiled too. Though vampires could not die of "natural causes," his forged death certificate indicated as much. The undying ceremony, the decision to die and to do so peacefully with the aid of necromancy, was as close to natural causes as vampires could achieve. Zarah had seen such practices on Arda, but not on Earth.

There were laws against assisted suicide in the United States, but the Supernatural Law Act and its many amendments, specified the undying ceremony could only be used on vampires who murdered, became ravenous, or who's mental capacity weathered, which was a nice way of saying the vampire lost their mind. It happened with the old, like Lizabeth LaBelle, her former master, a thousand-year-old—or at least that was what Zarah had chosen to believe.

Before Harvey made the reform, Zarah had worked as an enforcer for LaBelle—easy work for a vampire who had grown and trained in the Last Empire on Arda. Earth's squeamish people thought simple torture was unnecessary and volatile. They had never served under Emperor Zerth, who set his own people on fire as punishment, knowing it would not kill them. Zarah could still smell the burnt flesh from the caged vampires hoisted in rows along the bridges into the castle.

LaBelle enjoyed inflicting pain. She enjoyed the screams and writhing bodies of her victims, but it had worsened over time. Trudy Coristor had said LaBelle wasn't such a sadist during their time in Greenbrooke Estates. Perhaps the master there had kept LaBelle in check. Zarah didn't know, but she had witnessed her master's mind erode until only the desire for power and blood remained. She couldn't forget the way LaBelle had squished Harvey's heart in her hands. She had been smiling—*smiling*.

A shaky breath shuddered Zarah's body. LaBelle was dead. She couldn't hurt anyone. Misplaced Stream was safe from the tyranny of a master vampire—for now.

It wasn't lost on the community what LaBelle had achieved. She had accumulated a large court by simply absorbing smaller ones, either by eliminating a court's master or by threatening them into submission. Zarah wondered how long until another master tried the same strategy to gain numbers and power. A large court threatened any neighbors. Although numbers did not necessarily make a court strong, it provided cannon fodder to throw at a problem. It was why the first emperor compelled masters in his reign to force-turn all humans in their charge. Smaller courts could not fight such a large army and hope to win.

She disconnected her phone from the computer, navigating to her contacts until she found Lucius Hilan's name. It rang three times before a baritone voice purred through the receiver.

"Yes, my goddess." She could feel his smile through the phone. "What service can I perform for you today?"

"I received the information from your contact," she replied. "This is the journalist, wishing to uncover the truth about Tatiana Smith."

"And why do we care about her so much?"

"She's saved more of the community than you pretend to," Zarah said.

"That hurts my heart to hear," Lucius gasped dramatically. "Though, my cats might disagree."

Zarah waved her hand, realizing quickly he couldn't see her. "The journalist."

"Yes, my cats are following him as you requested," he explained. "George Zeilberg as described in your care package is a seasoned journalist working for the *Streaming Enquirer*. He's lived a rather lucrative life, exploiting people for exclusives, but his gambling addiction has thrown him into a world of debt."

"Which is why he needs an exclusive with Tatiana immediately."

"Do you want me to send some friends to change his mind?"

"I handled that myself."

"Oh?"

She explained the exchange with the journalist.

"You are a woman of action, Zarah Dellawood."

She threaded her fingers through her hair, ignoring the pain squeezing her heart every time she heard her last name—Harvey's last name. He would follow her around whenever she signed her name or made a reservation or introduced herself to someone new. She could change her last name, but how could she erase him?

"Have you heard of a ritual killing in the serpent community?" she asked, wishing the tension would ease in her chest.

"Aw yes," Lucius said. "Tragic."

"What have you heard about it?"

"Serpents aren't part of *your* community. Why concern yourself with it?"

"A friend of mine is part of it."

"Is your new friend in the legal world involved?"

"Do you have information or not?" She exhaled loudly, letting him know her patience thinned.

Lucius chuckled, a delicious sound that hummed through her body. She hated how he could affect her in such a way. She didn't want him, not really. Loneliness was an empty glass, desperate for the smallest drop of water. Her glass was a desert starved of moisture, a barren wasteland—and it had been that way long before Harvey had died.

"What I know is limited," he said, "but if you would like my contacts to investigate, just say the word."

"How much?"

"For you, everything is free."

"Lucius."

"You still owe me that dinner."

"I'm aware." She kicked off her heels, massaging her feet. "A deal is a deal, but you must allow me time for mourning."

"I am a patient man."

She frowned. Lucius was a respected man, who owned a lucrative business, although completely illegal. For all his good qualities, he viewed her as a prize, something beholden, and to which he was entitled. It left a bad taste in her mouth, but her body responded to his boldness. He wanted her. He'd made that plainly clear. She admired his confidence, but that didn't mean she wanted what he did. Still, she would attend that dinner, paying off her debt to one of the leaders of the Underground.

"Let me know what you find out about the serpent ritual," she said, voice neutral.

Lucius chuckled again and she wanted to taste that sound on her tongue. "Anything for you, my goddess," he replied before hanging up.

She sat in Vaiden's house enclosed in silence, surrounded by his scent, hoping it would distract her. It didn't, but it made her miss him and what she knew he could do to ease the tension in her body.

She exhaled. At the apartment, she had glanced over Tatiana's case. There were a lot of questions surrounding the ritual, the suspect, and the victim. Perhaps Lucius could shed some light on it and Zarah could steer Tatiana in the right direction. She knew it was manipulative, but whatever kept Tatiana from taking to the streets in the underbelly. Vaiden wouldn't let her do it, so neither would Zarah. She had to keep Tatiana safe. That was her priority—that was what she promised Vaiden. If she failed? A shiver cascaded down her body.

She tilted back her head, closing her eyes, relaxing against the computer chair. Silence carried, but it didn't last long—not as images of LaBelle crushing Harvey's heart flooded her mind. She shot upright, threading her fingers through her hair again. It was her punishment, LaBelle had said—to live.

14

The horn sounded, waking soldiers from their beds. Experienced fighters of wars past guided the new blood toward the armory for their armor and weapons. The soldiers on the walls stayed vigilant, giving their siblings-in-arms plenty of time to prepare. Vaiden sat on his bed, listening to the commotion—listening with his expanded hearing to the whispers of wind beyond the walls. They were coming.

He climbed to his feet and began fastening his belt and sword sheaths. Short swords were handy in a fight and lighter than the long sword Gabriel preferred. Vaiden strapped the swords to his thighs, emptying his head of thought. He sank into the void deep inside himself, letting the blackness welcome him with shadowed arms. He was a Shade, a warrior of Wara. To rid the world of the Corrupted was his purpose, or he would die trying.

Outside, the smell of rain greeted him. Great, he thought. Nothing like a battle in a storm with impaired vision and sound. He refrained from activating his nocturnal sight close to the torches lighting the path around the keep. A group of squires carried arrows to the archers. They would need more, he thought, observing others on the ground, assembling arrows, lances, and other weapons they may need in battle. A few practitioners pressed their hands to the walls, reciting enchantments of protection and warding. Vaiden stayed clear of those High Elves, knowing his closeness would nullify their efforts.

"Vaiden." Gabriel's voice forced him to whirl around, finding the ambassador fitted with his standard chainmail and light armor, covered in his cloak. Vaiden wore nothing, beyond his usual black garb. If it slowed down or restricted his movements, he wouldn't wear it in a fight. Though, he missed his leather jacket with its many slots for weapons.

"Did Caroline get out?" the Shade asked.

"Yes, she and the families are taking the farmer's path east. There's a tavern out there where she'll wait for word," Gabriel replied. Despite his neutral tone, his eyes clouded with worry. "I sent my company with them just in case."

Vaiden nodded, knowing Gabriel had hand picked his men. They had to be skilled, patient, and loyal to travel the far reaches of Arda into the swamplands of the serpent kingdom, the mountainous terrains to visit the trolls, and if they were fortunate enough to sail and climb the treacherous rocks to the orc mines, they would find a flourished people, wealthy in iron, salt, and community.

"You should have gone with them," the Shade said.

"And listen to you call me a coward for not staying until the end of time." Gabriel shook his head. "Not a chance."

Vaiden opened his mouth to argue, but another horn sounded from atop the keep. "We should get up there," he said instead. "Glades could probably use some guidance."

"He's a general, Vaiden. He didn't climb to that rank without understanding battle strategy."

The Shade frowned at his friend. Glades knew how to fight vampire armies and, perhaps, a few swarms, but these Corrupted were not like others. Their specialness offended Corrupted nature. They needed to be destroyed at all costs before they became too powerful and organized.

Atop the walls, they found Alvez updating the general on the fort's readiness. Glades had decided not to send soldiers and instead instructed scouts to spy on the Corrupted and report back. They hadn't returned, but that wasn't surprising to Vaiden.

He looked out into the perpetual darkness beyond the walls. Only the soft orange glow of the torches kept it from swallowing them whole. Hopefully, none of the Corrupted scouted the farmer's path, where families searched for salvation. The farms would take them in, but he knew if it came down to a fight, Gabriel's men would protect Caroline with their lives. Hopefully, it would be enough.

Lightning danced along the clouds breaking the illusion of impenetrable darkness. Soft rumbles of thunder followed. The storm surged miles away, but it wouldn't wait for them to fight this battle. It would invade with a speed and force no one could stop.

Vaiden exhaled, turning on his nocturnal sight to evaluate the tree line. He ignored the flash of lightning and the glow from the torches, stepping as close to the balustrade as the stone allowed. The gray tones swept past the clearing into the woods beyond the southern gate. Figures stood immobile by the trees, donning hoods to hide their identities. Not that it mattered. They were all one identity, the Corrupted. It didn't matter what riches they had in their early lives. They had chosen the path of dark magic and allowed it to consume and infect their minds.

Vaiden's eyes searched for the blood mage, the one they needed to stop before eliminating the necromancer. He gathered they could try to kill both simultaneously, but he wouldn't want to pull away efforts from a being that could literally summon meteors. Without the fort's walls, they would be vulnerable.

"Do you see it yet?" Glades asked.

"It will show eventually. The others are standing fast at the tree line."

Thunder boomed. The wind grew stronger, carrying scents of rain and greenery from the far south. Vaiden had watched enough weather forecasts on Earth to know a low had drifted up from the southern ocean, bringing all its moisture northeast. He wondered how weather might be different from the two worlds, considering Arda didn't traverse through seasons like much of Earth.

They had magic. It lived in the very ground they walked upon. Jana blessed certain places with fair weather, perfect for crops and animals. The mountains were never without snow, stuck in perpetual winter. In the lowlands, heat and humidity clung to the air, creating a wet and sticky swamp perfect for serpents. Jana gave them their ideal environments and expected them to be maintained. He wondered if expunging the world of vampires unbalanced those biomes.

He shook his head. A nest of Corrupted stood at their gates, armed with a deadly staff and a necromancer capable of creating monstrosities, and he was thinking about the weather.

"Rain's rolling in," Alvez said. "We're going to be drenched in minutes."

"I can see that, captain," muttered Glades. "The Corrupted are using the storm as shielding."

"How so?"

"How well can you hear in the rain?" Vaiden asked. "Or see?"

"Is that why they're not moving?" the captain asked.

The Shade nodded.

"These Corrupted are smart."

"They are unnatural," grumbled the general.

Purpose swelled inside Vaiden, pumping through his veins, igniting the need to draw his swords and meet the Corrupted on the battlefield. They were safer behind the walls. It was a better strategy, but Vaiden longed to pound the ground with his feet as he charged through the clearing, lofting heads from the shoulders of their enemies.

The horn sounded again, announcing the arrival of the blood mage. In the grayscale of his vision, it radiated with its red cloak. The staff was in hand. It leaned against it as one might a walking stick, but that was no ordinary piece of oak. An educated High Elf might be able to identify the staff, but they had no scholars from Mysogus.

"Steady," Glades bellowed at his men lined along the balustrade. They had their bows at the ready. No arrows drawn yet, but the night was still young.

Lightning struck, quaking the ground. He heard swears underneath the breaths of the soldiers. No one liked fighting in a storm, especially in the flatlands. The keep was the tallest structure in the region. Perhaps it, or the horn atop it, would act as a lightning rod and spare those farther below.

"The horn blower should probably retreat from his position," Vaiden said.

"Not until the battle is won," Glades answered.

The Shade spared a glance at the general, temporarily blinding himself with torchlight. Glades stood strong in his armor, looking like the fierce warrior he'd known in the past. In this moment he appeared to be the general the fort needed, confident and immovable, years of battle experience aging his eyes. He'd fought the vampires, creatures much faster and stronger than the average elf. Against those odds, he had prevailed. What were the Corrupted?

Raindrops splattered against the stone beside Vaiden's hand. Then another and another, until a light shower dampened his hair and clothes. The Shade glanced at Gabriel with his hood raised over his head, a slight smile gracing his lips. Vaiden rolled his eyes, returning his gaze to the enemy.

The blood mage raised its staff and the Corrupted moved out. A shriek pierced through the air, louder than the thunder, shuddering every elf standing on the wall. Vaiden fought the instinct to cover his ears as another banshee wailed over the rain.

His eyes fixed on the movement of the Corrupted, pushing everything else aside. He let his pulse deafen the sounds of rain and the cry of monstrosities. He counted ten of them racing through the clearing, not as big as the monstrosity they defeated in the woods, but sizable. They had heads of cows and horses—clearly this necromancer had a love of animals, or perhaps, a hatred to mangle them into unnatural abominations.

"Surnuna guide us with your light," Gabriel recited. "Wara bless us with the strength to withstand this night."

"You better ask Grita to make sure those wards hold," Vaiden said. "Or ask Moren to damn our enemies."

"I don't think Moren is going to curse those who she helped make," Alvez chuckled.

"Then you know nothing of Moren."

The captain opened his mouth to reply when lightning struck the keep behind them. Not lightning, Vaiden thought, watching rubble fall. He turned back to the blood mage with its staff raised, a red glow surrounding its body like a halo.

"Archers!" Glades shouted. They drew arrows, notching them on their bows. "May your aim be true."

They loosed. Gravity pulled the arrows down like a shower of death, striking a few Corrupted, but nowhere near the blood mage. Vaiden witnessed a few of those arrows bounce off an invisible force.

"Target the Corrupted around the blood mage," he said. "They're protecting it."

Glades relayed the suggestion and another round of arrows loosed, fighting wind and rain. The stronger the storm grew, the harder it would be for the archers. Shiny blue erupted from below, stealing his attention. He looked over the balustrade finding the monstrosities hammering their mangled limbs against the wards. With so few practitioners at the fort, the magic only covered twenty feet up the wall. On top of it, Vaiden didn't affect it, but he knew the Corrupted would think of something to help their monsters.

At Glades's order, a unit of archers fired on the monstrosities, leaving the experienced longbow experts to concentrate on the blood mage and Corrupted. The arrows did nothing to the thick-skinned beasts at the walls. They were dead, immune to pain and fear.

From the woods, more dead marched into the clearing—some of Alvez's men, Vaiden knew. There were loads more than a small unit though. Where had they found these dead? Vaiden's heart quaked, searching the faces for anyone familiar. They couldn't have had time to find those on the farmer's path.

"They're climbing the walls!" someone shouted.

Vaiden blinked, returning his gaze down the wall. There was nothing below him, but he searched far left, finding the Corrupted using their magic to create ladders of vines for their monstrosities to climb.

"Shoot the Corrupted!" Vaiden ordered, marching toward archers. They listened, but the Corrupted smartly protected each other with their own wards.

The Shade turned inward, finding their practitioners putting every effort into protecting the walls. They didn't have enough High Elves to make wards and use arcane magic to fight the Corrupted. Why were they so unprepared?

"Glades!" Vaiden fought through a sea of squires refilling bins with arrows. "We need the High Elves to break the Corrupted's wards."

"Without our wards, they'll cut through," the general returned.

Before Vaiden could argue, a monstrosity leaped over the balustrade. The Shade drew a sword, watching its limbs flick a few men off the wall, another one it flattened. Vaiden evaded its strike, driving his blade through its stomach, slicing open its belly and spilling the contents onto the wall. The stench of shit and dead filled his nostrils, but he pushed it away evading another strike. The monstrosity whirled around as other soldiers attacked it.

The Shade scaled its unnatural shape, using arrows lodged into its skin to help him climb. It bucked, a mustang refusing to be tamed, making Vaiden lose his footing. He clung to its diseased skin, his blade hand sinking into it. He didn't want to think about what he was touching, or if the smell would be burned into his nose forever. Purpose swelled inside him, making him stronger, steadier, emptier. He found his footing and punched his blade through the horse's skull. It fell forward, propelling him with it. Vaiden tumbled, using momentum to flip back to his feet.

There was no time to catch his breath as more dead and monstrosities had scaled the wall. He unsheathed his other sword, plunging it into a mangled soldier—a fresh one, one of theirs. The necromancer worked quickly.

He climbed atop of the balustrade, searching with his nocturnal sight for the green glow of necromancy, but the dead didn't give him the chance. He hacked at their arms, freeing his ankles before running down the balustrade. It was narrow, but he kept his balance aiming for one of the Corrupted's vine ladders. Its magic waned the closer he became, sending dead and a monstrosity back to the ground. Vaiden kept running, targeting the next ladder.

A blast shook the wall, making him slip, luckily toppling back onto the wall. He hit the stone hard, losing one of his blades in the carnage and decay. Another blast spattered him with debris, but he forced himself up, ears ringing, making him lose his balance. He blinked, his nocturnal sight flickering through his eyes. He shook his head, willing it to focus.

Bodies littered the ground, some of them moving, despite their egregious injuries. The rain mixed with puddles of blood, torn flesh, and bits of bone. The wide eyes of a young soldier looked at the sky, his mouth agape, filling with water. He would drown. Vaiden shook his head, leaning against the balustrade to help him steady. There was no light in the boy's eyes. He was dead.

He turned to the Corrupted huddled around the blood mage in the middle of the clearing. It raised the staff high above its head, shooting a beam of light into the sky.

"Fuck," Vaiden breathed. They were going to lose.

15

Glades dragged Gabriel away from the wall and down the stairs of the connecting tower. Gabriel fought him every step, ripping his cloak clean off his body. The general was bigger and stronger than the ambassador, but Gabriel had a sword, though he wasn't sure if he was willing to fight Glades.

Rubble exploded with every meteor hammering the fort. The battle was lost. They couldn't win this fight, not without a squadron of Shades and High Elves working in tandem to stop the dead and Corrupted. Vaiden was on the wall, still fighting. Gabriel should have been at his side, like he had in the Forty-Second.

The rain assaulted them in the courtyard, soaking Gabriel to the bone. He wrenched his arm, finally breaking free of the general's grip. Glades whirled on him, his nostrils flaring.

"You are too important to leave behind," he growled. "Come willingly, ambassador."

"We can't abandon the men," Gabriel returned, stunned that Glades would leave his post. "Vaiden's still up there!"

Another meteor smashed into the keep. It wouldn't last much longer.

"Leave him!" The general drew his sword. "He's *just* a Shade."

Gabriel unsheathed a long sword. "I'm responsible for him."

"He's as good as dead on that wall."

The ambassador raised his sword, pointing it at the general, like an extension of his arm. It had been in his family for generations, had killed many enemies and Corrupted—none of which were as esteemed as Glades, but Gabriel wouldn't run. He wouldn't abandon these soldiers or leave Vaiden behind. He was the moon to his sun. If one fell, they both did.

Glades glowered at the white steel shining in the lightning. He knew the blade too and what Gabriel could do with it.

"I tried," he said.

"There's still time to turn this around," Gabriel replied. "We can gather the soldiers…"

A red glow lit Glades's face, spreading until all the fort was visible, like the clouds had parted and the morning sun split the darkness. The clouds hadn't parted while the rain fell, and it was late into the night. Their eyes drifted to the sky, finding a cluster of meteors aiming for Fort Khali.

It crashed into the keep and the southern gate, shattering through stone, turning rock into rubble and debris into projectiles. Gabriel dove behind the nearest shelter, a cart. The keep collapsed toward the north gate, crushing all in its wake. His home—no match for the heavy keep—was obliterated.

His chest tightened. The magical fire burned through the rain, lighting the devastation. Squires raced around the courtyard, helping each other and the practitioners. They were yelling—screaming, but Gabriel's pulse thundered in his ears, muting their pleas, as he stared at the life he'd built with his wife.

Caroline was on the farmer's path. Safe—she was safe. They could rebuild.

He blinked, climbing to his feet. His gaze swept over Fort Khali, flattened by meteors, until his eyes fixed on the southern gate in ruins. Nothing moved, not even the dead.

"Vaiden!" He ran sword in hand, cutting down the dead. A monstrosity charged him, but the ambassador evaded, slicing the blade through its side. He kept running, his boots squashing through mud and blood.

A shadowy figure caught his eye, standing in the middle of bodies. It raised its hands, a green halo showcasing its magic—the necromancer. Gabriel ignored it. Without Vaiden, he couldn't hope to defeat such a powerful Corrupted.

Bodies rose all around him, forcing him to stop in his tracks. He was surrounded. Perhaps he couldn't ignore it. If he killed the necromancer, maybe they could formulate a plan to stop the blood mage. Separately they were powerful. Together—near unstoppable.

Gabriel turned on his heel, facing the direction he'd seen the necromancer. A sea of dead stood between him and the Corrupted. Its head tilted at the ambassador; the green glow of its power condensed to its hands. It lifted one of those gloved hands, pointing one finger at him.

"Wara, give me strength," he gritted.

The mob of dead attacked. Gabriel cut down those closest, making short work, giving him space. His sword sliced through flesh and bone, ridding the dead of arms and legs. They fell, writhing against the ground. Gabriel stepped on their bodies, giving him a semblance of high ground.

His arms tired from lofting heads, but he pushed on. He couldn't keep this up all night. The necromancer could mangle the dead back together and form new monstrosities. He needed to push through the crowd, make a path, something—

"Gabriel!" someone shouted. He whirled toward that familiar voice. His sword cut down another dead, finding a figure standing near the stables—too small to be Glades.

A practitioner came to Gabriel's rescue, using her wards to push the dead aside. A couple of soldiers assisted, slicing through the dead, giving Gabriel a path. He rallied his strength, cutting down the last few dead standing between him and rescue.

A soldier grabbed his arm, pulling the ambassador behind him. Gabriel focused on the voice who called his name. The slender frame waved frantically, reminding him of only one person.

"Alvez?"

"I can't hold this ward much longer," the High Elf claimed.

"Retreat," Gabriel ordered.

One of the soldiers grabbed the ambassador's shoulder before he could flee. Gabriel raised brow at him, but he stared into the face of a stranger. He knew most of the soldiers, or at least, recognized them. Not this man or the others in his company. Then he realized they weren't wearing the standard uniforms. They were not soldiers.

The man watched the realization pass over Gabriel's face. "Come with us, ambassador." He gestured with his blade to a break in the wall.

"We insist," another said, raising his sword.

Gabriel pushed away, lifting his own blade. "You don't want to do this."

"Hurry up!" the High Elf spat. Already the ward shimmered, the first signs of failure, then the dead would overwhelm them.

Another practitioner managed to join them, followed by more strangers. There were ten of them. Ten blades to his one. Gabriel believed in his abilities, but he wasn't arrogant enough to believe he could win this fight.

"Gabriel!" Alvez shouted again.

He couldn't give his back to these people. They weren't the Corrupted, but they weren't his people either. Gabriel had heard of rebels kidnapping important leaders in the military to learn the king's plans. Reports detailed the mutilation of their bodies that would make even the strongest stomach churn. Torture didn't scare Gabriel, but he knew his limits and he didn't want the enemy to find out.

He ran toward the captain. "Alvez!" His eyes frantically studied the stables, searching for any other survivors. Vaiden stumbled into the firelight, easing a heaviness in Gabriel's chest. The Shade shouldered a column, holding his side, but he didn't run to Gabriel. He didn't assist. Could he not see—

Something slammed into Gabriel, sending him to the ground hard. He rolled over, launching his fist at the attacker. Bone crunched under the impact, blistering his hand in pain, but Gabriel didn't stop there. He pushed the man aside before two more overwhelmed him, holding him down. Another picked up his sword, admiring the white steel, caked in mud and blood.

"Pretty," the man said before reversing his grip and slamming the hilt into Gabriel's head.

16

Tatiana drove down Maple Avenue, a district devoted to Ardan faiths. On one side of the street, structures built in whimsical styles with glass roofs, airy courtyards, and plush gardens, were everything children thought when imagining a perfect fairytale. Tatiana counted the nine separate gardens, representing each elven goddess donned with a ten-foot marble statue for elves to kneel before with their prayers.

The dark, more intimate buildings on the other side of the street, no less lovely or intricate, contrasted greatly. They were closed from the public's eyes, no gardens, or statues. Red banners, marked with a serpent's eye, hung over the windows. The outside walls looked like stone, engraved with shields and spears while snakes slithered between them—something that greatly attracted tourists. Serpents valued their privacy. Their practices were sacred. No outsider may enter the den without the direct consent of the head of the congregation, known as the *daehekans*.

While elves worshiped on Fridays, serpents dedicated every night of the week to praise. Of course, Arda didn't have a calendar like Earth. Their months were divided by moon cycles and harvest. The serpents were dedicated to spending each night, reading scripture and praising their god, Shoresleen, which translated to "sky serpent."

Coastal claimed there were depictions in elven history of such a being, but from the illustrations Tatiana only saw a dragon. Serpents despised human obsession with dragons, but to Tatiana, it only made sense why humans imagined such a creature. Like with the vampires, the fables derived from somewhere.

She continued driving to the lower-class neighborhoods beyond Maple Avenue. The den Mr. Slaseezor led was much smaller and plainer than the main den. The simple two-story building could have been mistaken for apartments, if not for the red banners hanging over the windows. Luckily, a parking space out front was empty.

A breeze played with her hair while she approached the main doors. A sign was posted with an arrow pointing toward the alley right of the building. Tatiana frowned, but a lot of religious places started using side entrances and exits to avoid crowded sidewalks picketed by anti-Ardan protestors. Although no one picketed the sidewalk that day, she followed the arrow.

It was a clean alley, all things considered. A dumpster with padlocks sat against a brick wall to the joining building. Tatiana expected a few felines to scatter when she approached, but no one, not even a stray cat hung around the trash. Peculiar, she thought, glancing down at the rest of the alleyway. It was abandoned, or it appeared that way. She wouldn't try her luck, not even to test her training with the blue fire, especially not in broad daylight.

She approached the red door with a painted serpent eye. It looked spray painted, but whoever marked the door did a good job with the details. She knocked, retrieving her phone from her jacket pocket. After constructing a simple text explaining where she was, she sent it to Logan. If anything happened, he would know where she was and at what time she had arrived. Not that she believed anything would happen, but she'd picked up this habit when she had dated. If Josie hadn't heard back from her, she would search for her. A few times she'd pulled Tatiana from some bad situations.

Tatiana took a deep breath and exhaled, slipping the phone back into her pocket. Even in the shade between the buildings, sweat slid between her shoulder blades. She would rather be wearing shorts and a tank top than the blazer and slacks in the heat, but that wouldn't be professional.

The door finally cracked open, a chartreuse eye peering into the alley. "Who are you?" the serpent asked.

"My name is Tatiana Smith, I am representing Mr. Slaseezor in his case," she explained. "He gave me permission to enter the den and speak to his wife."

The serpent opened the door wider, bowing her head. Tatiana did the same. "Come in," said the serpent, gesturing with black claws for fingers. The attorney did as instructed, following the brown-scaled serpent down a narrow hall, past the kitchens, to another door. Inside, the smell of incense greeted them. Pillows scattered around a low table where a round bowl surrounded by cups sat in the middle.

The serpent kept walking, leading her to another room where others tended a raised garden. Most of the greenery Tatiana knew was foreign to Earth, but she spied a few rose bushes and tulips. "Ms. Smith to see Rocahn," announced the serpent.

"Oh!" A serpent threw down her shears and wiped her claws against a gray apron. "Ms. Smith, I did receive word you would be joining us. Please." She gestured back into the previous room.

"Looks like you have your hands full with that garden." Tatiana smiled, trying to ease the tension as she kneeled on one of the pillows around the table. After spending months with Vaiden in his cabin, he had changed the way she thought about sitting in a room. He would never give his back to open space so she chose a spot with a wall to hers, where she could see both doors connecting to other rooms.

"It's coming along nicely," the serpent said, lifting a small cup beside the bowl and filling it. She placed it in front of Tatiana then poured herself a cup. "The plants from Arda are picky about certain fertilizers. I think it has something to do with the magic there, but I am pleased something is growing."

"How did you import them from Arda?" Tatiana knew some species were illegal to Earth, but most of those crimes were overlooked. They'd get a fine at best and have their wares destroyed.

"They all came from my husband's family when they made the great trip through the doors," she explained. "They've lived here for decades, you know. I was born here, but I do love learning about where our people came from."

Rocahn raised her cup, reciting something in serpent tongue before sipping. Tatiana joined her, but she didn't recite the passage before drinking the same amount as her host. The drink was sweet and tasted faintly like mango.

"How is my husband?" asked the serpent. "Is he sleeping?"

"He is doing his best."

Rocahn looked at her cup, carefully grasped between her claws. "He's a good man. Works hard to get the young ones interested in worship. They are wild. Many want to leave the old ways behind because they never lived on Arda, but we shouldn't let them forget."

"What happened that night of the ritual?"

Mrs. Slaseezor took another sip from her cup, her dark eyes looking away. "Everything went as planned before the ritual began. The den was filled. It isn't always, but it was a special night, and our community came together from all over to welcome the new members. I feared we wouldn't have enough room."

"Did you know the victim?"

"Koreen Tohlsee." She nodded. "He was one of the few young ones interested in the faith. He'd studied Ardan culture in school and wanted to feel closer to our people."

"Do you know if he had trouble with anyone in the community or outside of it?"

"We all have trouble from humans." She frowned at Tatiana, but then something shifted in her eyes. "Not *all* humans—just the ones who want us to go back to Arda. I never understood that. I'm not even from there."

"Any others? Any trouble with young ones against Koreen joining the faith?"

"Not that I know of," she sighed. "He kept mostly to himself."

"What about his family?"

"They returned to Arda years ago."

"Returned voluntarily?"

She nodded. "They couldn't cope with the technology here, but the den looked after Koreen. All the families did."

"Was he seeing anyone?"

"He was not yet the age of coupling."

Serpents did not "date" until they were in their mid-twenties. Anything else was unacceptable and would result in a member being shunned by the community. Even with the influence of culture in the United States, most serpents chose to stay traditional in this aspect.

They had arranged marriages, which usually took place after a year from the first coupling, which Tatiana knew to be a week of sharing interests, living together, and sex. If the coupling was unsuccessful, the families would not move forward with the marriage. Both families had to agree the coupling was a success or the marriage would also be off.

"Did anyone have an interest in Koreen for coupling?" Tatiana asked.

"Not that I am aware of," Rocahn answered, sipping more of the drink. "Ms. Smith, is there any way I can see my husband?"

"I'm afraid while Mr. Slaseezor is in custody, he is permitted no visitors other than his attorney."

She bowed her head. The spikes down the middle of her head fanned out, appearing like hair. Her features were softer than her husband's, but she had similar coloring, except her eyes. They were dark, almost black in the dim lighting.

"Mrs. Slaseezor," Tatiana said softly, "I am going to do everything I can to prove your husband had no knowledge about the blades, and that he could not have possibly committed this crime."

Rocahn raised her head, dabbing her snout with the end of her apron. "What can I do to help?"

"I will need your financial records for the den and also your personal ones," she explained. "This will prove that your family received no incentive to murder Koreen."

"We did get many donations the night of the ritual."

"That's fine. That shows community interest," Tatiana said, then she had a thought. "Were any of the donations made personally to your husband?"

She shook her head. "We are non-profit."

"I see." They spoke more about the night, but Mrs. Slaseezor wasn't present when her husband had cleaned the blades. She said it was part of his routine to clean them alone. It didn't help his case, but it would show this was a normal night and Mr. Slassezor never wavered from his routine.

By the end of the interview, Tatiana handed Rocahn her card and told her to call if she learned any more information. Mrs. Slaseezor promised to get the financial records to her immediately.

Safe in her car once again, Tatiana texted Logan, letting him know she had left the den and to look out for any deliveries, faxes, or emails of the financial records. He messaged back within minutes, asking if she had any other plans for the day. She lifted her brow at the text. Brave, she thought. He hadn't received his test scores yet.

Reviews, she sent back. It could mean anything from employee reviews to case file reviews. She sat waiting for his reply, but another thought crossed her mind. *We need to find more information on the victim*, she typed and sent.

She planned to pour over the books she had on serpents and their traditions. Perhaps there was a clue somewhere or a direction she could use to understand how the ritual went wrong. Ultimately, she was left with the question, why would someone want Koreen dead and for Mr. Slaseezor to take the fall. Maybe they were two separate questions, for what would someone want Koreen dead and who would want to hurt Mr. Slaseezor's reputation? She needed to brainstorm, to write every question in her head on a notepad.

Logan texted again. Tatiana stared at his message, her fingers hovering over the virtual keyboard, but she hesitated, swallowing hard. *Do you want to get coffee and talk about the case*, read the text.

She sighed, resting the phone on her lap and looked out the windshield. He was testing the water, fishing to see if she would bite. Part of her wanted to see what it'd be like, sitting in a coffee shop with a charming man, like Logan, who understood her work, who wouldn't be annoyed with how demanding her job was.

Her chest tightened. Gary never cared about her—not really. It was a ruse, an act to lure her to Jen. Nothing more. She was nothing to him—just a body, food for his soul sucker girlfriend. Then why did he have to make her fall in love with him?

Her fingers threaded through her hair, knowing the answer. She would do anything for someone she loved, even blindly following them into the arms of a notorious serial killer. They must have known about her past—the controlling boyfriends and parents. Was it that easy for them to fool her? Did she really want to know the answer to that question?

She took another deep breath, easing the tension in her chest. Logan wasn't Gary. He was *just* a guy—her paralegal at the moment. They were working on a case together. He wanted to get coffee and brainstorm. If he were any other colleague, especially another woman, would she have hesitated?

She picked up her phone, pressing on their conversation and let her fingers do the work. *Where do you want to meet*, she texted.

17

The rain poured in a heavy shower, covering the ground in thick puddles. Each drop washed away dirt and blood from Vaiden's body, but it couldn't wash away the failure cementing in his veins. Fort Khali was gone. Their soldiers lived on as corpses in a blood mage's army.

He did not understand these Corrupted. Their brains should have been warped, diseased beyond any repair, yet they were organized. They knew exactly how to invade the fort, which gate would be the weakest, and how to use the weather to their advantage. He wondered if they knew the Shades had been recalled to Kiji, but that seemed far fetched.

In all his years, he had never been bested by a swarm or nest. With every muddy step, it weighed on him. The fort was gone, one of the mightiest strongholds in all of Eskandor. It hadn't lasted an hour against that blood mage and its necromancer sidekick.

Vaiden grimaced, glancing at Alvez walking silently to his right. They followed the farmer's path, jumping at every sound whispering through the long grass. The dead had overwhelmed the surviving forces, picking them off one-by-one. The captain had dragged Vaiden away, purpose unwilling to let go of the fight.

Alvez was right to retreat. They couldn't win, but it left an uneasiness in the Shade—something he couldn't quite decipher. He'd lost fights before, but this was different. Gabriel was gone—taken.

He winced, his ribs aching. The wall had crumbled beneath his feet. He didn't remember the fall or the keep slamming to the ground. Alvez had been screaming in his face when he'd woken, but he hadn't heard the captain's words over the ringing in his ears or seen through the haze of magical fire and rain—not until he had heard Gabriel—not until he had witnessed the ambassador struggle against the clutches of the Corrupted and rebels alike. Vaiden couldn't move, could barely breathe, or stand on his own two feet. They'd taken Gabriel and Vaiden had done nothing but watch.

He'd find him. Moren knew what he would do when he did. Kill them all? Vaiden inhaled sharply, despite his protesting ribs. *Kill them all.*

They walked through the night, stopping to rest for no more than an hour. By dawn, they'd reached the tavern, nestled in the darkness of the tree line. Only a dirt path marked its existence to the passing route. The long rectangular building was constructed with heavy timber, but a layer of vine covered much of it, like nature had marked its claim, taking back what belonged to it. A faint glow in the tinted windows let them know it wasn't abandoned.

Alvez marched under the shelter of the slanted roof, glancing back at Vaiden before reaching the door. The Shade stood in the rain, letting it batter his sore muscles.

"Come on," the captain urged. "Let's get out of the rain."

But Vaiden's heavy feet wouldn't move. His heart pounded—not with purpose, but with something else. Ice bolted down his spine, tying his middle in knots. He didn't like whatever it was. It was foreign, something a Shade shouldn't feel.

"What's with you?" the captain asked, his brows knitting together.

Vaiden opened his mouth, his words coming out hoarse. "Caroline's in there."

Alvez licked his lips. "Do you want me to tell her?"

"What?"

"About the ambassador?"

Vaiden's jaw locked. Even a coward, like the captain, was brave enough to face her with news of Gabriel—*his* best friend.

The Shade brushed past him, throwing the door open. Soldiers scrambled to their feet, some drawing their weapons. Vaiden raised a brow at them, scanning their faces, but not seeing Caroline. Alvez pushed his way inside, his hands up in surrender.

"We're not Corrupted," he announced. "Just looking for shelter."

The soldiers sheathed their swords, returning to their games and drinking. Alvez scurried to the fireplace, warming his hands. He pulled off his cloak and draped it across the back of a chair, sitting to remove his boots. He would warm faster without the wet clothes, but Vaiden doubted he would strip that far in front of an audience.

The Shade studied the barkeep, a round-faced man with a build to match. He stared intently at Vaiden, though his expression remained pleasant.

"Good morrow," the barkeep said. "Welcome to the Shaking Tusk."

A young woman, who Vaiden could only guess was the man's daughter, shuffled out of the back with a tray of sliced bread and a kettle. She poured the tea, setting a cup before her father. He gestured at the Shade.

"You look weary, soldier," he said. "This will warm you up."

Vaiden leaned against the bar, picking up the cup in a salute before sipping it. Weak, but hot—he wouldn't complain. "Which one's the captain?" he asked, gesturing at the soldiers.

"Were you at Fort Khali?" the barkeep countered. "We've been waiting for news."

He wiped his apron on the counter, cleaning an invisible spill. His dark eyes stared at the Shade from under furrowed brows. "The soldiers haven't heard back from the scouts they sent."

Vaiden drained his tea, wanting something stronger, but it would only thin his blood, making his wounds bleed easier. The movement blistered pain from his ribs, clenching his jaw. He needed to get out of these wet clothes and tend to the damage.

"The fort's gone," he answered.

"What do you mean *gone*?"

The Shade leaned heavily on his forearms, bowing his head. "What do you think that means?"

"It's the mightiest stronghold in the east. No one has ever scaled its walls."

"Well, you don't need to scale walls, if you can smash them down."

"You." Vaiden glanced over his shoulder to find a man who held himself with confidence. His bright eyes bore into the Shade with precision, like they could laser through his flesh if he stared long enough. Of course, this man wouldn't know what a laser was. He'd never been to Earth.

He approached Vaiden, towering over him, using his size to intimidate, but the Shade wasn't biting. He knew if he stood at his full height, he'd be taller than this soldier, but his ribs wouldn't like that, and he didn't want to piss them off more.

"Who are you?" asked the Shade.

"Captain Windel," he replied. "What did you say about the fort?"

"It's gone," Vaiden exhaled. "The Corrupted came with their army of dead, blasted down the walls with meteors, and defeated the soldiers within."

"How many dead?"

"Who the fuck knows."

"By Moren," the barkeep gasped. "Surnuna save us."

"Where's the ambassador?" Windel asked.

Vaiden turned his whole body toward him, straightening as much as his ribs would allow. He met the soldier's gaze, letting his eyes grow dark and empty. "Where's his wife?"

The soldier shifted his gaze. "Lady Steel just woke," he said. "It'll be a moment before she receives an audience."

Vaiden nodded, leaning against the counter. The barkeep poured him more tea. He sipped it, letting it warm his body and relax his sore muscles.

"What happened to the families who escaped the fort with Lady Steel?" he asked.

"They are staying at a nearby farm," answered the soldier. "Some broke for north, aiming for White Star."

If they made it, they would be safe from the Corrupted, from any enemy. No one liked trudging up the mountain passes, even the diseased. Then again, these Corrupted weren't like any he had ever faced. Who was he to say what they would do?

"Surnuna light their path." Vaiden raised his glass.

"Wara protect them," echoed the soldier.

"Father," the young woman said, her eyes darting between the barkeep and the men at his counter.

"What is it, Surna?"

"The lady is ready for her guest."

"This way." The soldier waved his arm.

Vaiden followed, glancing at Alvez slumped in the chair, snoring softly. At least one of them could rest. The Shade wasn't sure if he should. Who knew what those bastard Corrupted would do? Maybe they would pick up their trail on the farmer's path, maybe they would push west and meet up with their buddies in Haven. Who knew? But Vaiden wasn't ready for another round, not just yet.

He needed more firepower, more Shades. Word needed to be sent to Mysogus and Kiji. They couldn't wait around for the king to act. The world would burn around them. Still, Casimere needed to know Fort Khali was lost.

With the fall of Haven, the next closest post to the eastern border was Duncan Village, a whole town built as tribute for Eskandor's most beloved king, Duncan. It was no stronghold, nor were its people soldiers. White Star and Abrita Shores were too far away. They needed to send a unit to make sure the Corrupted stayed within the border. The human settlements wouldn't stand a chance and that would only piss off their allies.

Windel led him down a narrow hall. Stationed at the farthest point of it was another soldier, guarding a door. The soldiers exchanged nods and the guard knocked on the door before opening it for Vaiden.

"Someone to see you, Lady Steel," Windel announced, sliding in first.

Caroline wrapped in a thick robe, clutched it at her throat. She stood from an armchair where a food tray sat on the table next to it. Her eyes darted between the captain and Vaiden behind him, her brows furrowing together.

"Where's Gabriel?" she asked.

Windel eyed the Shade, gesturing for him to move forward. Vaiden ignored him, stepping aside for the captain to leave. He didn't and that only irritated the Shade further.

"It's alright, Windel," Caroline said, voice gentle and calm. "Leave us."

He bowed slightly at the waist, casting a warning glare the Shade's way before finally leaving them alone in the room. Caroline approached Vaiden, her eyes sweeping over him, studying the state of his dirty body. She knew the damage of battle. As a healer, she'd been the only one brave enough to help the Shades—or the only one decent enough. Even if other High Elves had training in medicine without magic, they would let Shades die.

It was how Vaiden had met Caroline. She'd sifted through the dead, looking for survivors during the First Vampire War, screaming at other healers to do their jobs, calling them cowards when they refused. Vaiden had been close to death when she'd stumbled upon him. He owed her a life debt—something he would never forget. He didn't like owing people, but Caroline had claimed they were even when she'd married Gabriel. Vaiden had introduced them, but the Shade didn't believe the debt had been paid.

Staring into her bright eyes in this shabby room, Vaiden's chest tightened. She swallowed hard, her fingers loosening their grip on the robe.

"Vaiden, where's my husband?" she barely whispered into the silence.

"He's alive."

"Where is he?"

The Shade looked away, jaw locked. He hated this. He wanted to do anything, but tell her what had happened at the fort—what had happened to her husband.

"Vaiden, please," she begged, her hands sliding to her stomach. "Where is Gabriel?"

"I don't know," he exhaled, managing to meet her eyes again.

Her lips quivered. "What do you mean you don't know?"

"The rebels took him."

"The...rebels?" Tears slid down her flushed cheeks. She covered her face with both hands, a sob shaking her shoulders. Vaiden reached for her, but she moved away, leaning against the armchair. "You know he's on their list."

"He's too important to execute. They'll want information. They might even try to ransom him," Vaiden blurted. His mind raced with all the scenarios, knowing every outcome didn't end with Gabriel returning home. "The kingdom knows how important he is, even these rebels. Without Gabriel, ties will be cut with our allies. If the rebels win this war, they need those allies, especially in trade."

"Stop it!" Caroline whirled on him, forcing him to step back. The awkward and suddenness of the movement ignited fire around his ribs. He winced, doubling over, holding his side. A wave of nausea hit him, but he swallowed hard, fighting it back.

"You're hurt." Caroline's voice softened, her warm hand sliding over his shoulder. He opened his eyes, not knowing he'd closed them, or that he leaned against the wall. Its coolness soothed him, but he turned away from it, meeting her worried stare.

"I'll get him back," he breathed. Every word took effort, but he meant them. Her round eyes searched his. The look in them hurt worse than any injury he'd suffered. "I promise, Caroline. I'll get him back."

"You better."

"I will!"

"You don't understand." Her head shook, spilling her long hair over her shoulders nearly down to her waist. She rarely wore it down, claiming it got in the way of her work and she needed to cut it off, but she never did, knowing when Gabriel was home he loved to brush and braid it for her. She loved it too, though she would never admit it aloud.

"What don't I understand?" he asked.

She bit her lip, stepping away from him. Her hands sunk to her stomach, clutching the robe. "I'm with child."

A heaviness weighed in his chest, crushing against his ribs. He needed to breathe deeply, but that would hurt. His eyes flicked to her stomach then back to her face, etched in pain. Everything hurt. "Gabe doesn't know."

She shook her head. "I was going to tell him, but then the Corrupted..." She exhaled. "He needed to focus on the fort."

"He should have come here with you."

She opened her mouth to reply then closed it, her shoulders sloping. "I know," she said, fresh tears rolling down her cheeks. "This wasn't supposed to happen."

Vaiden reached for her and this time she didn't recoil. She collapsed into his arms, her warmth welcoming—her grip not so much. His jaw clenched, eyes tightly shutting as she held him.

"You're shaking," she said, stepping back. "Did I hurt you?"

He exhaled, groaning at the burst of fire in his side. "I think I've broken ribs."

"For the love of everything Surnuna holds dearly." She raced to the privy and returning with fresh linen. "Take off your clothes."

He licked his lips, wrenching his belt loose. "Well, when a lady asks so sweetly—"

"You're injured and I'm carrying another man's child."

He shrugged, regretting it immediately.

Caroline scowled, helping him remove his belt, sheaths, and bracers. She didn't bat an eyelash at the blood or the pieces of gore that fell to the ground removing his sheaths. Her hands gently guided his shirt over each shoulder and over his head, ignoring his groans. She discarded the wet shirt, her eyes widening at the trauma to his torso.

"It's going to take weeks to heal properly," she said.

"Just patch me up, doc."

She gave him a quizzical look, but went to work, tearing the linen. "I wish I could heal you."

"You and me both," he huffed, looking down his left leg where blood pooled beside his boot. "Shit."

"What?" she asked, following his gaze.

He smeared the blood with the toe of the boot, watching more drip to the wooden floor. "Guess it's pants off too?"

Caroline frowned at him, tearing another piece of linen. "You need to be more careful."

"Sure," he snorted, groaning at the blistering of his sides.

She helped him remove his boots and peel off his trousers, which was easier until he stepped out of them. Only his undershorts remained. He thought about making some kind of joke to relieve the tension, but Caroline's face remained focused on his wounds, especially the one down his left calf.

"I'll need to sew this," she said. "It's deep."

"Aw, just how she likes it."

She rolled her eyes, grabbing a pail of water. "Sit there." She pointed at the armchair. He did as he was told, despite the searing pain rippling through his body. His jaw clenched as she scrubbed his wound clean. A bath would have been more proficient, but the tavern didn't have a bathhouse or a private tub for its guests. They would have to make due with the bucket.

"Gabriel has been worried about this new you," Caroline said, readying her needle and thread. "But, I think I like Earth-Vaiden."

"Earth-Vaiden," he snorted, groaning again. "Gabe's been worried?"

"He says you've changed." She held the needle out, staring up the long line of his body. "Hold still now."

He nodded, letting the emptiness fill him. Shades didn't know pain—well, they could feel it. Everyone did, but Shades could tolerate it more than other elves.

"Be glad this is in the fatty part of your leg," she said, plunging the needle through his skin. He inhaled sharply. It was a bee sting, nothing more. "And that I'm a good seamstress."

She was. Even though they could afford to buy her any dresses she desired from merchants, she had chosen to make her own clothes. It helped her practice stitching, but mostly she preferred not to take apart dresses to make them fit her shape more precisely. Gabriel joked she was controlling, if only in tailoring.

"What happened at Fort Khali?" she asked.

"*To* Fort Khali, you mean," he sighed, his ribs aching. "There's a blood mage with this staff that can summon meteors. It crushed the keep and the walls. It was hopeless."

"Could the archers not take care of it?"

"The others protected it."

"Oh." She continued stitching, kneeled between his legs. Vaiden tilted his head back, closing his eyes for a moment. The world spun behind his eyelids, swirling toward the void of sleep. Hot electricity shot down his calf, making him bolt upright.

"Fuck!" He doubled over, a wave of nausea washing over him, strangled by the constricting of his ribs like a hungry python.

A knock rapped the door. "Lady Steel is everything alright?" Windel asked.

"Just fine, captain!" Her brows furrowed at Vaiden in that worried arch. "Are you OK?" she asked. He waved it off, not trusting his voice. She finished sewing up his wound, washing other rips along his legs. "The blood mage destroyed the fort."

He nodded, taking a shallow breath. "It had a necromancer as its second-in-command. They work well together."

"Is it strange for powerful Corrupted to pair up like that?"

"No, but it is strange for them to be so organized."

"Organized how?"

"Making targets, attacking strongholds," he explained. "This is not typical Corrupted behavior. There's something else going on."

"Like what?"

"I'm not sure."

Caroline's lips pursed, her eyes searching for something unseen. "In my training, we were taught the Corrupted targeted things for some type of gain, like food, resources, and the dead to make protection. What if their target is not something so simple?"

"What do you mean?"

"What if they want power?"

"They have magic."

"A different kind of power, like status or land or—"

"Ascendency?" Vaiden raised a brow at her. "These are the Corrupted, not an invading force."

"You said they aren't typical," she argued. "Therefore, you should treat them like any other enemy, who uses strategy in order to take control. They already closed our borders and diverted our supply routes both by land and water by seizing Haven first. It's in the middle of the kingdom and the center waterway."

The Shade blinked at her. She was right. That wasn't surprising, but, how obvious the Corrupted's plans were, hit him like one of the blood mage's meteors. While the kingdom fought each other, their real enemy picked them off slowly, gathering dead and power, surmounting for a true test. Fort Khali had been that test and they had won.

"Casimere needs to know about the fort," Vaiden said. "I think it's about time I pay our king a visit and get some answers."

"What about Gabe?" She stood, preparing the binding for his ribs.

"It'll take the rebels a while to decide what to do with him," he replied. "I mean what I said. He's too important to throw away. They also went to great lengths to recover him during the battle. They'll try to use him for some type of gain, even if that means ransoming him or getting our allies to turn against Altamost."

"So you confront the king, get him to release the Shades, and then go after my husband?"

Vaiden grimaced as he climbed to his feet. "That's the plan," he said, a dark smile spreading on his lips. "But when I see your husband, should I describe to him how you were kneeling between my thighs?"

She hit him with a wad of linen, a small smile playing with her lips. "Raise your arms. This is going to hurt."

He waggled his brows at her. "Kinky."

18

The coffee shop nestled at the bottom of an apartment complex on the north side of downtown. Very *Friends*, Tatiana thought bypassing the tables and chairs behind a gated iron fence. Despite the lunch rush on a Saturday, no one seemed in a great hurry. Soft jazz played through speakers mounted in the corners of the shop. Wooden tables each with different tablecloths spread throughout the main floor with padded mix and match chairs. Whimsical art hung on the walls, reminding her of *Alice in Wonderland*.

She found Logan tucked away in a corner, typing feverishly on his tablet. It was one of those surfaces that had a combinable keyboard. She'd wanted one for a couple of years, but hadn't made the switch yet. There was nothing wrong with her old laptop, but she noted how sleek and faster the newer machines were. It might be worth the investment.

Her eyes drifted up to the man sitting behind the screen. He swept away his long golden bangs from his furrowed brows. His features were handsome in that "surfer guy" kind of way, which probably didn't help the stereotype considering he did surf. She knew he skateboarded and snowboarded too, anything that worked on his core and balance. Her eyes swept over his lean torso in the white button up. The sleeves were pushed up to his elbows, revealing more of his golden-brown skin. She licked her lips, wondering why he'd stayed single these past few years.

Surely when Tatiana announced her engagement to Gary, he would have moved on. Maybe he was too busy? She remembered what it was like being a paralegal, especially considering she'd worked for their boss, Calvin Pearson. There was barely time to eat during the day, let alone think about dating. Josie had dragged her to blind double dates whenever she had a minute though. Many times Caden and Tatiana had discussed case files, much to their dates' displeasure or on the occasion, they both had passed out during movies.

Being a paralegal was rough, but Tatiana enjoyed busy work. It distracted her from the emptiness in her life, national and worldly dramas, and whatever crisis the media wanted to shove down everyone's throats. She didn't have time to think. She only had the work.

When the firm had allowed her to return to work, she had jumped at it, taking every file available. When her cases finished too quickly or thinned, she took any pro bono work that had come her way. The mountain of caseload she had worked in the last four months would make other attorneys green in the face, but Tatiana couldn't let herself be alone with her own thoughts.

"Hey." Logan smiled brightly at her, pushing away the tablet. "I ordered you a coffee." He gestured at the cup and empty chair across from him. "Creamer, no sugar or milk."

"Thanks." She slid into the chair, sipping it. The warmth filled her with renewed energy and comfort all at once. Coffee powered the workforce. It was the finest magic wrapped in a rich, smooth blend.

"How'd the interview go with Mrs. Slaseezor?" Logan asked.

She sat her cup down, holding it between her hands. "She was helpful, but she didn't have much information that could clear her husband."

"Is that surprising?"

Tatiana shook her head, then had a thought. "She said the victim was too young for coupling and had been active in pursuing their religion. I think he wanted to feel closer to his family since they returned to Arda without him."

"Why?"

"She didn't say, but my guess would be he was born here on Earth and what is born here, shall remain and doesn't belong on Arda. The serpent kingdom has strict rules about this. The den looked out for him."

"He was a legal adult." His eyes darted to his screen. He turned it around, revealing his research. "The blood ritual was used for sacrifice back in the kingdom. From what I found, one member of the family would be sacrificed so the rest could be protected by the den. Mostly the old or diseased would be chosen, but a few times, if the family had a bad reputation, they would take a healthy young person to cleanse their name."

"What if Koreen's family had a bad reputation?"

"You said they returned to Arda."

"What if the kingdom said they couldn't return without a sacrifice?"

"From what I've read the kingdom won't take anyone back who has traveled to Earth," he replied. "Rumors say they have been executing them."

"What if Koreen's family made a bargain?"

"Serpents do like to make them." He thought about it for a moment, turning the tablet back around while Tatiana sipped more of her coffee. "But why would they implicate Mr. Slaseezor in this bargain? Wouldn't the kingdom see *daehekans* as holymen and sacred?"

"Mr. Slaseezor lives on Earth though," Tatiana said. "They see him as a disgrace and disposable."

"Even as a leader of the faith?"

"You would have to factor in if they know and understand how our justice system works or if they care," she explained. "In their kingdom, it would be justifiable to kill Koreen to free his family of shame, at least in the old ways. The ritual doesn't use sacrifice anymore. Mr. Slaseezor said it was banned centuries ago."

"So maybe Koreen's family has influence or knows a loophole in the new laws and made a bargain for their return?"

"It's possible, but would they sacrifice one of their own, and how do we find proof of this when they're on Arda?"

"Someone had to stay behind to frame Mr. Slaseezor."

"And it takes a long time to acquire passage to Arda."

"Someone magical has to open the doors." Logan nodded. "From our informants in the Underground, it's quite expensive too, given the punishment for being caught smuggling people or cargo to Arda."

"Five years for smuggling into Earth," she said, "but if you are caught smuggling into Arda then they can execute you, considering the treaties for Earth technology and ideologies are banned from there."

"Do you know of any cases of people being caught on Arda's side?"

"No, but I doubt they'd inform us, considering they believe they would be within their rights to handle it how they see fit. I know they handle their own citizens similarly when they cross into other kingdoms. If you dare to go to that kingdom, then you must follow their laws, and if not, the consequences are yours alone to bear."

"Their laws are so different from ours."

"It's a different world."

"A harsh one."

She nodded, sipping more coffee, hoping it would relax the tension between her shoulders. Vaiden was on that world, fighting a war—in constant danger. Luckily, the elves didn't have such strict rules as the serpents. Their people wouldn't allow the sharing of Earth's cultures or religions, or discussions of technology, but they could return home without fear of execution.

Most immigration to and from Earth was done illegally, much like the southern border of the United States. If they could find a way to cross, they would. The doors were trickier than fences and rivers though. A magical person needed to activate them. Tatiana had watched a video on the spell work. It seemed complicated and would take someone with great knowledge of magic and possession of said magic to unlock it.

There was loads of misinformation on sorcery, stating if someone had it, they could learn all kinds of magic. Some could be learned, like abjuration to learn wards and other protective spells. Most were born with a natural alignment, like Tatiana's blue fire, which was arcane magic. Coastal possessed healing magic, which was the purest of white colors. She claimed not all healers had white magic, like hers, that the colors could have pigments of blue, pink, and sometimes yellow. The darker the color, the more malevolent the power. Jen's had been violet.

"Do you think our private investigator will lend aid on this case?" Logan asked.

She shook her head. "He doesn't like to take cases on the supernatural, especially not one going through an expedient trial."

"How are we going to investigate and construct a good defense then?"

"A little elbow grease," she scoffed. "Keep on your contacts in the Underground. The sooner we find a trail on this ritual angle, the sooner we can find whoever is responsible for Koreen's death."

"Shouldn't the police be doing that?"

"They think they got their guy," she replied. "They won't waste resources when there's thousands of other violent crimes to solve."

"Any investigator can see there's still a lot of questions in this case."

"I agree, but that doesn't change the fact Mr. Slaseezor is the one in the hot seat. His defense is the only one that matters. If we can't prove his innocence, then he gets sent back to Arda or he dies, and since we cannot guarantee Arda will take him back kindly, we must assume they will execute him too."

Logan nodded, a thought crossing his mind. "How was ladies night?"

She arched a brow at him, sweeping her eyes over him. "Why?"

He wet his lips, raking a hand through his hair. "Just curious." A smile played with his lips. "From what Darling told me before she left yesterday, it was going to be a night to remember."

Tatiana looked down at her empty cup between her hands. The ceramic had gone cold without coffee to warm it. She thought about getting herself a refill, but that would mean visiting with Logan longer. Not that she didn't enjoy his company, she didn't want to give him the wrong impression. She liked him, but she wasn't sure how much. It was weeks away from learning if he passed the bar. They had to keep it professional—friendly, but professional.

"I didn't stay long," she answered.

"Oh? What happened?"

"I was tired, but it was a good night all things considered." He didn't push, which she appreciated. Everyone wanted to know her business of late—the media, her friends, even those tight suits up in HR. She wanted to be left alone, to work, and free Mr. Slaseezor from persecution. Was that too much to ask for?

It was the price of fame, she knew. Not that she asked to be popular, but the media wouldn't let an attractive successful woman be missed from their star profiles. She used to revel in being recognized as a feminist icon, for inspiring other young women into law and shedding light on preternatural rights, but after the events six months ago, she couldn't muster the strength to speak at events or look at social media. Her name had been forever linked with Jen. Too many people were obsessed with serial killers and not cognizant of the pain and devastation they left behind.

"Well, at least one of us had fun last night," he chuckled. "I'm on a social media ban for a month."

"What did you do?"

"Oh, you know." He leaned forward with elbows on the table. "Got into an argument with some bigot that doesn't understand the law, but thinks because they watch certain news channels and cop shows, they are the smartest person in the world."

She rolled her eyes. "You should ignore those trolls."

"I try." He shrugged. "But it really grinds my gears when people don't understand the atrocities that happen to preternaturals. I mean, Mr. Slaseezor might be executed for a crime he didn't knowingly commit."

"It's our job to make sure that doesn't happen."

"Have you ever thought what would happen if they caught a Shade here on Earth?" He leaned back in his chair with his hands behind his head. "What a media storm that would be."

She rubbed at her chest, trying to soothe the uneasiness spreading through it. "Yeah," she managed softly. Vaiden wasn't on Earth, but he planned to return. He wasn't a registered Ardan, but that was the least of his worries as a Shade. There was no trial, no formal investigation when one was discovered. They were to be executed on the spot.

As an officer of the court, she was supposed to report any unlawful acts or illegal statuses of Ardans, but she'd found charities like Home-Away-From-Home to be more beneficial to helping preternaturals register and find a legal path to becoming a citizen of the United States. Shades were permitted no leeway. Technically, she should have reported Vaiden's identity and whereabouts to the authorities, but Tatiana couldn't bring herself to betray him, not after he'd saved her life.

She agreed Shades were dangerous. They took direct orders from the king and would stop at nothing to fulfill those orders. Purpose also forced them to take action against any Corrupted that crossed their paths, ignoring any laws set in place by Earth's governments. Earth couldn't control Shades, which was one of the reasons for their strict laws about them.

Generally, she agreed with those laws, though she had never agreed to no trial or representation, but the fact they would be executed without deportation or imprisonment had always bothered her. She argued these laws needed to be changed. It was against the rights of the people of the United States not to have their day in court with proper representation and fight for their lives.

"My buddy, who works down in the state building, says there's rumors of California introducing a bill to allow Shades," Logan said. "I'm not sure if the governor is ready for that kind of argument, especially with the presidential election coming up."

"She hasn't announced her candidacy."

"We all know she's going to run. I don't think announcing this kind of legislation will have a good reaction."

"It won't pass in the house," Tatiana said. "I'm not sure anyone wants to get in legal fights with the federal government and the UN. It's a concern of more than just the U.S. when it comes to Shades."

He leaned forward again. "Come on, Ana, you don't agree with the Shade laws either."

"No, but even if it was repealed correctly at the federal level, our government would have to create treaties with the UN over this. I don't see other countries being comfortable with the idea of allowing Shades to run freely in our country, no more than we would in theirs."

He frowned. "Now you sound like the DA."

"I am insulted," she gasped, flinging back a lock of her hair for dramatic effect. "At least, I think about the issues. Leanger is just prejudice."

"It's a wonder how he won his election."

"A lot of people are still uneasy about preternaturals in our society and the crimes they commit. It makes people feel unsafe."

"Humans commit the same crimes."

"True, but sorcery wasn't publicly known in humans until after the Supernatural Law Act."

"I meant murder," he chuckled. "Every crime in our world can be committed by humans just as easily as the supernatural."

"I wouldn't say 'as easily,'" she said. "Last time I checked, we don't have the same claws and teeth as some of our clients."

"Unless you buy the synthetic substitute."

"Knives, but teeth?"

"I've seen the prosthetics." He made a face. "I'm still not sure how they fit without surgeries to enlarge the mouth."

Tatiana shook her head. She knew people had cosmetic surgeries all the time to appear more feline or serpent. An article, she'd read, discussed how more than ever humans paid to have false vampire fangs implanted. It was their bodies. They could do what they wanted to them, but she hoped they truly wanted such a transformation. Sometimes there was no going back.

Logan's phone chimed, grabbing his attention. She watched him sweep away his bangs again, staring at the device. He was handsome, articulate, and someone who shared many of her same politics. They could talk for hours about legislation and law. She truly enjoyed his company.

Yet, nothing happened while she gazed at him. No tingling through her body or fluttering of her heart. She had more of a reaction in Caden's company than Logan's and Caden was her best friend. Maybe Caden made her feel safe, but shouldn't a forbidden office romance awaken excitement within her? Not that she would date Logan while she was his boss. She'd been clear about that.

She exhaled, her eyes trailing over his slender build and soft hands, holding the smartphone. Gary was shorter than Logan, but thicker in muscle. His hands were manicured, much like his entire person. Nothing was without a place from his hair to the knots in his shoelaces—immaculate. She'd loved that about him. He'd kept a tidy space and had understood she liked her stuff a certain way. They had argued about how the toilet paper should unroll, but that seemed like normal couple disagreements.

Their fights about sex were not normal. He'd hurt her a few times, even talked her into liking it rough. She did sometimes, but not his idea of what that meant. Then there were things she hadn't told anyone, not even her closest friends—things that she looked back at recently, knowing they were red flags. No meant no. She'd forgotten, or she had thought he was her safety, that he loved her, and it was OK, but it wasn't.

He had video taped some of it for Jen, pleasuring her through Tatiana's fear and pain. She'd shown one of the more violent experiences to Vaiden in an attempt to distract him. It had, but Vaiden had finished the job. He'd told Tatiana he'd destroyed the rest of the films, but that she needed to seek therapy. So far, she'd ignored his advice—everyone's advice.

"I got a lead," Logan announced, rising from the table and gathering his devices. "A feline claims to have some information."

"Do you want me to go with you?"

He shook his head. "They spook easily, especially around us humans."

"I know a feline," she said. "Maybe they would be more comfortable if one of their kind vouches for us."

"I've got it, boss." He smiled sweetly, but there was something hidden in it. Trust me, it said. She bit her lip, the uneasiness spreading through her chest again. She didn't like the idea of Logan trudging alone through the underbelly. It was dangerous, but what alley in the ghetto wasn't? Maybe she wasn't as progressive as she thought she was, or maybe she had common sense. He shouldn't go alone.

"You need back up." She climbed to her feet, standing in his way to leave.

His smile faltered. "Don't worry," he said. "I've done this many times in the past. It's nothing."

"Meet where others can see you and text me when you arrive and when you leave."

"Ana." He exhaled, deflating his entire body. "I'll be fine."

She stepped forward, leaning in to whisper. "Do you have a weapon?"

"What?" His brows shot up underneath his bangs.

"You need something to protect yourself with. Get a weapon. Keep it in a pocket or some place easily accessible." She grabbed the sides of his arms, shaking them slightly. "Just protect yourself."

"Are you OK?" he asked, worry etching across his brow.

She stepped back, pinching the top of her nose. "Just promise to at least text."

"Yeah, of course," he said. "It's going to be OK. I've done this before."

"And I've met with a thousand clients, but it only took the wrong one to put a bounty on my head."

His face twisted with confusion. "What do you mean?"

She opened her mouth to explain about Harvey and LaBelle, realizing that wasn't public information. According to her own statement, Harvey had nothing to do with her disappearance those months ago. It was all about Jen and Gary.

Her fingers threaded through her hair, trying to think of a bad case. "Serpents don't like to be insulted," she said instead. "I've been banned from some establishments because of my breakout case."

His face softened into something resembling sympathy. "I know you're just looking out for me, trying to avoid the mistakes you made early on, but trust me, I'll be OK. You've taught me well."

A weight lifted from her shoulders, relieved he didn't push about the holes in her story. "I mean it. Text me before and after the meeting."

"Will do, boss." He smiled that teasing grin she'd grown fond of over the years. The fluttering from her heart was not from excitement, but dread.

"Be careful," she commanded as he slipped past her. He saluted, moving through the tables for the exit. She studied the other customers, ignorantly drinking coffee, blissfully unaware that a serpent might be executed because they needed proof he didn't knowingly plunge a dagger through someone's chest. If they knew, would they even care?

Tatiana cared for them all. Cared enough she wouldn't sleep well, if at all, during the upcoming week. Mr. Slaseezor was innocent. She knew it in her bones, but she couldn't let anyone else get hurt, especially someone with whom she was responsible.

In her car, she retrieved her smartphone and scrolled through a list of contacts for the only feline she knew.

19

The farmers agreed to take in the families from Fort Khali, but Caroline was too important to leave at that tavern or one of the farms. Captain Windel agreed. The smartest place to bring her was Mysogus, but how to get there. Fort Khali stood in the way west. To the south, the Wildlands would be unsafe. If they gave a wide berth by going north and over to White Star, the road would lead them to Haven. During this time of year, mountain passes to other destinations would be unreachable. Vaiden had stared at the map long enough his eyes started to cross.

"We'll go south," Caroline had finally ordered. "The Corrupted have already moved north to Fort Khali. The only sensible route is south."

"There's more Corrupted than just those accompanying the blood mage," Vaiden had replied. "The closer you get to Aegan's shrine, the more will arrive."

"We won't go that far south."

"There is the trader's path," Windel had offered.

Vaiden hadn't liked it, but Caroline was right. The Corrupted would be divided between the fort and the shrine. Likely, they could go undetected through the trader's path that led to Cobble Road. The Shade would take no chances though. He instructed the ambassador's men on a few rules of traveling through the Wildlands.

"Everyone sticks together. We stay quiet. If I say jump, you jump."

They had stared at him with bored eyes, but after their captain had asked if anyone objected to the instructions, they had come to attention. "It is our duty to keep Lady Steel safe," he'd said. "Any man not fit for this task, declare it now."

None had voiced their objections. It was over a week's journey to Cobble Road on horse, but they didn't want to give the Corrupted more bodies to make monstrosities from. Horses made noise and needed nourishment too. They couldn't take any chances. The men hadn't liked the idea of walking, but once they had entered the Wildlands, no one had complained.

The utter quietness of the long grass fields made the hair on Vaiden's arms stand up, but he ignored it, using his senses to study the areas. They were in the wide open. Anyone with a good pair of eyes could have seen them for miles. Likely, the Corrupted, or some other predator, had already spotted them and were tracking their movements. Given their company of ten soldiers, most predators wouldn't attack, but weirder things had happened recently. He wouldn't risk their safety on what was considered normal or not.

It started raining on the third day. Drenched, cold, and aching with every step from his ribs to sore muscles, Vaiden pressed on, focusing all his energy on signs of an attack. The fifth day a lorapod, a giant lizard with shark-like teeth, attacked. The soldiers had easily defeated it and later roasted its meat for a much needed meal.

Vaiden prowled in the darkness, watching the fields with his nocturnal sight. The rain had subsided, but the air was plenty humid. By the fire, Alvez sat alongside the men, whispering stories about their adventures. He was interested in their trips to the serpent kingdom while eating something that may or may not be related to them. The men laughed, but their captain demanded silence. They sobered, remembering this was no errand to meet emissaries in faraway kingdoms.

"Drink this," Caroline's voice said. Vaiden eyed the waterskin she'd brushed against his arm. "You need to keep hydrated."

He took it, thinking of no reason to turn her down. The water was cool and welcomed in the heat, but he kept moving, checking their perimeter.

"Slow down," she groaned. "My legs aren't as long as yours."

"You don't have to walk with me," he replied quietly. "You should be with the men, protected."

In the darkness, even without his added sight, he could depict her frown. She made no move toward the fire. Dressed in trousers and knee high boots, she knew at any moment she may need to run. It was hard to run in a dress, especially long ones with heavy, awkward skirts. Most women traveled in trousers for that reason, but a few traversing short distances would wear dresses, especially on the west side of the kingdom between Brevene and Casimere.

"After we part ways, how are you going to get around Haven?" she asked.

"Don't worry about it."

"Of course, I will. That's why I'm asking."

"It'll be easier to fool the Corrupted by myself."

"But you won't be alone. Alvez will be with you."

Vaiden exhaled, his ribs violently protesting. "You should convince him to stay with you," he said.

"He won't. His father lives in Casimere."

"I'm aware."

"He wants to see the king and tell him about Fort Khali. He was stationed there. He'll support your report."

"Glades got out. He'll tell the king. The general's word is worth more than a lowly captain and a Shade."

"What if Glades doesn't make it to Casimere?"

Vaiden scoffed. "He can take care of himself, which is something that can't be said for the captain."

"Even more reason he goes with you, instead of traveling on his own."

She had a point, but Vaiden hated it. Truly he didn't like the idea of going near Haven, especially after what they'd experienced at Fort Khali. He expected the blood mage's nest would join with them, but that could take weeks. Just because both groups were Corrupted, that didn't mean they wanted the same things. Maybe they did. Caroline thought it was all a grand scheme for the Corrupted to gain power and control of the kingdom.

Part of him agreed with her, but the other half needed proof. Attacking Haven and the fort wasn't enough for him. It should have been, but that part of him needed more. How did the nests correspond? Where was their base of operations? Who was giving them orders?

***

Over the next few days, heading farther west their trip in the Wildlands finally ended. Woods greeted them with shade during the hot days and shelter through the nights. Eventually the trader's path brought them to a small village where they rented rooms at a tavern. Caroline bathed alone, both Vaiden and Captain Windel standing guard. When she finished, she helped Vaiden wash his hair.

"Don't tell my husband about this," she chuckled. "He'll get rightly jealous that my fingers were in your hair."

"You two have a fetish," Vaiden snorted. He relaxed against the back of the tub with his eyes closed, letting her fingers soothe the headache he'd been carrying around for days.

"What is a fetish?" she asked.

"Oh." His eyelids flew open. "Something of an obsession on a sexual level."

She scoffed, but in the reflection of the water, he spied a teasing smile spread on her lips. "Earth seems to have a saying for everything."

"Or they'll invent new ones. Believe me when I tell you, learning a language there is not easy."

"Gabriel will be the judge of that," she said. "My husband does have the most brilliant tongue in all the land."

"Yes, his linguistics are unmatched."

"Among other things."

He tilted his head back, grinning. "Oh?"

She shrugged, though her expression was quite proud. "You haven't said how life is on Earth or about your mother or Lewej."

"Coastal's living large," he said, dipping his head forward to a more natural position. "I don't care about Lewej."

"Asiram was a good woman. It was nice of Coastal to take in her daughter."

Vaiden was quiet for a moment, thinking of his mother. She would be at a bar or club this time of night, cozying up to some attractive young woman. Coastal was boastful about her one-night stands. He didn't know why, but it did make him think of someone else.

"Zarah lives in the same city as we do."

"Really?" He didn't mistake the excitement in her voice. "How is she? How does she like Earth? What does she do for work there?"

He chuckled. "She was married, but the guy died not too long ago. I'm not sure what she's doing with her life now that he's gone."

"That's—sad," Caroline said and meant it. "Do you think she's close to the undying?"

He shook his head. "She loved the guy, but I doubt she loved him *that* much."

"What do you know of love, Vaiden? It can drive you mad, make you do impossible things, and be someone you don't even recognize."

"I know she didn't have what you and Gabe do."

"Are we a measuring stick?"

"You're mine."

"I don't know if I should be honored or slightly disturbed that a Shade would create such a unit of measurement."

"You're my example of what love looks like," he said, "of how strong it is, and no matter what happens, you find a way."

She was quiet for a moment, rinsing his hair, and then drying her hands. "After this war is over, do you think you can help me convince Gabriel to retire?"

"I won't have to."

"What do you mean?"

"You're having a baby, Caro, but I'm not going to sugarcoat the process," he said. "It takes time to train a replacement. He might miss some things. It'll eat at him, but once the process is over, he'll be all yours. Then you'll write to me about how you need him to go away."

She hit him with her towel. "Do you need help getting out?"

He shook his head, bracing his arms on the sides of the wooden tub. His legs still worked fine, but for some reason the inability to be flexible in his torso radiated pain throughout his whole body, making his legs forget how to work. Caroline didn't say anything. She took one of his arms, letting him use her as a crutch and helped him climb out of the tub.

"We are definitely not telling your husband about this," he groaned.

"I might," Windel said through the door.

"You won't," Caroline ordered, despite the smile on her lips.

Once he was dry and wearing undershorts again, Caroline applied a salve to his wounds and wrapped his ribs in fresh linen.

"This must be how people feel wearing corsets," he hissed as she pulled the fabric tightly. "Why would they freely do this to themselves?"

"Fashion."

Vaiden rolled his eyes. "Bunch of masochists."

"What is that?"

"Oh boy," he sighed. "You and I are not going to play one-hundred questions with every Earth-word or phrase."

"Well, can I at least ask one more question involving Earth?"

"Sure."

"Are you and Zarah—"

"No."

"You didn't even let me finish my question."

"That's because I know what you're asking," he said, slipping on his trousers as she held them for him. He pulled a black shirt over his head, his sides blistering in pain. Caroline assisted, saying nothing about how pathetic he was.

"Then can I ask—"

"You wasted your one question."

"If I didn't fully ask it, is it really a question?"

He narrowed his eyes at her.

"I helped you get out of the tub and dressed you." She put her hands on her hips. "One question."

He stifled a sigh, knowing it would only bring him pain. "Sure."

"Are you happy on Earth?"

"Happy?"

"Content, whatever the Shade-equivalent is."

His mouth opened ready to answer, but he considered her question more deeply. Happiness was a foreign concept to him. He had a job, though illegal, paid well enough he didn't have to worry if his lights stayed on. His car was cool, but he doubted Caroline would understand anything about automobiles and he wouldn't want to get her or Gabriel in trouble for knowing technology about Earth.

He had a home, food, and colleagues. Lucius might be a friend. He really didn't know. Zarah *could* be a friend. They had history and a previous sexual relationship. She was beautiful, but he didn't need such a relationship from her any more.

"Well?" Caroline asked, folding the towels they'd used.

"I don't worry about anything," he answered. "I have work and a roof over my head. Coastal is a constant in my life, though I'm not sure if that's a good thing or not."

She frowned at him. "She's your mother. She loves you. Besides, she gave up everything here to find you on Earth. You should be grateful to have someone who cares so much about you."

He held up his hands in surrender, not wanting to challenge a soon-to-be mother's insecurities.

***

Was he happy? It weighed on him when they finally reached Cobble Road days later. South would lead Caroline and Gabriel's men toward Abrita Shores, another road would take them to Mysogus, the magical school. Since she was a former student, she had clearance. He didn't know about the soldiers, but they were her escorts. Perhaps the practitioners wouldn't mind extra hands during this Corrupted blight.

When they said their good-byes, Caroline reminded Vaiden to be nice to Alvez and for the young captain to stay strong. Vaiden hugged his friend tightly, despite his ribs, promising again that he would find Gabriel. She smiled at him, something sad shining in her eyes.

"I believe in you," she said. "Write when you can."

Vaiden watched the men escort Caroline away. They were all capable soldiers, who would give their lives for her. Gabriel had chosen them well, especially Windel. He saluted the Shade with a short nod and shook Alvez's hand.

"Wara keep you safe on your travels," he said before joining his men.

A heaviness weighed in Vaiden's chest while he watched Caroline disappear into the distance. She would be fine, he thought. The Corrupted weren't stupid enough to attack Mysogus, even with a magical staff. The practitioners at the magical school would have more firepower than that blood mage could imagine. They would do everything and anything to avoid another High Tower incident.

"Let's go," Vaiden said. "We're burning daylight."

The captain's nose wrinkled. "How can daylight burn?"

"It's a saying from a cowboy I like."

"What's a cowboy?"

The Shade groaned. It was going to be a long two weeks to Casimere.

20

J ay Wishland lived in a rather sketchy part of town that Tatiana wouldn't
visit unless she believed it was truly necessary. Her body shivered against the
feeling of eyes watching her every move when she parked her car and climbed
the stairs to the complex doors. She pushed a button under Jay's name, a
buzzing sound followed.

"Yeah?" His voice sounded sleepy over the intercom.

"It's Tatiana."

"What are you doing here?"

"You didn't answer your phone."

Another buzzing sound let her know the door unlocked and she was clear to
enter. Inside, the smell of feet and mildew filled her nostrils. She scratched her
nose, fighting a sneeze while she took to the stairs. Jay lived on the third floor.
A litter of kittens passed her, holding a basketball. She pressed herself against
the wall, smiling as they ran down the stairs at a graceful speed she admired.
They didn't seem to mind her, but a parent chased after them, casting a wary
glance her way.

At the top of the stairs, Jay leaned against his door frame, picking something
out of his teeth with a claw. "What's up?" he asked.

She frowned at him, her eyes sweeping over his graphic tank top and baggy
joggers. He wore nothing on his feet. His claws tapping the tiled flooring.

"You don't look so good, counselor," he said quietly. "Not sleeping?"

"Jay, get inside." She gestured at his apartment.

He shrugged, but did as he was told. The apartment had off white colored
walls and brown carpet throughout the main room, except the little hall
impersonating as a kitchen. It had cream colored linoleum, which probably

matched the flooring in the bathroom, if she dared to enter it. The main room doubled as a living room and bedroom.

Jay sat on his unmade bed, his legs spread wide. "Nice for you to visit." He threaded claws through his shaggy brown mane. His silver cat eyes studied her outfit.

"It's too hot to be wearing a suit," he said. "I'd be melting."

"I met with a client's wife today," she answered, leaning against the back of his sofa. "It's a pretty bad case and I was wondering if you would be willing to help."

He looked down. His foot playing with dirty clothes on the floor. For some reason, it was too hard for him to dispose of them in a laundry hamper. "I don't know," he exhaled. "What would I have to do?"

"Talk to some people."

"In the underbelly?"

She shifted in her heels, wishing she'd worn sneakers instead. "Just a few about a serpent."

"A serpent?" He raised his head, his face scrunched like he'd smelled something foul.

"It's really important, Jay. This man is up for a murder he didn't commit."

"Are you sure?"

"Of course, I am."

He seemed to think about it. "I got everything squared with Fluffy Tails. Tom Cat's off my back."

"That's good."

"But now you want me to go sniffing around those alleys again." He crossed his arms. "It took me years to leave the alley cats behind."

"I know." Her shoulders slumped. "You've been doing great."

"So why?" He jumped to his feet, stalking toward her. "Last time I helped you, I lost my car and broke my shoulder."

"*Desolocated*," she corrected. "And Vaiden bought you a new car."

"Don't try to make it sound like everything's fine, Tati," he growled. "I still have nightmares about that night—of that bitch dragging you away and no matter how many buildings I jump to, I'm never able to catch up with her to save you."

"Jay." Guilt washed over her like a tidal wave. He was one of the only witnesses she had named in her statement. He had tried to save her. That was true. His car was the one found at the incident so he had to be involved. His part in the story was pursuing Jen's car in his own after he had witnessed the elf move Tatiana from her art gallery to a limo. The limo then had driven them to a secluded cabin south where Gary had waited for them to begin their killing ritual. Street cameras had confirmed the limo and the route it had taken to support Jay's story.

The public knew nothing about the blue fire or that Jen was a soul sucker. They didn't know about Jen's assistant Marcie Marr, the guards Vaiden had killed, or that Mystic Crane had shown up. Tatiana had fallen unconscious so she didn't have the pleasure of meeting them.

Jay had. He'd watched them contain the magic from both the blue fire and Jen's magic so it didn't catch the surrounding forest on fire. It was a sight, he'd said. One that had him chewing on his own claws.

"I don't want you to fall back into that life," Tatiana said.

"OK, then don't send me back there."

She opened her mouth to argue, but his round eyes begged her to drop it. What was she doing? Did she not trust Logan to do his job? Or was she afraid he'd get hurt? The latter was real paranoia. Logan could get hurt, but he'd been working the alleys for years—like she had as a paralegal. It was how she had built trust within the community.

The police wouldn't do it. They didn't care, nor did they have the resources to follow-up, not on supernatural cases at least. It wasn't all their fault. Expedient trials didn't allow time to gather evidence and find witnesses willing to exonerate suspects. Another right the preternatural community deserved—due process.

They had a watered down version instated by the Supernatural Law Act, but every trial Tatiana won demonstrated why the preternatural deserved true due process. It was a waste of the court's time and caused distrust between the police, legal fields, and the citizens they served.

Her phone chimed within her pants pocket. She retrieved it, seeing Logan's text. He was at the meeting. She knew the street, not the worst alley, but that didn't mean it was safe.

"Why do you want me to go talk to the cats when your firm has an investigator?" Jay asked. "He can do it."

"He won't." She slipped the phone back into her pocket. "My paralegal is down Row, meeting with a feline who claims to have information."

"Row isn't a bad place. Just where most get strung out."

"I just..." She folded her arms over her stomach. "I don't like him being out there, especially alone."

"I get it, but he's got to spread his wings and do the dirty work, show face, or the underbelly won't respect him, like they do you."

"A lot of good that did me," she grumbled, chewing on her lip.

He gently pushed her arm, leading her toward the door. "Tati, the community loves you. What LaBelle and Jen did, does not represent us. You should be one of the untouchables. Even those brutes over at Fluffy Tails think that."

"Thanks, Jay."

He shrugged. "Anytime, but really not—not that I don't love you, but just because you and I have different definitions of what Saturdays are for."

"It's in the afternoon, Jacob. I can't help that you party until the sun rises."

"My first name is just Jay. It's not short for anything."

"Really?"

"You've seen my paperwork."

"Caden's your lawyer, so I'm not privy to that information."

He made a face. "Maybe you should be my lawyer?"

"Only if you commit a big enough crime."

"Maybe not." He grabbed the door handle, pulling it open. "Tati, good seeing you, but..."

A noise from inside the apartment alerted their attention. "What was that?" she asked, turning toward the bathroom. "Is someone else here?"

"No," he said too quickly, like a kid caught with chocolate on their face, but denied they had any cake. Another bang, followed by cursing sounded from the bathroom. Tatiana cocked a brow at him.

"You sure?" she asked.

"It's just the neighbors."

"I live in a apartment too. I can tell if sounds are coming from inside, outside, or neighbors." She marched to the bathroom, despite Jay's pleas for her to stop. She knocked. "Who's in there?"

The door flung open, revealing a familiar face. "Surnuna, who taught you to knock? The police?" Lewej scowled, rubbing her head.

"What happened?" Jay asked, sliding between Tatiana and his guest.

"I slipped," she groaned. "Your tub sucks."

Tatiana's eyes noted her dry hair and the fact she was wearing the same outfit from the night before. "Why were you hiding?"

"Because." Lewej pursed her lips, striding from the bathroom. Jay jumped back, giving her space. "I don't want people to make a big deal about this."

"About what exactly?"

Lewej turned on her heel, giving the attorney a bored expression. "You know what."

"Not unless you say it aloud."

"We don't have to do that." Jay rushed between them again. "Thank you so much for stopping by, Tati. It's nice to see you. Let's get together some *other* time."

Tatiana crossed her arms defiantly. "Does Coastal know about this?"

"Ugh! No, of course not," Lewej whined. "She's so old school. Like, I know she's two thousand years old, but hello! We live on Earth. It's perfectly fine that I see Jay. There's no harm in it."

He smiled white needle-like teeth at her.

"Age has nothing to do with it, Lewej," Tatiana said. "You know it's a death sentence still on Arda to couple between races."

She rolled her eyes. "Yes, thanks for Earth-splaining to me my own world, but last I checked, we're not on Arda."

"When did this happen?" Tatiana pointed between the two of them. "I don't really remember you meeting each other."

"At the hospital," Jay said. "Before Vaiden left, I had dinner at his place too. They showed up and..." He smiled again at Lewej.

"Please don't tell Coastal," she begged.

"Technically, you're in her charge," Tatiana replied.

"I'm a legal adult here on Earth."

"Not to the elves and not by your immigration status. She's responsible for you."

"OK, but what is this hurting?" She motioned between them. "It's no one's business."

"I agree," Tatiana said, "but that doesn't change the fact you're lying to Coastal, even by omission. Where does she think you are right now?"

"Look. I don't want to make a big deal about it," Lewej said. "We're just hooking up, being safe and responsible, two consenting adults. I like him. He likes me. Why involve anyone else?"

"Again, I agree."

"Then why are you being such a pain in the ass?" Lewej asked. "If Vaiden was here..."

"Hey, OK, we're not bringing the big guy into this." Jay put up his hands. "He's not here to defend himself and tell us all how much he doesn't care, even though he does."

Lewej rolled her eyes. "He's not your friend."

Jay gasped, pressing his paw against his chest. "He's my *best* friend."

"Tell that to Gabriel."

"Who's that?"

"You just like Vaiden because he bought you that little car."

"My Skyline is awesome! It's blue with a big wing and..."

"OK!" She waved her hands. "You're just as bad as he is about *his* stupid car."

Jay gasped again. "You take that back! His Viper is so cool."

Tatiana burst out laughing, pushing past them. They continued to argue about cars, ignoring her completely, even when she opened the apartment door. She didn't know what to think about them as a couple, but she knew they'd never run out of things to complain about.

By the time she returned to her vehicle, Logan had texted her again. The meeting went smoothly, he said, but the contact's information wasn't helpful. She cursed under her breath, wishing someone would come forward with evidence to help Mr. Slaseezor.

She took a deep breath, staring at the apps on her phone. Her eyes caressed the social media ones. She could take it into her own hands. Ask the public for aid. Sometimes it worked. Sometimes freaks came out of the woodwork to gain attention and waste their time.

What would the serpents think? Most of them didn't adhere to technology in this way. The young ones used it though. Maybe someone saw something, but didn't know it. She could help refresh their memory.

She opened the most popular of the apps. Her fingers navigated, using its features to make a new post. She typed out a simple message, asking for anyone with information about the crime to come forward. As she stared at the message, she wondered if PR needed to approve it before posting. In the past, they had forced her to take down certain statements, but nothing that she would make a fuss about. Mr. Slaseezor's life was at stake.

She posted it, throwing her phone in the passenger seat and running her hands through her hair. It was done. Hopefully, someone came forward.

21

Fog rolled in the closer they traveled to Haven. Vaiden stayed alert, his skin nearly on fire with purpose as they trotted through the woods. The main road was unsafe. The Corrupted would be watching it, wishing for the stupid and unfortunate to use it, headed to Casimere.

Vaiden wasn't stupid. He hid in the shadows of the woods, using the brush and trees as cover. They had seen a lot of swarms during their journey—more than Vaiden had seen during his years with the Forty-Second. This blight was out of control. The Shades needed to do something or they would lose the whole damn kingdom.

Alvez stayed vigilant at his side, retreating when told. He'd learned quickly Vaiden didn't care for back talk and second-guesses. When he made a command, it was followed or there were consequences. After the second time Vaiden had slapped the back of Alvez's head, it was wired into his brain to move, not talk.

Despite Alvez's quick learning, Vaiden hated having a rookie, like the young captain, at his back. The kid was no Gabriel Steel. He didn't have the battle experience or knowledge when it came to their enemy. The Corrupted wouldn't give them mercy or second chances. They only had the heat of the moment. Either they died or the Corrupted did. Alvez understood this, but he was squeamish about fighting them.

"Either kill or be killed," Vaiden said as they settled for the night. The giant tree served as a nice shelter. The large trunk formed around rock, creating a massive cave that could have fit a whole midsize SUV. With no obvious signs animals lived there, it was the perfect place to hide.

Alvez handed him a bowl of rabbit stew. Not Vaiden's favorite, but he wouldn't complain. Supplies were scarce with no villages between them and Casimere. They would ration what the tavern had provided them, but it wasn't much. Alvez wasn't a bad hunter or cook either. He seemed to prefer these jobs to the responsibilities at the fort or taking commands from Vaiden.

"I'm willing to protect myself and others," the captain said, spooning his stew.

"Protecting and killing are two different things."

Alvez ate, muttering something under his breath.

"What was that?"

"I don't know why you are making a big deal about this."

"Because you are the only one I can depend on out here besides myself," the Shade explained. "I need to know you will do whatever it takes to have my back."

"I didn't come on this journey for endless lectures," Alvez scowled. "Has anyone ever told you what a complete horse's ass you are?"

Vaiden frowned at him. "Name calling doesn't change the fact you are a soldier," he said. "Part of the job is killing when necessary."

"*When* necessary."

"You want to stress that, but the truth is—"

"The truth is I saved you at the fort!" The captain stood, throwing his bowl aside. "A little gratitude would be appreciated."

"How embarrassing you think basic decency should be applauded."

"Glades saved himself, but I didn't. I knew we needed you and Gabriel. I just couldn't get to the ambassador."

"Didn't want to."

"You didn't do anything either!" His anger hit Vaiden like a hot whip, searing and tearing all at the same time. The Shade sat, an immovable mountain. Alvez turned away from him, studying the forest beyond their cave.

There wasn't much to see in the darkness without nocturnal sight, but even with such a special ability, details were lost in the fog. It was why Vaiden hadn't bothered. He would rely on his hearing.

"That wasn't fair," Alvez barely whispered. "You were hurt."

"Probably concussed too."

The captain turned to him with a raised brow. "You say the weirdest things."

"It's an injury to the brain." He pointed at his head. "Like a bruise or something."

Alvez sat back down, leaning with his back against the tree. "I know you don't want me here. You think you would be better off alone on this journey."

"I'm a Shade."

"And for some reason that makes you better than me and everyone else?"

"No, it means the Corrupted's magic cannot hurt me."

"But their dead can and if they know how to fight, their weapons can."

"You'll find they rarely know how to use weapons because their diseased brains only think about the power," he explained. "But yes, the dead can attack me."

"If their magic can't hurt you then how can the dead hurt you? Isn't it their magic that brings them back?"

"Sure, but I see you're uneducated in how necromancy works. The magic hijacks the soul, bringing the person back as the undead. They're not exactly alive, but they're not dead either, just walking shells made to destroy. Even if you killed the necromancer who raised them, it wouldn't kill the undead. They'd have to be put down individually."

"Does it ever bother you—killing so many?"

"I've been killing since I was ten years old. It's muscle memory at this point."

Alvez stared at him for a long minute, his brows furrowed thinking. Realization slid behind his eyes, shining with empathy. "I've heard stories of how they train Shade children. I didn't know it started that young."

"They should make us a school and train us at earlier ages, learning basic hunting and weapons training, but the tradition for millennia has been gathering us before we turn ten."

"Why would you want kids that young training?"

"Because most Shade children go to Kiji completely unprepared and end up as some predator's lunch," he replied. "I blame the parents. They should prepare their children for their roles in this kingdom."

"I'm guessing your mother prepared you."

Vaiden opened his mouth to correct him, but he pressed his lips into a fine line. Alvez didn't deserve his life's story, no more than he wanted to hear why Alvez's father had him assigned to Fort Khali. They didn't need to be best friends on this journey. They needed to work together.

"Do you have my back?" the Shade asked instead.

"Of course."

Vaiden narrowed his eyes at him, weighing if Alvez had what it took to do the job. Casimere was a week's walk away. They didn't know what would be waiting there either. Maybe they would be welcomed with open arms as survivors of Fort Khali. Maybe they would be shunned for retreating and not fighting to their last breath. Vaiden didn't care. He wanted to look the king in the eye and ask important questions—questions Gabriel had written, but who knew if the letter would ever reach the king's desk.

"Get some sleep," the Shade said instead, wrapping a cowl over his shoulders. "I'll take first watch."

Alvez didn't argue. He expertly extinguished the fire and covered up with his own cloak, snuggling against a stump. Within minutes, he was snoring. Vaiden tuned it out, focusing on the forest. His ribs ached as he settled against stone at the mouth of the cave. It hurt to take a deep breath, but at least his muscles weren't sore. Shades healed faster than the average elf. He was thankful for that, but he would have preferred a magical heal, bones and all.

He exhaled. Perhaps it was the only time he was jealous of other kinds of elves. Caroline would have been able to heal him if he wasn't a Shade. It would have made everything—including this journey—easier. At least he didn't need help doing menial tasks anymore, like gathering firewood and refilling waterskins. Alvez had taken on those chores without complaint.

Vaiden glanced at his sleeping companion. He wasn't a bad kid, but he had lots of learning and maturing to do, especially during civil war. Hopefully, he would get the opportunity to grow up. Vaiden would return him to his father, but after that, it was out of his hands.

He blinked into the darkness, snapping on his nocturnal sight, wondering why it was important to him that Alvez returned home safely. He was technically an adult by Earth's standards. On Arda, it wasn't uncommon for whole villages to be filled with multi-generational families. With the exception of Shades, children stayed with their parents until they married, were accepted into Mysogus, or joined the military. Those in the military were under the direct guardianship of their ranking officer, serving as a proxy to a parent. Vaiden wondered if Glades realized how many children he'd lost at Fort Khali or if he cared.

Vaiden loosed another breath. If Glades survived the fort and the journey to Casimere, he was ahead of them. He'd get to the king first. It wasn't a bad thing, but Vaiden wondered how the general would explain his survival and why he returned with no soldiers. The king would be displeased to learn not only had he lost a stronghold, but a chunk of his army too.

Surely some of the soldiers had survived, but they would hide at the farms or travel to White Star or Abrita Shores. Both were rebel leaning. They would take in the soldiers, claiming the king had turned their backs on the fort, leaving it without proper defenses. They weren't wrong, but using a tragedy to further divide the kingdom didn't make them right.

Vaiden leaned his back against the stone, his eyes heavy, but his watch was far from over. The rebels had taken Gabriel. They'd risked infiltrating Fort Khali during a Corrupted attack to snatch Gabriel in the chaos. He wondered if the ambassador had been the only target. It seemed so from his perspective, but he couldn't be sure.

If the rebels wanted to be on the right side of history, helping the soldiers defend against the Corrupted would have been a good start, but that hadn't been their mission. It was sneaky—something that reminded him of operations in the Forty-Second. The Corrupted could have killed Gabriel without the rebels helping. If their goal was to eliminate him, they would have let him die. They didn't want him dead then. Something had changed their minds.

Perhaps they wanted to ransom him or use him to gain allies within the other kingdoms. Whatever their plan was, Vaiden didn't care. He would leave Casimere in search of Gabriel and when he found him—

"No!" Alvez screamed, bolting up from sleep.

Vaiden glanced at him as the captain blinked into the darkness. "I'm here," the Shade whispered.

"It-it-it was a nightmare. It wasn't real," he panted, wiping the sweat from his brow.

"What happened?"

"The-the cart," he sharply exhaled. "The oxen turned into one of those monstrosities and it tore through my men."

"Go back to sleep," Vaiden said.

"How can I sleep, knowing those men are still walking around as undead slaves to the Corrupted?" Though a child revealed himself in Alvez's round eyes, the fire blazing in them reflected the soldier deep within. He was proud to serve his kingdom and lead those men, but he'd failed them—like Vaiden had failed Gabriel.

"You can't free them from their prison if you don't get some rest," the Shade replied. "We make it to Casimere, inform the king, get this blight under control, and then set things right."

Alvez nodded, swallowing hard. "Do you think we will be able to stop the Corrupted?"

"That's what we Shades were made to do."

He nodded again, relaxing against the stump. "Free the Shades, end the blight, make things right," he said, closing his eyes. Within minutes, he was fast asleep again.

Vaiden watched over him for a moment, wishing the nightmares away. Let them plague someone more deserving—like the fools in control of the civil war or the Corrupted destroying the kingdom. Did the Corrupted dream? Vaiden didn't know and he didn't care.

He silently cursed their brains with a world of misery—when they finally took that leap to meet their goddess, they would find Aegan had turned her back on them, leaving them in agony within her realm. Nothing would hurt the Corrupted more than knowing their sacrificial mission was for naught. It was. They just didn't know it yet.

Besides Alvez's outburst, the rest of the night remained quiet and still. Vaiden let the captain rest through both watches. The kid needed it. By late morning, they needed to clear Haven, through the nest of Corrupted that had begun the damn blight.

22

Monday morning eroded away through a rush of meetings, updating her case files, and wishing she had a minute to get some good coffee. Logan remedied the latter, bringing her a to-go cup on her way out of the office. She needed to touch base with Mr. Slaseezor. He'd been locked up all weekend. Nothing was more lonely than waiting in a jail cell, locked underground, surrounded by concrete, waiting for the day he would either be set free or sentenced to death.

The judge could deport Mr. Slaseezor, but that also could be a death sentence, considering the rumors that the serpent kingdom killed any of their kind who returned from Earth. Tatiana didn't understand why they would do such a horrible thing, but from her knowledge of the serpents, they didn't like outsiders or those tainted by other faiths. Perhaps that was the reason, but why wouldn't they allow those serpents to live elsewhere? Arda was a big place. The human settlements were particularly welcoming to outsiders, or at least, that was what she'd been led to believe.

Before she could reach the elevator, a hand grabbed her arm, whirling her around to stare into Caden's wide eyes. "Did you see this yet?" he asked, pushing the screen of his smartphone into her face.

She grabbed it, frowning. "What?"

Her eyes drank in the feed from a social app. A hashtag was trending across the United States, *#FreeTheDaehekans*. Both sides of the argument seemed to be using the hashtag to make a point. Many of the supporters had reposted her message asking for assistance in Mr. Slaseezor's case. She hadn't used his name or named which particular den the stabbing had taken place.

Her chest tightened at the number of people calling for Mr. Slaseezor's execution. Most of them vilified the faith, comparing them to non-religious spaces which had "never hurt anyone." She scowled. It was a fallacy. These spaces had nothing to do with each other. The situations were nothing alike. They could not be compared.

"Where are you going?" Caden asked.

"To see my client." She handed him back the phone with a raised brow. "Why?"

"You may want to swing by the den first. A few of these posts show protests outside of them."

"Shit." She scrambled into the elevator, pushing the button for the garage. "Tell Logan to comb through the feed. Someone might post something useful."

The doors closed before he could reply. Her pulse thudded in her ears, negating the silence of the elevator. She knew posting was risky, but she hadn't expected this kind of reaction from the public. Maybe that was her ignorance. She hadn't posted in half a year. Of course her first message back on social media would trend. How could she be so careless?

She swallowed hard as the doors opened to the garage. The security officer locked eyes with her and nodded. She smiled slightly, hurrying to her car. Thank goodness she'd opted for the loafers instead of heels. Her feet had needed the break.

Her heart dropped to her stomach when she spotted George Zeilberg waiting by her car. "You can't be here," she announced, hoping to catch the security guard's attention. "This is a private garage."

"Yet it has access to the public." He gestured at the sidewalk, snaking around the edges of the concrete structure.

She frowned at him. "What do you want?"

"I'm sure you know how popular your post was," he said, wetting his lips. "Might an old friend ask for more information about what happened and at which den?"

Part of her was glad he'd finally moved on from her personal life, but she didn't have time to engage with this vulture and his need for attention. "I've got to go," she said instead, opening her door and sliding into the driver's seat. Before she could slam it, he grabbed the door, using his round body to block her from closing it.

He adjusted his square-framed glasses on his wide nose. "You said it was murder."

"*Alleged* murder," she corrected. "I've got an appointment, George. I need to go."

"A stabbing gone wrong?" George made a face. "I can see the headlines now and how the clickbait will make the public believe this *daehekans* used a ceremony as the perfect time to kill one of its congregation. You know most people don't actually click to read the stories. They just absorb the headline and move on."

"So what good would it be to give you information to write a story?" she countered. "I need to leave. Move away." She added the right amount of venom in her voice to lift his brows.

"I thought we were friends, Tatiana." He pouted. "We used to help each other. My stories helped shed light on your cases to bring people forward with information. It was mutually beneficial for both of us."

She frowned at him, summoning a rendition of Vaiden's bored expression. George straightened, taking the hint.

"Hey," the security guard called. The click-clack of his boots, soothing her pulse.

"Tell your pet vampire to back off," George said.

She raised a brow at him. "What does that mean?"

"I'll stop pursuing the story about Jen, but I will not stand for her threats."

"Her?"

"Don't play dumb, Tatiana."

"Sir," the guard's voice said, pulling George away from her door. "This is a restricted area. Only employees of the firm are allowed in here."

"Oh, sorry, just catching up with an old friend." That good ole boy grin plastered across his face, meaning to instill ease and trust as he glanced at her then back to the guard. Tatiana scowled, finally pulling her door close. She'd let the guard handle the situation. It was his job and she was in a hurry.

They moved to the sidewalk. George talked animatedly, but the guard put up his hand gesturing toward the exit. He wasn't having any of what the journalist was selling. Tatiana smirked, starting her car and shifting the gears into reverse.

When George and the firm disappeared into the distance, she toggled the phone options in her car. "Call Zarah," she said, prompting a screen on her dash.

An automated voice returned, "Calling Zarah." It had taken hours for it to recognize the pronunciation of her name when Tatiana had first programmed her information into the smartphone. She wanted to pull out her hair every time it had responded with "calling Sarah."

After several rings, Zarah's voice filled the car. "Hello?"

"Did you threaten George Zeilberg?"

"He's been stalking you," she replied. "I caught him outside your apartment the other night and decided it was time to confront him."

"Did you *threaten* him?"

"I might have eluded that you could file a restraining order against him or even sue his paper for the harassment, but an open threat against his very person? No."

Tatiana loosed a breath.

"I gather he approached you again," Zarah said.

"He wanted to know about my case, but he did let me know a vampire was threatening him. *My* pet vampire, as he put it."

Her laugh caressed Tatiana's skin like velvet. "It's nice to know I rattled him."

"If you want to make threats on my behalf, perhaps let me know beforehand." When Zarah didn't reply, she continued. "I know you're just looking out for me, but I can take care of myself."

"Vaiden—"

"Vaiden's on Arda."

"He asked me to look after you. I promised him I would."

"That doesn't mean threatening people."

"So it is fine for this journalist to follow you everywhere through the city? To the courthouse, to the firm, to your home? Or would it be better that he understands boundaries and when and where it is appropriate for him to approach you?"

She opened her mouth to argue, but she did agree. George needed boundaries. It was her fault for letting him believe he was entitled to her. Even Gary had argued that the journalist was blackmailing her, using the dire situations of her cases for exclusives in exchange for information.

Her chest tightened, thinking back to the night Bailyn Rosenhouse had shot Gary in her house. It hadn't killed him. Gary had explained in his statement it was some type of spell Jen had cast making it appear he had died, thus faking his own death.

A siren wailed through her ears. She winced, her eyes instantly checking her mirrors. There were no officers or emergency vehicles behind her. It was only in her head. She took a deep breath, the siren dulling to echo the beats of her heart.

"You're right," she finally said. "George needs boundaries. He's needed them for a long time, but I need to do that on my own."

"How did that pan out today?" Zarah asked.

"I let the security guard handle it."

"In my experience, unless he understands his actions have real consequences, he won't stop."

She nodded, turning the car down another street into traffic stopped at a red light. "Promise you won't threaten him again."

Zarah exhaled. "Fine, but for you to understand Vaiden wouldn't let this man harass you. I let him live. Vaiden would have eliminated the threat."

"And you don't want to let him down?"

"I wouldn't want to disappoint him, no."

"You both need to remember I am an attorney, an officer of the court," Tatiana said. "I'm duty bound to report threats to the authorities."

"I understand, but whatever threat George implied from our conversation was in his own head. I never said any words that would harm his person."

"But you're a vampire." Traffic moved across the intersection. Tatiana followed them through. "Remember if George feels the least bit threatened by you, he can spin it."

Zarah scoffed. "He said, she said."

"*Human* said versus *supernatural* said." The weight of Tatiana's words hung in the air, thick enough to taste. "I don't want to be dragged into a civil dispute. That's not my area of expertise."

"I'll keep that in mind."

"Just don't do anything that will make me have to visit you down in those basements." She shivered, despite the hot sunlight pouring through her windshield. "I hate it down there."

"I promise."

She steered the car down Maple Avenue, her attention immediately drawn to the crowds littering the sidewalks, holding signs and chanting.

"I've got to go." She hung up, surveying the Anti-Arda group, yelling at the other crowd across the avenue. Police had been called and stood at the ready for the protest to become violent. Tatiana carefully drove with traffic, wishing these people would go home and leave the preternatural community alone.

At every den she passed, more protestors filled the sidewalk. She exhaled sharply, knowing the police would first protect the wealthier establishments down Maple Avenue. If anything happened in the poorer neighborhoods it would be fifteen to thirty minutes, maybe longer, before an officer arrived to intervene.

Her chest tightened to see the entrance of Mr. Slaseezor's den crowded with Anti-Arda groups, chanting for the serpents to "go back home." She knew many of them weren't from Arda, like Rocahn, but it didn't matter their origin. They were home. This was their place of worship, and they deserved peace.

Parking was near impossible that time of day, but she eventually found a spot and marched toward the alley. A few serpents stood at the entrance, tensing as she approached. Their detestation ate through her like fire destroying a forest.

"I'm Tatiana Smith," she said. "I am representing Mr. Slaseezor in his case."

"You're the reason for this," growled one of the guards.

"It wasn't my intention to—"

"You humans need to learn to stay out of *our* business and just leave us alone."

"Sleed." Another serpent, who Tatiana recognized as the one who let her enter the den before, stood with the door ajar. "Come in, Ms. Smith. Rocahn has been awaiting your arrival."

The attorney walked between the guards like a mouse trotting between vipers. She didn't blame them for their anger or distrust. It was a shit show that she'd caused with a simple message requesting help. She should have known better.

The serpent led her through the halls like the first time she'd entered the den. Mrs. Slaseezor kneeled around the table with other serpents, murmuring too quietly for Tatiana to hear. When the other serpent announced her arrival, their heads snapped up—all of them sneering at her.

"Ms. Smith." Rocahn's tongue slipped between her lips, tasting the air. "I knew you'd come."

"I'm sorry for the scene outside," she said. "I didn't think a call for help would—"

"You humans never think," one of the other serpents spat. Rocahn hissed at them, making the others shrink back.

"Leave us," she said. They quickly made for their exit, each keeping an eye on Tatiana while they slipped through the other door. Tatiana glimpsed into the next room where the plants had been, but the room appeared vacant. The last serpent shut the door, leaving her alone with Mrs. Slaseezor.

"I would like to apologize," Tatiana began. "I should have expected the public to react, but—"

"The news had already broadcasted about the stabbing," Rocahn said, "but it fell on deaf ears, like all the other crimes against our kind. Your post brought lots of attention. Not all of it bad."

"Has anyone come forward?"

"Not to our den, but my cousin says one of her friends from another den told her about rumors."

"What rumors?"

"About the ones involved," she answered. "They believe my husband was set up."

"It is our best theory. We are trying to determine who set him up, but with the limited time—"

"That's why you made the post."

"Yes, I needed the public to help narrow down our list of suspects."

"There's a list?"

"Not a concrete one," she explained. "We start with being suspicious of everyone and then narrow it down. I have been looking into Koreen and his list of potential enemies."

"He was a good boy."

"But his family returned to Arda without him."

"He was born here so he could not go with them."

"Is it possible that the kingdom asked for them to make a sacrifice to wipe their slate clean so they could start fresh again in Arda?"

Rocahn rubbed her hands together, her tongue tasting the air again. "I'm not sure. I'm not as versed in the kingdom's policies as my husband."

"Would anyone here know?"

She shook her head. "We're mostly from Earth. My husband built this den in hopes to connect the worlds through our faith. We are one people." She spoke in serpent-tongue, a word Tatiana knew to mean "the serpents."

"Were Koreen's family still in contact with the kingdom while they were here on Earth?"

"They have family who live there." She paused, a light bulb lighting between her eyes. "You think they had Koreen killed to grant them entrance back to the kingdom?"

"It is one theory."

Rocahn shook her head, standing. "He was a good boy, loved by his family. It hurt them to leave him behind."

"But they were still willing to leave him behind."

"You don't understand," she said. "They argued about taking the risk of bringing him there, but he wouldn't go. Earth was his home. He wouldn't leave."

Tatiana tilted her head. "But you said he was very interested in the faith, of your culture on Arda. Why wouldn't he want to go?"

Rocahn flinched, recovering by picking up the bowl gingerly between her claws. She brought it to a counter to the left of the room and refilled it from a pitcher. "I do not know why he decided to stay."

Tatiana moved toward the serpent. "Mrs. Slaseezor, is there something you're not telling me?" She grasped the other woman's arm, softening her voice. "Please, tell me. I need to know everything to help your husband."

Rocahn's tongue slipped between her lips again quickly, a nervous gesture perhaps. "I—" She exhaled. "There." She pointed at a stack of files. "All the financial records from our personal accounts and the den."

Tatiana retrieved them, eying the serpent. "If you know something, please tell me."

"I know nothing more."

"Mrs. Slaseezor, your husband—"

"I know very well of my husband's situation, Ms. Smith," hissed the serpent. "He didn't do this." A tiredness shined in her eyes and drooped with her shoulders. "I just want him home."

Tatiana shifted the files to one arm and patted Rocahn's arm. "I will do everything I can to set him free, but I need all the help I can get. Talk to the others, see what they know and can learn from the other dens."

"I will try."

"If you learn anything, call me."

The serpent nodded, gesturing for Tatiana to leave. She did, eying the guards who glared at her. The protestors' chants echoed down the alley, wishing for the serpents to go back "home." Tatiana clenched her jaw, returning to her car. These serpents had done nothing to deserve such harassment. It fueled the fire at her core—not the blue fire, but the anger and drive to crack this case. Mr. Slaseezor deserved justice. He deserved his freedom. Anti-Arda groups be damned. She would free him.

23

They had slipped past Haven, nearly undetected when a mountain lion intercepted them. Vaiden knew by the way it swiped at him, it had cubs nearby. Alvez unsheathed his sword, but the Shade put up his hand, shaking his head. The cat wouldn't hurt them as long as they left. Quickly, but with no sudden movement as Vaiden had instructed, they followed an unmarked trail out of the woods. Eventually, they found the road and the cat returned to its cubs.

"Highland Road," Alvez panted, resting his hands on his knees. "I'm so happy to see you."

Vaiden rolled his eyes, threading his fingers through his hair. The movement made his ribs groan, but he ignored it. "It's a few days until Casimere."

"Yeah, but at least it's a straight shot and no more tripping on rocks and limbs."

"We'll still have to make camp."

"There's taverns and farms on the way."

"Do you have coin?"

The captain straightened, his mouth open, but he promptly shut it, exhaling sharply.

"I didn't think so," the Shade said. "We'll camp when needed."

The sun shone as they marched down the road. Its warmth was welcomed. He'd spent too many days soaked to the bone through the last couple of months. It was a wonder if he would ever dry.

Alvez stretched his arms to the sky, bathing in the light. A grin plastered across his face, as he recited a passage from Surnuna's slate.

In light, we find peace.
In light, we find protection.
In light, we find our path.
We find our goddess, Surnuna, Light of All Paths.

Vaiden pushed his shoulder, making the captain stumble. He whirled on the Shade, his eyes wide and alarmed.

"What was that for?" he demanded.

"Keep an eye out," Vaiden replied. "Just because we aren't marching through the woods, doesn't necessarily mean we are *out* of the woods yet."

The captain blinked at him. "What?"

"There's still Corrupted outside of Haven. There's no reason to believe they haven't moved west."

"The Corrupted came up from Aegan's shrine."

"And they're trending this way."

"Trending?"

"*Coming* this way," Vaiden scowled. "Keep alert. We're not safe out here."

"I hadn't assumed we were." Alvez's shoulders slumped. "I just wanted to take a moment and thank Surnuna for watching over us on this journey."

Vaiden rolled his eyes, continuing down the road. "Remember that the Corrupted ambush."

The captain hurried to his side, glancing at the forest over his shoulder. "I'm surprised you would allow us to be out in the open then."

"This route is more direct, and you're not the only one tired of the rocky terrain."

They elapsed into a moment of silence, listening to the forest surrounding them. Insects sang a chorus, but unfortunately the different species of them couldn't decide on one song or the same genre, so the noise might as well have been nails on a chalkboard. Vaiden pulled on his ears, disengaging his expanded hearing. He should have known better.

"You have that special kind of hearing," Alvez said.

"You don't?"

"Nope. My tutors tried, but no matter how hard I concentrated, it never surfaced."

"Huh." Vaiden knew not every elf had super hearing. All of them had better hearing than humans, but the expanded hearing was a special talent. All Shades had it and the nocturnal sight. Vaiden wasn't sure why, but he expected Wara gave them such gifts to level the playing field against her sisters' creations, including the vampires.

"Do you have nocturnal sight too?"

"It comes with the Wara package."

"I suppose the guards of the kingdom do need every weapon at their disposal," he mused. "Is it true that Shades learn to fight with any weapon available to them?"

"Shouldn't all soldiers learn that?"

Alvez raised his hands in surrender.

"We aren't taught anything," Vaiden explained. "We are brought to Kiji Village, given the choice of weapons and supplies, then sent into the forest to survive for five years on our own. That's our training until we return and are assigned to a unit."

"I thought all of your kind had to join the Shade battalions."

"I served in the Forty-Second, alongside Gabriel, Glades, and many others, doing the bidding of the crown."

"How did you wind up guarding King Rothnar?"

"He liked my history, I guess," Vaiden said, "or maybe he liked that I was a Shade. I wouldn't object to his direct orders."

"Who would willingly defy a king?"

"More than you think."

Alvez pursed his lips, but he didn't push for more information.

Highland Road was mostly flat from the eastern border until Brevene. Farther west the land turned mountainous to the coast. There were some hills between Haven and Casimere—small ones that made Vaiden grimace, holding his side. He let Alvez move ahead, hoping the young captain stayed mindful. The Corrupted were out there. They couldn't forget.

Vaiden longed for air conditioner and soft mattresses, for burgers and cheap alcohol. Arda was his home, where he had grown and developed as a soldier, but he missed Earth—the different smells in the air, the convenience of vehicles and phones. While he didn't heavily rely on technology to do his work, it would make this journey to Casimere obsolete to call the king, telling him the news, and then use his locator apps to find Gabriel.

Yes, he missed the modern world, but he realized how lazy it had made him. Not that he had been in poor shape, but he'd gained more muscle, trimming down his body fat since returning to Arda. It was the constant walking, eating rabbit food, and fighting for his life, he'd gathered. Once he moved back to Earth, he would increase the cardio and strength training in his workout to stay in peak physical shape. He'd have to find something challenging to train his mind.

The constant interpreting emotions should have been challenging enough, but that frustrated him in a different way. He knew when he returned to Earth, there were people who could help him, especially his mother. Not that he didn't appreciate Coastal's eagerness, but he thought it would be more beneficial to the bind to learn from the one who'd cast it.

Despite her staple as the region's top preternatural attorney, Tatiana was a surprisingly powerful sorceress. She hadn't known of the sorcery in her blood when she'd cast the bind or when she had blown up his cabin with the blue fire. He'd forgiven her for both incidents, much to everyone's shock.

He had spent his last week on Earth with her, learning about the bind and teaching her what he knew about magic. She'd given him a crash course on facial expressions. He knew some, but her training as a trial attorney proved useful for recognizing people's moods, which could affect someone throughout an entire day.

Emotions were exhausting, but he liked the way Tatiana affected him—lighter, freer, and comfortable. It took a long time for him to recognize and sort his confusion, but he'd never been confused around her.

"What's that?" Alvez cocked a brow at him. "Are you smiling?"

Vaiden frowned. "I smile."

The captain made a face, illustrating how unbelievable the Shade must have sounded. The boy was good practice for learning different emotions and how people expressed or repressed them. His anger and pride being two of the best examples. Vaiden noted his outbursts, embarrassment, and sorrow. He was a complicated person with a range of emotions, like the soap opera actors Tatiana had introduced him to.

I wonder if Cindy has revealed her secret to Douglas yet, Vaiden thought. He wondered how many episodes he'd missed of that hot mess, and if Tatiana had recorded them like she'd promised. Maybe they were on a streaming app. They could spend the entire week he returned binge watching the show. He'd like that—to lounge beside her, engulfed by her minty scent. Maybe she would lay her head on his shoulder and he would rest his head on top of hers. It sounded cozy, simple, and warm.

"There it is again!" Alvez pointed at him. "What are you thinking about?" The Shade scowled at him. "Mind your own business."

"Shouldn't your focus be on the Corrupted that might ambush us?"

"Should I remind you, injured or not, I could wipe the ground with you?" Alvez rolled his eyes. "Was it about Earth? Or *someone* on Earth? A girl?" Vaiden shook his head.

"OK, a guy then." He held up his hands in surrender. "I won't say anything."

"Being attracted to the same sex isn't a crime here on Arda."

"No, but it's frowned upon. There are those who want to preserve family legacies, like my aunt. She's old-fashioned that way," Alvez explained. "I suppose that does make sense why the ambassador is comfortable letting you share intimate spaces with his wife."

"Wait," Vaiden chuckled, waving his hands. "I'm not attracted to men."

"Sure." The captain's sarcastic tone revealed how much he believed the Shade. "Explain why you look at Gabriel so longingly then? I mean, you're really obsessed with him, even pouting about him, and promising to find him."

"Don't be an ass. He's my brother-in-arms."

"Why the defensive tone then?"

"I'm not defensive, nor am I insulted. My mother is attracted to only women," Vaiden said. "I just don't like my words to be misconstrued."

Alvez looked him up and down. "I'm not buying it. There's something going on between you and the ambassador and maybe his wife too. She bathed you."

"*Helped* bathe me," he corrected. "And that's none of your business."

The captain seemed to think about it. "Your mother is attracted to only women. How did that work with your father then?"

A shadow lunged from the trees. He grabbed the captain, throwing him aside and drawing his blade in time to parry the monstrosity's attack. It was at least eight feet tall with the face of a mountain lion. The Corrupted had followed them.

The Shade evaded the next attack, slicing his blade through the monstrosity's side. It yelped, other smaller mouths on its back screaming at him. The clang of metal let him know Alvez was in his own fight, but he didn't dare take his eyes off the abomination before him. Its limbs an entanglement of claws, flailed at him, striking air then the ground. He kept moving, ignoring the pain blistering in his sides.

A Corrupted charged out of the forest, a sword raised high above its head. Vaiden threw his blade, spearing the Corrupted through the middle. He returned his attention to the monstrosity in time to evade another attack. Sliding on his feet, forcing the monster to turn, he inched closer to his weapon. The Corrupted's sword laid on the ground by its body, an easier target.

The monstrosity roared, charging for the Shade. He evaded, rolling on the ground, snatching the sword in his hand and using momentum to propel himself back to his feet. He stumbled, casting a glance at Alvez, clutched in a fight with the dead.

"Vaiden!"

"A moment," breathed the Shade. Purpose swelled through his veins as the monstrosity charged again. He gripped the sword, feeling its weight—heavier than he liked his weapons, but something was better than nothing. He sidestepped the monster's charge, letting the blade do the work, cleaving through its side. It shuddered, its insides spilling on the road before it finally fell. Vaiden wasted no time chopping off its head before turning to Alvez.

He grabbed the captain's tunic, pulling him away from the dead before lobbing off its head.

"It's dead!" he shouted at Alvez. "It feels no pain. Put it down before it kills you *or* me!"

The captain winced. His eyes brimmed with tears. "He was my friend."

The Shade glanced at the beheaded soldier on the ground. "He wasn't your friend anymore," he said softer. "He wouldn't want you to suffer the same fate as he did."

Alvez wiped his eyes with the back of his hand. "I know. I just—"

Vaiden pushed past him, recovering his blade from the body of the Corrupted. Its diseased eyes watched the sky, seeing nothing at all. He didn't like the longsword, but another weapon could be useful, considering he'd lost one of his blades at the fort. The Corrupted didn't have a sheath. It wasn't uncommon to carry swords around naked, but Vaiden found it inconvenient for one of his hands to be occupied all the time. He'd have to reconfigure one of his sheaths to make it fit.

The Shade grabbed the Corrupted's ankles, dragging it onto the road.

"What are you doing?" sniffled the captain.

"Burning the bodies." He heaved the cloaked corpse onto the monstrosity. "I don't know about you, but I hate fighting things again, especially when I've already killed it once."

Alvez surveyed the bodies, anchored in place. Vaiden exhaled, shuddering at the pain in his ribs. "Will you bring that one?" He pointed at the soldier. "We need to lay him to rest."

"And burning the body will do that?"

"It's the only way to make sure a necromancer doesn't bring him back."

"I-I can't do it."

"Do you want him to come back and be used by the Corrupted? For his soul forever to be trapped in a decaying body and unable to cross to Paradise?"

"Of course not!"

"Then bring him to the pile."

The captain's round eyes shifted to where Vaiden leaned, holding his side. "You hurt yourself again."

"Ribs don't heal quickly. I just aggravated my injuries. I'll be fine, but your friend won't be, unless we burn him."

Alvez closed his eyes tightly. "He's really trapped in that body."

"His mind isn't, but his soul is," the Shade explained. "If it helps, think of him as a shell, a weapon, nothing more than a plaything for the Corrupted to kill more of your friends and innocents across the kingdom."

The captain took a deep breath, opening his eyes. He wet his lips before grabbing the soldier's ankles and dragging him toward the pile. "Sorry," he whispered, propping him against the monstrosity then fetching the head.

Something rustled in the trees. Before Vaiden could reach for his blade, he saw the Corrupted rush for the captain with a dagger raised. "Alvez!"

He reacted as he had been trained, unsheathing his sword, countering his opponent's attack. His blade sliced through the Corrupted's arm, disarming it, before it returned, ramming through its chest. It was a beautiful move. Something Alvez must have practiced endlessly.

The captain's mouth hung agape, watching the Corrupted's pained expression relax, emptying of life. He dropped his blade, the corpse falling down atop it. His lungs caved, needing air, as his arms hung suspended, shaking. Vaiden stepped toward him, but the captain backed away, stumbling for the edge of the road. His legs gave out as heaved his breakfast into a bush.

Vaiden's eyes scanned the surrounding woods for any more surprises. He didn't hear anything aside from Alvez's vomiting. Maybe they were alone, but he doubted it. No one was truly alone in the woods.

"You good?" he asked.

Alvez shuddered, panting in response. Vaiden left him alone and finished dragging the corpse and the head to the pile. He found some dried brush and kindling near the road, then retrieved the flint from Alvez's bag that he'd dropped during the fight. Within minutes, the bodies were on fire, smelling worse than ever.

"Let's go." Vaiden grabbed the captain's shoulder, pulling him to his feet. Alvez pushed away from him, snatching his bag from the Shade's hand. Vaiden watched him march away, not taking his attitude personally.

First kills affected everyone differently. Vaiden had killed another Shade in Kiji. Everyone was a threat in the wild, even their own kind. It was to teach Shades that they could trust no one, not even other elves. The Corrupted *were* elves after all. They might have reduced them to "things" and "its", but they were people once. The same people the Shades were expected to protect—until they crossed that line in the sand, drowning in a pool of dark magic from which they could never surface.

"That's one down," Vaiden said gently when the smoke faded in the distance.

Alvez lifted his head, brows knitted together over a pools of unending sorrow.

"You said we needed to put all your friends to rest," he explained. "That's one."

"Nine more to go."

24

Tatiana skipped lunch and drove straight to the office. Darling's brows scrunched with suspicion when she caught her in the parking garage.

"What are you doing back, Ana?" she asked, clutching a list of lunch orders. She held up the files of the financial reports, rushing to catch the elevator. "Did you find something?"

"I don't know," Tatiana said as the doors closed behind her.

She exhaled into the silence of the elevator. Generally, she would have gone straight to her client during the morning, but it was already noon. She needed to have Logan comb through the financials to determine if the Slaseezors were honest about the den's nonprofit status and if they had received any suspicious amounts of money. Tatiana didn't truly believe Mr. Slaseezor had anything to do with the murder, besides being the patsy. She needed to prove it though. Gut feelings weren't evidence.

The doors chimed open. She exited as a few other attorneys and assistants raced for the elevator. It was lunch time. Logan might already be gone. She searched the usual areas. The cubicles, where the paralegals worked, were a ghost town. Laughter filled the break room, but when she peeked through the door, finding most of the paralegals engaged in some type of game, Logan wasn't there. She thought about asking them where he was, but she didn't want to interrupt their fun. She remembered her paralegal days well. They needed to blow off some steam.

He was out for lunch, she decided, returning to Command Central. It was eerie for no one to be present at the secretarial station during the middle of the day, but all staff deserved a break. Calls would redirect to the first floor and be put on hold until they were back.

She headed to her office, deciding to drop off the files and to text Logan to go through them before she raced off to meet with Mr. Slaseezor. She hadn't forgotten about him, alone in that cell. The door swung open as she reached for the handle.

"Oh!" She startled, nearing colliding into Logan. "There you are!"

He wet his lips, his hazel blue eyes softening his surprised expression. "Looking for me?" He grinned.

"Have you had lunch?"

"I ate a sandwich while looking through social media," he said. "What do you need?"

She eyed her opened office door. "What were you doing in there?" she asked.

"I am ashamed to admit," he chuckled, "but I ran out of sticky notes and wanted to see if you had any extras."

"Command Central didn't have any?"

"Darling was supposed to ask Supply to bring some up, but she went to lunch."

Tatiana scooted past him, aiming for her desk. "I'm sure I have some," she said, pulling open a bottom drawer and rummaging through loose papers. "Aw, here. The bread and butter of organizing every great lawyer's life."

She held out an unopened package of sticky notes. "Thanks," he replied, gently taking them from her hand. His eyes swept over the exposed skin of her wrist and up her jacket sleeve to the files she held in her other arm. "What are those?"

"Oh." She threaded her hair behind an ear. "The financials from the Slaseezors."

"How did the visit go with our client?"

"I haven't made it over there yet," she sighed. "The whole den is pretty upset with me over my post."

He made a face. "Because you asked for help?"

"Because protestors are outside every den in the city, either demanding Mr. Slaseezor be set free or executed. They didn't want the attention."

"But if they're not helping then the public may be able to."

"I should have okayed it with the den first," she said. "I didn't even ask PR if it was a good idea before I posted it."

"It's your case."

"It's not my life." She held out the files to him. "Go through these, though. See if there's anything suspicious or worth noting."

He took them, his brows knitting together with questions, but he didn't push.

"How is the research on social media going?" she asked, sitting. He took one of the chairs opposite her. "Any leads?"

"There's thousands of posts," he said, frowning. "I have some saved from serpents in the area."

"Any threats?"

"Threats? To you?"

"No, to the dens or the Slaseezors?"

He shook his head. "No one has speculated who the *daehekans* is yet, which I guess is odd, but there are plenty of Earth-born serpents asking for the traditions of Arda to go home."

"Really?" Tatiana leaned back in her chair, crossing her arms. She wanted out of the blazer, but she hadn't planned to stay long. "I didn't realize there was a movement against their traditions."

"From what I've seen and my contacts have said, the young serpents are embracing more of Earth's faiths, or the lack of faith," he explained. "Many of them want to live as humans."

"To be accepted?"

"I think it's more on the lines of freedom—to not let religious rules bind them to a certain way of living."

Tatiana nodded. She wished her magic would go away. That the blue fire would fizzle out and she could go back to living a normal life, without worry that her power could potentially incinerate her home or the people around her. She hadn't thought how the preternatural cultures from Arda might clash with those on Earth, like her parents' more conservative views versus her liberal ones.

As the world changed so did ideology, but adding another world that lived in medieval times to modern Earth caused another layer of disconnection. They were different worlds with different definitions of morality and civil rights. What they considered proper, others from Earth might view as archaic. It was an imbalance, but the preternatural community tried to share these opposing views with respect, especially those from Arda, unless she had missed something.

"Mrs. Slaseezor did say her husband was encouraging the young ones to join the faith," she said. "Maybe he rubbed someone the wrong way?"

"But why would they have killed Koreen?"

"Maybe the prank went wrong?"

Logan's eyes studied something unseen. "You said that Koreen wanted to be in their faith. Maybe he had friends that were against him joining the den and things got out of hand."

"We are still asking a lot of questions and not making any progress to finding answers." She exhaled, leaning forward to rest her elbows on the desk. "Did you find anything more on Koreen's family?"

He shook his head. "From what I can tell, they all left, leaving him behind and the den's been supporting him ever since."

"So what Mrs. Slaseezor told me today might be true," she said. "That the family wanted him to go to Arda, but he refused."

Logan shrugged.

"Did you research his social media?"

"I didn't see anything that stood out to me."

"There's something we're missing." Tatiana stood, gripping the back of her chair and staring at the ceiling. It was white with no pattern. She imagined it was her whiteboard, picturing photos and yarn tacked to each other like a conspiracy map. There *was* a conspiracy. Who wanted to frame Mr. Slaseezor for Koreen's murder? And for what reason? The problem was, no pictures hung under the marker for suspects.

"Not to change the subject," Logan said, wetting his lips again. "But there was something I meant to discuss with you the other day, but we got tangled up with work."

She raised a brow at him. "Oh?"

He stood, holding the files like a shield in his arms. "I know that people are making comments about me taking the bar and what that means." He paused. "For *us*."

"Oh." Her chest tightened. "Logan, I—"

He put up his hand to stop her. "I don't expect anything," he said. "It was over two years ago when we made that pact. It was silly and I think everyone is having too much fun obsessing over it, which is weird."

"It's only fun if it's at our expense," she snorted.

"Even if I pass the bar, don't worry about the pact." He waved it away. "You've gone through so much already—I mean, with Gary and all. You deserve to heal from that."

Her shoulders slumped, staring into his handsome face. Her heart didn't do any cartwheels gazing at him, but a new respect blossomed there. He was a good man, smart and polite with an amazing work ethnic. Why didn't she want him? Was it because they were colleagues?

"You know by rescinding the pact, it's really going to piss off a lot of our coworkers," she said.

"Let them be mad." He shrugged. "As long as we're good."

She smiled at him—a real one, not a business one—something that reached her eyes and brightened her face. He smiled back. "I'll get to work on these files," he said before sliding out the door.

"Thanks," she said, meaning for more than the work he did, but for giving her room to breathe. She was lucky he was so perfect. Her smile slipped. Once, she had thought the same about Gary. Maybe she wasn't the best judge of character.

A siren willed her into submission—a siren Gary had confessed to blaring in that room to torture her. She swallowed hard, taking slow deep breaths with her eyes closed. The siren faded, distant until finally the ringing stopped. She opened her eyes, finding the clock on her bookshelf. Half the day was over and she hadn't visited Mr. Slaseezor yet.

***

"I agree with my wife," her client announced. "Koreen's family loved him, but ultimately they understood why he wanted to stay."

"And why was that?" Tatiana asked.

"He wanted to help spread the word of our faith to the serpents here. It was important to him, as it is to me, for the young ones learn about our culture."

"Was there anyone who didn't like that Koreen wanted to join the faith?"

"What do you mean?" Mr. Slaseezor tilted his head. His dragon eyes narrowed, the pupils becoming slits in his irises.

"Did any of his friends not like the idea of him joining the den?"

"Not that I know of," he answered. "I knew him, but we did not talk about things outside of the faith and the den."

Tatiana nodded, though it frustrated her that no one seemed to know anything. She needed to dive more into Koreen's personal life. "Do you know any of his friends' names?"

He shook his head. "He was, what do you call, a loner? He did not have many friends."

"What about romantic interests?"

"Ms. Smith, I have already told you we did not talk about things like that."

"Surely, since your den was supporting Koreen, you would know if any families were interested in him for coupling."

"He was too young."

"We both know researching for possible couplings starts long before reaching the appropriate age," she countered. "I know serpents who were introduced to each other in grade school."

"It is not uncommon."

"Then do you know of anyone interested in Koreen?"

He bowed his head, his eyes darting across the metal table between them. "I met Koreen shortly after his family left, but my duties keep me busy with the den. My wife and the other women look after the children. She would know of anyone interested in him."

"She claims she doesn't know."

"Then she does not."

Tatiana crossed her arms. "We are running out of time, Mr. Slaseezor. Is there anything at all, no matter how small, about Koreen, the ritual, any members of the den, or not of the den, that might want to hurt you and Koreen?"

He shook his head, his shoulders slumping. "I have spent all my time in this cell thinking what drove me here."

"What about threats from Anti-Arda groups?"

"We don't really receive many threats. The ones we get are like most other dens, wanting us to return to Arda."

"Do you know any serpents that are particularly angry with your faith?"

His head snapped up. "What do you mean?"

"I posted a message on social media, asking the public for help regarding your case." Before he could say anything, she put up her hands to stop him. "I did not name you or the den, but I did ask for information."

"Have you found any?"

"What we have found is many younger serpents denouncing the faith."

He hung his head again. "They have adopted the human ways and want to bring down our kind's cultures. They do not know what they are saying. They do not understand."

"Understand what exactly?"

He remained quiet for a moment. His dragon eyes closed while he took a few deep breaths. Finally, he opened them, raising his head, turning it to the side to see her better. "We are not humans. We need different things than they do."

"I've heard vampires advocate the same."

"It is true." He nodded. "Our world is very different, but it was *made* for us. Coming here was a risk, but an adventure. We want to help the young ones understand where they came from. They may have been born on Earth, but their kind is from Arda."

"Did Koreen feel the same as you do about the problems with the young ones?"

"Yes, he spoke how joining the faith had opened his eyes and helped him fix his anger from within."

"He was angry?"

"Aren't all young ones? Especially those lost and cannot seem to find control in their lives?"

"Koreen was out of control?"

"He felt lonely, even when his family was still here," he replied. "One of the reasons he wanted to join our den was because we were a close group. He enjoyed our traditions, the worship, and our togetherness. He was happy with us." His eyes welled with tears. "He was finally happy."

"I'm sorry." Tatiana reached her hand across the table, not touching him per the rules, but letting it rest there as a comfort. She was there for him.

He bowed his head again. "Thank you."

She nodded, slowly returning her hand to her side of the table. It was a complicated case and filled with many questions. Every visit with the Slaseezors, her list grew instead of shortened.

"I know you said you did not know much about Koreen's time away from the den, but would you happen to remember if he said anything about places he liked to visit?" she asked.

His eyes scanned the table again, reading something unseen. "There was a park he talked about," he said. "I believe it was off Maple Avenue. He liked to visit the Grand Den on his way back from it."

"Did he plan to join the Grand Den?"

"No, he just liked the way it looked."

"It is lovely."

"He liked to walk by the elves' gardens too. Their faith also interested him because the goddesses have a lot of influence on Arda. Moren, in particular, is part of our faith and the vampires."

"She is the mother of vampires, if I remember."

He nodded, a thought flashing across his stare. "I remember Rocahn asking him what he liked about this park, but he never really answered the question. It was odd at the time. He was an honest young man. When I asked him about it later, he had said he liked to go there to think. I didn't question him." His lips curled back, revealing his sharp teeth. "I should have pushed for more."

"I don't know," Tatiana said, "but I will check out the park to see if anyone there knows him. Maybe we will find something."

"I need to understand why this happened, Ms. Smith." His dragon eyes pleaded, somehow soft despite their devious appearance. "He didn't deserve this. He was a good boy."

It weighed on her mind when she returned to her car. Both the Slaseezors had said Koreen was a good boy. Gary had seemed like a good man too, but he had been a lie, a wolf in sheep's clothing, who had fooled her. Maybe Koreen had fooled the Slaseezors?

She clicked on her phone, noting messages from Logan that claimed he had found nothing in the financials deemed suspicious. She didn't doubt that. Her fingers swiped away his messages, aiming for another conversation with Zarah.

Want to play bodyguard? she messaged. Within seconds, her phone chimed. *When and where?*

25

Casimere sat at the foot of the kingdom's tallest mountain, *Duna A'anar*, which loosely translated to Rise to Sun. At the summit of the mountain, Surnuna's shrine overlooked the capital, judging the people and their political games. She was the Goddess of Life. Vaiden imagined she frowned at how they'd squandered the blessing she had given them.

"One day I'll make the climb," Alvez said as they gazed up the mountain side.

"Why?" Vaiden asked. "The climb could kill you, not to mention what the lack of oxygen might do to your brain, or the fact the frigid temperatures could freeze you solid."

"Sounds like you lack the convention of the faithful."

"No, I'm just not stupid."

"You believe those of the faithful are stupid?"

"Not all of them," replied the Shade. "Just the ones who want to climb a mountain known for killing people who climb it."

"Some might call that brave."

"Trust me, as a person who has scaled a mountain with his bare hands, it is dumb."

"What are you talking about?" Alvez cocked a brow at him. "What mountain?"

"White Star to High Tower."

"There's a path that leads from the city to the school around the Specter Peaks."

"Yeah, but I wanted to see if it was quicker to climb the side of the mountain than take the path."

"Was it?"

"Fuck no," the Shade scowled as a wagon, carrying barrels raced past them. It was the first time in two weeks, they had shared the road with someone other than animals and bugs. Vaiden's eyes descended from the mountain, sweeping across the farmlands between them and Casimere. They were hours from entering the city, but he could already see the traffic cluttering the intersecting roads.

Alvez nodded at a young woman and her friend, carrying baskets as they tended a field. He smiled, like he had at Caroline, making the girl and her giggling friend blush. Vaiden shot him a look, wiping the smile from his face.

"What?" he asked.

"You're confident around women," the Shade said.

The young captain shrugged, a different kind of smile spread with his lips—something playful and ambiguous—meant to frustrate Vaiden or throw him off. He wasn't sure.

"I find it strange that such a coward wouldn't be scared around them."

"Why would I be scared of women?" Alvez asked. "They're wonderful."

"Have you asked one out?"

His smile turned mischievous. "They like a man in uniform, especially a superior officer."

"There's nothing *superior* about you."

"I'm a captain. I've led soldiers."

"Not well."

"Says the man who has never led anyone in his entire life."

"I've led you here, haven't I?"

The captain laughed. "We are on this journey *together*. I'm not following you."

"And yet, if I didn't come this way, you wouldn't have."

"You don't know that."

"Don't I?" The Shade gave him a measured look. "Face it, kid, you would have never made this journey alone."

"Doesn't mean you would have either."

It was Vaiden's turn to laugh. "I don't need a holding hand."

"Like you didn't need Lady Steel to bathe you?"

"Well, if you don't like beautiful women bathing you, then that's your problem."

Alvez frowned, increasing his pace. "Now I'm in the lead," he grumbled. Vaiden shook his head, letting the kid pout.

The closer they journeyed to the city, the more people littered the road. Some parked their carts to the side, selling wares. Vaiden spotted fruits and vegetables, notably cabbages. One vendor displayed maps with locations circled, promising to find buried treasure or relics of long ago. The Shade rolled his eyes at the man's pitch. The nerve he had to convince people to go on quests during a Corrupted blight.

At the corner of intersecting roads, a priest lectured strangers about scripture. "Surnuna warned us!" he shouted. "When the darkness takes over again, we shall know it was because we let ourselves give into weakness. We allowed the darkness into our hearts and thus shall it take over our world."

"Not him again," groaned a woman, pushing her children onward.

"The Dark Age approaches!" exclaimed the priest. "Prepare, friends! We must stand in the light before it disappears forever."

Vaiden locked eyes with the priest and he paused, blinking as if he'd seen a ghost. By the weathered sun tattoos on his hands and forehead, the priest had served Surnuna. His tattered robes said he hadn't lived at the fane for a long time, but that wasn't surprising given his behavior.

The Shade moved on, his eyes scanning the crowded road ahead for Alvez. The priest made sure Vaiden had moved a great distance away before beginning his lecture again. Let him believe the Dark Age was returning. Arda had survived it once before. It could again, but the priest was missing a huge chunk of reality. They were already shrouded in darkness while the Corrupted controlled parts of the kingdom.

He found the captain, chatting briefly with another soldier before she moved on. She wore a blue uniform, symbolizing specialized guards, like the king's men or Gabriel's unit. They served important leaders of the kingdom. Vaiden approached, wondering who she guarded.

"Who was that?"

"A friend, someone I met in basic training. She's a guard for one of the council now," Alvez replied. "She wanted to know if the rumors are true about Fort Khali."

"So news has already made it here."

"She said that General Glades arrived a couple of days ago, but the king hasn't made any announcements."

"She must have overheard conversations between the council members then."

Alvez nodded, but then a thought crossed his mind. "Why hasn't the king announced anything?"

"He doesn't want there to be panic."

"But this would be the perfect time to band the kingdom together and call the Shades back to destroy the Corrupted."

"I agree."

"Then why doesn't he do that?"

"I don't know."

They continued down the road to Casimere, engulfed by aromas of food and manure. The sun shone high in the sky when they approached the eastern gate. The city was built in five rings. Each ring climbed up the side of the mountain's foot, the base layer being the biggest, like a pyramid.

The outer wall was fifty feet feet high and at least twenty feet thick of hard stone. There were three gatehouses: south, east, and west, with two towers for each one. Between the gatehouses stood ward turrets, which were twenty feet taller than the wall. The turrets created a shield against magical attacks. They could also launch arcane strikes against enemies, but practitioners only used this ability as a last resort considering it could weaken the wards.

While enemies from other kingdoms had never penetrated through the outer wall, rebels in the kingdom had. Before Vaiden had arrived, Kanaris had led an attack on the city and pushed through two of the five rings before being overwhelmed to retreat.

This was the wake up call for King Altamost to allow Vaiden's return to the kingdom. He wanted Kanaris dead, yet, his orders had deterred Vaiden from completing his mission. The Shade wanted to know why. If he could end this civil war with Kanaris's death, why not let him do his part?

Gabriel didn't think ending Kanaris would settle anything. It would drive the rebels further in their pursuit for Altamost's head. Maybe it would, or they would understand they were outmatched. The king commanded an army, who believed they were protecting the kingdom—even from itself.

Those who supported the crown and military were powerful players, not just in wealth and respect, but magic too. It was why they wanted the ear of the king. He had direct control of the Shades. Corruption was a snake endlessly swallowing its tail. Unless the head was destroyed, nothing would change.

Vaiden studied the closed east gatehouse. He'd never known a time in the past when any of Casimere's gates were closed. The murder holes stared back at him, unseen eyes watching his movements. Alvez tugged on his arm, whisking him toward the south gate, but Vaiden gazed up the towers, over arrow loops, to the balustrade where guards patrolled, watching the masses for anyone suspicious. The Shade spied a few practitioners chatting at the base of a turret.

It wasn't the show of force expected after months of civil unrest, especially since Kanaris had bullied his forces into the city. Vaiden expected Altamost to beef up security, but it appeared relaxed to him. Perhaps the king thought closing two gatehouses would suffice.

Funneling citizens through one gate didn't necessarily make it easier to spot the enemy, especially since they looked like every elf. Vaiden didn't know how the guards could sort ally from foe until he saw the lines of people waiting outside the gates.

"I forgot about this." Alvez raked a hand through his hair. "You need papers into the city now."

"Papers?"

"Yeah, it details who you are, where you're from, and where you're going, all verified through an approved chancery," he explained. "It's a pain, but it's kept the city safe since the rebels attacked."

Vaiden cocked a brow, watching guards take these papers from citizens. They glanced at them, mostly studying the seal before moving on. He didn't know how proficient such a system would be, or how they could recognize a forged paper or seal in a glance, but Alvez claimed it had worked—or the rebels had remained hidden.

Who was to say a chancery couldn't be bought? If Vaiden thought this, so had the rebels. Maybe they were already inside the city, scouting for alternate routes to the castle. Vaiden could tell them. He'd been ordered by King Rothnar to find all the weaknesses in the city, any place a potential assassin could hide or use to traverse through the walls unseen. The Shade had used some of these paths to rendezvous with Zarah when she had visited.

The more he thought about it, the more it made sense the king had them scouting the cities throughout the kingdom. He wanted to know which ones were loyal to figure out which chanceries would help the rebels, narrowing down his list of potential enemies and traitors. It was smart, but the civil war was the least of their problems during a Corrupted blight.

"We need to get inside," the Shade said.

"Let me talk to the guards," Alvez replied. "I know some of them."

They moved to the gatehouse, keeping their hands away from their weapons. With his expanded hearing, Vaiden heard arrows notch in the tower loops. He didn't blame them. Cutting line was a dick move, but they were on a mission.

"Hey, Bardy!" Alvez waved at one of the guards checking papers. The guard eyed them in his standard brown tunic, his hand resting on the hilt of his sword. A slow smile crept on his lips.

"Well, isn't it the youngest captain of all the land," he snorted. "What are you doing here?"

Alvez clapped him on the back, grinning wide, but it quickly slipped. "You heard about Fort Khali, right?"

"Damn shame." Bardy nodded.

"We were there." Alvez gestured at Vaiden behind him. "We need to speak to his majesty."

The guard's eyes darted to the Shade, drinking in his tall lean frame and the weapons on his hip. "Do you have papers?" he asked.

"Bardy, how could I get them? The fort was destroyed. We barely escaped with our lives."

"You, I know." The guard pointed at Alvez then Vaiden. "You, I don't and I can't vouch for people I don't know."

"A good policy," the Shade replied.

"He's Vaiden Zarren," the captain said. "He's with me. I'll vouch for him."

Vaiden wasn't sure if the guard heard anything after Alvez's said his name. He'd gone pale, but alert, standing taller and with eyes wide, like a child longing for a treat.

"Vaiden...Zarren?" he breathed. "King Rothnar's personal guard?"

The Shade dipped his chin at the guard, knowing his reputation proceeded him. "I need to speak to the king," he said. "He needs to know the intimate details of the Corrupted nest that attacked the fort and how it was destroyed."

"Of course!" Bardy gestured for them to follow. Another guard pointed at them, but Bardy waved him away. "They're cleared," he announced, adding, "Surnuna guide you."

"Wara give you strength," Alvez returned, saluting his friend before passing through the gates.

Vaiden said nothing. He followed the captain, ignoring the angry glares of those who had no doubt waited in line for hours. Karma might get them for that, but he knew their business was more important than the average merchant and consumer. The cabbages could wait.

26

Nathalu Park overlooked a natural creek. Trees, hundreds of years old, hung their limbs lazily over people enjoying the shade they provided. Manicured paths zig-zagged through freshly cut grass, kept green and full, despite the heatwave hammering the west. A group of joggers rested at a pair of benches, rehydrating while children enjoyed a game of frisbee. It was a peaceful, joyful place where someone may have plotted to kill an innocent serpent.

Zarah wasn't sure about the "innocent" part, not as Tatiana had brought her up to speed on the case. Many of the details, the vampire already knew from her contacts in the Underground. Koreen's family had left him on Earth, although they had begged him to go with them to Arda. He had been excited to join the den and influence other young serpents to also join the faith.

It was rather strange for someone originally from Arda to find serpents not interested in their religion. They were one of the more traditional and conservative creatures in the alternate world. Perhaps Arda was wise to ensure Earth's influence did not change their cultures.

Zarah had never been a religious person, not even as a human. She knew little about the goddesses aside what she'd overheard from elves during her time as an ambassador. Coastal had preached about Alumpius, even though the goddess had been banned centuries ago. Zarah only knew details about Wara because Vaiden was a Shade, but he didn't seem keen on his goddess. Zarah didn't blame him. Moren was her "mother" as a vampire, or at least, that was what scripture claimed.

In truth, Zarah didn't hold loyalty to any deity. Why would they want to make creatures like vampires, who preyed on the blood of others? What was the purpose? As Tatiana smacked a mosquito on her arm, cursing at the little "bloodsucker," Zarah snorted.

"Sorry." Tatiana sighed, slumping against the bench they shared. "I know that's been labeled a slur recently."

"Your 'sorry' does nothing for my cousin who you just killed," the vampire teased. "I've been called worse things than 'bloodsucker.' If anything, it is accurate; although, there is now plasma fruit to consume instead."

Tatiana nodded, pursing her lips. Her steady pulse gently throbbed in Zarah's ears. Delightful, but the vampire schooled her features. Her thirst had been long conquered. It was music to her—delicious, *delicious* music.

"I'm not sure if we'll find anything here," Tatiana said, "but Mr. Slaseezor claimed Koreen hung around this park. Maybe he met someone here."

"A drug dealer?" the vampire offered, her hand gesturing at a shady meeting between felines near the outskirts of the park.

"Serpents generally stick together," the attorney returned. "Koreen wanted to inspire other young ones to join the den. Maybe they still hang out here."

"You want to ask around?"

"Here, I'll send you his picture. We want to know if anyone knows him," she said, fingers flying across her smartphone. Within seconds, Zarah's phone chimed with the received picture. She glanced at the photo of a young serpent. Their spikes or quills didn't generally form until their mid-twenties. The nubs at the top of his head would have been spikes eventually, signifying he was ready for coupling. Koreen had gray scales with splashes of red along his snout and around his dark eyes, giving him a menacing appearance, but the same could be said for most of his kind.

"How old was he?"

"Twenty-one," Tatiana replied, her eyes solemn.

"So young," Zarah mused, thinking back to when she'd been that age as a human. It was a long time ago in a different world. She barely remembered her early life, like a hazy dream. The older she grew, the details of her adult human life chipped away, along with the pain she'd endured.

"I'll go this way." Tatiana pointed.

The vampire clicked her tongue. "You asked for me to be your guard."

"It's broad daylight."

"And crimes don't happen during the day?"

"We'll cover more ground faster separately."

Zarah crossed her arms. "I'm beginning to believe you tricked me here, making me think there was danger, so I can spend my afternoon canvassing an entire park."

"Not the *entire* park." A teasing smile spread on Tatiana's lips. "I've got this side."

"Fine, but you owe me." She stood, waving her phone.

The sun glared down at the park, coating those in its wake with a thin layer of sweat. Zarah rolled her shoulders in the silky blouse, wishing she'd worn a tank top. Not that she would get hot or sweaty in the blouse and skirt, but it would help her blend in with those in the park and make her appear less "official."

After asking a couple of serpents walking their child, who she'd mistaken for a pet at first glance, the vampire's eyes swept over the corner of the park searching for more of their kind. Lots of felines and humans scattered around doing various activities, but serpents were scarce. It was hot and cold-blooded creatures preferred the shade or indoors during these hours. She refocused her efforts toward the water and under the trees.

Within minutes, she found young ones near the waterline. They tossed stones into the creek, laughing loudly at some unheard joke, or at least, Zarah didn't hear it. She had pretty average hearing for a vampire. With concentration she could depict voices through phone calls, heart beats, and other useful noises, but they had proved Vaiden's expanded hearing was better—something she truly wished they hadn't discovered because anytime he was able to brag about it, he would.

"Excuse me," she said, trying her best to sound pleasant and not-at-all brimming with boredom.

"Yeah?" A serpent with yellow eyes slid his tongue between his lips, tasting the air and more likely her perfume.

"Can you help me?" she asked, smiling, careful not to spread her lips too wide or she'd show fang. Though the preternatural community claimed they were most afraid of the humans and their government, Zarah found the community still responded poorest to vampires—even other vampires. "I'm looking for someone."

The serpent glanced at his friends who all shrugged. He stepped forward, holding his baggy jeans at the waist. It was odd to see serpents out of their simple robes or armor. Modern clothes looked awkward on their slight builds, or perhaps they didn't have good tailors. She knew there were designers who'd focused only on the supernatural, but she'd always thought the clothes impractical or gaudy.

"He's a serpent, maybe you've seen him around here." She clicked on her phone and aimed it at him. His tongue slithered between his lips again.

"Yeah, he looks familiar," he said, gesturing for his friends to come forward. They slinked over, crossing their arms as each took a turn looking at Koreen's picture.

"Hey Cedith, that's the guy who passed out those flyers," said another. "For that den."

"Haven't seen him in a few days," Cedith, the baggy jean serpent, claimed. "He's missing or something?"

"Or something," Zarah answered. "Do you know anything about him?"

"Just that he's into the faith."

"He's not a bad guy," one with long quills said. "Though I did see him get into an argument with some chick last week."

"What chick?" one of the friends asked before Zarah could.

"That rich one, what's her name?" It tapped its chin with a black claw. "The one with the family that attends the Grand Den."

"Arkella," another one offered.

"Yep, that's the one. She's too good for these parts. That's why I thought it was weird she was here in the park."

"She doesn't visit it?" Zarah asked.

They shook their heads. "Her family's got money and keeps her in the Grand Den or at home," Cedith explained. "They don't want her befriending those beneath her."

"I heard they are already looking for matches to coupling her ," the quill one grinned.

"It's a bit early," another said.

Cedith shrugged. "Matches can start pretty early for the ones with influence."

"Does her family have influence?" Zarah asked.

"They're one of those old families," the quill one replied. "They only want to join families with blood from Arda."

"I see." Zarah hadn't realized serpents had their own flavor of politics. It was foolish to think vampires were the only preternaturals with complex dramas that spilled over from Arda. Serpents at least didn't continue the archaic rules applied by their kingdom on Earth.

They'd embraced the laws and boundaries each country adhered, many of them being significantly less fatal than their own kingdom. Only the serpent kingdom proved equally brutal as the Last Empire. Vampires had barely held an empire for six hundred years. The serpents had ruled for millennia, second to only the elves.

"Is there anything else you remember about Arkella?" she asked.

They shook their heads. "Sorry, that's all," Cedith said. "Hope you can help him. He's a good guy."

She should have told him he'd died, but that seemed cruel since they'd been so helpful. Instead, she thanked them and found Tatiana, hopelessly wandering the park in search of serpents. After Zarah had relayed everything the young ones had told her, she asked if they should go to the Grand Den.

"I'd have to get clearance from someone." Tatiana held the back of her hair up, the bottom layer slick in sweat. "After posting that message, I'm not sure if the den is willing to help me more."

"Even for their *daehekans*?"

She shrugged. "Serpents are finicky that way."

"What about this girl, Arkella?" Zarah asked. "Maybe she has social media and we can reach out to her that way?"

"That seems inappropriate."

"I'll do it." The vampire shrugged. "Of course I'll have to make a profile, or maybe someone in my contacts can do it for me."

"I don't think the Underground should get involved in this."

Zarah bit her tongue from replying that they already were. Tatiana didn't need to know that. She would get upset that Zarah had asked for information.

"Then I'll make my own profile," she said instead. The lawyer shifted on her heels, furrowing her brows. "I'll be nice and professional."

"That makes it even more suspicious."

"I'll pose as a private investigator or something."

"For the den?"

"Of public interest."

"I doubt serpents would believe that." Tatiana frowned. "I'll try to get permission from the den."

"Maybe explain to Mrs. Slaseezor what we've learned today?"

"I'll try, but, like I said, serpents are finicky. They believe I have already betrayed them."

"Her husband's fate rests on the ability for you to do your job. That means investigating this family at the Grand Den. If Mrs. Slaseezor truly loves her husband, she'll do whatever it takes to set him free."

Tatiana tilted her head, the pools of her eyes crashing against Zarah like ocean waves. "You did everything you could for Harvey."

"I know." She was surprised by the tightness in her voice and the stingy behind her eyes. It had been months since Harvey's name had made her cry. She would not embarrass herself at this park, in front of so many witnesses. Not that crying was something of which to be ashamed, but Zarah had created a mask of strength and poise. She would not let him ruin that for her too.

"I'll talk to Mrs. Slaseezor," Tatiana said. "Hopefully, she'll come through."

"In the meantime, I'll scare a young woman into telling me all her secrets." A dark smile spread on the vampire's lips. "Hopefully, she'll confess to murder and we can put all of this behind us."

The attorney crossed her arms, her lips pressing into a fine line.

"Fine, I'll be polite," huffed Zarah, "but one day you'll let me have my fun."

"You don't have to be an enforcer anymore. Those days are gone now that LaBelle's court has dissolved."

"It didn't dissolve, darling. LaBelle died."

"Jen killed her."

Zarah nodded, recalling what the Coristors had told her at Harvey's funeral—how they had tricked their master into trusting them and using Jen to kill her. She didn't know how to feel about Trudy and Harry Coristor. They had left a mess helping Harvey then saving themselves. As far as Zarah knew, they'd returned to Harry's home in England. Hopefully, she never saw them again.

Something painful slipped behind Tatiana's eyes, making Zarah take her hand. She had never been the affectionate friend, but she found one of her important roles in taking care of Tatiana was soft assurances. For a top class attorney and powerful sorceress, she was a sensitive soul.

"Both of them are dead," the vampire whispered, though no one was close enough to hear her. "They can't hurt you."

Tatiana wet her lips, nodding her head. "I'll call Mrs. Slaseezor and see if she can grant me access to the Grand Den."

"Keep me updated," Zarah said, letting go of her hand. "If you can't get in your way, then I'll try my way."

"You're liking this too much." Despite the suspicion in her voice, Tatiana grinned.

"Darling, it was once my job to investigate anything an emperor found threatening. That included a few affairs, which was fun, though they ended pretty horribly."

"I thought you were an ambassador to the elves."

"That was during Zerth's reign. Before that, I was the personal guard to the emperor—not Zerth, his predecessor."

"Zerth was the last emperor."

Zarah nodded, wishing someone would have staked him before he had the chance to gain power. The empire wasn't perfect, but it was all Zarah knew before the other kingdoms united and ended vampires in Arda altogether. Gabriel had gotten her out—had given her the choice between going through the door or being executed. She hadn't known (neither had he) the door would lead her to Earth.

During those times, no one truly knew where the doors had led, but no one had returned. They had assumed those who crossed had died, but given the choice between a quick death and whatever the elves had planned for her, she hadn't stayed to become entertainment for a populace that hungered for her suffering. She had chosen the door and emerged in a land quite different from Arda.

Part of her missed her home, but she would never trade Earth's technology for the beauty of Arda. Maybe for a vacation, but she couldn't be caught or she'd be executed for being a vampire.

"I'll message you later if I get in," Tatiana said, walking toward her vehicle.

"Best of luck," Zarah returned, truly meaning every word.

27

The smell of shit and bullshit filled the air in the lowest ring of Casimere. It was where the market could be found. Vendors from across the world traveled to the city to intrigue elves with splendors from faraway places. Vaiden glanced around the wagons, missing the vampires' weaponry stand and the orcs' armor. He didn't really care for the serpent spices or whatever random things the felines brought to the kingdom, but with the borders closed, the only vendors of different kingdoms were those who lived permanently in Eskandor.

He didn't know if they had gotten stuck before the borders closed or if they had chosen to live in Casimere, but their presence brought great crowds to the market. Perhaps it was a strategy knowing cowards would run back to their respected kingdoms, but who truly with a reasonable mind wanted to stay when the Corrupted ran amok? Vaiden gave props to the merchants who one-finger saluted opportunity and split. They knew whatever profits they made in the city weren't worth their lives.

Vaiden's ears rang with the hammering of blacksmiths and whinnying of horses in the stables, forcing him to disengage his expanded hearing. Those in the market would park their carts then check their animals into the stables where they would be groomed and fed, courtesy of the city for vendors journeying there.

Alvez ogled the trinkets, his hands needing to touch everything they passed by. Vaiden grabbed his arm, pulling him toward the huts where the impoverished lived. They were simple one-room homes with thatched roofs and wooden doors. They scattered around the outskirts of the lowest ring pushing toward the second ring. A few children played between them, kicking around a leather ball. Their parents would be at work, selling at the market or whatever menial labor the city required, like scooping shit from the streets.

"We don't have time to look at every damn thing," the Shade growled. "Or have you already forgotten why we're here?"

"Easy!" The captain wrenched his arm from his grasp. "I just got caught up in the festivities. It's been a long time since I've been home. I've missed the excitement."

"You can play after we talk to the king."

"Should we visit a bathhouse before going to the castle?" Alvez wrinkled his nose. "One of us smells like an oxen."

"Why would we bathe first?"

"To be more presentable for the king?"

Vaiden rolled his eyes. "What part of 'after we talk to the king' do you not understand?"

"Just that." The captain bit his lip, looking ever younger than he was. "I've never met or spoken to the king."

"I have. It's not that great."

Alvez frowned at him, aging immediately. "I remind you. He is our king. You will show him respect."

"I've known Alty a lot longer than you. Hell, probably longer than his council has known him."

"I don't think you should address the king by nicknames. He has a revered title."

"You're right. I should not use nicknames and go straight to pet names. Asshole, fuckface, shithead—"

"Vaiden! He is your king. Have respect!"

"Fine. Richard Cranium."

Alvez blinked at him. "I don't know what that means."

A smile spread on the Shade's lips. "Well, you see, 'cranium' means 'head' and on Earth another name for Richard is Di–"

"I thought we were in a hurry to see the king." Heat crawled up the captain's neck, his face pinching into a tight, serious expression.

"Glad you're up to speed." Vaiden clapped him on the shoulder, marching toward the second ring. Alvez scowled, muttering something under his breath. He followed Vaiden up the stairs to where wooden and stone buildings formed a lively commercial district with taverns, shops, and the occasional bard, entertaining a crowd with upbeat music.

No animals were allowed past the first ring with the exception of pets. A couple walked their domesticated lorapod, whose hisses and tongue flapping might as well have been coos of happiness. It was spoiled from its round body to the expensive leather leash and halter strapped to its scaly form.

Alvez smiled at young ladies as they passed the tailors. Many of them smiled back, twirling their skirts, before their eyes landed on Vaiden. One girl managed not to look away. Her bright eyes stared him down, her mouth hanging agape.

"Seems like you have a fan," whispered the captain, elbowing his arm. Vaiden didn't look back, knowing Alvez had mistaken her expression for mysticism when fear had shined in her eyes. The Shade knew the look well. He'd seen it around High Elves all his life. He didn't blame the girl. He'd killed many of her kind in his time, not all of them Corrupted.

The crowds were more relaxed in the second ring. No one was in a hurry to catch a deal before the market closed. The butchers took special orders while bakers lined their windows with fresh goods. The smell of pies filled Vaiden's nose, his stomach grumbling. They hadn't eaten since sunrise, a breakfast of jerky, chewy and tasteless. The Shade grabbed Alvez's arm, guiding him away from the bakeries.

He half-expected to see homeless stealing a few of those pies, or tents pitched between the narrow alleys, but Casimere had no homeless. Everyone worked and had homes. Those in poverty were supported by a tax the rich paid to cover the expenses of the huts down in ring one. The wealthy believed it was their duty and privilege to help those less fortunate, providing them simple dignities. It was one of the things he respected about this city.

In the center of the ring, a ten-foot statue erected of Leeth the Rightful. Long before Kanaris's rebels had invaded the city, the only other time Casimere's defenses had failed was during the Second Age. Leeth's army reclaimed it from Knoran, a Grand Priest, who had murdered Leeth's brother, King Jarviski. The priest had ruled Casimere for six years before Leeth was able to enact his revenge. His statue stood in the middle of a fountain where many gathered to cast coins into the water, wishing for peace or whatever their hearts desired.

Like all soldiers, Alvez saluted the statue when they approached it, a sign of respect and admiration for the kingdom's legendary general. Vaiden didn't bother. Leeth had been dead for millennia. He didn't care who remembered him, especially not while he lived in Paradise.

"My father's estate is down there." Alvez pointed down a gated alley left of the fountain. Most of the merchants lived behind their businesses or above them. Tall stone buildings lined the walls of the ring where the bulk of Casimere's citizens lived in apartments. If he hadn't lived on Earth and witnessed the glory of skyscrapers, he might think these were the tallest residential buildings he'd ever seen. Vaiden expected a man with a chair at the king's table to own wealthier accommodations, but Alvez had claimed his father lived modestly.

The third ring, the middle level of the city, belonged to the wealthy. All the buildings were made of stone, draped with greenery and stained glass windows. Even at this busy hour, the streets remained sparse. Guards patrolled down the main arteries, dipping their heads at citizens they passed. Children played a game of marbles and sticks that Vaiden didn't quite understand.

A group of women gossiped around the entrance of the gardens. It wrapped through the middle of the ring, a dedication to the goddesses. Surnuna had the biggest shrine, but elves attended the other shrines too, asking for blessings of harvest from Jana and fertility from Layetta. Only Alumpius's shrine was absent, for King Rothnar had banned her worship when Vaiden was a small child.

Moren's section had been turned into a graveyard where the Goddess of Death could guide those worthy to Paradise. Strangely, Vaiden thought her section was the most beautiful with the stone carvings signifying each noble family and their mausoleums. The royal section of the graveyard was filled with statues and stone benches for elves to praise their fallen monarchs. Notable generals and heroes of old's graves were decorated with foliage and sculpted stone caskets with their resting likeness, holding their favored weapons.

They strolled over the stone bridge at the center of the ring where most of the children gathered, learning from tutors about their city, history, and other kingdoms. One of the children cast a stone into the engineered stream that flowed underneath the bridge. The stream snaked through the ring down to the sewers for filtration before finally emerging to the river that they had crossed a day earlier. Most thought to enter the sewers in an attempt to infiltrate the city, but Vaiden had inspected their access points to find them superbly secure. If given the option, he would never attempt to enter Casimere through those tunnels. It would be quite disappointing and a waste of time and energy—not to mention the assault to his nose.

"This is my favorite place in all our kingdom," Alvez said, walking lazily with his hand resting on his hip.

"Not Brevene?" Vaiden mused. "How refreshing."

"The pink trees are beautiful, but there's something about the magic in this place that always takes my breath away."

"Magic?"

"Not magic like *that*, but the way the greenery and stone mix, like civilization and nature bonded. It's peaceful. Before my mother fell ill, she loved to walk the gardens and teach me about each goddess," he explained, adding quietly. "Even Alumpius."

"What illness did she catch that couldn't be healed?"

Alvez was quiet for a moment while they cleared the bridge, aiming for the stairs that would lead them to the next ring. Vaiden hated stairs, especially the next set. He'd climbed them more times than he cared to count, escorting Rothnar to and from the gardens. Even as paranoid as the king had been about assassinations, he had believed snubbing the goddesses their weekly praise would surmount into deadly consequences. Though that seemed hypocritical given he had banned worship of one of them.

"We had been visiting my aunt, clearing brush when she was scratched by nightbloom," Alvez explained, his eyes shiny with unshed tears. He looked away, admiring one of the statues carved into a building. "She died the next week."

"I'm sorry," Vaiden said and meant it.

He shook his head, his voice quiet. "When the High Elves did arrive for burial, they said there wasn't much they could have done besides make her more comfortable."

Then she had died in agony, Vaiden thought. Nightbloom was rare in Eskandor, but by absorbing parts of the vampire kingdom after its collapse, they had inherited a slither of the deadly vine with its razor sharp leaves and their mesmerizing blooms, said to attract prey with an intoxicating scent. Vaiden remembered Emperor Zerth had decorated his palace with it, wrapping them around columns leading to his throne. Nightbloom couldn't hurt vampires, but Zerth had forced emissaries to cut themselves on the vines. Poor bastards. It was one of the reasons why the serpents had reduced the entire palace to ashes—the only way to truly kill the vine.

"I was glad I was stationed at Fort Khali so I could visit her resting place during leave."

"Your father didn't move her here?"

"No, she's buried with our family's ancestors."

Vaiden nodded, knowing it was common for elves to keep their dead in private graveyards. He briefly wondered where Coastal's family had been buried or his father's. Perhaps near White Star where they had both lived? He made a mental note to ask Coastal when he returned.

"Why didn't your father teach you about necromancy?" Alvez asked. Vaiden's head snapped up, meeting his eyes. "You said he taught you nothing and said he wasn't in your life."

"Correct."

"Why?"

"Why do you think?"

The captain's brows furrowed together, a thought crossing his mind. "Not all High Elves hate Shades."

"How many necromancers do you know that are fond of them?"

"But necromancy is a natural ability," he argued. "They aren't born Corrupted."

The kid was right, but necromancers started life with a handicap—a head start to that line in the sand where dark magic corrupted their brains. It wasn't fair, but it was the hand they had to play. Those who devoted their lives to research and the faith, often didn't cross that line, but it would be an eternal lifespan filled with discipline and denying temptation. The more he thought about it, the more they sounded like recovering alcoholics.

"My father decided when he met me he didn't want anything to do with a Shade," Vaiden explained. "I've only seen him a handful of times during my life."

"That must be hard."

"I don't care."

"Right." Alvez snapped his fingers. "You're a Shade. You don't have feelings."

Vaiden scoffed.

"Then explain why you—" He seemed to search for the right word.

"I was trained to mirror and impersonate those around me," the Shade interceded. "It appears that I emulate the behavior of regular people." It wasn't a lie. Before Tatiana's bind, it was how he blended into the Forty-Second and society.

"Is that hard?" the captain asked. "How can you know if someone is happy, if you've never been happy?"

It was a good question. Vaiden opened his mouth to explain mirroring when shouting grabbed their attention from the fourth ring. They raced up the steps into the military level. Clashing metal rang in the air.

"You're wrong!" shouted a man. "I'm not with the rebels. I don't know what he's talking about!"

"You're lying," barked another man, restrained by a couple of guards. Blood streamed down the right side of his face. Vaiden searched for the threat—for the swords. Another guard had the point of his blade pressed to a man's chest. He wore simple clothes and sandals, a short sword laid at his feet.

"You're disarmed," said the guard. "Surrender."

"I am not a rebel!" spat the man.

"He's a liar!"

"No, *you're* the liar!"

"Enough!" The guard shoved his sword harder into the man's chest, making him wince. "Surrender peacefully or—"

Before the guard could finish, the man bolted, a fierce grin spread across his face, but slipped quickly when an arrow loosed into his shoulder. Somehow he kept running toward the third ring—toward Alvez and Vaiden. The captain unsheathed his sword, but Vaiden grabbed his arm. This wasn't their fight.

The archer perched on the stairs leading to the wall notched another arrow, firing at will. It pierced through the accused's thigh, forcing him to the ground.

"I'm not a rebel!" cried the man. "I didn't do anything!"

The guards ignored his pleas. They scooped up his arms, dragging him toward the gallows. If he'd surrendered, he would have had his day to argue against the accusation, but he'd fled. By rule, only the guilty flee, and the guilty hang.

Alvez sheathed his sword. "What was that all about?" he asked in a whisper.

"Obviously, the one man accused the other of being a rebel," Vaiden replied. "If it was true or not, we'll never know."

The captain watched the guards return to their posts or whatever business proceeded the conflict. His brows scrunched together, watching the other man accept help from a healer. The practitioner hovered their hands, radiating with cyan magic, over the man's wounds. Within seconds, he was healed, thanking the High Elf for their time.

"This is the third person you've accused of being a rebel this week," the guard, who'd fought the fleeing man, said.

"I overheard him talking about the rebels, about ransacking the city, and—"

"Talk is talk." The guard waved his hand. "That man will die for his actions against His Majesty's men, but you must present proof before making another accusation, or you will be the one we investigate next."

The man visibly swallowed, watching the guard sheath his weapon and wondering if he would soon be in the same shoes as the man he'd accused. He didn't have to be, but by his messy hair and shabby attire, this man wasn't well. The dark shadows under his wide eyes told the story of a person who hadn't had a goodnight's sleep in some time. The attack on the capital had widened his eyes. They weren't safe in Casimere.

Could have fooled me, Vaiden thought. Besides the paper inspection at the gates, the Shade hadn't seen any increased security throughout the tiers of the city. Did they really believe those papers would keep them safe? Alvez and Vaiden had walked inside without them. Who was to say others hadn't either?

"You there," the guard said, leaving behind the paranoid accuser. "This is no place for spectating. Be on your way."

"We have business with the king," Vaiden returned.

"We're survivors from Fort Khali," Alvez added. "I'm Captain Alvez Kazquer and this is—"

"A Shade." The guard clicked his tongue. "All Shades are to report to Kiji Village at once."

"On my way, but first, I must speak to the king."

"It is the king's order, Shade."

Vaiden's jaw locked, inhaling sharply. The guard wasn't wrong, but his tone rubbed Vaiden the wrong way. "It's imperative that we speak to the king," he managed, voice neutral.

"We have information about the ambassador and the Corrupted," Alvez offered.

The guard's brows shot up. "What about the ambassador?"

"He's been—"

"For the *king*'s ear only," Vaiden said dryly. The guard sized him up, the way some men did before deciding if they could win that fight. The Shade let his eyes empty of any light—of a void black as night, endless and uncaring. He was tired of the formality. They'd arrived with information about the fort, of the Corrupted, and Gabriel. Any guard worth their tunic would understand the dire situation besieged on the kingdom. He should be escorting them to the palace, not hindering them from entering it.

"The Shade goes alone," the guard finally returned.

"What?" Alvez blinked, exchanging a glance with Vaiden. "I am—"

"I know who you are," the guard replied. "Callum Kazquer's son, but the palace is closed. Only certain individuals are allowed access. You are not one of them."

"Excuse me. I am a captain. I outrank you."

"He's a king's man," Vaiden said, gesturing at the blue tunic. "His job is to ensure the safety of the palace and the king. He outranks anyone from this level on."

Alvez glared at him, his nostrils flaring. "I didn't come all the way here to be sidelined," he growled, returning his gaze back to the guard. "Why can he enter, but not me?"

It was a fair question. If the guard had any sense, he'd know Vaiden was the more dangerous of the two of them. Looks could be deceiving, though. Lizabeth LaBelle had appeared like an innocent sixteen-year-old girl with a heart-shaped face and a sweet smile that could make anyone drop their guard. She'd killed many doing just that.

"Shades are bound by the direct order of the king," he explained. "They cannot hurt him."

Vaiden bit his tongue from correcting him. Shades were bound by the order of the king. That much was true. It had never been tested if they could hurt the monarch or not. There had been no reason to and Shades didn't do anything without cause. He wouldn't clue the king's man on that distinction though. He needed to see Altamost and get some answers.

Vaiden grabbed Alvez's arm before he could argue with the guard. "I got you here," he said quietly. "That's what matters. Go to your father's estate and tell him, if he's there, what's happened. After I'm done, I'll seek you out."

Alvez nodded, a thought flashing across his face. "It's the house with the yellow door."

"This way." The guard gestured. Vaiden wanted to tell him he knew the way. He'd walked these paths for decades, escorting King Rothnar the Daunting or searching for ghostly assassins. But the Shade said nothing in return. He silently followed the guard through the fourth ring, studying the soldiers around them. Shift change was soon to follow. Tired soldiers would be filing into the barracks while the others began their duties. In the chaos, a Shade would meet with the king and learn what the hell was going on.

28

The den claimed Rocahn wasn't available to take Tatiana's call. She asked if any of the members could get her access to the Grand Den, but they stated only the *daehekans* or his partner could grant access with their blessing.

Purple and red hues flooded her office with the sunset. It had been a long day, running around the city looking for answers that she hadn't found. They were a step closer though. Koreen was seen arguing with another serpent named Arkella, a member of the Grand Den. Maybe it had something to do with his death? Maybe it did not. Either way, Tatiana needed to know the truth. Mr. Slaseezor's life depended on it.

A knock drew her attention to the opened door. Logan leaned against it. Having shed his suit jacket, he'd rolled up his sleeves to his elbows, holding up a stack of papers with a triumphant grin.

"The files you asked for," he said, placing them on her desk.

"Thanks." She skimmed the top sheet. "I haven't been able to track down any sole member to the Grand Den named Arkella, but that's not surprising since the majority of them admit under their family names instead of individual names."

Logan nodded. "I've reached out to my contacts again to see if they know anything about this girl or her family, but so far I've heard nothing. Did the den give you permission yet?"

"I still haven't heard back. They assured me Mrs. Slaseezor would return my call."

He looked at his watch, frowning. "It's getting late, Ana. Regular business hours closed a couple of hours ago. You should go home. She'll probably call in the morning after she's met with the Grand Den or whoever she needs to contact to get you access."

"Maybe." She chewed on her lip, thankful her lipstick had worn off near midday. Sometimes she reapplied it, but after spending most of the day in the hot sun, she decided vanity wasn't worth it. "My worry is her pride will not let her pursue this."

"Why? Her husband's life is at stake."

"But to insult a powerful family within the Grand Den can have bad consequences," she explained. "Rocahn might hesitate. If her husband is found guilty, she inherits the den and all the responsibility, which means she doesn't want to insult the Grand Den. They could expel the Slaseezors and their den, impacting everyone depending on it."

"Would the Grand Den do that, shun them for doing the right thing?"

"It depends on how important Arkella's family is," Tatiana said. "I've known serpents expelled by the Grand Den. It's not easy for those of the faith to be denied access to worship. Those against the faith will shun them too."

"Why?"

She shrugged. "That's serpent culture."

"The young ones were pretty helpful though," he said. "Maybe stepping away from that culture isn't such a bad thing."

"Maybe, but when they're up against enemies, their tribe is all they have," she replied. "If you have no tribe then you're alone."

He nodded, his eyes looking at something unseen. "Have you ever been part of some type of religious organization?"

"No, but I know what abusive relationships look like, especially the ones that make you believe you are dependent on them, making you lie for them."

"Do you think Rocahn has been lying?"

"I think she's not telling the whole truth about something, but I'm not sure what." Tatiana leaned back in her chair, crossing her arms. "Have your contacts found any other leads?"

He shook his head. "It's gone dark, they said. Nothing that stands out and nothing through the Underground."

"That's what's troubling about this case," she said. "If it was through the Underground, I could understand why we can't get our hands on evidence, but it's just the dens keeping the truth from us. One of their own might die because they're either too afraid to say anything or too prideful to do the right thing. Either way Mr. Slaseezor doesn't deserve this."

"No, he doesn't."

Logan bid her goodnight, telling her to go home once more. There was no use in waiting around at the office, especially when the only light on in the entire floor was her desk lamp. She exhaled, finally pushing away from the desk and gathered her things.

Her phone chimed with a new message, drawing her attention. She put her bag down, retrieving it from her pocket. It was Zarah, asking if she found anything with the new lead.

Not yet, Tatiana replied. *Waiting on a call for permission to enter the Grand Den.*

No fun, she returned, followed by a frowning emoji. *Want me to do it my way?*

Tatiana's thumbs hesitated over the virtual keyboard. It wasn't illegal for Zarah to contact Arkella. She was a legal adult in the eyes of California law. The reasons might be a slippery slope, but that would be up to Arkella to investigate. Zarah didn't work for Tatiana. They exchanged no money. As long as Zarah made no threats...Tatiana shook her head. If the Grand Den ever learned she had anything to do with it, she would never be allowed inside, and members of the faith would be prohibited from talking to her. She could not allow that to happen.

No, she typed. *Let's wait.*

She stared at her phone, waiting for the message to send, but the little circle kept turning as if she'd lost signal. Her eyes panned to the full bars atop her screen. Why was it having a hard time sending the message? She clicked it off, gathering her things again and finally slipped away from the office.

It was common for her to be one of the last to leave, even before the events of six months ago. She looked for Emil, the custodian, to let him know she was headed out, but when she didn't spy him or his cleaning cart, she carried onto the elevator. He would see her light off and understand she'd left.

It had been nice of him to check on her through long nights, researching and finding leads during her time on the second floor. She wondered how his son's baseball season was going and if scouts had taken an interest in him yet. Although she didn't know much about baseball, she loved hearing Emil gush about his son and the rest of his family. It must have been nice having so much family, leaning on each other and knowing someone waited for him at home.

Her chest tightened when she emerged from the elevator. She needed to call her parents—to check on them. Although they had lied to her repeatedly, they were her only family. She should try again. Coastal had told her she needed a magical teacher, who specialized in destructive arcanes. Her parents weren't, but perhaps they knew someone they could trust.

The garage was quiet and empty, besides a few employee cars. She peered into the security booth, but didn't see the guard. He must have been patrolling. Not odd, she thought, hurrying to her vehicle. It was a coincidence that two people who she frequently saw every night weren't around. She slipped her hand into her pocket, feeling for her keys. Her heart raced, but nothing was there. It was quiet and empty—the kind of emptiness she'd experienced in that cell between sessions of that glaring siren. Icy fingers of dread danced across her skin.

"Here kitty, kitty," whispered in her ear.

She sprinted to her car and slipped inside. Her hands shook, finding the ignition and inserting the key. It started, purring like the cool breath she'd felt on her neck. Her eyes darted to the mirrors and then through the windows. Nothing. The garage was empty.

She leaned against the headrest, closing her eyes and working on her breathing. Jen was dead. Her voice was a figment of her imagination, haunting her, torturing her.

"The brain is powerful," a voice of golden silk said, forcing her eyes open. Her car was gone, replaced by an airy visage, some kind of luxury rooftop far away from Misplaced Stream. Greece came to mind. She sat at a glass table filled with fruits and wine glasses. How did she get here and if so, how was it real?

A noise brought her attention to the man sitting across from her. He was dressed in silk robes adorned with jeweled rings on almost every finger and golden chains hanging around his neck. From his ears hung more jewelry, all sparkling and mystifying like the Cave of Wonders beckoning for her to touch them. He blinked dark eyes at her, a bright smile widening with his lips. It appeared almost kind, if not for the darkness slithering behind it.

"Who are you?" she asked.

He chuckled at some unheard joke, stroking his beard. "I see my reputation does *not* proceed me." He added something in a foreign language, which Tatiana thought might be Arabic from the clothes and turban he wore. "I am Ackrim of Mystic Crane."

"Mystic Crane," she barely breathed. Her heart pounded against her chest and she swallowed hard, trying to soothe it. "What do you want?"

He snapped his fingers. A waiter appeared, pouring white wine in his glass then hers. With a wave of Ackrim's hand the waiter disappeared, gone like a ghost. Was he even real? Had Tatiana imagined him too?

"No, he is very real," Ackrim said. "This is a 'projection' from my location to you. I've been wanting to meet, but your friends are in the way."

"My friends?"

"The elf and vampire and some others," he said, sipping his wine. "The elf made it clear if I approached you, he would act. Since he'd killed one the most powerful beings I've ever met, I did not doubt his ability or his threat. He seems quite fond of you."

Vaiden, she thought, remembering when he'd spoken about meeting Mystic Crane while she was unconscious after the fight with Jen.

"Yes, that's his name. A colorful fellow, wouldn't you say? Loyal. Strong. And with confidence we all should envy. He's made you a priority."

"And when he finds out about this?" She gestured between them.

"Well, I have broken no promises. I am not in Misplaced Stream so no physical threat to you."

"I don't think that's what Vaiden meant."

He waved his hand, saying something else in Arabic. "I told him we would monitor you and we would eventually reach out to hear your answer."

"My answer to what?"

"To join us, of course." His face shined with glee, like a child on Christmas morning. "You need a teacher, someone specialized in arcane magic. We have many who can teach you everything you need to know about your power."

To harness it, she thought. *To use me as a weapon.*

"Aw, yes, that fable." He drained his wine, tossing the glass aside. "We are an organization of many—hundreds really. Every person swears allegiance. If we need to deal with a problem, we are all—how did you characterize it—used? It is a privilege to be a member, to even be considered.

"We don't need weapons, Tatiana. We need people, voices, knowledge, and, yes, with enough time our organization has needed power. We have many powerful practitioners, many knowledgeable researchers, who work tirelessly to find ways to keep our kind safe."

"*Our* kind?"

"The magical," he offered. "Sorcery is rare in humans, as you know. It spreads through so few family lines, dating back to ancient times. It is our theory that these humans came from Arda where they must have copulated with elves and eventually their children's children and so forth, became the sorcerers living here on Earth today."

"If you have so many practitioners, why do you need me?" she asked.

"We do not *need* you," he chuckled. "You need us."

"I'm fine on my own."

"Are you?" He cocked a brow at her. "Coastal Coster is a fine High Elf, a high priestess of Alumpius, but she is no teacher of the arcane. What happens when your power becomes unstable again, like it was at that cabin, or another such as Jen tries to take it from you? Will you always be able to depend on the elf or that vampire, or will one of them be your next victim?"

She opened her mouth to argue, but he wasn't wrong. He knew it by the smug smile spreading on his lips. If she lost control over the blue fire, people would perish. Every second she put people's lives in danger. How could she do that?

"It is hard living amongst those who do not have power, who do not understand it and will look at you like you are something alien, something horrifying, but we forgive their ignorance. Don't we, Ms. Smith? It's why you've grown fond of the preternatural community. You were always an outsider to the petty world of humans."

Her thoughts turned to Josie, Caden, and Darling, and their many other friends. She'd spent the majority of her twenties with them, eating dinners, dancing, laughing, and living enjoyable lives. She wasn't an outsider among them. She was their friend.

"If you trust them so much, why haven't you told them about the blue fire?" Ackrim asked. "Is it because you know they'll look at you the same way they look at your clients? Like they're waiting for them to snap, like some rabid dog?"

"It's not like that," she said, a weight bearing down in her chest.

"Then why, Ms. Smith? Doesn't your employer deserve to know there's a bomb working on floor two of his building? Do you think the insurance will cover you or the damage you might inflict if your power erupts? How could they possibly allow such a liability to work there?"

She pushed away from the table, standing, heat crawling through her veins. "One, it would be discrimination to fire me for being supernatural. I would sue them and win. Two, I would be the perfect PR story to introduce their preternatural division in law. My success is already nationally recognized, adding sorcery to my resume would only strengthen the community's trust in me. And three—"

"I have heard no reason why you haven't told your so-called friends about your magic." His smile was blinding, but also mesmerizing, reminding her of the time when a vampire had tried to glamour her. She turned away, counting back from ten. He wasn't a vampire. He didn't have that kind of power.

"I'm not ready," she said. "It's no one's business."

"And yet, there's a registry for supernatural people in the U.S.A. for the government to keep track of them." He spread his hands wide. "Do you not want to be tracked, Ms. Smith?"

"The media already does a good job of that."

"Aw, yes, Mr. Zeilberg."

"George?"

"He's been snooping around where he shouldn't. We could end his search with a simple spell that would make him believe he was wrong and there was nothing to find. He would even apologize to you, publicly, if you wish."

"Why would it matter to you if he's in my business?" she asked.

"Because once you are a member of Mystic Crane, it is the organization's business to protect its members, even from the media," he replied. "No harm would come of the journalist. He's only human after all. They're easy to manipulate."

"I expect an organization as powerful as Mystic Crane has effectively been manipulating the public for a long time."

"You make it sound like a bad thing to protect our kind." Something sad shined in his eyes. "Like so many other minorities in the world, we only want to exist."

"And you do that by commanding the Marshals to take out your competition."

"The Marshals only intervene when called upon," he explained. "We only bound them to us to ensure they aren't used to exterminate us. You know how governments can be. Look at that incident in Nebraska. They left no one alive, not even innocent bystanders. They are overpowered by human standards, and yet, unlike every other police force in this world, they are celebrated. Why do you think that is, Ms. Smith?"

She sat back down. "Because people see them as white knights."

"Taking down the boogeyman, are they?" He shook his head. "They can slay whole courts of vampires. What says they don't one day decide to murder us all?"

"Are you saying that's why you bound them to your organization? Insurance?"

He shrugged. "Is it survival of the fittest, or is knowledge the most powerful weapon in the world?"

"It sounds to me like you've pulled the strings, you have the power, and you want someone weaker minded with less resources to believe they need you."

"I don't think of you as someone weak."

"I'm not," she shot. "I'm a survivor."

"Why not be more than a survivor?" he asked. "Wouldn't you rather live comfortably than having to worry daily if you are safe, if you are in control, and if the Underground will come for you again? I assure you, with our protection, you'll never have to worry about such things again."

"Is that your best pitch?" she laughed, leaning back in her chair, crossing her arms. "I've heard better from car salesmen."

"It's not a pitch, Ms. Smith. It is a promise," Ackrim said. "If you join Mystic Crane, we will ensure your safety. You will never have to worry about the media or scoundrels, like George Zeilberg, being in your business. You will never have to worry about your power becoming erratic. We will teach you to control it."

"And the only catch is when you call upon your banners, I must answer?" She lifted a brow at him.

"It's a good trade, no?"

"What else would I have to give up? My job, friends, family?"

"We are an exclusive organization, I'm afraid, but you are an asset to us in the legal field."

"So, if one of your members gets caught then I have to represent them?"

"You would get paid." He popped a few grapes into his mouth, savoring them like he'd tasted flavor for the first time in his life. "We take care of our own. You'll never have to worry."

"Yeah, you said that already." It would be nice not to worry, she thought, bringing that wide smile to his face. These were the same people who had brought danger into her life—who had led Jen straight to her—who had done nothing while LaBelle chased her from the city to the mountains and back. They would have let her die. Only her friends had kept that from happening.

His smile slipped. "We do not know everything, Ms. Smith. We cannot be everywhere all at once."

"The Dellawoods approached you, asking for protection, but you rejected them, knowing LaBelle aimed to kill me."

"She would have never gotten you."

"She didn't need to. She had associates who got to me. Coristors' man almost drowned me in a lake. When he failed, Bailyn Rosenhouse was going to deliver me to Jen."

"But you survived."

"Not because of you," she argued. "Vaiden was there for me. He killed Jen while your organization sat on the sidelines."

"We contained the magic." His nostrils flared. The mask he'd carefully sculpted slipped, showcasing the darkness behind it. "Without our intervention, the forest would have burned, bringing unneeded attention from the authorities."

"What did you have to fear when you know the Marshals will do nothing to you?"

"It is more than that, Ms. Smith. We must live aside the magicless of this world. If they learn of our existence, do you think they would open their arms to us? They would believe we are dangerous."

"You are dangerous."

"We only want to *exist*."

"Then there *is* something to worry about."

Confusion etched across his forehead. "What?"

"You said I wouldn't have to worry anymore, but that's not true. As long as there's something to fear, there's something to worry about," she explained.

His face struggled to find a comfortable expression. "Very good, Ms. Smith," he laughed dryly. "I can see why you're a formidable attorney, but as you know, we in management always do the worrying for our members so they may live blissfully."

"Ignorantly, you mean," she corrected. "There's nothing about your deal that I find attractive."

"Not even learning what you need to control the blue fire?"

"I can find my own teacher." She blinked and was sitting in her car again. A shaky breath escaped her lips as her fingertips caressed the smooth surface of the steering wheel. "This is real."

Her phone chimed within her pocket and she fished it out, staring at a new message. *Sorry for the disconnection*, the unknown number read. *We'll chat another time.*

"Bullshit," she huffed, swiping the message away, and making a mental note to ask Coastal about spells to fortify her mind from whatever Ackrim had done. While she had her phone out, she thought to text Coastal at that moment, but another text from an unknown number caught her eye.

I have information you want to know.

29

Zarah frowned at her phone, waiting for Tatiana to return her text. Ten minutes ticked away before she finally casting it aside. Investigating legally was a nightmare. She would have already had this case solved if Tatiana allowed her to do it her way—but her way was archaic, even downright medieval at times.

Squeamish humans, she thought. What was a little spilled blood, if it wasn't their blood? Why did it matter how answers were given as long as answers were given? *Coerced* answers, Tatiana would object. No one could be completely believed under duress, but Zarah disagreed. She'd never received bad information from someone desperately clinging to life.

She turned to Vaiden's computer, unlocking it with the passcode he'd nicely jotted down for her eyes only. He had loads of software she didn't understand, but she'd become increasingly fond of the locator app. She'd used it to follow George Zeilberg. As smart as that man believed himself to be, how easy it was to swipe his phone and use its location software to keep tabs on him.

Immediately, her eyes drew to his location on the map—at his home where he ought to spend every evening, instead of stalking her friend. She understood George's suspicion around the events six months ago. Any investigator would want to know the truth, but that wasn't George's motive.

He needed money for his gambling addiction, but he was also addicted to blackmailing people into giving him information. Like any good addict, he needed boundaries and for his source to be cut off. He hadn't gotten what he wanted. Zarah would make sure he never did. Maybe George could have an early retirement? His knees weren't what they used to be or his articles. Times were changing too quickly for the aging man, forcing him to hang up his hat.

Many would believe such a story. She could even glamour people into nudging him that direction, making him feel like he wasn't needed and letting him make that decision to cash in his check. It was manipulative, mean even, but Zarah was charged with protecting Tatiana. Who knew how long Vaiden would be on Arda. George was a threat.

Vaiden would have already taken care of him quickly, silently, without any room for suspicion. A heart attack in the middle of the night? A stroke? The man wasn't in the best health. He lived an unhealthy lifestyle from his eating habits to his lack of exercise. It was plausible for such decisions to have deadly consequences.

She exhaled into the quiet of Vaiden's house. Tatiana would suspect something, especially given the fact George had already reported Zarah's threats. She needed Tatiana to trust her, killing a man would only hinder their relationship.

The more she thought about it, the more she'd realized she liked Tatiana and she didn't want to lose her. She didn't know when this change happened. Was it because they'd grown close because Vaiden was away, or did Zarah need someone to protect, like she had Harvey? What good was she though? He was dead, like her emperor and his successor. Everyone she'd ever vowed to protect was dead.

Her chest tightened and she rubbed at it, trying her best to soothe the aching organ within. It was soft and tender, easy to squish, like a peach. LaBelle had enjoyed squishing Harvey's heart, allowing the muscle to crumble beneath her touch and for the blood to slide down her arm. She'd smiled.

Zarah screamed, pushing away from the computer. She couldn't sit and do nothing. A murder needed solving. A serpent had answers. It was simple. LaBelle would have sent her to find that serpent and rip her to shreds, if needed, to get those answers. Zarah would do it too. Whatever it took to please her master—to complete the mission and protect the court.

Her phone chimed. She retrieved it, relieved to find a message from Tatiana. More than one message, she realized, scrolling.

Meet me. She read the location, sweeping across the room for the door, but her hand hesitated. It was late. Why were they meeting at the park where those young ones had given them information about Koreen? Did it matter, she asked herself. Tatiana needed backup in a preternatural neighborhood and Zarah was charged with keeping her safe.

She pulled open the door and raced to the car. A short ride later, she found Tatiana sitting in her own car in the lot adjacent to the park.

"What's this about?" Zarah asked when Tatiana slide into her passenger seat. "Not another canvassing I hope."

"Someone texted me about information regarding the murder," she answered. "They wanted to meet here."

"What did they tell you?"

"Nothing yet." She paused, a thought crossing her mind. "I met Ackrim."

"Ackrim?" Why did that name sound familiar to Zarah? She searched the great passages of her mind for the name and where she'd learned it. Blindly light greeted her with a smile. "Mystic Crane!"

Tatiana held up her hands. "He wasn't actually present. Well, he said it was a 'projection.' Whatever that means."

"When was this?"

"Just before I came here."

"What did he want?"

"For me to join his organization," she answered. "I rejected him. He said we would talk again at a later date."

"They want your power," Zarah said. "They'll stop at nothing from getting it, even if that means resorting to Jen's way of stealing it."

She shivered, a haunting expression crumpling her face. "I know."

"Don't go near him again."

"I didn't really have a choice," she scowled. "He was in my mind or something. Before you say anything, I already texted Coastal. She'll come up with something to protect me, I'm sure."

Zarah exhaled loudly in the car. "Vaiden isn't going to like this."

"I mentioned that to Ackrim." A smile spread on her lips, chasing away that haunted stare. "He's scared of him."

"As he should be."

"But I think he also respects Vaiden, like a hunter might admire a lion."

Zarah nodded. There were many killers she admired. Vaiden was one of them. The Underground had a codename for him, Silent Death. She wasn't sure how they came up with that name, but whenever it was used, agents of the Underground paused, like they were afraid to breathe. Vaiden was a successful contractor for their business. Only an effective asset like him could be regarded as both respected and dangerous, much like the king of the big cats.

"We won't believe that his fear or admiration of Vaiden will keep you safe," Zarah said. "We will research spells to protect you and if I have to, I will be your personal guard."

"That's not necessary."

"Like hell it isn't, Tatiana!" the vampire growled. "Mystic Crane is powerful. We will not underestimate them and their resolve."

"I'm not saying ignore them," she said. "If you're following me around all day, people are going to notice and then there will be questions."

"Tell your work there's a threat against you. It can be vague and that you feel more comfortable with security."

"We have security."

"Well, I can put in an application and bully my way to being your personal guard."

"Zarah."

"Whatever we need to do to keep you safe, we will do," she said softer. "Besides, if you were so confident then why did you invite me here tonight?"

"I didn't say I felt safe. I said it would bring a lot of attention." Tatiana frowned. "Also, thank you. I'm not stupid. I know these neighborhoods are more dangerous at night and I think a highly trained vampire, like yourself, would be good backup, but if you rather—"

"I have nothing better to do."

"Glad I'm not inconveniencing you."

Zarah stared out the windshield into the dimly lit park. Could they not afford better bulbs? City funds were rubbish, she thought. Harvey had won his initial council seat by promising upgrades to preternatural neighborhoods. He had, but not all of them. This one included, it seemed—or since his departure from the council—they had cut his budget and programs. *Snakes.*

"Do you see anything?" Tatiana asked.

"The street lights overwhelm my night vision," she said. "We'll have to go further into the darkness for my sight to be more effective."

"I guess I thought it would equalize the light."

"No, the light disrupts it, the same for Vaiden's sight."

"He has night vision?"

"It's called nocturnal sight. All Shades have it."

A figure stepped below one of the park lights, wearing a robe with the hood drawn up to hide their identity. Zarah didn't like the vast space between them and the figure. Too open. If this was Ardra, it would be the perfect place for archers to hide in the trees and on buildings to target that field.

"That must be them," Tatiana said, grabbing the door handle. Zarah pulled on her arm, keeping her inside the car. She raised a brow at the vampire.

"Do you have a weapon?"

"I have magic."

She nodded, considering for a second that Tatiana wasn't a trained practitioner, but no one wanted to fight magic, especially if they didn't have it. "Let's move together and slowly," she instructed. "If anything happens, you run for the cars and defend yourself when needed."

They drifted into the field, away from traffic cruising down the streets. Zarah didn't mind privacy, but the further they moved from the public, the more likely others would be willing to fight. Her eyes adjusted to the darkness of the park, searching the shadows. The lights frustratingly kept her from seeing anything in great detail, but despite the itch someone was watching them, the park appeared empty—not that she would trust appearances.

When they crossed the midway point in the widest, most open part of the field, Zarah concentrated on her hearing and smell. A light breeze played with her hair, forcing Tatiana's minty scent to infiltrate her nose. She pushed it away, searching wider for anything else. The smell of grass and dirt she expected. Salt hung in the air—moisture from the ocean. It would rain eventually. They needed it to drown the heat.

Flapping caught her attention, whirling her attention to the sky where the silhouette of a bird blackened the stars. She returned her stare to their target. They too searched the shadows for something suspicious.

"Hello," Tatiana said, approaching them. They startled, chartreuse eyes darting from underneath the hood. "I know you from the den."

"Zabetha," the serpent said, bowing her head. Tatiana did the same, a sign of respect.

"What information do you want to tell me?"

The serpent's tongue flicked between her lips. Her eyes swept over Zarah then back to Tatiana. "I don't know this one."

"She's my associate. You can trust her."

"I do not even trust you."

"Then why meet with me? Why go through all this trouble?"

"Because Mr. Slaseezor is innocent."

"Then help me prove he is and set him free."

A quiet growl quaked deep in the serpent's throat. Most would find it threatening, but Zarah had been around enough serpents to know it was just a thinking noise, like how humans made a "hmm" sound.

"Rocahn lied about Koreen," Zabetha said. "He was a desired candidate for coupling. Many of the Grand Den wanted him to join so the families could discuss futures with their daughters."

"But Koreen's family moved to Arda," Tatiana replied.

"They did not like Earth's ways. They missed the simplicity of home."

"Did their return to Arda affect any promises of coupling with Koreen?" Zarah asked.

Zabetha nodded.

"Was a girl named Arkella promised?"

"Rocahn told me her family believed Koreen was beneath them because they were not members of the Grand Den," she explained. "I know Koreen met Arkella through mutual families from our den."

"Let me guess." Zarah crossed her arms. "They hit it off."

"It is against custom for the young ones to become interested in each other in such ways," Zabetha replied. "But yes, they liked each other. I remember Koreen expressing to Rocahn his feelings for Arkella, but Rocahn said it would not matter. Arkella's family had already rejected him as a match."

"I imagine that upset him," Tatiana said.

"He did not let it show," she replied. "He dove into his studies of the faith. I believe he shoved away that future with Arkella, but she had different ideas."

"Like what?"

The serpent spread her arms wide. "Like all young people, they believe running away together will solve everything."

"I imagine her family did not like that idea," Zarah said.

"I don't know. I am not part of their den, but I know Koreen met Arkella in this park because Rocahn had me follow him. She said we needed to watch him like one of the family, but I think she thought he would get into trouble. He did get into an argument with Arkella here that day."

"About what exactly?" Tatiana asked.

She shook her head. "I was too far away to hear, but Arkella was furious with him. She struck him before running away."

"He must have rejected her plan," Zarah offered.

"I do not know," Zabetha said, her tongue tasting the air. She stiffened, her eyes darting, searching for something in the darkness. "They followed me."

"Who?"

Zabetha did not answer. She ran, only making it a few paces before something slammed into her. A figure mounted her smaller frame, plunging a dagger into her body—a killing blow. The serpent shrieked.

"No!" Tatiana reached out toward her with electric blue lines snaking down her arms. Zarah grabbed her shirt, pulling her in retreat.

"It's too late," the vampire said, staring into the blank stare of Zabetha. Her assailant stood, its hood casting shadows to hide its face, but Zarah could see, through the gray tones of her night vision, its snarling sharp teeth. "Go! Run!"

Tatiana smartly ran. "There's more of them!"

Zarah twisted her head, her peripherals catching glimpses of more hooded figures crossing the open field. "Keep going!"

The assailant attacked, slashing his dagger. Zarah easily evaded, squatting down and punching him in the gut. He doubled over, giving her the perfect opportunity to grab the blade from his hand, stabbing him several times through the chest.

His body fell as a flash of blue caught her attention. She whirled around. Two figures rolled on the ground, trying to extinguish the blue flames. It wouldn't help. Not even water could.

Tatiana cried out as she struggled with a third figure. A sweet smell filled Zarah's nostrils, watering her mouth and breathing life into an endless hunger dead within her bones. If she was newly turned, it would have sprung her into a demented state, but Zarah focused her attention on the attacker, flinging the blade in her hand. It struck true, slicing through its arm, making it drop the dagger. Tatiana kicked the attacker between the legs, making *him* crumple to the ground.

Zarah rushed forward, grabbing his head and twisting it with a sick crack. Her eyes darted to where Tatiana grabbed her left side. Blood caked her hand where she held pressure. "Shit. Can you make it?"

"We can't leave her like this." Sweat slid down Tatiana's face. Her eyes wide and frightened.

"She's dead. It's my job to ensure you don't die too." She grabbed Tatiana's right arm, pulling her toward the vehicles. "Can you run?"

"I don't—" Zarah didn't wait for her to reply. She scooped Tatiana up, throwing her over a shoulder. She cried out.

"Sorry," the vampire said, running for the cars. "Close your eyes." She glided through the field, hoping her speed wouldn't irritate Tatiana's wound too badly.

At the cars, she threw Tatiana in the backseat of her BMW and jumped into the driver's seat.

"We shouldn't leave her like that!" Tatiana exclaimed.

"Between her or you, I pick you." The vampire slammed the car into reverse, peeling out of the parking lot. She switched gears and stomped on the gas, speeding into traffic.

"Where are you going? The hospital is the other way."

"Do you want to explain how you got stabbed?" Zarah asked. When Tatiana didn't respond, she continued. "We're going to Coastal. She'll heal you."

30

King Jarviski named the palace the Crystal Keep for the giant glass dome atop the throne room. It shone for miles away, a beacon of beauty, life, and the center of Eskandor's power. While most palaces were made into impenetrable strongholds, the arrogant elves built theirs open and airy. Rothnar the Daunting had boarded most of it up, but the kings who had replaced him had restored the palace back to its original glory.

The palace was designed in intricate, elegant shapes that Vaiden imagined were hand-carved by the world's most patient artists. No archway, column, or square tile was left naked of vines, flowers, impressions of the goddesses and other mythical creatures. Water joined themes as the main medium for magic, supplier of life, and the most powerful force of nature. It was represented in murals, fountains, and engineered waterfalls.

Vaiden followed the king's man through archways art nouveau enthusiasts would kill to own back on Earth. He spotted other guards watching them through the halls, each wondering who visited the palace and if he was a threat. Vaiden mentally counted them, finding more guards present than ever before. Altamost had beefed up security, but only for himself.

Laughter invited them into the throne room where the king sat atop a raised dais surrounded by nobles, generals, and a few others Vaiden didn't recognize. Altamost's personal guards noted who'd entered the dome. Their stares studied every inch of him, spying where his weapons could be located and how easily they might disarm him. The Shade frowned, knowing well what their position beside the king required. *Poor bastards.* At least, those days were far behind him.

His brow arched at General Glades, who watched the Shade with laser focus. What had he told the king? Why wasn't the city more prepared for an attack? They needed to contact Mysogus and get the Grand Priestess to—

Vaiden's stare jumped to the woman leaning against the left side of Altamost's wooden throne. A red floor length dress with off the shoulder sleeves that belled over her hands hugged her body like a dream. Her honey-colored eyes studied every detail of the king's face, drinking in his words like a woman dying of thirst. She tossed back a lock of hair, dark enough some might believe it was black, if not for the sunlight shining through the glass dome, highlighting the auburn strands of her hair. Who was this woman so close to Altamost and why had the guards not intervened?

"Your Majesty." The king's man bowed before the throne. "An arrival from Fort Khali."

"Another one? Thank Surnuna." King Altamost exhaled, his blue eyes drooping with exhaustion and pain. Theater, Vaiden thought as the king lifted his stare, fixating on the Shade. The welcoming warmth he'd conjured in his mask slipped at once, replaced by surprise then confusion. Vaiden was getting better at reading facial expressions. Thank Alvez and his moods.

"Vaiden," breathed the king. "What are you doing here? You were at Fort Khali. Why? You should be tracking down the rebel's leader."

The Shade crossed his arms. "Hello to you too, Alty."

The king's man shot Vaiden an unfriendly look. His hand gripped the hilt of his sword, ready to discipline the Shade for not properly addressing a royal. The others' eyes darted between the Shade and the king. No one dared to make a sound, some didn't even breathe.

King Altamost chuckled, easing the tension immediately. A few nobles exhaled, covering their anxiety with laughter. The king's man loosened his grip, his features relaxing.

"You always were one of my favorites," the king said. "I'm amazed King Rothnar allowed such a personality, but as always, it is good to see you, old friend."

He commanded the throne room to empty. The nobles pouted, hating to miss the hot gossip. The generals and commanders left as well, all but Glades, who, despite the friendly atmosphere, remained serious and focused on the Shade. Was he worried Vaiden would turn him in? And for what exactly? Retreating against far superior odds? Vaiden didn't blame him, though he should have ordered the retreat formally to the rest of the soldiers. For all the concussed Shade knew, he had. Perhaps he'd missed it between meteor strikes.

"You come with news of Fort Khali," the king said once the nobles were gone, except *her*. She combed back his hair with her fingers, licking her lips while marveling at his bone structure. It made Vaiden's skin crawl.

"General Glades has given a rather detailed account of the attack already," the king claimed. "Any new information you provide will be greatly appreciated, especially given your expertise."

"He told you about the blood mage?" Vaiden asked.

"Yes, the one with the meteor summoning staff and the necromancer who can form multiple monstrosities. It's quite the feat for the Corrupted, wouldn't you say?"

"I would say they aren't normal, and I can relay they are journeying this way."

"They followed you," Glades said, his voice oddly accusatory.

The king raised a brow at the general, his stare sweeping from him then back to Vaiden. A friendly smile spread with his goatee. "Vaiden is one of the best that has come out of Kiji. If he didn't want to be followed, he wouldn't be."

"I crossed paths with the same Corrupted, who attacked the fort east of Haven."

"How do you know they are the same ones?" the king's man asked.

"Tor." Altamost clicked his tongue.

The guard bowed his head. "Apologies, my king."

"How do you know?" he asked, gesturing at the Shade.

"The monstrosities are made from animals, generally larger ones, like horses. It is the necromancer's signature," Vaiden explained. "These Corrupted work as one. The few I killed on the road, I believe were scouts sent ahead of the group. It is my theory they wish to combine with the nest in Haven before journeying here."

"Casimere is well guarded," the king said.

"So was Fort Khali."

"Not the same in the slightest, as you know."

"I know this city has been infiltrated by the rebels with no aid from magic." The king's jaw locked at the Shade's words. "This blood mage is powerful and calculated. It thinks with a military mind."

"That's not possible," Glades said. "Its brain is diseased, rotten."

"And yet, it destroyed your fort like a sandcastle," Vaiden shot, making the general flinch. "I wouldn't underestimate it, Alty. I would have around the clock double duty on these walls, in every sector. You can't give them a chance to break into the city."

The king took a deep breath, his eyes rereading Vaiden's words in the air. "Unlike Fort Khali, we have the turrets and the practitioners."

"Why aren't the Shades being utilized?" Vaiden asked. "Against the Corrupted, there is no greater force."

Altamost smiled at Vaiden, almost sweetly, if not for the anger darkening his eyes. "That is part of a greater plan," he said, standing. The lady pushed away, fetching his walking cane. He took it, leaning heavily on his left side.

When the king was a lad, he was involved in a terrible rockslide. A boulder had crushed his leg, but the practitioners were able to recover it. Unfortunately the injury was so severe he suffered some permanent damage. Despite the misinformation Earth liked to spread across social media, magic could only do so much. It depended on the practitioner's ability and how long ago the damage was inflicted.

Those following Aegan believed nothing was impossible. They could cure any disease and heal any wound. Vaiden thought it was ironic, considering their goddess was the *Creator* of Disease and Famine, but their misguided ignorance would never admit wrongdoing, even whilst using blood magic to prove their point. Dark magic had consequences. It eroded the brain or it took something else, mostly sacrifices and lives. Curing one life while taking another was not the miracle they thought it was.

"Now that this business of the Corrupted is behind us," the king said, stepping off the dais.

"Is it?" Vaiden asked, furrowing his brow. The king was shorter than the Shade—maybe only five-foot-eight-inches tall. Even the crown of silver vines and golden leaves added nothing to his height, but like Alvez had said, the king was a revered title. It demanded respect.

No one ascended to such a position doing nothing, at least not in Eskandor where blood did not necessarily grant power. It took work and earning recognition from the people and those who spoke for them. It was why Rothnar's brother didn't inherit the crown after his passing. Chorlee earned it through his years of service and dedication to the people. It was sad his reign prematurely ended before it really began.

Vaiden had suspected Altamost or his supporters had something to do with the tragic death of King Chorlee. There was no proof aside from his gut feeling, but guts were full of shit so they had no merit. The council had tasked Vaiden with finding proof, but Altamost's guards had discovered them colluding and charged them all with treason.

The council had been pardoned, stating their caution was misplaced, but appreciated for the welfare of the kingdom, which was political jargon for "I'll let you live, but now I own you." Vaiden was pushed through the doors, given no other options. He didn't know why Altamost didn't execute him, but maybe the new king didn't want to kill a decorated soldier, or he didn't want to find out if the Shades would turn on the monarch, or, perhaps, like he'd mentioned, Vaiden was one of his favorites.

It was before the days of the *Discovery* so Earth wasn't known to Arda. For all the king knew, Vaiden was dead. What a shock it must have been when he learned the doors hadn't killed him. Then again, he might have not thought about it until Gabriel had suggested returning Vaiden to Arda to settle this war. Of course, Vaiden was a Shade. They didn't hold grudges.

Vaiden wasn't about to announce he wasn't the same Shade. The bind had changed him in ways that even surprised and confused him. Staring into the face of the man, who'd ignored Gabriel while he had begged the king to reconsider pushing Vaiden through those doors—yeah, it burned something deep in the Shade's middle. Gabriel had been on his knees. He had cried. The king had ordered his guards to push the Shade through. Vaiden hadn't struggled. He'd made it easy for them.

"I understand that purpose clouds your mind, but leave the Corrupted blight to me, old friend," the king said, patting the Shade's back. He limped toward the fountain in the middle of the throne room. A statue of Surnuna holding the sun above her head transformed her power into life, represented by the water. At the base of the fountain, murals had been carved into the stone of forests and civilization growing and multiplying.

"Surnuna guide us," Altamost whispered to the goddess before turning his attention back to the Shade. "Why aren't you tracking the rebels?" he asked. "It was my only order for you."

"But Gabriel—"

"Aw, yes, where is the good ambassador?" The king waved his cane, gesturing around them. "I should think you two joined at the hip because he is responsible for you. It was part of our agreement for your return to the kingdom."

"The ambassador was taken by the rebels at Fort Khali."

Surprised blinked into the king's eyes. "The rebels were at the fort?"

"They came late in the fight," Vaiden answered. "We thought they were assisting, but it seems their true mission was to take the ambassador."

"Take or recover?"

"What do you mean?"

"You weren't supposed to be at the fort." He pointed his cane at Vaiden. "You were supposed to pick up Kanaris's trail and hunt him down. General Glades reported to me that it was clear to him that Gabriel has kept you from carrying out that mission."

A knot tightened in Vaiden's middle. "That's not—"

"Did the ambassador tell you my orders had changed?" Vaiden tried to mask his confusion, but failed. The king smiled slightly, finding what he wanted. "I wonder why he would keep you from completing this mission."

Vaiden relaxed his features, letting his eyes empty. "Gabriel brought me here to assist the crown."

"'To help the kingdom,' I believe were his exact words," the king corrected. "Exactly *who* does the ambassador want to help?"

"I don't follow."

"My only conclusion is that Gabriel Steel has been working for the rebels this whole time, giving them information from the crown, allowing them to steal our resources. When my order came for you to eliminate Kanaris, *their* leader, he steered you away, lying about my orders, knowing you could end this civil war with a swing of your blade."

"Gabriel is one of the most loyal servants this kingdom has ever had," Vaiden argued. "The problem is not with the rebels, Alty. The problem is the Corrupted. Take them out and you will gain the trust of the people and restore faith in the crown."

"Faith?" He gestured behind Vaiden. The woman in red stood patiently beside General Glades. "I have *the* faith."

Vaiden arched a brow at him.

"Allow me to introduce the Grand Priestess, Dallia," he grinned, striding to her. She offered her hand and he laid a small kiss upon it, his face tilting up to meet her smile. "My most humble supporter."

234

"How long has she been here?" Vaiden asked, not of the king, but to the guards. They said nothing in return. Tor studied the Shade with a question welling in his eyes. "The Leader of the Faith is only welcome in this palace during the coronation and to celebrate the Magnificent Harvest. Unless my timeline has been wrapped by my time on Earth, it's well past both of those occasions."

"I've repealed those laws," Altamost said.

"You can't," Vaiden shot. "They were set in stone by Leeth."

"Nothing is forever, old friend," said the king. "Do you dare question my authority?"

"No, but I question your motivation or rather hers."

Altamost laughed. "Yes, Leeth set those guidelines because Grand Priest Knoran used his influence of the faith and magic to ensnare King Jarviski, killing him to take over the kingdom. There's nothing to fear *now*. I invited Dallia to extend her stay."

"Why?"

"We have much to deliberate about the blight and this civil war." He smiled up at her, taking her hand and kissing it again. "Her support has been deeply appreciated."

"Do you not see that something is wrong here?" Vaiden gestured at the guards then settled his stare on General Glades. "She's influencing the king."

"Some might say the words of nobles might influence me too."

"She's *magically* influencing you. Glades, back me up here."

"The Grand Priestess has been an admirable addition to the king's council," the general replied. "With Mysogus's support, we will win the rebellion."

Vaiden's ribs protested as he whirled back to the guards. "Are you *all* under her influence?"

They stood there like sentries, waiting for the king's orders. These weren't Shades. These were Novices. They should have emotion, have suspicion, but their stares were as blank as dolls.

"I'm beginning to think Gabriel sent you here," the king said, gazing at the beauty of the glass dome. "Yes, that makes perfect sense. His rebels collected him and he sent you here as a scout. He's probably scheming with Kanaris right now."

"What?" Vaiden pivoted so he could see all the occupants in the room. His pulse raced, not with purpose, but something else that he didn't like. "Gabriel isn't a rebel, Alty. He fought them at the fort. Why would he fight them if he was working with them?"

"Aw, yes, he had to make it look like a struggle so others would believe they were taking him by force." The king stroked his beard. "Yes, it's true. The ambassador has turned on us."

"This is insane! Listen to what you're saying, Altamost. Gabriel would never turn on the kingdom."

"I am the kingdom." The king stood tall, his face falling into a serious expression. "It is my judgment that has passed. Gabriel Steel is a traitor and those who defend him are as guilty of treason." He tilted his head. "Weren't you already guilty of that once? Wasn't he the one who talked me into letting you return? I see it clearly now. You are here to assassinate me."

"Your Majesty." Vaiden shook his head. "Listen to me. I—"

"Seize him."

The guards sprang from their posts, wielding blades, slashing in fury. Vaiden dodged. These men were under the combined control of the Grand Priestess's power and the king's direct order. They could not refuse. Vaiden didn't believe they should reap the consequences, but they didn't feel the same about him.

They were highly trained soldiers—the *best* to guard the king, but he was also another handpicked personal guard of a king. A king who was a soldier, not some nobleman. Rothnar didn't want any guard at his side. He wanted the most dangerous, skilled, and relentless soldiers he could find. Many he brought over from his command as a general, but he'd plucked Vaiden straight from the Forty-Second. If there was an upper hand between a one-versus-three fight, it was his age, experience, and, the fact, he was a Shade.

He punched one in the face, grabbing his sword in time to block another's attack. His ribs ached, but he pushed it away, focusing on the next move. He evaded a strike from Tor, kicking the other's guard knee. It crunched, forcing a cry from the man as he fell to the floor. He would live.

The king's man whirled around, his blade slicing through the air. His attacks were more precise, the sign of an experienced fighter. Vaiden felt—more than saw—the other guard at his back. He ducked, metal striking ringing above his head. He kicked the guard in the stomach, rolling off balance to miss Tor's next attack.

"Fuck," Vaiden groaned at the pain erupting from his sides when he got to his feet. He shouldn't be fighting with damaged ribs, but irritating them was the least of his problems under assault by the king's man's blade. Vaiden evaded, but when his foot hit the dais, he knew he was running out of room. Tor was good, cornering the Shade. Smart, but also stupid to think Vaiden would let himself be cornered.

He unsheathed his hunting knife from its hidden slot in his boot, ramming it into the soldier's thigh. Tor fell, grimacing, but he didn't quit, picking up his sword for another slash. Vaiden admired that, but he cut the man's attack short by kicking him in the face. His head bounced against the tiled flooring, clearly out cold. The Shade retrieved his hunting blade. He'd never leave it behind.

Glades unhooked his battle ax, but Dallia raised her hand, stopping him. She glided forward, her hands glowing with purple power. Vaiden stood fast, adjusting his grip on the knife, daring her to come closer.

"This ends now," she said, obliging him, but she suddenly stopped in her tracks. Her purple magic dissolved into mist. She stared at her hands, blinking at them then down at her clothes before returning her gaze to the Shade. "What?" The confusion deepened lines on her face, her wide eyes swept around the dome.

"Get him!" ordered the king. Soldiers piled into the room quickly, each drawing a weapon.

"Time to go," he said under his breath, racing for the exit. It was blocked so he turned for the next best route. Maps of the palace flashed before his eyes, recalculating like an app on his phone. If he could get to the servant quarters, he could take a shaft down to the—Guards blocked the path. Around and around he went, running through the arches, evading blades and arrows.

Fire erupted from his side but he ignored it, pushing his legs. Light hit him in blinding sunbeams when he emerged into the open. Arrows whistled past him, making him wonder how he could outrun them. The guards on the ground didn't prove as effective. Shift change had begun and the tired soldiers barely raised their heads as he raced past them through the fourth ring.

"Stop him!" someone shouted, but Vaiden continued, staring ahead at the gate. The ones standing by got the clue and slammed it shut. He one finger saluted them, turning toward the right barracks. An arrow grazed his shoulder, but at least it didn't stick him.

The elevation climbed this side of the ring, giving him the high ground. He dug deeper seeing the old route he used to rendezvous with Zarah hadn't changed. A smile spread on his lips as he mounted a crate parkouring to the wall before launching himself over the balustrade into the third ring.

31

"I'm too old for this shit," Vaiden groaned, his sides blistering in pain while his hand blindly searched for the knife. His blurry vision fought to focus, tuning in and out of his nocturnal sight. It was darker in the graveyard, aided by the giant shady trees, hundreds of years old. Their thick branches and leaves shielded the guards up in the fourth ring from spotting him in the hedges, the softest landing spot he could hope for surrounded by all the stone sculptures and mausoleums.

He needed to get up though. The soldiers would open the gates and rush into the gardens. Thankfully the graveyard was on the edge, furthest away from the entrances. Vaiden grabbed his blade, untangling from the hedges. When he moved far enough, magic restored them to their glory, erasing any indication he'd fallen there.

Distant shouting let him know the soldiers infiltrated the third ring. They would stop at nothing to find him. He stuck to the shadows, moving in a crouched position behind bushes and stone-carved memorials, invisible and silent as the air. Training kicked in, his expanded hearing searching through the corners of the graveyard for movement. Soft steps near the entrance let him know someone had entered Moren's garden.

His hand tightened around the grip of his knife, shouldering a mausoleum. He glanced around the corner, spotting the soldier. His sword was drawn, held out from his body, parting a curtain of vines. More voices spread through the gardens, like wildfire, blocking his way. He couldn't run through fire—not through the soldiers either. It wasn't their fault King Altamost had gone crazy. Magic and power warped his ambition into something truly dangerous. Grand

Priestess Dallia had accomplished something the Leader of the Faith hadn't since Knoran's days. She could not be underestimated.

No, these soldiers could not be at fault for their possessed king's orders, Vaiden thought, sheathing his knife. He needed to sneak past them without killing them. More bloodshed would only solidify his and Gabriel's guilt in stone. Only the guilty run, whispered through his mind. Yeah, that may be the law on Arda, but Vaiden knew a lawyer who could argue, so did the frightened. Was that why his heart was thudding against his chest? Was he scared?

He pushed the thought away, focusing on the tremendous task ahead of him. More guards poured into the garden, fanning out, searching every shadow. They knew the routine, especially during a civil war. How many had been executed as rebels during Altamost's possession? They wouldn't hesitate to kill him, but he wouldn't make it easy.

As light as the breeze and quick as a mouse scurrying across the floor, Vaiden hurried from grave to grave, using the sculptures as a shield. He wasn't a small man, but the elves weren't humble with celebrating their dead. Each needed to be remembered with elaborate, enormous pieces, showcasing how important their family or station was. Vaiden thanked Opretta for their vanity, shifting with the shadows.

"What's the story with this one?" a soldier asked his partner, scanning the headstones.

"Assassination attempt is what I heard." The partner opened the door to a mausoleum and peeked inside. "He made a mess of the king's guards."

"Who let him in?"

"He came from the gate is what I heard."

"*We* let him in?"

"We didn't do anything."

"Tor is going to have a fit."

"Tor's one of the injured."

"Surnuna help us."

They turned their backs, giving Vaiden the opening he needed. He crouch-walked behind the sculptures to the stone resting place of a general sleeping on his back. He paused only letting his hearing search for footsteps. When the coast appeared clear, he moved, whisking past the whining guards to the garden entrance. Soldiers heavily patrolled outside. It would be impossible to sneak past them.

Shit, he mouthed, searching for the next possible exit. His eyes darted up one of the shady trees, searching for access to the border wall. One limb hung over the stream. Not a soft landing, but softer than the hedges. He ran behind the cover of vine curtains, shadowed, but not invisible—a calculated risk, but it was the direct route.

"Over there!" someone shouted, forcing Vaiden to push his legs. His sides ached, but he ignored them as an arrow whizzed through the vines striking the stone behind him.

"Fuck," he groaned, hurdling over stone dividers. A flash of metal caught his eye, forcing him to the ground, sliding on his knees as a sword sliced the air above him. He unsheathed his sword, parrying the next attack. His foot tripped the soldier, granting him enough time to climb to his feet and run. He didn't like retreating, but the odds were not in his favor, especially after he spotted the soldiers pouring through the gates.

Another arrow struck a stone close to him. Their aim was improving. He sheathed his sword, picking up speed. The tree—the route of escape—was in sight. He visualized it, evading another arrow. The soldiers were closing in. He could hear their footsteps closely behind him, but it was his expanded hearing amplifying their steps he knew. He had time.

His boot hit the bark and he launched himself up, grabbing a hold of a branch. An arrow whistled by, barely missing him. A sigh of relief escaped his lips as he hurled himself over the branch to the trunk of the tree. He climbed, rotating so the tree was between him and the archers. Orders shouted in a mixture of panic that he tuned out, focusing on his hand and feet placements. He'd climbed a mountain with his bare hands. What was a tree?

Of course, he had been a teenager with perfectly healthy ribs when he'd climbed the mountain. He cringed, pulling his body higher, fighting the fatigue in his upper body. There was no time to rest, to shake out his arms, and no place to safely pause until he reached the limb overlooking the water. He focused on it, pushing away all the pain and doubt circling his mind.

The soldiers would figure out his plan shortly. They would run to the bridge and have archers waiting on the high ground. He would be a sitting duck in the water until he washed to the shallow ends east where he was sure more soldiers would be waiting to retrieve him, but he would disappoint them.

A smile spread with his lips when he finally reached the branch and pulled himself on it. He took a deep breath, his eyes shifting to the water below. It was white rapids this time of day, not a relaxing bubbling stream like during the night. The sound drowned out the bustle of the work day so those going to school or strolling over the bridge could enjoy peace from the noise.

His heart raced, staring at the violent water. As a kid from White Star, swimming was foreign to him in the cold. Gabriel had described using water as cover in Abrita Shores along the vast docks of the floating city. He wouldn't hesitate to dive into the water. Neither could Vaiden. The longer he waited, the more prepared the soldiers would become.

"Move!" He heard, but didn't wait to see who made the order before he jumped into the water. A thousand needles pricked his skin, stunning his body immediately. He opened his eyes into the black of the water, searching the base for a grate.

His nocturnal sight blinked on, fixating on something metal near the bottom. Vaiden swam toward it, moving laterally through the current until he broke free of it. His lungs constricted with the need for air, forcing him to swim faster, broader strokes, stronger kicks. He grabbed the bars, the hinges sighing as he forced the grate open, crawling through the narrow passage until light poured into a chasm. He surged through the waterline, a rush of air desperately pouring into his lungs.

"Fuck," he growled, blinking at the firelight blazing through his nocturnal sight. He turned it off, finding an enclosure where an old blanket still laid beside the water. He grabbed the sides of the pool and pulled himself over the dry, hard stone.

On his back, he stared at the ceiling, finally understanding why Zarah complained about this certain rendezvous point. It was one of the secret places Vaiden found by Rothnar's order, but one he'd neglected to report. He'd never before taken the stream access. It had been Zarah's path, but she didn't need to breathe. Something he should have added in his calculations before considering it.

He closed his eyes, his limp body exhausted and sore. This was a safe place. No one knew it existed. Even if the soldiers jumped in the water, unless they had nocturnal sight, they would never find it. At this hour, they wouldn't dare. They would wait until the evening when the water settled and use the practitioner's magic to light their way. By then, Vaiden would be long gone.

A heaviness weighed him down, slipping him into numbing darkness, but he didn't move. He let it take him, soothing his wounds, drifting him to peace and Paradise.

***

Vaiden jolted awake, groaning with his ribs. Visions of sandy beaches and the bright sun faded behind his blinking eyes. He looked at his hands, missing the warmth of the fingers that had been entwined with his, or when they had brushed through her blonde hair, or when his arms had wrapped around her soft body. A sigh escaped his lips. It had been a dream—only a dream. Tatiana was a vast world away.

He climbed to his feet, staggering against a nearby wall. "Shit." How long had he been asleep?

A series of tunnels and iron gates led him to the increasing foul smell of shit until he found the stairs. It was a steep climb, but at least he would leave the sewers behind.

With every step, he pieced together his escape route. Under the cover of darkness it would be easier, but he didn't know if the soldiers would let him wait for nightfall. Their plan would be to force him out. To go through each home and business, if needed. The longer he remained in the city, the more likely they would find him. He couldn't run forever and he doubted after his earlier stunts, if they would take any more chances.

Light faded from the skies by the time he reached the city. It was quiet in the third ring, only a few strays braved the streets, each hurrying home. The city might be on lockdown, he thought. Would Altamost allow such panic though? Maybe people were tired after the market and their work days that they wanted to be home. Vaiden didn't know, but he couldn't hear any music playing in taverns, which could only mean they were vacated, or that all the bards in the city had suddenly vanished. The Shade doubted the latter. The citizens of Casimere were big tippers. A bard made a decent living on song requests, if they didn't squander it all on wine.

The deep shadows from the ring's wall made it easier to hide, but the bare streets bathed in silence forced him to move soundlessly, which took effort and thought. He spotted guards patrolling through the streets. They visited residents, checking each home down a line. Vaiden watched, mentally taking note how long it took to search a house. They made the residents stay outside. Most looked impatient. Others worried. Vaiden wasn't sure why. What did they have to hide?

He waited for them to visit Alvez's home in the second ring. His father stood fast by the door, unmoved by the soldiers entering his house or the ones standing outside with him. They chatted, apologizing to the king's council. He nodded at them, remaining stoic, though the men towered over him. His gray-streaked hair was pulled into a high bun, leaving his clean-shaven face unframed. He didn't need it. Like Alvez, he had good genetics, though his complexion was lighter than his son.

When the first soldier returned, Vaiden realized Lord Kazquer stood alone. Panic rippled through his chest. Where was Alvez?

After the rest of the soldiers exited the home, they nodded at their supervisor, giving the all clear. The soldiers moved onto the next house while the king's council looked on, wishing them luck. He slipped inside the yellow door, closing it soundly behind him. Vaiden couldn't enter through the front door. He needed to find an alternative route.

His eyes searched the three levels of the home, no balconies or opened windows from the front. Unfortunate, he thought. Unlike the buildings built into the wall surrounding the ring, the Kazquer family was lucky enough to purchase one of the townhouses along the street. It had a shared courtyard with other homes, but Vaiden managed to traverse through the open streets quieter than a mouse. It helped the guards moved routinely down the streets, but his luck would run out eventually.

Greenery filled the courtyard, making it more private than he'd expected. Vines climbed up the back of the home, but Vaiden didn't spy any opened windows. Not that he wanted to climb more. The higher he was, the more exposed he would be to the guards below. He gently checked the backdoor, pleading for it to be unlocked.

Shit, he mouthed. Locked. His luck was running out.

"Hey," someone whispered. His eyes searched through the woods finding a figure, waving.

"Alvez?"

"This way." He hurried to the cellar doors, unlocking them. Vaiden followed, a weight lifting from deep in his chest. The kid was OK. They hadn't taken him.

Inside, Alvez lit a torch, his eyes studying the Shade. "What happened?"

"The Grand Priestess seems to have influence over the king," Vaiden explained. "It's made him paranoid. He thinks Gabriel sent me to assassinate him."

"What?" Alvez shook his head. "That's crazy."

"Exactly." He snapped his fingers. "Gabriel is absolutely loyal."

Internally, he wasn't as sure. Crazy or not, Altamost stood firm that he'd ordered Vaiden to pursue and kill Kanaris. Gabriel had lied about his orders being changed. The Shade didn't know why, but he planned to ask—if he could escape Casimere first. Then he had another thought.

"Why are you hiding?" Vaiden asked.

"Father thought since I was seen with you that the king might believe I was a part of the ploy too," he answered. "He thought it best for them not to find me."

"Son," Callum Kazquer's voice filled the basement, drawing their attention. "Is this—"

"Vaiden Zarren."

The king's council stepped off the stairs, exchanging a glance with his son before returning his stare to Vaiden. "It seems I owe you a debt for returning my son to me," he said, "but it also appears things went folly with the king."

"Do you understand that the Grand Priestess has power over him?"

He shook his head. "I don't think it's that simple, but I do understand why you would think that. You are a Shade. Magic is the enemy."

"Magic isn't the enemy." Vaiden crossed his arms. "The irresponsible people wielding it are."

A smile tugged at the counselor's lips. "A wise correction," he said. "To make myself more clear, the king's antics started much before Dallia arrived."

"Before the Magnificent Harvest?"

"Let's go upstairs," he said. "You look like you could use a cup of hot tea."

The smells of spices greeted them atop the stairs. Vaiden's stomach grumbled, famished. He hadn't eaten since breakfast—before the sun had risen. Alvez scurried to the pot hanging in the open fireplace. He stirred the contents, wafting hearty smells into Vaiden's nostrils. He held his stomach, trying to soothe its neediness.

"It'll be done soon," Alvez announced. "I'm sure you're hungry."

Vaiden didn't say anything. He followed Callum to the sitting room, noting the banners of Surnuna hanging on the walls and her symbols and likeness carved into tiling and wooden arches alike.

"You're quite devoted," the Shade said.

"Surnuna is a symbol of life and prosperity," Callum replied, sitting in a cushioned high back chair. He gestured at the empty one across from him, both angled toward a small fireplace. Its golden flames, played with the light in Callum's eyes, making them appear brighter. "She protects us with her warmth and lights the path so we will never be lost."

"I suppose she abandoned those who lived through the Dark Ages."

The king's council shifted in his seat, crossing his legs. "We do not know why she forsook the world during that age, but the sins of our ancestors have long been paid."

"Some might think we're falling into a new kind of Dark Age."

"Let us hope that is not true. Magic was the only thing that kept the world alive, plants growing, and food harvestable. Without it, we would have been a barren world."

Vaiden nodded, finally sliding into the empty chair. It was comfortable, or it would have been if his ribs would let him relax. No matter how he sat, he couldn't seem to find a position that didn't cause some sort of discomfort.

"You're injured." Callum gestured at the wound on his shoulder. He'd forgotten about it.

"Just a graze," he said. "The archers were relentless."

"Alvez."

The captain slid through the archway. "Yes, Father?"

"Fetch my kit," he replied. "Our guest needs tending."

He nodded, vanishing from sight again.

"That's not necessary," Vaiden said. "I don't plan on being here long."

"Nonsense," Callum scoffed. "You have an open wound. It must be cleaned."

Alvez returned with a leather pouch, which he laid out on the table between the chairs. It had many instruments Vaiden recognized from Caroline's medic bag. Others he'd never seen before and didn't want to know what they did.

"You're a healer," Vaiden announced.

"A long time ago," he said, "back in the Last Empire War. I've long retired to a life of serving the crown, but I assure you, my hands are still quite steady."

"Shades are used to hatchet jobs."

Callum's brows furrowed, something sad reflecting in his eyes. "An unfortunate fact and a shame that those, who didn't treat our kingdom's protectors with respect, shall forever be haunted by."

"I doubt it."

He chuckled. "It seems Alvez did not exaggerate your cynicism."

"It's not cynicism. I'm a realist."

"I'm not sure what that means, but if you would allow me?" He held his hands wide, gesturing at the wound. "It would be easier to remove the shirt."

"Not for me," the Shade grumbled.

"He has broken ribs," Alvez announced, placing a steaming bowl of water on the ground between them. He laid cloth on the table too. "I can help you remove it, if you want."

"We should replace the binding anyway," Vaiden said, standing. He unhooked his belt and tossed it and the swords on the chair.

"Son, get the linen for the binding. Use the spare sheets upstairs."

Alvez did as requested, leaving Callum to help Vaiden to peel off his shirt. Callum gently cut off the binding with a small knife from his kit. The Shade growled at the purple and red blotches dominating his torso. Fighting with the guards had reaggravated his injuries, setting him back a couple more weeks.

"I imagine you are in pain," Callum said, his eyes focused on the injuries.

"Not the worst I've endured," he answered, sliding back in his chair. "Before I returned to the kingdom, I had a run in with a court of vampires, who kicked the crap out of me at their master's command."

"I can't imagine the damage they might have caused." Callum dipped cloth into the hot water and began scrubbing the wound.

"It wasn't fun." Vaiden left out he'd healed rather quickly. He had theories of why. Though he didn't have magic and couldn't harness it, Tatiana had magic. The bind had perks. One of which he assumed might be healing. He'd always healed faster than the average elf, but not as fast as he had since the bind. Being cut off from Tatiana, had plunged him back into normal Shade healing, but he'd managed to keep the emotions. It was strange and something else he needed to discuss with Coastal upon his return.

"Tell me what happened with the king," Callum said, preparing the needle and thread. Vaiden explained how the king had twisted his words and turned on him. The king's council said nothing, besides the occasional head bob while he sewed up the wound. Alvez returned during the story, asking questions, forcing Vaiden to repeat himself—something he hated.

"I don't understand why the king believes Gabriel has turned traitor," the captain said. "He's been an ambassador for a long time. He fought his best against those Corrupted at the fort. It was overwhelming."

Vaiden clenched down his jaw as Callum secured the binding. "It appears the king has reasons to distrust the ambassador, but I wouldn't go as far to believe he has flipped. Gabriel Steel is an honorable man, but why would he ignore the king's order?"

"Killing Kanaris won't change anything," the Shade exhaled, testing the strength of the binding. It was tight. Council Kazquer didn't disappoint. "If anything, it might make the rebels more determined to cut off Alty's head."

"Alty?" Callum's face twisted in delightful confusion. "I haven't heard that one. Though, it is more kind than other names the nobles call him."

"Tiny Tim?"

"No, but they do poke fun at his bad leg."

Vaiden opened his mouth to explain who Tiny Tim was then decided against it. Altamost didn't deserve to be bullied for his bum leg when his mishandling of the Corrupted blight was front and center.

"Why are the Shades in Kiji?" he asked instead.

Callum returned to his seat, folding up the instruments of his kit before sliding them back into the leather pouch. "The announcement was made some time after Dallia arrived," he explained. "He did not discuss it with the council. He signed the order and sent it to every post."

"And none of you argued against it?"

"I assure you, we did." He leaned back in his chair, clasping his hands together. "There's not much we can do after an order is made. I have continued to request the Shades return to their posts, but he keeps saying there's a larger plan."

"He said something similar to me," Vaiden said, sitting. It was harder to sit with the restricted binding, like wearing a corset. He didn't understand why anyone would willingly torture themselves like that. Damn masochists. "Dallia made him send the Shades away then."

"I'm not sure," Callum returned. "I've never seen her animated, like you described, mostly she just stares at him, transfixed, bewitched in a way. It's strange, eerie at times."

"Do you know which magic is her focus?"

"To ascend to Grand Priestess, as you no doubt know, you must possess each flavor of magic. It must be tested and controlled," he explained. "Dallia was born under the sign of Jana, but she can harness the powers of all the goddesses. It makes sense why she transcended after the passing of the former Grand Priest."

"What happened to him?"

"He chose his time."

"Meaning he decided to die."

Callum nodded. "He was in his thousands."

"My mother is in her two thousands."

"It is rare to find elves living so long," he said. "We used to be the most eternal race in this world. I suppose, we are again now that the vampires are gone, but it seems not many stay past their first millennia. Your mother is a rare subject."

"She likes her life."

"Does she remain in the kingdom or has she traveled to Earth?"

"The latter."

"I suppose a new world does bring excitement."

"What are we going to do about Dallia?" Alvez asked, sitting quietly on the floor by the fireplace. Vaiden had forgotten about him. He'd been oddly quiet.

"We can do nothing," Callum answered. "There's not enough evidence to support that she's influencing the king."

"I beg to differ." Vaiden cocked a brow at him. "She's obviously influencing him. The level of infatuation alone suggests—"

"There's still nothing you can do." Callum held his gaze for a couple of seconds before looking at his son. "See if the stew is ready."

He opened his mouth to protest, but ultimately did as his father requested. For a complainer, he seemed well-mannered at home.

"If Dallia has control over Altamost, wouldn't it have broken the closer you reached him?"

Vaiden thought about it. He had stood within touching distance of the king at one point, but whatever hold Dallia had on him hadn't broken. Perhaps it was a more intricate spell. A bewitched item he wore or—Vaiden tried to think of an instance where elven magic overrode his shadeness, but he couldn't think of one.

"There's still something going on."

"I agree," Callum said, "but I don't believe we have the full picture yet." He paused. "You cannot stay in Casimere. If they find you, they will execute you. The number of those accused of being rebel is unfathomable, but the king has charged you with treason. By running, you know, there will be no opportunity to argue."

"There was none to begin with."

"So what will you do?"

"I promised Gabriel's wife that I would find him," Vaiden replied. "I keep my promises."

"I suppose you can ask him for the truth when you see him."

He nodded.

"I'm also guessing you have a plan to escape the city." His brows raised with questions. "The fact they weren't able to find you this afternoon, speaks volumes of your abilities."

Vaiden shrugged, wanting to give away none of his secrets. In truth, there was only one route he knew that led outside of the city. It would be risky, but the market provided plenty of cover in the bustle of the day. Guards would be checking every vendor cart, but Vaiden wasn't sure how thorough they would be with the animals.

Horses and oxen were bulky, but the serpents traveled with long-haired sloth-like creatures called rousens. They weren't slow like sloths, but they were friendly and extremely dumb. There would be plenty of hair to hide him, but it would be stinky. Not to mention a test of his strength, but what was new?

"I'm guessing by sheltering me here, you don't agree with how the king is handling things," Vaiden said. "Is the kingdom looking at the wrong official for treason?"

Callum smiled. "I'm not working with the rebels, but someone needs to look after our citizens. It is mine and the rest of the council's duty to ensure things do not get worse."

"They will."

"Yes, I expect they will." His smile vanished.

Alvez poked his head through the archway. "Food's done."

"Thank Jana," Vaiden sighed, his stomach rumbling in celebration. "I'm starving."

32

Tatiana opened her eyes. The smell of salt and the sea lingered in her nose. She lifted her hands, confused not to find a layer of sand coating them. It had been comfortable on the beach, not dreadfully hot or cold, just right for a swim, but they had never made it in the water.

They. She exhaled, missing the strength of Vaiden's arms, the solidness of his body, and his earthy musk. They hadn't spoken in the dream, holding each other and gazing into one another's eyes, like they were the pieces missing from a puzzle. She missed him. *God*, did she miss him. Her hand found that invisible golden rope that bound them together. She tugged, but no response had returned—for six months.

"She's awake," someone whispered, tilting her head toward the voice to find Zarah on the phone and an elf, cleaning her hands with a washcloth.

"Coastal," she managed, her voice weak. The elf's liquid black hair had been pulled back into a braid that fell nearly to her waist, exposing her pleasing features. It was difficult for Tatiana to gaze into her almost lineless face and believe this person had lived for two thousand years.

"Lie still." She brushed back Tatiana's hair. Coastal's eyes softened, letting Tatiana know her condition had been worse than she thought. "You've lost a lot of blood."

"The park." Tatiana's tongue was like sandpaper against the roof of her mouth.

"I've taken care of it," Zarah announced, finished with her phone call. Her hair was slicked back from her face and wet. She had changed into a T-shirt and sweatpants—more than likely loaned from Coastal. "The scene will be cleaned up."

"Zabetha?" Her heart weighed heavily, thinking of the serpent who'd risked everything to tell Tatiana the truth. Rocahn had lied. Koreen had been a desirable candidate for coupling, pointing them toward any rejected serpent for motive in his death.

In New York City, the powerful serpents lived like the mob. She had read articles about entire families wiped out because a coupling contract had been broken. What if Koreen's family had moved back to Arda out of fear? It seemed desperate given the rumors that the kingdom killed those returning from Earth.

"I'm sorry, Ana." Zarah frowned. "She was part of the scene."

"So her family doesn't even get to know she's gone?" Tatiana tried to sit up, but Coastal gently pushed her back down.

"You need rest," the elf said. "I have healed your wound, but your body must deal with the trauma."

"I'll send a discreet note to the family," Zarah added.

"And what will it say?" Tatiana asked, the pit of her stomach blackening. "Your daughter's dead?"

"Something more eloquent, I'm sure."

Tatiana let out an exasperated sound, slamming her fist against the table she laid upon. "So this is what the Underground does. It sends notes."

"What do you want me to do?" the vampire asked. "I can't bring her back. I can't deliver her body to the family. We would be targets of the police."

"We are the victims! We *defended* ourselves."

"You used magic, Tatiana. Are you ready to tell the public about your little secret?"

"That's enough!" Coastal pushed between them, forcing Zarah away. She threw her hands in the air, muttering something in a foreign language—more than likely the vampire language from Arda. Coastal pivoted back to Tatiana, her brows arching. "It is sad what happened to Zabetha, but Zarah is right. She had killed at the scene. Judges won't care about who attacked who when it comes to supernatural crimes. You know that, Ana."

"I can make arguments. I'm an attorney. I know how to speak to judges and juries."

"Is that a risk you want to take?" Coastal asked softer. "They will look at you differently for having magic, especially since you have failed to register yourself as a practitioner."

Tatiana opened her mouth to argue, but she was right. The laws concerning magic were strict. It was a foreign power with no way for the government to regulate it, so the only way legislators could fight it was to place strict laws, prohibiting certain magic and forcing practitioners to register themselves for monitoring. To violate these laws could mean spending time in a supernatural prison or, if the practitioner was especially malicious, they could be executed.

"Zabetha deserves better," she said instead, letting her weight settle back on the table. Her middle was sore from both the trauma and healing. It took energy to heal, something she'd learned from Coastal's lessons. It was why the elderly weren't as receptive to healing magic. They had less energy to give.

"The letter will give her family some closure," Coastal said. "At least, they will know she is gone and not just disappeared."

"Without a body, you know, she cannot enter the Morenlands."

"Their faith does indicate that."

"We'll bury her," Zarah voiced somewhere beyond her field of vision. "The letter will specify she had a proper burial required by their faith."

"Good." The elf crossed her arms, emphasizing her impressive chest in the satiny nightgown. Like most of her clothes, it was a variant of purple, which Coastal had informed Tatiana was the sacred color of her goddess, Alumpius. She'd worn the color the majority of her life; though, during her time on Earth, she had allowed other hues to enter her wardrobe.

"Now, it is late," Coastal said. "Stay here tonight, rest, and tomorrow figure out what you need to do. Zarah, why don't you help Ana to the guest room?"

"I can do it myself." Tatiana pushed off the table using her elbows. She grimaced at the soreness of her abdominal muscles while Zarah lingered within reaching distance. Her feet touched the cool tiled flooring, her knees wobbling.

"Let me—"

"I'm fine!" she hissed before her right leg slipped from underneath her. Zarah grabbed her waist, keeping her from falling.

"You're not fine," the vampire pressed, helping her stand again. "You were stabbed."

While Tatiana remained upset about the park and that the Underground was involved, she couldn't blame Zarah. She'd only come along because Tatiana had asked for her help. What had she expected? Not this, she thought. Zabetha didn't deserve to die. No *one* should have died. Now that the

Underground had protected Tatiana, what would they want in return? A favor? Nothing could ever be that simple.

Zarah helped her to the guest bedroom. It was an awkward crawl, considering the vampire was much shorter than her. She wrapped her left arm around Zarah's shoulders, leaning heavily against her. Fire radiated through her side, engulfing her ribs and hips in the inferno. She focused on her breathing with each step, in through her nose and out her mouth. Zarah remained patient until they finally reached the bedroom.

"I'm sorry I failed you," she said, her voice as controlled as her expression. "It was my job to protect you and I couldn't even do that."

"We were outnumbered," Tatiana answered, sinking into the bed. "You couldn't have been in two places at once."

"Vaiden wouldn't have let it happen."

"You need to stop comparing yourself to him."

She shook her head. "I'm a vampire. I should have easily disposed of those serpents."

"And if I hadn't hesitated to use my magic, they wouldn't have gotten the opportunity to overwhelm me." There were three of them. She had self-defense training, but nothing compared to Zarah and Vaiden. Even with her arms glowing electric blue—a clear warning, they had bravely continued their assault.

She hadn't heard the one flanking her, a tactical ambush while the other two had distracted her. The blue fire had reacted to the knife, surging out of her like a bomb. It had done that before—when Jen had stabbed her through the stomach, but the blast hadn't been as powerful as the last time. Her wound hadn't cauterized like it had six months ago either.

"Still." Zarah clicked her tongue, shifting on her heels. "You got hurt. I failed. Vaiden would be disappointed. I can hear him now. 'You couldn't even stop a band of serpents. The emperor must be so proud of his star guard.' He'll hold this over my head forever."

"I'm fine." She reached out her hand and Zarah gently took it. "And Vaiden's in Arda. He doesn't have to know."

"Coastal will tell him."

She hadn't thought about that. Coastal was his mother, a fact that baffled Tatiana. One, the High Elf was a lesbian—on Arda there was no science to help women get pregnant without a man—but also because Coastal appeared youthful. She barely looked thirty, yet she had a son, who was two hundred years old—something that also baffled Tatiana.

She understood that elves were eternal. They aged to a certain point. Vaiden claimed they did age, but the process moved immeasurably slow. Vampires were somewhat different. The turned appeared frozen at the age they became vampires, while the natural borns grew like the elves, and seemed to stop aging. While there wasn't any scientific explanation for their ageless states, Tatiana wondered if magic played a part in it. Shades were void of magic though, which weakened her theory.

"It doesn't matter." Tatiana let go of her hand. "You aren't responsible for stabbing me. The serpent, who stabbed me, is."

Zarah crossed her arms over the white T-shirt Coastal had lent her. Bold letters across it read, "if you are reading this, you're welcome." It was baggy on Zarah's smaller, more athletic frame, but she wagered, the vampire appreciated not being caked in blood. Not that she didn't trust Zarah's control, but being covered in someone else's body fluids was gross.

She looked down at her stomach where Coastal had cut away her shirt. Dried blood clung to her skin where her side had been sliced open, but the wound had disappeared. Not even a scar remained, thanks to Coastal's magic.

"Would you like a different shirt?" Zarah asked.

"No, it's fine," she exhaled, but it grew into a yawn. "I'm just tired."

"I am sorry about Zabetha. I wish I could do more, but it is out of my hands now."

Tatiana's eyes flicked up to meet Zarah's softened gaze. Pressure bubbled in her chest. She fought from raising her voice. "*You* called in the Underground."

"I had to protect you."

"You had to protect *you*."

She shook her head. "I wasn't worried about me, but if anyone—cameras or a witness—saw you and put you at a crime scene, then you were in danger. I couldn't let that happen."

"So what now?" Tatiana asked, throwing her legs on the bed. "I owe the Underground a debt? I don't want to be in their debt. I don't want anything to do with them."

"It's on me," she replied. "You weren't mentioned."

The pressure building in Tatiana's chest eased, liquifying into something warm and light. How could she be so selfish? Zarah had protected her. She meant everything that entailed from physical to reputational preservation. Tatiana could be jailed for lying about her magic and even disbarred. Zarah had put herself at the mercy of the Underground to ensure it didn't come to that. And the thanks she got?

"Zarah," she sighed. "I'm sorry. I should be thanking you—*thank you* for saving me and covering for me."

"I promised Vaiden to look after you. I owe him."

"But this is more than paying Vaiden back. You're putting yourself in the Underground's path and that's a risk."

Zarah plopped down next to her. "Don't worry about that." She smirked. "One of the big wigs is quite infatuated with me."

"Oh?" She raised a brow at her. "When did this happen?"

"I'm not sure *when*, but I'm supposed to go to dinner with him some time." She shrugged. "It's part of a past deal, but I might be stringing him along for more perks."

"That's a dangerous road to walk. What if he wants more than just dinner?"

"Well, he's human. He won't push or I'll rip out his throat."

Tatiana pursed her lips.

Zarah slapped her leg. "I'm joking." She grinned. "He's not that stupid. He knows what I'm capable of, or if he doesn't, then he's quite arrogant to think he could handle me."

"It seems like he's extorting you for this date."

The vampire waved it away. "Do you need anything?"

Tatiana wanted to push for more details about this deal she'd made with a leader of the Underground, but there was a more urgent matter stretching her bladder. Zarah helped her to the bathroom, allowing Tatiana privacy while she relieved herself and freshened up. There was a lot more blood than she'd originally thought, wondering if Coastal hadn't healed her, would she have survived? Not that she didn't believe in science and medicine, but her wound had been serious and Coastal's apartment had been much closer than the hospital. Zarah retrieved her some fresh pajamas, which did not seem to be clothes that would fit Coastal.

"It probably belonged to one of her girlfriends," the vampire said, helping Tatiana pull the maroon tank top over her head.

"Why does everything hurt?" she groaned.

"You use your core for a lot more than you think."

When she finished dressing, Zarah helped her back to the bed, forcing her to sleep on the left side away from the door.

"I'll be fine," Tatiana argued.

"Serpents tried to kill you. I'm not letting you out of my sight until this is all finished."

"What does that mean?"

"It means, get used to seeing this face." She gestured at herself. "Because I will be at your side everywhere you go."

"You can't come to work with me."

"Try to stop me." There was an edge to Zarah's voice, something that made Tatiana pause from arguing. Tonight had surprised the vampire, something that rarely happened. Zarah called herself a failure because she had gotten hurt. Maybe it was an overreaction to stay in her sights until the trial was finished, but the serpents had made it clear they would kill to bury the truth about this case. They couldn't take any chances.

"We'll iron out the details tomorrow," Tatiana said, laying her head against the pillow.

"Really?" Zarah's brows raised in surprise. "You're giving up that easily?"

"Zabetha is dead. Whoever is behind Koreen's death is cleaning up loose ends and Mr. Slaseezor is the fall guy. I can't let him be the next victim in this case."

"We need access to the Grand Den," Zarah said, pulling the covers over her legs. "Maybe we should do it my way?"

"I need proof, using force will only get us in trouble with the court."

"I was thinking more on the lines of guilting a young one into sharing the truth."

"We don't even know what Arkella looks like."

"I found her social media page. I could send her an anonymous message, claiming that I know who killed Koreen and why."

Despite the implication of witness tampering and an outright lie, Tatiana snickered. "That would definitely get her attention."

"We should try, at least, to force her out in the open."

It was a risk, but they were running out of time. By the end of the week, Tatiana needed a witness or proof that Mr. Slaseezor didn't knowingly kill Koreen. Without it, he could be executed or sent back to Arda. Both options had to be treated like a death sentence. Arda was a different world where she couldn't protect him.

"Let's do it."

33

The wind cut through Vaiden like a million icicles carved into unseen arrows. It swirled around the trees—through them—like their massive trunks and thick limbs were nothing more than sheets, hanging on a line. Vaiden sniffled, no longer feeling the tip of his nose or his feet and hands. His cheeks blazed despite the cowl he wore, covering all his face, but his eyes, which watered to no end.

He'd left Casimere with nothing more than the clothes on his back and his weapons. Callum had offered him supplies, but it would be too heavy to carry, hanging on the underside of a *rousen*. His plan worked, but it'd cost him half a day when the serpents traveled west of Casimere. When they had finally stopped for lunch, he'd untied himself from the creature and scurried into the forest, not before helping himself to a bag of food and a cloak. He'd since picked up more supplies from villages and cottages along the way.

The best path to White Star with the road to Haven under siege of Corrupted was through the mountain passes. He knew they would be ravished by winter, but the further he climbed north, the more he cursed himself for not cutting through Haven again. It would be stupid, but as his lungs raged against the cold thin air and his bones rattled deep inside his body, he knew this wasn't any smarter.

Only his thoughts kept him company those last few days, hiking through ghostly paths. Alvez had offered to accompany him, though his father had protested. It made sense why he thought to run with Vaiden. Guards and witnesses had seen them together. Anyone would think they had conspired to assassinate the king over the fall of Fort Khali or whatever story Altamost planned to spin.

In the end, Callum had won the argument. He could keep his son safe—keep him hidden, as long as Alvez remained quiet and did as instructed. The young captain had looked to Vaiden, pleading for aid in his defense, but the Shade truly didn't want to chaperone the kid again. He had enough problems without adding him as a liability; though, as he trekked through the snow and ice, stealing Alvez's warmth might have been worth it.

His anger was the only thing left keeping him warm. Gabriel had lied to him—had kept him from fulfilling his purpose. It burned a hole through his middle, flaring his nostrils while he pushed his legs onward. Altamost was right to find it suspicious. Hell, Vaiden did. Why else would Gabriel keep him from pursuing Kanaris, if not to protect him? What did that mean? Was Gabriel a traitor? He had claimed killing the rebel leader would change nothing. How could he know that?

Vaiden shook his head. Gabriel had been an ambassador for over a century. He'd counseled kings and emperors, chieftains, and war leaders alike. At the end of the Last Empire War, he'd been the deciding vote to end the vampires. He knew how politicians thought and how the people following them would react to certain news. It made him useful and also vital in negotiations.

Vaiden dissected every conversation he'd had with Gabriel these past few months, trying to pinpoint one conversation that proved his friend's betrayal. Maybe he was blinded by that friendship, but he couldn't believe Gabriel would help the rebels. They hadn't appeared friendly toward him at Fort Khali. Maybe it was the illusion they had wanted to create, but Gabriel was a bad liar. Vaiden knew all his tells.

It nagged him that Gabriel had lied about the king's order, and Vaiden had missed it. Maybe he trusted Gabriel too much? After all their years in service, fighting side-by-side, protecting another one, bleeding for each other—how could he not? Maybe that trust had been taken advantage of. Maybe Gabriel had only brought Vaiden back to Arda for selfish reasons. He'd missed him. Such sentiment Vaiden hadn't understood until he'd seen his friend's smiling face and then Caroline. He'd missed them too—something impossible without the bind.

Despite the numbness spreading through his face, he frowned. He had returned to Arda for Gabriel— to end this damn civil war and stop the Corrupted blight. The king had ordered him to kill Kanaris, but the Shade's true purpose would always be to eliminate the Corrupted. A secondary mission had been added by promising Caroline to return Gabriel to her. Vaiden would. He needed answers.

The wind howled, making him thankful for the cowl covering his ears. It would be senseless to use his expanded hearing in such harsh conditions, but even his sight was useless in the barrage of snow and ice plaguing the mountain. He was effectively blind in this hellscape, only his sense of direction and instinct guided him through the passes.

This far north, the only real danger was freezing to death. Hypothermia silently stalked its prey, disorienting it, cutting off oxygen, and exhausting it to no end. Well, to only *one* end, Vaiden shivered. He sent his thanks to Surnuna, grateful that his body still produced heat. As long as he kept moving, shivering, and thinking, everything would be fine.

The beach was warm. Concrete on a summer day was scolding hot. What would he give for a bowl of bubbling stew or a proper winter coat? The furs draped tightly around his shoulders might as well have been an old T-shirt, thinned from years of wear. Maybe he should have let Alvez tag along. At least his annoying voice would have kept Vaiden's temper boiling.

There were better ways to keep warm, he thought, envisioning Tatiana's long silky legs tangled with his beneath thick blankets. She radiated with heat of the flesh and power. It'd burned down his cabin and nearly the woods surrounding Jen's hideout, if not for Mystic Crane.

He exhaled, a cloud of his frozen breath swirled around him. Numbness crept up his legs, covering his knees. He would need to stop soon and find shelter. The weather worsened at night. He hadn't forgotten.

Then he saw it, something that would have made him wept if he didn't think his eyes would freeze shut—the pillars to Alumpius. He'd long forgotten the purpose of the pillars and why someone spent time and energy hauling the stones north to carve them, but they symbolized salvation for Vaiden in that moment.

Each pillar was placed along natural stairs that led to the shrine of Alumpius. In the haze of snow and wind, Vaiden couldn't depict her forty-foot statue, but he knew her arms would be open, holding a horn in one hand, and an unrolled scroll in the other. Her blind eyes would be shielded by a headdress of pearls that some sociopath took the time to carve during similar conditions. How had their hands not shook in such perilous weather?

At the top of the stairs the land evened out, but Vaiden couldn't see much through the white whirling around him. He used his gloved hands to shield his eyes, but little good did they do. Dark smudges through the white embodied his memory of where the shacks would be placed. While the smaller one on the left would be more ideal to warm faster, he knew the larger building on the right had a fireplace and beds.

The wind harassed him up the steps where he clung to the railing before reaching the door. Smartly the architects had built the doors to open inwards so he didn't have to remove a foot of snow before spilling into the shrine's dormitory.

His mother had lived there the majority of her early life, praising the goddess and helping the faithful, who'd journeyed to each shrine. She described it as a home, a family, and a place of fun, warmth, and peace. He stared at the shabby conditions, the worn grayed wood with complete indifference. His legs carried him as far to the fireplace before collapsing, throwing the pack from his back.

"Fuck," he breathed, opening the damper. Air rushed through the chimney, letting him know the contraption still worked. Pieces of old wood and ash filled the fireplace, but he turned to the rest of the room, frantically searching for something better to burn.

He crawled to the nearest bed, ripping the sheet from the straw-stuffed mattress. His numb fingers shredded it into strips, filling the firebox. He returned to the mattress, unsheathing his knife and stabbed through the material to reveal the straw within. It was dry, much to his pleasure. He chucked a healthy handful into the fireplace.

"Come on, come on, come on," he whispered, becoming increasingly more annoyed while he searched for his flint. "Gotcha!" His hands shook violently while he hovered it and his knife at the base of the fireplace. After the first few attempts, he took off his gloves, stretching his fingers and warming them with his breath.

He shivered against the cold, huddled in his furs, pouring all his concentration into lighting the fire. Three more attempts. Nothing. The cold sunk deeper into his bones, gripping its icy hand around his heart. Why fight, it whispered with the wind. Wouldn't it be easier to bundle in the blankets the dormitories had to offer and just rest? After all his journeying, he needed sleep—deep sleep, engulfed in peace and darkness, no worries of the rebellion, the Corrupted, or returning to Earth.

Like hell. He struck the flint hard. Sparks flew, igniting the straw. A pent up breath rushed through him as needle pricks ignited across his hands, warmed by the fire. He tended to it, making sure it burned thoroughly before gathering more fuel. Luckily, someone had brought in an arm load of chopped wood before the shrine had been abandoned.

Once the fire was roaring, he searched through the rest of the building for supplies. It had been picked clean of most resources, but at least a few blankets had been left behind. He pushed a bed in front of the fireplace before opening his pack for dinner. His own supplies were dwindling, he thought, chewing on a piece of bread.

It was a few days hike to White Star. He didn't know what he would find there. Maybe the duke in charge had closed their gates, allowing none of Altamost's loyalists entry. Gabriel had claimed Kanaris sheltered there. It would mean the duke of the city more than likely housed the rebel leader. Any other scenario would be strange, unless Kanaris and his bunch were able to bully the guards and take over White Star. They would have heard if the rebels had officially taken over a city though. There would be new demands and a submission of victory, something the rebels hadn't accomplished through their efforts.

While Vaiden shivered in front of the fire, melting snow in a metal cup for some water, he thought White Star was a smart and dumb city to take. If they were allies with the duke, fine, but if the rebels focused their efforts to take the one city no enemies of the entire world cared to occupy, it was a joke. Altamost wouldn't waste time fighting in such weather. He'd wait for the rebels to grow tired of the cold and abandon the city, which they would because who wouldn't? He remembered occasionally living in White Star as a child. It sucked.

Different scenarios raced through his mind of how he might infiltrate the city. There wouldn't be *rousen* fur to hide in. Though if one did travel this far north, he might skin it for its fur.

He doubted the gates would be open, especially if Altamost knew Kanaris was in the city. The outer walls weren't too high. He could watch guard shifts, learn their routine, and then find a particular unsecured patch of the wall and scale it. He'd need rope and a hook, but it was doable, though he wasn't sure what his ribs might think about that.

A breath shuddered through his lips. There was no sense in strategizing until he knew specifics about the guards, the gates, and the presence of the rebels. If they housed there, they would help keep their friends safe—if they were truly friends and not hostages.

Too many questions, Vaiden thought. Inside, it would be a piece of cake to navigate. He'd spent a great amount of time in his younger years learning the inner workings of the city—the best places to hide and blind spots from guard posts. He wondered if other children thought to do the same. If he'd had the ability of emotions when he was a teenager, perhaps he would have been a nuisance, like Gabriel had been in Abrita Shores.

He snorted. Sun and moon. Gabriel had been chaotic in his early years while Vaiden had been controlled and calculated. When had they eclipsed and Gabriel had become the stable one while Vaiden ran around like an idiot, dodging swords and arrows?

He laid on the bed, bundled in his furs and blankets. The journey was long and far from over. Rescuing Gabriel wouldn't solve the Corrupted crisis or the civil war. He wasn't sure why it mattered to him that the kingdom's issues be resolved before he returned to Earth. Given the option, he would choose for the Corrupted blight to be over.

The people would feel safer, but it wouldn't end the paranoia, especially in Casimere where they seemed more concerned if their neighbors were rebels or not. He thought it was silly, given the fact the Corrupted could turn people into monstrosities. Perhaps the people believed the Corrupted blight was far away and they were safe behind stone walls. They hadn't heard the truth about Fort Khali, he'd wagered. He doubted Brevene had either.

He wondered what the rebels thought. Some of them had risked their lives to capture Gabriel. They knew who the true enemy of the kingdom was. Would they put behind their pride and help destroy the Corrupted? He imagined yes, but no. There would be stipulations and one of those demands would be Altamost's head.

They didn't know about Grand Priestess Dallia's hold over him though, or whatever else was going on there. All Vaiden's instincts screamed something was wrong, yet the other guards had remained unaffected. Maybe they were under a spell too. He couldn't know. He couldn't feel magic, but Callum had brought up a good point. When he had approached them, the spell should have broken. If it wasn't magic, then what the hell was going on in Casimere?

Too many questions, he thought again. Sleep poured over him like a tidal wave, forcing him to relax. The fire was strong. It would be fine. He could sleep. The wind howled beyond the shack's walls, rattling the boards, but he pushed the sound away. Alumpius would watch over him, like she had his mother before him. Perhaps she wouldn't mind that he was one of her sister's creations.

***

Vaiden crouched behind a tree, watching the guards atop White Star's walls, lazily strutting from post to post. There was no sense of urgency to their posture, not that the Shade thought they needed to worry about an assault on the city. It did seem odd to find guards laughing, sharing a smoke, and flirting.

His eyes studied the opened gates, another surprise. The pompous guards he might believe, but opened gates? They were at war, housing the enemy of the crown. Maybe Gabriel's contacts had been wrong, or maybe Kanaris had decided not to stay in White Star for the winter. Vaiden wouldn't blame him. The cold sucked.

He surveyed another guard shift before the cold bit through his bones, encouraging him to move. With his furs wrapped tightly around him, he slithered to the road, joining a band of merchants for added protection. His fingers tightened around the grip of his sword while he watched the guards posted at the gates. They smiled at the merchants, quipping to the ones they recognized. None of them remarked on the Shade entering their walls, but perhaps the brown furs helped create the illusion he was a Novice, like most of the populace.

White Star wasn't a grand city, like Casimere. There wasn't much enticement to live in the north, besides the fact no one wanted to fight in the ice and snow. The Corrupted wouldn't come this far north either, perhaps making White Star a bit more attractive. Mostly hunters and their families lived in the city. The outer wall was made of stone, but the inner walls dividing the city between the residential and commercial zones were wooden.

Hammering rang in his ears as he passed the blacksmith. The fire glow casting orange hues reflecting in the snow. Vaiden admired their craft and envied the hot environment they worked in. He followed the merchants to the stables, splitting off toward the market. It was a small crowd of local vendors, selling meat, bread, and other valuable wares. A few of them stood at their booths outside, while the lucky ones, like the baker, had a store from which to sell.

Most of the buildings in White Star were made of stone. Vaiden thought cabins would be warmer, but the architects of the city had wanted the citizens to have homes as impenetrable as the mountain at its back. Who cared about their comfort?

Despite the cold, the city bustled. Vaiden didn't remember it ever being so lively or crowded, especially after midday. A bard played her lute, sitting on a fountain filled with snow. Her angelic voice carried a soft melody, a tune of how a tyrant wronged a goddess and how she would have her vengeance. He could only imagine this bard was a child of Alumpius, like so many angry with Rothnar's ban of their goddess.

"What did the scouts say?" a woman whispered to his left. He leaned against a wall, pretending to listen to the bard's next song.

"Perry claims the Corrupted are moving west," a younger woman answered. Younger because the other one had visible lines on her eternal face.

"After Fort Khali, the crown should be panicked to get this blight under control."

"Perry says there's been no direction from Casimere."

"By the goddesses," sighed the older woman. "When will the people of Casimere stand up to their king? Do they not know what's happening in the east?"

"They don't care. They think they're safe behind their city walls. Who knows if the king is telling them the truth? Fort Khali was flattened. Even a garrison filled with soldiers was no match for the Corrupted."

"Surnuna save us."

"At least we have the ambassador." Vaiden's chest tightened with her words. Gabriel was there. The rebels had him.

"Thank Wara, Perry's scouts were able to get him. Maybe Casimere will finally understand how serious we are."

The younger one pulled her hood over strawberry blonde hair. A sad smile spread across her face. "We can only hope."

These women were standing in the open while guards patrolled closely by. They didn't seem afraid their conversation would be overheard. In Casimere, they would have been arrested for conspiracy. Gabriel had been right. White Star had indeed aligned with the rebels.

Vaiden slipped into the tavern, evading any suspicion of the stranger lingering in the market. He ordered tea, paying with the coin Callum had graciously given him. The hot liquid warmed his core while he listened to more gossip in the tavern. They all seemed to be in agreement. Altamost was a bad king, who wouldn't help his people. Fort Khali's destruction was a tragedy. He was surprised by how these rebel sympathizers mourned the king's soldiers, but perhaps they too understood the Corrupted were the real enemy.

After he finished his tea and warmed his bones, he set off into the streets again. Like he'd never left, he navigated the windy alleys through the residential district to the wooden barrier between the city and the manor where the duke lodged. To his credit, he didn't live alone. Soldiers, not on city watch, lived in the lower levels. The cellar had been long converted into a three cell prison for criminals.

Vaiden didn't remember many arrests during his youth, but he recalled Coastal and her friends celebrating when a rapist had been caught. Rape was one of the most serious crimes in Eskandor. In Layetta's scripture, she called for anyone who lay with another against their will to be burned of their evil, coated in stone, denied Paradise, and sent to Aegan's realm for unending agony. They had taken the Goddess of Fertility's words literally when sentencing that particular rapist.

His fingers glided down the wooden wall, searching for air. He found it behind a thick winterberry bush. Even after all these years, they hadn't patched the broken boards. He slid them aside, creating a space big enough for him to slip through, but not with all his gear. His eyes searched the surrounding buildings. It would be suspicious to find a pile of furs and a pack laying on the ground. The guards would sound an alarm, knowing they had an interloper in their midst.

He stuffed the furs and pack behind some brush, burying them in a layer of snow. Not that he believed he would have time to recover them after rescuing Gabriel, but given the option, he didn't want to leave White Star without proper gear. Food they could find in nature, but they would freeze to death in the harsh climate without cover.

It was a tight squeeze, but he slipped between the broken boards, crawling belly down in the snow. More brush covered his grand entrance, thankfully. Wearing only his Shade black clothes and cowl made him stick out like a sore thumb in the white of winter, but he wasn't about to strip naked in the freezing cold.

He stayed low, crouch-walking through the brush growing along the wooden wall. His eyes stayed fixed on the guards, carefreely strolling along the gatehouse and patrolling the courtyard. The outer wall had joined with the mountain at the manor's back, blackening the sky, but providing darkness and cover when Vaiden finally reached the gardens.

When the guards shifted, he ran across the courtyard, slamming his back against the hard stone of the manor. His ribs groaned, reminding him of their existence. He pushed the pain away, his eyes searching for easy access. None, as expected.

He grimaced, sliding off his gloves and stretching his fingers. Most of the activity would be in the lower levels of the manor. The best route to go undetected was to infiltrate through the upper floors. Vaiden gripped the dark stone, realizing quickly it was quite slippery. Ice, he frowned. *Of course.*

Wind slapped his exposed skin, forcing him to slip his gloves back on. It was the best plan, but he needed a different route inside. His eyes searched the gardens, searching for something as simple as a ladder. Nothing, but across the way, he spied lattice where ice vine snaked up a section of the manor with pale blooms.

Excellent, he smiled, darting across the way. The windows were boarded up this time of winter, but he was mindful of the doors and the patrolling guards. The lattice hadn't been there last time he'd visited White Star. Maybe this duke was partial to plants. Something odd, considering he chose to live in a winter hellscape.

The climb brought him to the third level. Far enough he thought, swinging to a terrace. He dropped low, whirling around to watch the guards for sudden movement. They carried on, blissfully ignorant of the Shade infiltrating their manor. What clowns.

He tried the door, knowing full well only an idiot wouldn't lock all their doors and windows in full winter. The wind could blow that shit open with a backhand. The nob twisted and twisted and finally clicked. *Unlocked.* Vaiden snorted. The duke needed to hire better staff.

The Shade slipped inside, shutting the door behind him quiet as a whisper. The wind cooperated, letting him lock it into place. An opened door would only invite suspicion. Even if the staff forgot this particular exit, he would do their job for them in the name of self-preservation.

The corridor was only lit by a few strategically placed candelabra along the corners. His training kicked in, sticking to the shadows and toggling his nocturnal sight to see through the darkness. This part of the manor belonged to the duke and his family as their personal apartments. Vaiden expected them to be empty that time of day, except for the occasional servant tending to chores.

He turned on his expanded hearing, searching for others on the level. There was shuffling in rooms far east of him, so he headed in the opposite direction. Through all his years living in White Star, he'd never explored the duke's manor. Perhaps an oversight, but how would he have known it might have been vital information later in his life?

He found the stairs leading to the lower levels and quickly descended, using his hearing to ensure no one would spot him. Floral arrangements decorated the balcony of the second level, overlooking the grand hall. Soldiers, courtiers, and others flooded downstairs. Vaiden hid behind an archway, covered by shadows and a bouquet of flowers that wilted the longer he remained. Of course they would use magic to keep blooms alive during the harsh winter. The Shade crouched, following the railing of the balcony across the way. The main doors pushed open, forcing him to stop in his tracks.

"Aw, cousin!" A finely dressed man approached the descendent of someone with giant blood in his veins. He was dressed in furs, a full beard covering his face, but he smiled at the smaller man, softening his features. "Come, come," he said. "I have news from our friends."

Vaiden followed them until they disappeared from his field of view, leaving him and the chatter in the grand hall. He disengaged his expanded hearing, following the routes of the balconies to the other side of the manor. Inside the dark corridor, he stood straight, groaning with his aching ribs. He opened doors, peering inside long enough to find closets, bedrooms, and storage. Most of the clothes belonged to women or men much smaller than him. A disguise could help him navigate to the cellar, but the main hall was packed. Someone would spot him.

He followed the sound of voices, using the servant stairs to traverse to the main floor. The men had entered the viewing hall, a glorified throne room for someone without a crown, where citizens of the city could be granted audience with the duke. Footsteps approached, forcing Vaiden into a side room. He listened as the steps moved onward and disappeared in the distance.

Exhaling into the dark room, he found a round table with a few chairs scattered around it. On the opposite wall hung a map of Arda. An old one, Vaiden noted, spotting lines dividing the vampire's land amongst the surviving kingdoms. He approached the table where flag markers sat arranged on a detailed map carved into its surface.

Black flags were pinned to Fort Khali and Haven, making Vaiden realize these were places destroyed by the Corrupted. Red flags symbolized those loyal to the crown, which had been placed on Casimere, Brevene, and Duncan Village. The rebels' yellow banners occupied Abrita Shores, White Star, and a few other villages. Mysogus waved a white flag—perhaps neutral ground. Kiji was notably empty. He memorized the map, wondering if Altamost had a similar ensemble in his war room.

Voices grew louder behind a curtain on the right side of the room. The Shade peeked, finding the viewing hall crowded with soldiers, rebels, and citizens of White Star. They gossiped, sharing mugs of ale, and seemed unbothered by the cold. Perhaps the manor was magically heated. It would make sense why no one walked around in furs.

At the heart of the hall where the duke stood in front of his wooden throne, he raised his mug saluting the bigger man by his side. "To Kanaris, my cousin, our friend..."

Vaiden didn't hear the rest of his speech. Purpose swelled inside him, flooding his veins in adrenaline and a call to action. He unsheathed his short sword, his eyes locking on the target. The crowd shifted, blocking his view momentarily, but when they parted—his heart sank.

"Gabriel," he breathed. The ambassador stood with his hands behind his back. Vaiden was surprised they hadn't gagged him, considering Gabriel's quick tongue. The sun to his moon watched the crowd and the men at center stage with calculation. He didn't appear hurt, but it had been nearly a month since Fort Khali. A practitioner could have healed him too. Vaiden was grateful he was in one piece.

"Enough with the inaction!" the duke announced. "We will remove King Altamost. We will defeat the Corrupted and we will reunite this great kingdom once again!"

The men cheered as the duke basked in their praise. Vaiden wondered who wanted to replace the king on the throne. Two guesses who, he thought, his eyes sliding back to Kanaris. Purpose drummed through his chest, radiating a great need through his limbs. He wet his lips, his fingers tightened around the grip of his short sword, waiting as the big man turned his back.

"We will rise and take back this kingdom," the duke said. "Down with Altamost. Down with the Corrupted. For Haven!"

The men chanted "for Haven," pumping their fists to the sky.

Go time.

34

The men chanted, celebrating the declaration made by Duke Heiron. It was an inspiring speech made to entice the visceral reaction of every face crowding the viewing hall. Kanaris and his cousin, the duke, had forged a great alliance. They'd recruited many of the smaller villages, growing their numbers. The crown had no idea how many of its citizens had turned against it. Even Brevene's allegiance quivered upon hearing the news about Fort Khali.

Heiron stayed in contact with all the dukes and duchesses of the land, communicating with lower lords and ladies too. They needed to know what was going on in the kingdom, how the Corrupted blight grew, and the facts—not propaganda from the crown. Gabriel agreed with most of it, but he saw through the duke too. He wanted power.

The station of White Star wasn't good enough for a man as decorated as Heiron, a former general with noble blood and real influence in the kingdom and abroad. He'd bragged about his friends in the serpent kingdom and the alliances he'd forged with the trolls throughout his military years. Gabriel listened, internally rolling his eyes.

The duke was talk. Where were the invitations from other kingdoms? Where was the aid of these "friends" of his? From what Gabriel had witnessed, the only friends the duke had collected were within White Star's walls. He'd made these alliances in effort to take Casimere. Something he'd failed to do over a year ago.

However, he would not deny the duke's accomplishments. In his own way, he had made an effort to unite the kingdom in hopes to stop the Corrupted blight. The only one standing in the way of that success was King Altamost. On that, Gabriel agreed.

A gasp sliced through the crowd, draining the hall of air and sound. Gabriel blinked at the frozen faces of the rebels, confused by their expressions until his eyes fell upon Kanaris and the blade against his throat.

"Hiya, Gabe." Vaiden smiled behind the rebel leader, holding the short sword with an iron grip. It was heavier than a dagger, but even as tall as the Shade was, Kanaris was much larger.

"Stop this at once!" the duke exclaimed. "Unhand him!"

The soldiers unsheathed their weapons. Controlled rage sparkled in their eyes. The rebels had fought side-by-side with Kanaris. They had survived Haven together. Each of them would give their lives for him. If they rushed Vaiden, not only would he kill their leader, but he would make good on their fealty.

Emotion drained from Vaiden's face, replaced by an unending emptiness Gabriel knew well. He turned Kanaris, who had his hands raised wide and naked. "Why would I do that?" asked the Shade.

"The ambassador has not been harmed," Kanaris's deep voice rumbled.

"Tell your men to lay down their arms."

"They will do nothing of the sort," the duke said. "You are surrounded. If you aim to survive this night, release my cousin."

Kanaris hissed, the tip of the blade digging into his skin. "That's just a shaving accident," Vaiden growled. "Push me. I *dare* you."

One of the rebels stepped forward. An elf with a shaved head, short, but built in solid muscle that he no doubt had developed from years of hard labor on the docks of Haven.

"You got some luck, friend," announced the elf, adjusting his hand around the grip of his sword. "Make it inside this city, fairing the weather, just to be cut down by our lot. Is that how your king rewards his best?"

The Shade replied, his voice dark as night, "I have no king,"

"Then you are lost, boy," spat the elf, pointing his sword at Vaiden like a finger. "And a pawn for a king you don't even follow."

"My arm is getting really tired. It would be tragic if I slipped."

"Perry," Kanaris warned.

He stepped back, holding his arms wide with the sword. His arrogant face silently beckoned for the Shade to come play.

"Good doggie." Vaiden smirked. "Tell your friends to do the same."

"You heard the man," Perry said. "Back up!"

The crowd did as instructed, but no one sheathed their weapons.

"Where do we go from here?" the duke asked. "You are obviously a capable soldier. If you are not aligned with the crown, why oppose us? We strive to better this kingdom. To take it back from the Corrupted and—"

"Save your breath, Heiron." Gabriel waved his hands. "He's only here for me."

Vaiden shifted his grip where he could face his friend. "Caroline's safe. I sent her to Mysogus."

Gabriel loosened a pent-up breath. It'd been the first news he'd heard about his wife. The rebels gathered a few families who had fled from Fort Khali, but no news had reached White Star of those who'd traveled the farmer's path. "Thank Surnuna."

"Now tell me the truth, Gabe." Something in Vaiden's voice made the ambassador feel like the blade was truly against his neck. "Did Altamost order me to Fort Khali?"

Gabriel's heart sank. There was only one reason why he'd question that. "You've talked to the king."

"Did you lie to me?"

"I delayed you."

"Are you a rebel?"

Gabriel's brows furrowed together. "Of course not. You saw them take me at the fort."

The Shade stepped away from Kanaris, the point of his sword still lodged against his throat. "The king believes differently and his argument is damn compelling."

Perry rushed forward, swinging for Vaiden's head, but the Shade evaded, dipping under his swing. Kanaris retreated to his cousin's side. A wall of guards formed between them and the men's clashing swords. Though Perry had fury and passion on his side, the Shade had something more—battle experience.

He disarmed the fisherman, pushing him to the ground. Perry bared his teeth at the Shade. "Come on now! Get it over with!"

Vaiden relaxed, the point of his sword slinging Perry's weapon out of reach. "You're not my mark," he said, casting a grave look over his shoulder at Gabriel.

"Did the king send you here to kill me?"

"Don't be silly." Vaiden sheathed his sword, turning his back on Perry. "Caroline sent me here."

The rebel scrambled for his weapon, climbing to his feet, arms swinging to strike.

"Perry, no!" Kanaris ordered.

The Shade turned, hands on his hips, staring down at the man with his sword raised. Sweat slid down his creased forehead while he struggled between striking the Shade or following his leader's orders.

"Easy, Perr," another soldier said.

"He came here to kill you!" Perry spat, his words obviously aimed at Kanaris.

"If he wanted to kill me, he would have."

"The king sent him here!"

"I have no king," the Shade repeated.

"Bollocks! You came here on a mission and I don't believe for a second it has anything to do with that pansy ass ambassador. He's not worth the trouble."

Vaiden raised a brow at Gabriel then turned back to the fisherman. "He grows on you."

"Give me one reason why I shouldn't cut down this piece of shit!"

"You need him," Gabriel replied, drawing everyone's attention. "To clarify, he is Vaiden Zarren, the personal guard to King Rothnar, and the prized assassin of the Forty-Second. He can get you into Casimere."

Whispers erupted through the hall. Gabriel knew of Vaiden's fame amongst soldiers. He'd stopped more assassination attempts than any other guard in their history. He also knew secrets of Casimere's structure, but that was lesser known, by only those closest to him.

Perry's tight expression softened, his eyes widening with great realization as he lowered his weapon. He would have never won that fight. Vaiden had gone easy on him.

Duke Heiron's eyes scanned the crowd, weighing their feelings on this new information. He leaned into his cousin's shoulder, whispering something too quietly for Gabriel to hear over the rumbles of discomfort through the hall. Kanaris pawed his throat where the blade had cut through his skin. It wasn't a deep cut, but the rebel leader had been rattled. Vaiden had infiltrated their city and put a blade against his throat in the middle of a crowded room. If that didn't rattle someone, they had to be as empty as the Shades.

"We have a lot to catch up on," Vaiden's voice whispered across Gabriel's skin. He nodded, relaxing with the moon to his sun returned to his side.

"I'm glad you're here," the ambassador admitted. "It's good to see a friendly face."

"I'm not friendly."

"I know you're mad, but you will come to understand."

"No, I will not."

"Vaiden," he exhaled. "We are surrounded by enemies. Don't you think you should be worried if they'll let us live?"

"They will, but you and I have other business."

"What does that mean?"

"Later."

"Vaiden Zarren," the duke began, his jeweled hands clasped in front of him. He rolled his thumbs over each other, a nervous gesture or a thinking one. "It seems we could benefit from one another."

"How do I benefit from you?" He crossed his arms, a small pained noise escaping deep in his chest. Gabriel fought from glancing at him.

"You want the ambassador," Heiron returned. "I can promise his safety. In return, you tell us how to sneak into Casimere."

"Why would I do that?"

"So we can end this bloody war," Perry growled.

"And how will breaking into Casimere accomplish that?" Vaiden fired back. "You think killing the king will solve this crisis. That's no different a strategy than me killing your leader to end the rebellion."

"He's right," Kanaris said. "Altamost is only one part of the problem in our kingdom."

"What's your plan to destroy the Corrupted?" the Shade asked.

"Does Altamost have one?" The duke tilted his head, his eyebrows raising in amusement. "Last I heard, he sent the Shades to Kiji."

"He did, but if you don't have a plan to defeat the Corrupted, what good are you to me?"

"You seem to misunderstand this situation." Heiron snapped his fingers and his guards surrounded Vaiden and Gabriel. "You came into my house and threatened my cousin. I am within my rights to have you jailed and sentenced for attempted assassination."

"Is that so?"

"Vaiden," Gabriel warned.

The Shade shrugged. "I guess you're not getting into Casimere then."

"There's ways we can *extract* that information from you." The ends of Heiron's lips curled, like a cat toying with a mouse. Part of him liked the idea of chaining Vaiden up and seeing what it would take to break him.

"He's a Shade," Kanaris whispered.

"You think that because he's wearing black," the duke said. "He's not like any Shade I've ever met."

"Vaiden *is* a Shade," Gabriel urged, "with the highest kill count in Kiji. It was the reason of why he was drafted into the Forty-Second and the reason Rothnar wanted him by his side. If you wish to break him, you will be sorely disappointed. Shades don't break. They don't feel pain, like we do, and they do not care about our lives."

"They do care about the welfare of Eskandor." Heiron put his hands on his hips, shifting his gaze to Vaiden. "You are tasked with protecting the kingdom. The same as any other Shade."

Vaiden looked at Gabriel, gesturing for him to answer. "Shades are tasked with destroying the Corrupted," he explained. "We give them titles like the kingdom's protectors to ease others, especially the High Elves. It's not in their abilities to care what happens to our kingdom, only that it is cleansed of the Corrupted. That is their purpose—their *only* true purpose."

"So this scum." Perry pointed at Vaiden. "Doesn't care if our homes are burned to dust or our children are murdered, as long as the Corrupted are destroyed."

"Yes."

The soldiers murmured, casting sidelong looks at the only Shade in the hall. Vaiden stood tall, his hands relaxed on the hilt of his swords. His dark eyes scanned their faces with complete indifference before landing on Kanaris. The rebel leader stroked his beard, his expression tight as he studied his men and their guests.

"Vaiden is right, though," Gabriel said. "Without a plan to rid this kingdom of the Corrupted, what good is it to tear each other down?"

"Get the king out of the way and we can have more soldiers and the Shades," Perry replied.

"Murdering the king doesn't give you the allegiance of his soldiers or the people of Casimere. Brevene would not back a usurper and you will find neither will our allies."

"You'd make sure of that. Wouldn't ya, ambassador?"

"There is a decorum between the rulers of the world," Gabriel explained, "one of respect and mutual assurances. They do not kill each other, and they do not support their murderer's succession."

Duke Heiron flinched with his words, recovering quickly by clearing his throat and raising his hands. The soldiers quietened, turning to their leaders with questions glittering in their eyes. How could they trust Vaiden and Gabriel? They weren't allies. Until this meeting, they had Gabriel locked in a cell. His only contact had been with guards who had brought his meals and the occasional visit from Heiron.

The duke wanted power, which meant influence in the neighboring kingdoms. He wanted to use Gabriel to obtain that influence and eventually gain the crown. His ambition was clear, but Kanaris did not seem to have the same goals. From this meeting, he appeared to be a quiet man, a thinking one. He had the rebels' loyalty and, without him, Heiron didn't have an army strong enough to take Casimere. The duke had to know that. It was why he had made a spectacle of Kanaris's return to White Star. He'd returned with the scouts. From what, Gabriel didn't know.

"We have the same goals ultimately," Heiron said, his voice controlled and soft. "We all want the Corrupted destroyed. We all want the kingdom united and free of this infighting. We can work together to resolve this blight and end our people's suffering."

"Then what's your plan?" Vaiden asked.

"We need to free the Shades."

"They're not chained."

"The king's orders keep them in Kiji Village."

"You're not the king. You can't override his orders."

"Yes, but perhaps we could fake his orders."

Gabriel raised a brow at the duke. "The Shades documents are sealed with a special insignia that only the king has. It is one of the few items passed down between our monarchs."

"I'm aware." Heiron nodded. "Only a handful of appointed officials even know what the insignia looks like."

"Yes, I—" His next words trapped in his throat as he gazed into the duke's smiling face. "That's why you need me, to make this insignia, but I assure you, my memory is not—"

"That won't be necessary, but we will need you, ambassador, to deliver this message and convince the Shades it is an order from the king."

"Why not send him?" Perry thumbed at Vaiden.

"I will not go to Kiji," he growled.

"We will need him to get our forces into Casimere," Kanaris replied.

"I'm telling you already that's not going to be easy," Vaiden said. "It'll require a small team, but they'll have to be your best. Even so, I'm enemy number one in the city. If I'm spotted, the operation is dead. They'll know you're coming."

"Then you show us the way and you stay behind," Perry offered.

His shoulders slumped, a pout forming on his lips. "And here I was planning to give you a tour of the palace."

The rebel scowled at him, but a thought crossed his mind. "You could get us over the walls and into the palace?"

"Sure." Vaiden shrugged, like he could do it in his sleep. Gabriel knew it wouldn't be that easy, especially since the guards of the city would be looking for him, but Vaiden had never backed down from adversity. Gabriel thought it was because his shadeness made him void of fear, but recently, he wondered if it derived from Vaiden's competitive nature to be the best—if Shades could desire. Why else would they keep score in Kiji?

"Let us break for dinner," Heiron announced. "Our guest needs to clean up from his travels, I'm sure."

"I go wherever Gabriel goes," Vaiden replied.

"Of course." The duke gestured at one of his men. "Take them upstairs and keep guards on their doors. I don't want to take any chances on them getting cold feet or for one of our own to take their frustrations out on them. We will reconvene after dinner."

Gabriel and Vaiden kindly went with four armed guards upstairs, two in front and two behind them. They led them to a room far nicer than the cell Gabriel had lived in. The windows were boarded up for winter, giving no hope they could escape without fighting the army outside.

Once the doors closed, Vaiden marched to the bed, wrapping a blanket of fur tightly around his body. "It's fucking freezing." He grimaced, watching the flowers in a vase beside him wilt.

Gabriel snorted. Not for a second had he believed Vaiden would abandon him. If he was alive, he'd find Gabriel and he had. Sun and moon, Surnuna and Moren, reunited once again.

35

The smell of lavender and citrus woke Tatiana. She groaned; her eyelids slit open to find the bed empty. Her hand patted the space where Zarah had laid, facing the door—protecting Tatiana in case more serpents had followed them and planned to attack while they had slept. The bed was cold, letting her know Zarah had been up for a while.

She sat up, grimacing at the soreness of her middle, but it didn't hurt as much as the night before. If anything, it felt like a bruise or a bad sunburn, but there were no marks on her as she studied her side in the bathroom mirror. Her hair was wild in her reflection, frizzy and tangled, but she ignored it. Dark circles had formed under her eyes, emphasized by her blanched skin—side effects from healing, but she would rather look awful than spend days in the hospital and subsequent weeks recovering.

Off white walls led her to the main room, an open concept of living room, dining, and kitchen. Her feet dragged across the marbled floors, making her wonder what product was used to keep them shiny and clean. She needed it for her countertops. Thick violet curtains draped across the large windows, shielding the room from the bright morning sun, but the room wasn't dark by any means. Recessed lighting expertly placed along the high vaulted ceiling shone a spacious, clean area, smelling much like the bed she'd slept in.

Tatiana noted the ten foot statue of Alumpius, standing in a corner where spot lights illuminated her shielded eyes by a head dress of pearls. Coastal claimed it was a miniature depiction of the goddess's statue at her shrine on Arda. The piece carved from stone would have set Coastal back a pretty penny, but Tatiana knew it had been gifted to her from a friend. Since the former High Priestess was quite popular, she wondered which of her friends had that kind of money to give something outrageously intricate and specialized. It had to be worth a fortune. Other depictions of Alumpius hung in the form of banners and tapestries adorning the walls amongst modern furniture.

Coastal sipped from a mug at the dining table, cleaned of Tatiana's blood. "Tea?" she asked.

"Please." Tatiana sat adjacent to her, taking the cup her magical teacher offered. The warm liquid soothed her scratchy throat. She'd slept hard and dreamless, letting her body heal away the trauma and pain. As she shifted in the chair, discomfort blooming in her middle, she knew she could handle it and not let it distract her from her job.

"Thank you for healing me," she said.

Coastal dipped her chin in a nod. "I'm glad I was here," she replied, her eyes softening. They were silver, not gray, enhanced by her white magic. It was why Tatiana's eyes were a vibrant blue and why Jen's had been violet. Coastal claimed not everyone's eyes symbolized the kind of power they held, but it was common.

"I've given some thought to the situation with Mystic Crane," Coastal announced. "We can work on warding magic, but there's no spell that I can cast that will protect you. You would have to do it yourself."

"OK, what kind of spell would I need to learn?"

"There's different kinds. We can discuss it when you have time for training."

"Ackrim took over my mind, and suddenly I was sitting somewhere far away. He could read my thoughts. I have to protect myself from him and Mystic Crane."

"Magic takes time to learn," she replied. "What Ackrim did is called projection. It hijacks the mind and brings it somewhere else. Illusionary magic is mostly harmless, though I do know of stories where someone had used it to torture another's mind."

"Great." Tatiana slumped in her chair, wondering if Ackrim was behind Jen's manifestation at the club. "So Mystic Crane can make me hallucinate until I agree to join them."

Coastal patted her knee. "If they wanted to do that, they would have already," she said. "After this case is over, we will work on warding magic."

After this case, but the case wasn't solved. By the end of the week, she would be standing in front of a judge, needing proof to set Mr. Slaseezor free or his execution trial would begin with the state explaining how he had the opportunity and means to kill Koreen, and how the ceremony was the perfect cover. By the end of the day, would the jury believe her when she said Mr. Slaseezor didn't kill Koreen? He was set up with no proof to who set him up or why. She took a deep breath. Arkella had the information they needed. She knew Koreen in ways the others didn't. They needed to talk to her.

"Hey," a voice startled her. She found a young woman sliding into Coastal's lap. The High Elf pushed back the brunette's hair, looking deeply into her eyes and smiling softly. They kissed, forcing Tatiana's stare to sink to her mug. The girl appeared in her early twenties and by how she dressed in a crop top and mini skirt, they had hit the club last night. Had she seen Coastal heal her? It was a lot of blood, which meant a lot of questions—not to mention a vampire had delivered her to Coastal.

"I'll text you," the girl said, standing. Her eyes swept over Tatiana, making her aware of how awful she looked. She threaded her fingers through her hair, hoping to soften the frizziness. The girl's expression stayed pleasant as she kissed Coastal once more before leaving the apartment.

"She seems nice," Tatiana said, smiling weakly into her mug.

"I don't even remember her name," Coastal snorted.

The front door opened and closed, making Tatiana wonder if the girl had forgotten something. Zarah strolled inside, wearing the same T-shirt from the night before and a pair of leggings.

"Oh good, you're up," she announced, looking up from her phone.

"Where were you?" Tatiana asked. "What happened to 'I'm not letting you out of my sight?'"

She held up a paper bag and plopped it on the table. "Breakfast for you."

Tatiana raised a brow at her then looked inside, a croissant. "Thanks, but I'm not really hungry."

"It'll give you energy to help you heal." Coastal pushed the bag closer to her. "Eat."

She wouldn't argue with the two-thousand-year-old High Elf who had healed countless wounds. It was the equivalent of arguing with a mechanic about how to change the oil in a car. The mechanic had all the experience and education. Tatiana could ask questions and get a second opinion, but she had never changed the oil in a car, so she had to put her faith in the mechanic's abilities—and Coastal's knowledge.

Her teeth ripped into the croissant, admiring the flaky texture and buttery taste. It was good. She wondered how Zarah decided on it. Had she ever eaten a croissant? Had they made them on Arda when she was human?

"I messaged Arkella," Zarah said. "She has yet to respond to my vague accusation of her involvement in Koreen's murder."

"You accused her?" Tatiana put down her empty cup . "That's not—"

"I simply said that I knew about her and Koreen and the reason he was murdered," she interceded. "She'll draw her own conclusions from such a statement."

"She may be the witness we need for this case. Let's remember not to—"

"Intimidate witnesses."

"Or?"

Zarah spread her hands wide. "I'm just trying to help, Ana."

She finished her croissant, knowing a decision had been made the night before about Arkella. Maybe her family or the Grand Den wouldn't allow her to come forward with information, but whatever the reason, Mr. Slaseezor did not deserve to be found guilty for something he did not knowingly do. Tatiana was tasked with making the court and a jury understand he was innocent. She could not do that without proof or enough deniability that he had anything to do with the switch of the prop knife for the real thing.

"We don't want to break any laws," Tatiana said.

"Asking questions is not breaking laws." The vampire crossed her arms, frowning. It would be easier to let Zarah do what she wanted, to gather information by any means necessary, but Tatiana had seen what that meant to the Underground. She wouldn't be responsible for what that "by any means necessary" could mean.

"Harassment and stalking, threatening harm, and targeting certain demographics are also violations of the law," she explained. "I don't want to have to defend two clients this week." A smile pulled on Zarah's lips, but it slipped when Tatiana continued. "Or explain to the State Bar of California why my friend has been claiming to be my associate, questioning and intimidating people for my gain."

"Do you want my help or not?"

"I want you to understand the limits of helping. We talk to Arkella, if she allows it, but we do not suggest we will hurt her or others for answers. We don't push ourselves into her home or follow her until she gives us information."

The vampire's nose wrinkled as if she smelled something foul. "We don't have that kind of time."

"No, but we also cannot afford to waste time on a witness who doesn't want to help. We can kindly ask for that help, but if they don't want to, they won't help."

"What about a subpoena?"

"That is not helpful without knowing the information she might have because if she doesn't know anything then I'll look incompetent to the judge and jury."

"Is it not a great honor to speak the truth and give the dead dignity?" Coastal asked.

"Some people are willing to live with shame rather than tell the truth," Tatiana explained. "It might be because they're afraid or don't want the attention, and sometimes, sadly, because people just don't want to deal with it."

Coastal threaded her fingers through her hair, thinking. "That's somehow worse?"

"Ignoring a problem, not wanting to take responsibility, or not wanting to help someone because of an inconvenience to your day, I find selfish, especially when a person's life is at risk."

"And Arkella might be the key to your client's release?"

"Might be, but we won't know for sure unless she tells us what she knows."

"It seems there's a lot of questions in this case." Coastal patted Tatiana's knee again, smiling weakly. "It's Tuesday. I expect by Friday, you need to prove your client's innocence."

"By Thursday," she corrected. "It's easier to get a judge to agree to a motion of dismal than a jury to acquit a supernatural," she explained. "I need solid proof though, or it goes to an expedient trial."

"And you don't want to leave it to a jury."

"It's only a one day trial per the rules of the Supernatural Law Act."

Coastal shook her head. "So much for fairness."

"The emperor wouldn't even give them a trial," Zarah said. "He'd just execute them."

"This isn't Arda," Coastal replied, "and the vampire empire is no more."

Tatiana pushed away from the table, standing. "I need to get to work," she said, gazing at Zarah. "Can you drop me off at my car?"

"I had it moved to your apartment."

"You had it moved?"

She nodded. "I'll take you home, but like I said last night, I'm with you until this trial is over."

Tatiana frowned, wishing Zarah had forgotten. She should have been relieved that someone as able as Zarah wanted to protect her, but she hadn't figured out how to explain it to her coworkers and the staff at Pearson and Associates. By public knowledge, Zarah was the widow of Harvey Dellawood. They were friends, but Zarah didn't have an occupation—or at least a known one, especially not as an agent of the Underground.

"Be careful," Coastal said, rising from her chair. She hugged Tatiana, which made her have to stoop from their height difference. Without shoes, Coastal was only five-foot-four.

"We will," Zarah answered, her voice somehow comforting. Tatiana didn't have to do this alone. As much as she hated lying, she hated the idea of being stabbed again more. If Zarah wasn't there or if Tatiana hadn't used the blue fire, those serpents would have killed her.

Coastal gave her a gentle squeeze and stepped back, her silver eyes soft and filled with age that her body did not reflect. "If Mystic Crane tries anything, call me and if you need more help..."

"I don't plan on meeting in any parks at night again," she snorted. "I'll call if Ackrim tries to speak to me again."

"If he does happen to use projection again, just remember you are not really where he is," Coastal said. "Think about your real surroundings, if it's cold or hot, if you are standing or sitting, and use it to break the connection. It's not a cure all, but it can work with a strong enough mind."

"I broke a vampire's gaze when they used glamour on me," she replied.

"Mr. Thomas was a master." Zarah pointed out.

"Be careful," Coastal repeated.

They drove to Tatiana's apartment, almost in near silence if not for the radio. Tatiana's car sat in her parking space, like she'd never left home the night before. She inspected it, finding nothing out of place. Her eyes shifted to the underside of the car, squatting down and feeling with her hand for hiding crevices.

"What are you searching for?" Zarah asked, her arms crossed.

"Trackers," she answered.

"I promise the agents of the Underground aren't that sophisticated."

"It's for my own paranoia's sake."

The vampire let her finish the inspection, watching the parking lot like security might do. Tatiana stood, hands on her hips. She wondered if Zarah had told the Underground who it belonged to, but the vampire had already confessed she'd left out Tatiana's name. They could run her plates though and learn she'd been there and lived in the building.

"How much do you trust the Underground?" Tatiana asked as they proceeded inside the apartment complex, finding her keys as they rode the elevator.

"I don't, but I know their people only do as directed," she explained. "They are discreet because to know information may lead to consequences later."

"You don't believe their natural curiosity will get the better of them?"

"I know what it's like to be in a position where you do as ordered and not to ask questions."

"As the ambassador or the emperor's personal guard?"

"As an enforcer for a court."

The elevator's doors slid open, revealing other tenants waiting to board. They exited, navigating their way to Tatiana's apartment. She breathed in the familiar scent of her home, clean cotton which misted periodically from a dispenser.

"I need to take a shower," Tatiana said. "Would you like a change of clothes? I'm not sure if I have something that will fit you, but a blazer can transform a look."

"It's ninety degrees outside." Zarah followed her into the bedroom. "I'm not wearing a jacket."

"A blouse and a skirt?"

"Take your shower," she said as they moved to the closet. "I'll find something."

Tatiana grabbed fresh undergarments, a satiny tank top, a blazer with three-fourth sleeves, and some gray slacks. She would have preferred a dress in the summer heat, but she wanted to wear something practical if she needed to run or fight. Not that she expected attacks in broad daylight, but she wouldn't put it past the serpents. Whatever their motivations, they didn't want the public to learn the truth about Koreen's death. It couldn't be good. If people resorted to murder in a cover up, then they were protecting something or someone.

While she scrubbed away the dried blood from her skin, she wondered if those serpents had been sent by the Grand Den or Arkella's family to silence Zabetha. Her chest tightened thinking about her and how she bravely had come forward to reveal Rocahn's deception. Did Rocahn know that her friend was dead? How far would she go to keep the truth from Tatiana and her husband?

They needed to talk. She hadn't returned Tatiana's call for getting permission to enter the Grand Den. Something was wrong. Rocahn had been forthcoming and willing to talk, but she'd dodged Tatiana's call and had hidden the truth about Koreen's coupling desirability. Had the Grand Den or Arkella's family threatened her? They were wealthy from what Zabetha had explained and they had looked down at Koreen, dismissing him as a match for their daughter.

Tatiana dressed, questions drafting in her head. How could the police close this case so easily? Maybe they didn't want to deal with the headache or maybe they truly believed Mr. Slaseezor was guilty. His fingerprints were on the blade. He'd performed the ceremony in front of innumerable witnesses. It appeared cut and dry, but the more Tatiana sank into this case, the more questions she was left with.

Maybe that was a good defense. She could argue the police only did half the job and didn't investigate further for the truth. From what she'd learned, Mr. Slaseezor never had any issues or resentment toward Koreen. He had no reason to hurt him. He had admired a young one's passion to learn about their faith and culture from Arda. That didn't sound like someone who wanted Koreen dead. That sounded like someone who'd taken a young man under his wing and had given him the opportunity to learn what he desired.

She emerged from the bathroom, finding Zarah dressed in a short sleeve dress that would have been form fitting on Tatiana, but the vampire didn't have Tatiana's curves. It hung on her athletic build loosely, but with a belt fastened at her waist, it appeared fashionable and business acceptable, especially with her hair pulled into a low bun.

Tatiana cocked a brow at her. "You're wearing a dress."

"So?"

"What if you need to fight?"

"A true warrior can defend themselves under any circumstances, even in restrictive clothing," she explained, a cocky smirk pulling with her lips. "You forget I grew up in Arda, where wearing gowns is custom for most women."

"I picture you wearing them on occasions, like at special events, but not the majority of the time."

"Only when I was a guard of the emperor, did I generally wear pants."

"Good to know." Tatiana skipped accessories and makeup. It was too hot for either. A reason why she'd pulled her hair into a high ponytail. She selected a pair of black loafers and dress socks, sitting on the bed next to Zarah to slip them on. "Is it mandatory for women to wear dresses on Arda?"

"No, it is a choice," she answered. "Most who travel wear pants, but it's simpler to make dresses than pants when sewing by hand."

"Oh." Tatiana hadn't thought about simple things, like tailoring, in the medieval world. People would have to make their own clothes, unless they were wealthy enough to hire someone to do it for them. Sometimes she took for granted how easy life was in the modern era.

"I do miss the gowns sometimes." Zarah pursed her lips, her eyes studying something unseen. "And the world, but Earth is my home."

She left out that the other kingdoms of Arda had forced the vampires through the doors or had executed them on sight. Though her own experiences with Zarah's kind wasn't the best impression, Zarah wasn't a bad person. Vaiden trusted her so Tatiana had. After these last few months getting to know her, even though they disagreed about the Underground, she regarded her as a friend.

Tatiana's phone rang. She scooped it up, immediately recognizing the number as Mr. Slaseezor's den. "Hello, this is Tatiana Smith," she said automatically.

"It's Rocahn. We need to talk."

36

Emptiness filled Vaiden's core, draining the light in his eyes and relaxing his face into his natural frown. He stared at Gabriel, sitting across from him in front of the roaring fireplace of their shared room. It was nicer than any prison cell, but they didn't have true privacy with guards standing outside their door.

Relief had deflated Gabriel's body into his chair while Vaiden explained Caroline's journey from the tavern to Cobble Road. "There's more," the Shade said, keeping his voice neutral. He didn't want to bring Gabriel the news. It was his wife's place, but he deserved to know. "Caroline's with child."

A tidal wave of emotions poured over his friend's face, too fast for the Shade to read. "She's with child?" he asked, disbelieving. His eyes widened with realization as his next words barely left his lips in a whisper. "I'm going to be a father."

"So you understand why you must go to Mysogus."

His brows knitted together, crumpling his expression. "What?"

"Caroline needs you," Vaiden said. "Stop all this with the king and the rebels and go to your wife. Protect your family."

"Altamost declared me a traitor. I would never make it to Mysogus."

"You would. Just don't dress like Ambassador Steel. Dress like a beggar, a farmer, someone else in a lower station. Keep your head down, be smart, and you'll be fine."

"Vaiden, none of us are safe. Not with the Corrupted blight, not with this civil unrest," Gabriel argued. "I have to make sure my child has a future or what is the point?"

The Shade frowned at him, afraid that his fears had come true. Gabriel would never stop fighting. He would never abandon his oath to protect this kingdom, even from itself. "This isn't on you."

"How is the duke or the rebels going to convince the Shades' command to unleash the battalions?" He stood, his hands waving animatedly. "Heiron isn't in the king's circle. If anything, Casimere already knows his allegiance is with the rebels. The Shades would kill him on sight."

"It's difficult to get information to Kiji," Vaiden returned, settling in his furs. His muscles ached from all the journeying and climbing the manor. He needed rest. Sleep pulled at his eyes. He rubbed at them, hoping to wake them up.

"Then they do not yet know I have been cast out." Gabriel crossed his arms. "I am still the ambassador in their eyes. It's the best plan to unleash the Shades."

"And if you're wrong?" he asked. "Then your child grows up only knowing stories of their father and never truly knowing the man."

Gabriel flinched, his expression sobering into something painful and deep—sorrow, Vaiden thought. Gabriel's mother had died giving birth to him. He knew what it was like growing up with only one parent. Vaiden too, but his father was alive—or, as far as he knew, he was alive.

He could send a letter to the fane north of Mysogus where followers of Moren lived and worshiped their goddess. Her statue was located in Abrita Shores, but the dormitories and fane had been moved outside of its walls, deep in the woods, away from the bustle of city life and nosy neighbors. It did seem an odd choice for the goddess's shrine to be located. The old Shadowed Mountains of the original vampire lands were more appropriate, but that was deep in troll country.

"I want to be with Caroline," Gabriel insisted, "but if we cannot release the Shades, then the Corrupted win."

"Why is that your responsibility?"

"Will you do it, Vaiden?" He pointed a finger at him, his nostrils flaring. "Will you go to Kiji and convince the command to move out the battalions?"

"You know I won't go to Kiji."

"Then someone has to."

"Why does that person have to be you?"

"Because I have the station and the ability."

"You are not the only one talented in negotiations, Gabe."

"Maybe not, but I am willing and able to do whatever is necessary for my child and for my kingdom to survive this blight."

Vaiden exhaled heavily, a small sound escaping his lips of the pain blistering from his ribs. As much as it would relieve him for Gabriel to be reunited with Caroline and for them to remain safe in Mysogus, it wasn't guaranteed the blood mage would not gather enough power to take on the magical school. If it attacked Casimere and won, it would be the test if it could fight the school. They needed to make sure it never came to that.

"Fine," the Shade breathed. "Go to Kiji. Do whatever you want, but answer me this, Gabriel. Why did you lie to me about the king's orders?"

He sat back down, wetting his lips, one of his rare nervous gestures. "The council reached out to me before you crossed over. They told me Altamost had a plan for the kingdom, but he wouldn't share it with them. We have been corresponding through these last few months and we believe the king is unfit for his station. That his mind and heart are not serving the best interest of our people."

"You're planning a coup."

He shook his head. "Leeth wrote laws in stone about the preservation of the crown, but if a monarchy is unwilling to protect his people, may he be removed and cast from the throne."

"Altamost has been rewriting laws."

"What do you mean?"

"I mean, he's mad with power and he thinks he's better than Leeth and that Leeth's words don't matter. I wouldn't be surprised if he repeals some of Duncan's laws too."

Alarm widened with Gabriel's eyes, but they quickly dissolved into thought, searching for something unseen on the stone floors beneath their feet. "It's worse than I thought if he's breaking stone laws."

"It takes quite the hammer to destroy those laws."

"Or a chisel," Gabriel said. "Slowly chipping away, shaping it to be something else, but for what? What is Altamost planning?"

Vaiden shrugged. "He didn't share it with me, but I'd say that priestess has something to do with it."

"Priestess?"

"Dallia."

"The Grand Priestess is in Casimere?"

"She's been there for a long time I think," Vaiden said then continued to explain everything that had happened in the Crystal Keep. "She's influencing the king, but I don't know how. My shadeness didn't seem to break any spells on the king or his guards, which reminds me. Glades made it out."

"Of course, he did," Gabriel glowered. "He tried to pull me with him during the fight at Fort Khali. I'm not sure why, but he said I was too important to leave behind."

"Maybe he knew the rebels planned to take you."

"Maybe, but I feel like his retreat was purposeful, like he'd been ordered to leave prematurely."

"A captain goes down with his ship."

"Exactly! It's been bugging me that he didn't order the retreat and save as many lives as he could have." Gabriel's lips pressed into a fine line, a thought crossing his mind. "You said Dallia is influencing the king, but you're not sure with magic. I know he fancied her when she toured the kingdom. It didn't appear she reciprocated his feelings."

"Maybe she used those feelings as weapons against him."

"I know Dallia. I've known her for decades. She's gentle and soft spoken. We were all delighted with her ascension to Grand Priestess. It might be the only thing the kingdom has agreed on in years."

Vaiden cocked a brow at him. "You never know people quite as much as you *think* you know them," he said. "Everyone has secrets, especially deceptive High Elves."

"That's just it, Vaiden," he replied. "What are *you* hiding?"

He scoffed, but clearly from his friend's face, he was serious. "What do you mean?"

It was Gabriel's turn to frown. His stare pierced through Vaiden's careful mask, searching for something the Shade couldn't decipher. "You've changed," he said. "I could tell when you first stepped through the door. Something was off."

He shrugged again. "That's Earth life for you."

Gabriel sat on the end of his chair, his elbows propped on his knees. He searched Vaiden's face. His own deepened with harsh shadows cast from the firelight. "Don't evade the question."

"I don't remember you asking one."

"What happened on Earth?"

Vaiden thought about being petty, forcing Gabriel to be more specific, but he knew what his friend meant. His eyes dark, like night, searched the sunny sky blue of Gabriel's eyes with opposing suspicion. Could he trust Gabriel, his best friend, his brother-in-arms with the truth? Would it be too much for him to handle? Vaiden had seen Gabriel fight monsters and battle odds stacked against his favor. He'd debated their enemies into submission and made hard choices on behalf of their kingdom. They had known each other since they were teenagers. If he couldn't trust Gabriel, who could he trust?

"I met a woman," Vaiden began. "I was hired to protect her from vampires on Earth, but it became complicated."

"Yes, women do seem to complicate things." A smile tugged on his lips.

"The woman is human, a sorceress, but she didn't know that when we met," he explained. "Her power is unpredictable and when it surfaced it became volatile, but our enemies found us and she almost died. We're not sure exactly how it happened, but our best guess is that her power switched into survival mode and latched onto the nearest thing to keep her alive."

Gabriel's brows furrowed, listening intently to his words. "What did it do?"

"It latched onto me, creating what Coastal calls a metaphysical bind," he answered. "It saved her life, but now we are connected."

"Connected how?" Despite his suspicious expression, Gabriel's voice managed to stay neutral.

"We can see through each other's perspective and Coastal said we can even share each other's thoughts with enough training. She explained that it is supposed to be used for transferring power between both people, but since I'm a Shade, that's not possible."

"She didn't break the bind? Why would she let this sorceress—why would *you* let this sorceress have power over you?"

Vaiden ran a hand through his hair. "It's complicated."

"Complicated how?" Gabriel asked. "You, of all people I know, would never want to be saddled with someone. You don't care—"

"That's the thing." Vaiden snapped his fingers. "The bind unlocked something inside me that allows me to feel—everything."

He blinked at his friend, downloading the information Vaiden had dropped on his head. "What do you mean you can feel?"

"You asked why I cared about things at Fort Khali. This is why. The bind allows me to experience emotions."

"Emotions?" Gabriel straightened, his eyes wide with alarm as he studied the Shade's face.

"Like sadness, happiness, anger, lots of anger. You don't know how angry I was with you on this trip to White Star. It was fucking cold and I blamed you for me having to go through the mountain passes. Though, I guess, I should blame Caroline. I promised to rescue you for her. Of course, you also lied to me, so there were many other reasons to be mad at you."

Gabriel shot to his feet, backing away slowly. He swallowed hard, his face paled even with the heat of the fire. "This is..." He took a deep breath in and out. "Incredible."

"Confusing, especially for me."

"Can you still communicate with this sorceress through the doors?"

Vaiden shook his head. "That line seems disconnected while I'm here."

"But the emotions remain."

"These last few months have given me plenty of practice reading people. It's been frustrating though."

"This makes so much sense." Gabriel paced the room, his eyes shooting to the ceiling, studying something Vaiden couldn't see. "You've been moody and rude. While that's not unusual when you are playing a part or mirroring, it's been more than that. It's been real, not faked. I thought so, but I couldn't believe it. You're a Shade. Shades don't feel, but you *are* changed. It's clear to me, but at the same time, I saw magic dissolve before you, so you still retain what makes you a Shade in that regard."

"It's a lot to process, even for me."

"I can't believe you would let someone with magic have power over you," Gabriel chuckled. "She must be someone special."

The bedroom door swung open, revealing one of their posted guards. He stepped inside surveying the room. Had he eavesdropped on their conversation?

"Dinner is served. You shall dine with the duke and his guests."

***

"*Rousens* are a delicacy," Duke Heiron said, sucking the juices from his fingertips. "It can be a tough meat, but our cooks slow roast them, making them tender and hearty."

Vaiden wouldn't lie, the stew was magnificent. The best thing he had tasted in a long time, but he remained silent, his bowl empty, its contents warming his belly while he stood at the large windows behind the duke's chair. Guards watched him, searching for any movements against their leaders. Kanaris sat on the far side of the room, at the other head of the table, surrounded by his entourage of fishermen turned rebel. They too watched the outsiders with great caution.

The Shade turned his attention to the snow, silently falling like ashes from the mountain. He stared up the behemoth peak, blackening the sky and casting White Star into shadow. As a teenager he'd conquered that mountain with his bare hands. A tremendous and dangerous task that he would never attempt again.

Atop the mountain sat Eskandor's original school of magic, High Tower. As he gazed up the mountain side, hoping to catch a glance of the magical building, his thoughts drifted to the years he'd spent in its halls, learning about magic and how to defend himself. A sad smile spread with his lips. In so many ways, it was his true home—the place he'd been born, the first place he'd thought to return after his time in Kiji.

It was owned by Latimere Greenbrooke, a master vampire and friend of his mother—friend of him too. He wondered how the old man was doing, especially after the death of Lizabeth LaBelle, his chosen daughter—something he hadn't known until after her death. Perhaps he should reach out to him when he returned to Earth, if only to see him.

High Tower was a symbol of evil from the Corrupted. A blood mage, disguised as a priest, had taken over the school, killing many of the faculty and students. The others he had tainted with his power and used their bodies as fodder from the soldiers, who'd first made contact. He'd corrupted over a hundred in the school. Each High Elf of great power had slaughtered those who'd tried to save them—until the Shades had arrived more than a month later. High Tower's fall had shaken the kingdom, shadowed High Elves in doubt of their safety in Sanctuary. It wouldn't be until King Duncan that the faith was restored in Mysogus—some three hundred years later.

Vaiden wasn't sure how Latimere had come to own the former magical school, but he knew the elves of the Second Age had wanted it destroyed, burned to the ground, and cleansed of the evil the Corrupted had inflicted on their people. Latimere had restored it to its former glory. Even though he had offered it back to the elves, they had refused. Well into the Fourth Age, they believed it to be cursed.

"Enough about the food," Perry said, flipping a knife in his hand. "When are we going to Casimere and ridding our kingdom of the cripple?"

Murmurs spread through the room, grunting in approval. They hungered for Altamost's blood, to avenge those they'd lost between Haven and their rebellion. Vaiden understood their disdain for the king. He'd never liked him.

"What about Dallia?" Vaiden asked.

"The Grand Priestess?" The duke shifted in his chair, casting a look at the Shade. "What does she have to do with all this?"

"She's in Casimere," he said. "She's sitting on the king's lap and showering him in praise."

"That doesn't sound like her," Heiron replied.

"I was there. I saw her completely enamored by Altamost and when push came to shove, she protected him."

The duke blinked at his cousin across from him. Kanaris stroked his lush beard with meaty fingers. "That means Mysogus has no leader."

"And?" Gabriel spread his hands wide. "They do have structure for subordinate staff to run the school while the Grand Priestess is away. If you are thinking of infiltrating it, I beg you caution. Some of the most powerful practitioners in our kingdom live there. They won't hesitate to protect the school from your forces."

"It would be foolish to attack the school." Heiron nodded. "Perhaps they might have some insight into why Dallia is in Casimere and when this love affair began with the king."

"You think she's controlling the king?" Perry asked.

"Something is wrong with their relationship," Vaiden answered. "There are reasons why the crown and faith are kept separate."

"One must lead the blind and the other speak for the voiceless," Kanaris said, nodding. "In this Leeth wrote in stone for history to not repeat itself."

"So we must ask ourselves, with the addition of the Grand Priestess, is history repeating?" Heiron asked.

Vaiden rolled his eyes. Of course, a man like the duke wanted to sound profound. He was campaigning. Although aligning with the rebels would alienate him from those in Casimere, the common people of Eskandor would reflect on the fact he had fought to unite the kingdom and to rid them of the Corrupted. If there was anything that made a candidate for the throne attractive, it was the right priorities.

"How will we communicate with Mysogus?" Perry asked. "It's hard enough getting letters to lords and ladies of the kingdom, but Mysogus? The chancery down in Abrita Shores has no access to the magical school and since the Grand Priestess is enthralled with the king, I'm betting she's placed orders to stay any messages that aren't from her or the king."

"You send it to someone not important to the school," Vaiden said.

"Caroline," Gabriel breathed. "She's there. She could find the information we need."

"Your wife is in Mysogus," Heiron said. "Could she be useful?"

"You are asking for her to put herself in danger," Gabriel said, not to the duke, but to Vaiden.

"She's a High Elf and it's her old stomping grounds. She knows how to be careful."

"If Altamost has declared the ambassador a traitor, won't they be inspecting letters addressed to her?" Perry asked.

It was a valid point. If Dallia sent word to the school about Gabriel's status, they may watch Caroline closely or even secure her to a room. Then again, the faithful were neutral to politics of the kingdom. It wasn't their place to pick sides. Maybe a few good ones ran things at Mysogus while their Grand Priestess was away.

"During the Last Empire War, I wrote to my wife under the guise of her cousin," Gabriel explained. "I can do it again. She'll understand."

"Sounds like a plan." Vaiden grinned.

"Sounds like a back up plan you thought through already." Gabriel narrowed his eyes at him. "Is that why you wanted me to go to the school?"

"You know why."

Gabriel searched his face for a moment, surveying if Vaiden's words were truthful. Shades didn't normally have any reason to lie. It was why they were regarded as the most honest kinds of elves, but it was more the lack of caring that made them so frank. Some people found their honesty to be brash.

He didn't know why anyone would be uncomfortable with the truth, but it happened.

"What would you have Caroline do?" the ambassador asked. "She won't be allowed into the meetings with the faithful and she won't be able to sneak into Dallia's chambers."

"She can let us know if the school is on the king's side," Heiron replied. "We need to know who will aid Altamost when we take Casimere."

Gabriel turned his whole body in his seat to glare at the duke. "You won't take Casimere. It doesn't matter how big an army you gather, the city is well defended, or have you forgotten what happened a year ago?"

"We penetrated through the walls."

"You snuck into them because Altamost didn't take your rebellion seriously. Now he has. You don't think the city is ready for another invasion?"

"They have closed all the gates, but the south one," Vaiden said. "Only approved papers of certain citizens may enter the city."

"You got in." Perry pointed out. "Why can't we?"

"I had the son of Callum Kazquer with me. The captain was able to talk the guards into letting me in," Vaiden explained. "I doubt that'll happen again."

"If we don't take Casimere, we can't win the war," Heiron said.

"I don't care about your rebellion," the Shade replied. "I only want the Corrupted destroyed."

"That should be the only priority," Gabriel added.

Heiron slumped in his chair, his expression unfriendly. As a former general, he wanted that victory. Casimere had only fallen once to an enemy and once recovered. Altamost was the sitting king. He'd been ordained by the faith and by the people. He was the rightful leader of the kingdom. Anyone else—even if their intentions were for the betterment of all elves—was a usurper.

"The council knows Altamost is hurting the kingdom," Gabriel said. "They plan to unseat him."

Heiron blinked at Gabriel, his eyes widening with questions. It would end his campaign for the council to overthrow the king. They would vote for one of them to take the crown.

"Who will sit the throne in his place?" Kanaris asked.

"That is unclear."

"Without a candidate, the council's argument will be weak," Heiron scoffed. "The candidate has to declare why they would be better suited for the throne and how Altamost has failed the kingdom."

"I'd say they have a good case," Vaiden replied.

Perry snorted. "All you'd have to say is he sent the Shades to Kiji during a Corrupted blight."

"Ding, ding!" The Shade rang an invisible bell.

"It's more complicated than that," Gabriel said. "The people of Casimere are still prospering. All the major cities in the kingdom have equal quality of life. The blight hasn't—"

"Piss on you!" Perry shot up. "Haven is gone! Burned to the ground. Our people were murdered and mutilated by those Corrupted!"

"It wasn't a *major* city and as far as cities go, none have fallen."

"Fort Khali doesn't count?" Vaiden cocked a brow at his friend.

"It was a stronghold, not a city for citizens."

"It was still part of our defense against any enemy and that includes the damn Corrupted!" spat Perry. Vaiden nodded in agreement.

Gabriel spread his hands wide. "I'm just giving you an example of how the king can counterpoint the council. By appearances, if you were to write down what the Corrupted have accomplished, it is miniscule compared to what an army from another kingdom may have done."

"They're not as organized," Vaiden said, "but they are gearing towards an assault on a major city—more than likely Casimere."

"How do you know that?"

"They followed me and Alvez through Haven."

"You went through Haven?"

"Around it."

"There's nothing to see." Perry sat back down, his jaw locking. "Just ashes."

Those last two words, simple as they were, forced every rebel in the room to look down. Their eyes clouded with something Vaiden couldn't decipher. Their home had been destroyed, but the structures and the village meant nothing in the face of their real losses. Vaiden wondered who Perry had lost. A wife, a father—children? Vaiden didn't know how that felt, not because he was a Shade, but because he'd never lost anyone important to him. It generally wouldn't have bothered him, but with the bind, a loss of someone significant would mean something new to him. He would feel it.

His eyes studied Gabriel, whose face filled with sympathy for the rebels of Haven. He'd lost soldiers, friends, and even his father during war. The ghosts of those lost hovered around him like a cloud, bursting with rain. Vaiden had never considered what his friend had lost through these years—Gabriel had even lost him once.

"The plan remains the same," Heiron announced. "We will have two fronts. The ambassador, escorted by our soldiers, will go to Kiji Village and release the Shades. Perry, you and your scouts will go with the Shade to Casimere."

"And do what?" Vaiden asked.

"Find us a way in," he replied. "Write to your wife, ambassador. The sooner we know Mysogus remains neutral and will not aid the king, the quicker we can secure the throne."

"We need the practitioners of the school to help defeat the Corrupted," Vaiden said.

"Why?" asked Perry. "Isn't that why we're getting the Shades?"

"While us Shades are immune to magic, we can't very well fight meteors falling from the sky."

"He's right, the practitioners will be needed to protect the people," Kanaris said.

"Can your wife convince Mysogus it needs to act against the Corrupted?" Heiron asked.

Gabriel studied the wood grains of the table. "She can try, but I make no guarantees."

"Then it's settled." The duke clapped his hands. "Tomorrow we save Eskandor!"

37

The guards on the door to the den wouldn't allow Zarah entry. Tatiana argued with them, but ultimately, Zarah hadn't received permission from the *daehekans*; therefore, she could not enter. The vampire didn't like the idea of Tatiana going inside alone, but they wagered the biggest and baddest serpents were outside guarding the entrance. They did have more security than usual, Tatiana noted the seven six-foot beefy serpents patrolling the small alley. Perhaps Rocahn had already learned of Zabetha's death.

Another serpent led her inside the den, taking her to the worshiping hall where Koreen had died. An ornate table-length altar sat centered on a dais. It appeared to be the base of a large tree trunk, but it had been carved that way and stained with a mahogany tint and varnished so it shined. The tree was red in the firelight of candles lit along the room. There were no windows in this room or modern electricity. Candles were the only form of light, covering the room in a warm glow, but the outskirts of the hall sank into shadows where any number of assassins could hide.

It was an odd thought from Tatiana, but perhaps Zarah was rubbing off on her, or being connected to Vaiden had given her his perception. Her skin crawled with the need to flip a switch to make the room brighter, but there was none to flip. She could summon the blue fire, but that would only make the serpents more afraid of her. She needed their cooperation. Mr. Slaseezor needed it. She would do nothing but stand at the altar, cleaned of Koreen's blood, waiting for Rocahn while a chill ran up her spine.

The heavy wooden doors sighed as Rocahn opened them. She stepped inside, her hands clasped in front of her, studying the attorney with dark eyes.

There was a shyness to her gate, like she would rather be anywhere but in this room with Tatiana.

"Mrs. Slaseezor," Tatiana said. "We have much to discuss."

"Yes, I imagine we do," Rocahn answered. She moved to the altar, curtsying before it and reciting something in a foreign language. "Koreen laid on this altar that night," she said in English, "surrounded by friends and patrons of the den. We were packed, not a place in this hall was empty. Everyone was so happy."

"Mrs. Slaseezor," Tatiana began. "I received information that Koreen was considered for coupling. My source said that he was highly desired. Why did you lie to me about it?"

"Koreen's family wished to return to Arda. There would be no coupling."

"But Koreen did have a relationship with a member of the Grand Den, a girl named Arkella."

She nodded. "It is unbecoming to engage with another before coupling. I only wanted to protect his memory."

"Mrs. Slaseezor—"

"Rocahn, please." She turned to face Tatiana. "I think we are past such formalities. I really didn't want to lie to you about Koreen, but I promised to look after him and that meant even from himself."

"Did you not think that perhaps Arkella or one of these other rejected families for coupling might have something to do with his death?"

Although she had no eyebrows, they seemed to furrow. "You think they might?"

"That is why I need access to the Grand Den. Arkella's family or one of the others might have information."

Rocahn bowed her head, her eyes studying something on the wooden floor. "I am afraid the Grand Den will not accept a request from us. My husband's arrest has cast us into shame. Until he is sentenced and the den cleared of his shame, we are banned."

"They have already decided he is guilty?"

"It is the best way for them to bargain peace with your kind and to keep the media appeased by denouncing us."

"They've publicly named you?"

She shook her head. "Only that the offending den is under investigation and is not associated with the Grand Den at this time."

"What did Koreen tell you about his relationship with Arkella?" Tatiana asked.

Rocahn stepped away from her, the serpent's eyes studying something in the darkness. "They were in love," she said barely a whisper. "It is against our customs for young ones to engage in certain activities before their families agree to coupling.

"Koreen wanted to join the faith. He would be barred from doing that if anyone learned what they had done. I told him to break it off with her, but he didn't listen, not at first."

Tatiana shifted on her heels. Her pulse steady as she listened to the serpent. They were finally getting somewhere. "What do you mean?"

Rocahn turned her body to look sidelong at the attorney. "Her family had learned of their secret relationship."

"What did they do?"

"If they revealed their secret, their only daughter's reputation would be ruined and they would be cast from the Grand Den." Rocahn approached Tatiana. Her dragon eyes softened with ghosts dancing in her eyes. "Arkella wanted him to run away with her, but he refused, stating they should fight for their love, but her family refused the coupling once, to do it again would be embarrassing. They contacted me and threatened that if we didn't get control of Koreen, the Grand Den would cut all ties with us and have our den shutdown."

"They can't do that."

"The rich and powerful can do anything in this world, Ms. Smith. All they need to do is make a call."

"Did they say what would happen if you did not control Koreen?"

She shook her head. "I made him break things off with Arkella, saying that if he didn't, we would not allow him to participate in the ritual and he would be barred from the den." She grabbed Tatiana's arm, squeezing gently. "I didn't want to do that, Ms. Smith. He was such a good boy. He'd already lost his family. He had nowhere to go."

"What proof do you have of this meeting with Arkella's family?"

She let go of her arm, stepping back. "I have none," she said. "I would have never thought to record them. It all happened so fast. I could not think they would actually hurt Koreen."

"You believe they switched the blades and framed your husband for Koreen's death?"

She nodded, looking down at her hands. "There were so many people in the den that night. Many we knew from the community. Any number of them could have been agents of Arkella's family or from the Grand Den. In the ritual, you pass the blade down a line. Someone must have switched the prop blade for the real one."

"Both blades circulated through the den that night?"

"Yes, it is theater for the audience to not know which blade is which, to make it believable that the ritual is of sacrifice to Shoresleen. In the olden days on Arda, one member of the family would be killed, feeding the blood to our god and if pleased, he would bless the family. Such sacrifice would enrich the den. The more families that joined—the more blood spilled—the greater the den would rise in status in the kingdom."

Tatiana nodded, recalling a version of this explanation from her research. She had never thought about how a den would gain status on Arda though. Serpents didn't have currency in their kingdom.

"But this practice has long ended on Arda," Rocahn said. "My husband had the prop knife made to resemble the real blade. The weight was even."

"How would Mr. Slaseezor know which blade was which by the time both ended up at the altar?"

"The prop blade always came from the right side of the room."

Before Tatiana could ask another question, the doors from the hall burst open. "Zabetha!" a serpent explained, waving a letter. "She's dead!"

"What!" Rocahn raced to the serpent, snatching the letter from her hands. "How?"

Tatiana's chest tightened as Zabetha's friends cried together, embracing. She could tell them how brave their friend was, that she didn't suffer, but that would only turn the serpents of the den on her, blaming her for their friend's death. In truth, Tatiana did blame herself, but the ones responsible for killing Zabetha were dead too. Whoever had attacked them that night were the true ones to blame. Did Arkella's family send those assailants? Or the Grand Den or were they one in the same?

A teary-eyed Rocahn approached Tatiana. "I'm sorry, but I must cut our visit short," she said.

"I understand. If there is anything more you can tell me, please call or email me." She paused. "I'm sorry for your loss."

Rocahn nodded. "She was my dear friend. One of the few people who I could truly trust through this process with my husband."

"What happened to her?" Tatiana's heart weighed on her chest like an anvil, making her ribs ache as if she'd broken them.

Tears slid down the serpent's cheeks, bowing her head, her voice hushed. "The Underground—I don't understand. She stayed away from places like that. Why would they do this?"

Tatiana wanted to tell her it wasn't the Underground; although, they had cleaned up the scene. Zabetha had been terrified of the serpents who'd attacked her, but she hadn't shared who they were or who they worked for. There hadn't been time. Tatiana wished she could change it all, protected Zabetha, and solved this case before anyone else got hurt.

Her core blackened, knowing she'd lied and stayed quiet for the Underground—for Zarah and Coastal, who'd helped her. She'd remained silent about six months ago to protect Vaiden. She hated lying. It complicated her life and put her career in jeopardy. Choosing between her friends and her work was difficult, but she couldn't punish those who'd saved her life. What kind of person did that? An honest one maybe, but not a grateful one.

She made excuses, she thought, passing through the den headed for the exit. Why couldn't she tell the world about Zarah and Vaiden—heroes? With the bind, it was likely Vaiden could pass the test for Shades—if anyone thought to test him. He wasn't registered, but that was a slap on the wrist for someone like him, who'd pass through the doors decades ago. Tatiana could help him register.

As for Zarah, it was to further hide the truth about her husband's death. Vampires didn't drop dead. They were either murdered or put to death. The Undying, assisted suicide, was allowed for their kind, given that the vast population of the country believed they were undead, therefore, not really alive. Tatiana thought it was splitting hairs. They were conscious. They had a conscience. She understood eternal lives were complicated though. Living multiple lifetimes wore people down. If they were a danger to society, they were put down.

She had many opinions about vampires, given what they had done to her six months ago. They were dangerous, even without being ravenous. Masters proved that every news cycle. They weren't willing to be normal citizens. Maybe it was their arrogance or maybe they believed they were above humans. LaBelle had thought so. She'd wanted to rule an entire city through terror.

Outside, the hot air clung to her like a plastic bag. She would not suffocate as long as she breathed. Whatever Zarah saw on her face made her come to attention. The security stared daggers at Tatiana's back, but she let them, not as much casting a glance their way.

In the car, Tatiana revealed everything Rocahn had told her about Arkella and Koreen. They'd been in love. Was that so terrible? Was that worth murdering him over? Tatiana knew that money, love, and drugs were the stereotypical reasons why people murdered each other, but a young man wouldn't get to live the rest of his life because he'd fallen in love. Why should that be a consequence of feeling?

She leaned back in her seat, massaging her forehead with both her hands, thankful for the air conditioner. This case weighed on her, not only in pressure to solve it, but on her soul. Mr. Slaseezor had a chance with his wife's admission that Arkella's family had threatened Koreen and the den. She could use that as motivation behind Koreen's death. Would it be enough though?

Not for the judge, she thought, but maybe for a jury. Expedient trials were challenging, especially one that only lasted one work day, typically eight hours. In those limited hours—four for each the defense and prosecution—how many details could be left unresolved? Tatiana had a winning record. It filled her with confidence, strutting into the courtroom, but she didn't know how she would feel if she couldn't find proof and not just speculation of Arkella's family or the Grand Den's involvement in this case. Anything Rocahn testified to could be labeled hearsay.

"What else did she say?" Zarah asked.

"Our meeting was cut short," Tatiana exhaled. "They received the letter about Zabetha's death."

The vampire's body stiffened, her eyes wide in shock. "What do you mean?" she asked. "I haven't sent the letter yet."

"Did the Underground take it upon themselves to do it?" Tatiana questioned. "I mean, I am surprised they would even take credit for killing her when they are, for once, innocent."

Zarah shook her head, typing feverishly on her smartphone. "They wouldn't do that," she said. "It was my task to send the letter. They were only charged with cleaning up the scene and burying Zabetha's body."

They sat quietly in the car while Zarah communicated back and forth with her Underground contact. Only the ding of incoming messages filled the car while Tatiana barely breathed. Whoever sent those serpents to kill Arkella had framed the Underground. Did they know who had cleaned up the scene? Did they know who Arkella had planned to meet that night? What if they had photos or footage of Tatiana at that park, using the blue fire? Her heart hammered against her chest. They needed to find out who did this and quickly.

Zarah's hand squeezed Tatiana's arm, making her startle. "It's OK," she said. "We'll figure this out."

"What did the Underground say?"

"They didn't send the letter."

"Shit."

"Indeed."

A familiar tune sounded, making Tatiana scramble for her phone in her purse. She found it, her eyes immediately recognizing the contact calling. "Logan, what do you need?"

"There's a young serpent here for you," he said. "She says she has information about Mr. Slasseezor's case."

"Did you get a name?" she asked, gesturing for Zarah to drive. The vampire had already put the car into gear, making Tatiana wonder if her hearing was good enough to listen in on phone calls. She would have to ask, especially given confidential information she may learn from clients through a call.

"Her name is Arkella," Logan said.

Tatiana's pulse raced. "Don't let her leave the office. I'll be right there."

She hung up, exchanging glances with Zarah. "Arkella's at the office."

The vampire smiled wide, revealing fang. "Looks like we smoked her out."

38

Moving an army was slow, especially on Arda, and even more apparent when maneuvering around the Corrupted. Vaiden's jaws clenched, watching Duke Heiron's captain give orders to his men. They didn't know anything about stealth or avoiding obstacles. They were raised in an isolated city on a steep mountain no enemy would bother to conquer. The only hardships they had truly experienced were from the weather and the occasional carnivore.

"Be patient," Gabriel said, clapping his back. "Even you said the route through Haven would be quickest."

Vaiden had, making him frown harder. His first thought was to avoid the blizzards through the mountain passes, mostly for his own health, but he hadn't thought what a logistical nightmare it would be for an army to pass through Haven. Duke Heiron planned to hide them in the farms outside of Casimere where he claimed they had reliable allies, but first they had to cross lands infected by the Corrupted.

"Did you finish your letter to Caroline?" Vaiden asked.

"Yes, this morning," Gabriel replied, standing while the Shade perched on a boulder. "A scout will bring it to the nearest chancery."

"I hope you didn't waste this opportunity sexting."

"What's sexting?" Perry asked, appearing at Gabriel's side. They glanced at him, measuring up the fishermen. He was a short man, maybe five-foot-six, but built in thick muscle. He wasn't a man to sit idle as they'd learned throughout the journey. He would go with his scouts ahead and journey back and forth with a restlessness Vaiden didn't quite understand. He'd meant to ask Gabriel about it, but the ambassador had been busy with his letter and perfecting arrangements for his travels to Kiji Village.

Vaiden wasn't happy about his friend going to the old village, especially without him, but he wouldn't return to Kiji, especially when Altamost had ordered the Shades there. They would trap and hold him until an order was given to move out. Vaiden couldn't be grounded. The rebels needed his help infiltrating Casimere.

"It's a sexual way of communicating on Earth," Vaiden answered.

Perry made a face. "What do you mean?"

Gabriel glared at him—a warning. He wasn't supposed to talk about Earth things, but did they care what Altamost had ordered when they were conspiring to remove him from the throne? It seemed silly to keep up the charade.

"Have you ever read a romance?" Vaiden asked. Before Perry could answer, he continued. "Pick one up and maybe learn something."

The rebel glowered at him, breaking away to his leader and the duke.

"When have you read romances?" Gabriel asked.

"I'm well read." The Shade smirked. "All kinds of stories."

"You shouldn't antagonize Perry. He's the leader of the scouts. You will be leading them inside Casimere. You'll need to work together."

"I don't like this plan," Vaiden confessed quietly. "We should stick together when we're surrounded by enemies."

"I agree, but what choice do we have? The Shades need to be freed from Kiji Village and we need to have eyes and ears on the king in Casimere."

Vaiden glanced at his friend then returned his gaze to Kanaris and the duke conversing with Perry between them. The scout crossed his arms, frowning while the men talked. He was a simple man, but angry. Vaiden wagered he'd lost friends and family in this war by both the Corrupted and the king's men. The way forward seemed easy to the Shade, but he wasn't complicated by the emotions of grief. He didn't know what that was like. He couldn't imagine it while staring into the face of someone deep inside it.

"It'll be a week before your party arrives at Casimere," Vaiden said. "I don't like what that means for us when the rebels decide to take the city."

"The plan does need clarifying." Gabriel nodded. "The rebels don't seem to think particulars through. They make a judgment and adjust to the environment once there."

"Sounds familiar," the Shade snorted. "We did a bunch of dumb shit in the Forty-Second."

"We did," mused the ambassador, "but we were young. Kanaris and Heiron are not young. This is over their heads."

"And they need us to fix it for them."

"We all need to work together to help the kingdom."

Vaiden's jaw locked. He didn't care about Eskandor, only that the Corrupted were defeated. What he truly cared about was back on Earth—the realization made him gaze at Gabriel. He mattered, Caroline, and their unborn child too. They would always matter to him—his best friends. They lived on Arda, a world he'd left behind. There was no place for him there anymore. Something he'd made peace with long ago. His home was on Earth, with his mother, work, and Tatiana.

"How comfortable are you being alone with Kanaris and his bunch?" Vaiden asked.

Gabriel shifted on his heels, gazing at the barren ground. It should have been covered in grass, but wherever evil grew, like around Aegan's shrine, death followed. The Corrupted had destroyed Haven over a year ago. The surrounding forest was almost unrecognizable, cloaked in darkness, fog, and decayed so only the trunks of trees remained. Vaiden briefly wondered what the environmentalists on Earth would think about the devastating effects of dark magic.

"I've traveled with less agreeable company in the past," the ambassador said. "I'll keep in mind we're not friends, but we do have a common goal. Maybe that will keep me alive when I've completed this task."

"Do you think you'll be able to convince the Shades the seal comes from the king?"

"I'll try."

"You know what they'll do if you fail."

Gabriel met his gaze, but his eyes shifted back to the ground, nodding slightly. "The Shades won't take kindly to someone impersonating a royal decree."

"They'll kill you, Gabe."

"They may hold us until we can be transported to Casimere."

"No, they'll kill you. When you're in the forest, you're in the wild where the rules of the kingdom are far removed. If they believe it is in the best interest of the kingdom, for whatever reason, they'll just end you and Kanaris's band of merry men."

Gabriel licked his lips, standing tall again. "Well, then they are putting a lot of trust into my abilities."

Vaiden wanted to tell him not to go to Kiji, to find a way to escape the rebels, and head to Mysogus, to find his old comrades in Abrita Shores, the pirates and the scoundrels, and sail away. Find a door and go to Earth. He'd be safe there. On Earth, Vaiden could protect him—only if he could escape his own men in tights.

Perry's scouts were small in number. Duke Heiron's army would be outside of Casimere, waiting for the signal to infiltrate. They hadn't explained how that would work to Vaiden yet, but he knew eventually their plan would surface and he'd be tasked with helping or watching them struggle. Either way an army awaited inside the city—one that dwarfed White Star's strong. He didn't feel like fighting a city, especially while the bigger, badder army currently surrounded them.

He could feel the Corrupted lurking in the shadows, filling the forest around Haven. Purpose raced through his veins, forcing every instinct into overdrive. Deep breaths soothed it, but while the stench of their corruption clung to the air, he would never be free of his one true purpose. It was like being surrounded by fire and withholding the water to a fireman's hose. It didn't make sense. He could put out the fire by killing the Corrupted, but he couldn't do that alone. They outnumbered him and he wasn't about to fight a blood mage capable of summoning meteors alone.

It was strange. Over fifty years ago he'd walked into the emperor's court alone, ready to slay one of the greatest psychopaths in all of Arda's history. He had surprise on his side and he hadn't been afraid to fight to the death—had that changed? Had the bind made him more vulnerable or more cowardly? Shades weren't afraid. They had no sense of self-preservation. What the bind had done was against nature. It should have bothered him, but it didn't. He wasn't expendable anymore. His goals had changed. He had a life on Earth and he damn well would return to it, preferably in one piece.

A shriek sliced through the air, making every soldier grab the hilt of their sword. Vaiden's nocturnal sight clicked on, searching the shadows of the woods. The fog was thick the closer they traveled toward Haven, but on the outskirts as far north as they could journey before the mountain slopes stopped them, it thinned. Vaiden didn't see anything that would make him draw his sword so he relaxed. Gabriel shadowed him until eventually the rest of the unit followed suit.

Kanaris studied Sun and Moon, his dark eyes blinking in the darkness. He gestured for them to join him by the fire. Gabriel elbowed Vaiden. The Shade grumbled to himself, standing and resisting the urge to grimace at the soreness in his ribs. They were almost healed. Part of him wanted to call timeout and tell everyone he needed to be one hundred percent before they tackled Casimere, but he doubted anyone would wait on him.

They sat across from the big man, taking account that Perry had gone back to scouting and the duke supervised the pitching of his tent. Only spoiled brats wanted a tent, Vaiden mused. Of course, this was a man fancying himself the king's replacement. He needed to appear as a man of stature. Gabriel had never traveled more luxurious than the soldiers accompanying him. It earned him their respect. Perhaps the duke thought his past heroics would buy that for him.

"I'm sure being this close to Haven bothers the soldiers," Gabriel said quietly, warming his hands by the fire.

Kanaris grunted, nodding his head. "The place where we lived and raised our families is unrecognizable. People don't know, or don't want to know, the evil that brewed here."

"I can imagine," Vaiden said.

"I'm sure you can." His dark eyes bore into the Shade, searching for something Vaiden couldn't decipher. "You could have killed me. Why didn't you?"

"It wouldn't have changed anything."

"You were ordered to by the king," he said. "Shades do what the king orders."

"I was once ordered by King Rothnar to find all the secret hiding spots in Casimere and report them to him, but I only reported a handful of the spots that I thought would actually endanger him. The rest, I kept to myself," Vaiden explained. "We have more freedom than the kingdom would like to admit."

"So Shades are not necessarily bound by the king." Kanaris stroked his thick beard. "This is the first I've heard of such a thing."

"We are bound by purpose," Vaiden said, resting his elbows on his knees. "Anything else is up to our discretion."

"Why would killing me not change anything?"

"It doesn't change the Corrupted blight," Gabriel replied, "and it doesn't necessarily end the rebellion either."

"It would change nothing." Kanaris nodded. "I am not the only one fighting for Haven and what we lost there."

Another shriek interrupted the silence of the woods, forcing everyone to come to attention, but the sound was farther away. Only a handful of the wary grabbed their hilts. Vaiden looked into the darkness, his eyes searching for anything unseen. Perhaps these Corrupted were a different breed, but by nature they ambushed. While sound directed the soldiers one way, the real danger could be from the opposite direction. Again, his nocturnal sight saw nothing in the shadows of dead trees mixed with the fog.

He returned his stare back to the rebel leader, clicking off his special sight to avoid blinding himself by the firelight. Kanaris gazed at him—still searching for something Vaiden didn't understand.

"What?" he asked, tired of the mental games.

"I remember when King Rothnar's personal guard was charged with treason and forced through the doors," Kanaris said. "It was a shock, considering you are a Shade and going against the new king."

"Altamost wasn't crowned yet."

"He wasn't, but he held the throne."

"The council tasked me to investigate King Chorlee's death."

"And what did you find?"

"I found it suspicious, but there was no evidence to prove he was murdered."

Kanaris's eyes widened, shock brightening them. "You think Altamost murdered him for the crown?"

Vaiden shrugged. "There was never a direction of who killed the king. Altamost had lots of supporters, many of them shady. He could have ordered it or one of them went out of their way to rid them of an obstacle. All I know is the council underestimated Altamost and believed they could get away with the investigation."

"They were careless," Gabriel agreed.

"They were pardoned," Kanaris said, "but the king forced you through the door."

"I suppose he didn't think he could trust me."

Kanaris nodded, his eyes sinking to the fire between them. "Altamost is cunning, but his disregard of this blight demonstrates a lack of integrity. He knew about the nest moving on Haven for weeks, but he did nothing."

A quiet rage grew in his voice with every word. His giant hands balled into fists on his thighs. The rebel leader had lots of reasons to hate the king, all of them well deserved. He wasn't wrong in his evaluation of Altamost. The blatant abandonment of Haven spoke volumes to how expendable the king thought of his people—or at least of the lower stationed ones. He'd kept the wealthier and more powerful close to his chest, but they were splitting off one-by-one the longer the war lingered. By Duke Heiron's account, even Brevene's leaders had become uneasy with their king's complacency.

"How many of your soldier's families survived?" Vaiden asked, motioning the general direction of Haven.

"Few," Kanaris said, sinking into his furs—the pain etched deeply on his face. He stared at the firelight, his eyes sullen despite the fire dancing in them.

"Who'd you lose?"

"Vaiden." Gabriel's voice forced him to gaze at his friend. His brows scrunched together, silently conveying a message to the Shade, but he didn't quite understand the expression.

"It's OK," Kanaris said. "I lost my wife and our son."

"How old was he?" Vaiden inquired.

"Old enough to have his own wife and children, two daughters. They were ten."

"Twins," Gabriel mused. "Rare for our kind."

"Our village priest said it was common for twins to be High Elves so we were not surprised when they showed signs of magic." The wrinkles on his forehead deepened as he stared at the fire.

"You must miss them."

"Every day," the rebel leader exhaled, his tired eyes finally lifting from the firelight, meeting Gabriel's gaze. "Altamost thinks we are rebelling because our village was destroyed. It was never about the village. The buildings and walls can be rebuilt, but nothing can replace our families. Their lives are gone." His voice fell into almost a whisper by the time he reached that final word. The weight of it pushed down on Vaiden, igniting purpose in a blaze the fire roaring between them could not match.

"The king does seem ignorant of this blight," Gabriel agreed. "The council doesn't believe he has the best interest for the kingdom. They will take action."

"Why haven't they?" Kanaris asked. "This war has gone on long enough."

"They've been waiting on me," he explained. "I've been touring the kingdom, meeting with leaders, and seeing the state of the cities. I have proof of the suffering around Eskandor. Without it, the arguments will fall on deaf ears."

"*Noble* ears," Vaiden scoffed.

"Without their support to remove Altamost, we do not win," Gabriel said. "They have the power and influence of the kingdom."

"You have outside allies," argued the Shade.

"And yet, the king had no problem labeling me a traitor." The ambassador spread his hands wide. "I am as expendable as any soldier, emissary, and servant of the crown."

Vaiden shook his head. "Not even close."

"I know you believe that, but Altamost sees me as any game piece on the board. If I am sacrificed for his greater plan, then so be it."

The Shade crossed his arms. Gabriel was right, but Vaiden refused to see him as anything but the greatest piece on the board. In chess, he would have been the bishop. Sure, the queen was an excellent piece, but an obvious one. If Altamost fancied himself as the king of the chess board, who was the queen? Dallia, he thought. Perhaps Glades was a knight? Was Kanaris the king across the board? Or Duke Heiron? What did that make the Corrupted? Did it matter when all the pawns were the people of this kingdom? By the king's efforts not to stop the blight, he might be willing to sacrifice them all.

"Why?" Vaiden asked aloud.

Gabriel's brows furrowed. "Why would Altamost sacrifice me?"

"No, why is Altamost unwilling to stop this blight?" he asked. "It strangles the kingdom, kills its people, and causes a logistical nightmare traveling from one city to another. Why would he want it to persist?"

"Control," Kanaris replied. "The people are being monitored."

"Maybe in Casimere, but not outside of it," Vaiden argued. "Abrita Shores is chaos. No one can control it, not even the duke who's overseen it for a century."

"A different kind of control then," Gabriel offered. "Fear is a way to keep people in line, to motivate submission."

"So you think the king wants to create distrust?" Kanaris asked.

"I don't know what Altamost wants, but by what Vaiden tells me of Casimere, it has fallen into a paranoid state, forcing neighbors to turn on each other."

"What do you mean?" the rebel leader asked.

"I witnessed someone accuse another of being a rebel," Vaiden explained. "It was clear this person had accused many in the past."

"It sounds like Altamost wants the people more afraid of us than the Corrupted." Kanaris crossed his massive arms in the furs. "We are fighting to save the kingdom."

"From Altamost or the Corrupted?" Vaiden asked.

"Altamost allowed the Corrupted to gain in numbers and strength. He did nothing. He is responsible for them. A better leader would have destroyed them in their infancy and not allowed something like a blood mage to manifest."

"And you would have destroyed them?"

"Without question."

Vaiden didn't doubt his words. Only idiots would have allowed the Corrupted to fester and gain power. He studied Kanaris's tight face covered in that thick beard. The rebel leader wasn't dumb, but he wasn't his ambitious cousin either. He was well grounded, thoughtful, and respected. Maybe Duke Heiron's greatest opponent wasn't one of the council or the king, but his own cousin.

"Dividing the kingdom does diverge power and resources," Gabriel mused. "Turning the people on each other blinds them from the real enemy in the Corrupted."

Kanaris relaxed, shaking his head. "Altamost is the enemy. He's the one who has created this blight."

"The Corrupted do not follow his orders," Vaiden said.

"But he enables their evil."

"I'm not arguing that part, but killing the king does not make the Corrupted stand down. They have no loyalty to him."

Before Kanaris could argue further, another shriek sliced through the air. Its venom hit Vaiden like a hot wind. The sound was much closer. He stood up, searching the darkness with his nocturnal sight. Purpose swelled inside of him, racing through his veins.

Shadows moved between the trees, hiding in the fog. Vaiden drew his longsword. Ringing metal let him know Gabriel followed his lead. The shadows darted through the trees. They were coming.

39

Ashes fell around them and could have easily been mistaken for snowflakes if not for the roaring fire roasting a mountain of bodies. Gabriel ignored the smell of burning flesh and settled on a tree trunk to clean his sword. In the moonlight, blood appeared black, but the firelight helped return its red sheen.

Vaiden stood by the fire watching soldiers pile the last of the Corrupted into the inferno. It was a large swarm, thirty by Gabriel's count. Too many. In years past, Gabriel would have called it a nest, but they knew the true nest lived in Haven, miles away. These Corrupted were a unit sent to eliminate interlopers. They had been discovered. It meant more would come when it was obvious this unit had failed—or at least that was how a military would address an invasion.

Gabriel shook his head. These were the Corrupted. They didn't have a military mindset, but he couldn't deny what had happened at Fort Khali or what he had learned from Duke Heiron and Kanaris about the fall of Haven. These were no ordinary Corrupted. How had they kept their wits?

"You good?" Vaiden asked, caked in blood and other body fluids Gabriel didn't care to identify. He looked rough—he had since Fort Khali. Gabriel knew he'd been injured, but Vaiden had never complained about it. He was standing at least.

Gabriel nodded, pointing his blade at Vaiden's head. "That's a bad cut, friend," he said. "You'll need a healer to sew that up."

Vaiden touched the wound through his left eyebrow, hissing as he studied the fresh blood on his hands. "More than likely a tetanus shot."

Gabriel frowned at what he assumed was another Earth term. "It's deep enough to scar."

"Aw, wouldn't want to blemish that pretty face, now would we?" Perry slapped Vaiden's shoulder. The scout leader grinned, triumph shining brightly in his eyes. Despite the black goo clinging to his skin from a monstrosity kill, his upbeat attitude radiated through the camp brighter than the bonfire of corpses.

The rebels completed their tasks, smiling and joking amongst each other. Before the attack, Gabriel would have said they were scared. Now—he looked at their happy faces, wondering where this energy was during their journey from White Star.

"Get yourself to a healer, friend," Perry said. "My girl, Alumpia, is over there."

He pointed at a slender lady with dark hair, wearing a blue tunic. Gabriel recognized her as one of the practitioners who had aided the scouts to take him from Fort Khali.

"Her magic will do nothing for me," Vaiden replied.

"Aw, but she's decent with a needle." Perry shrugged, his gaze sweeping over Gabriel. "Hurt too, are ya?"

He shook his head, standing and sheathing his sword. "The soldiers seem in good spirits now that they've killed something."

"A lot more to go, I'm afraid." His nose scrunched like he'd smelled something foul. "Haven's overrun, breeding like a damn plague. Only way to get rid of those bastards is a good blade and fire."

"The Shades will handle them once they're free," Gabriel said.

Perry stepped toward him, but Vaiden grabbed his shoulder, forcing the rebel back. He didn't seem threatening to Gabriel, but whatever his friend saw in the smaller man, he would trust. Perry batted away his arm, a fierce smile spreading across his face. It faltered quickly, melting into a snarl.

"You lot are not going to take this victory from me," he growled.

"Wouldn't dream of it," Vaiden said, his hand resting on the hilt of his sword. "Though, you should remember, the ambassador is the key to freeing the Shades."

"I'd do it myself," Perry scowled. "Kill all those damn Corrupted with my own hands."

"But you can't." Vaiden's eyes emptied into an unending darkness, not even the firelight could brighten them. "That's why you're going to Casimere instead."

The rebel's hands balled into fists, but he made no move to grab his weapon. "Piss on them," he spat. "That cripple caused all this. We'll have his head and nothing short!"

"Assassinating the king will only make the kingdom and our allies turn on you," Gabriel said. "Put him on trial. Let the weight of his crimes be heard and have him removed legitimately."

"Piss on you!" Perry's face darkened with rage. "Everyone in that city knows what he's doing! They think they are safe. They don't care about us lot out here getting slaughtered. We mean nothing to them. Our children meant nothing to them. Our old. Our homes. None of it mattered then. It means nothing to them now."

"Make it mean something then. Killing Altamost only makes him look like the victim and you the monster."

"I don't care what I look like to those sniveling nobles," Perry said. "They can cut me up, hang me at the gallows, or burn me at the stake. Doesn't matter as long as that prick is dead."

He pushed past Vaiden. Heat radiated off the rebel hotter than the fire. It was best they let him cool off.

"Well, that took a turn." Vaiden crossed his arms. "His grief blinds him from the bigger picture."

"He doesn't care about the bigger picture," Gabriel replied. "None of it matters because of what was taken from him."

"Should I be worried he'll jeopardize the mission?"

It was a fair question, Gabriel thought. Perry was unpredictable, but at the same time, they needed the scouts in Casimere. He was their leader. They wouldn't follow Vaiden without him.

"I'll talk to Kanaris," Gabriel said. "He'll make Perry see sense."

"And if he doesn't?"

"Then I believe you will know how to handle the situation when it arises."

"So you believe it will arise?"

Despite instinct telling him to give Vaiden a boost of confidence, Gabriel knew men like Perry well. He'd worked with many through the Forty-Second and as an ambassador. Like any wounded animal, they could not be trusted.

He dipped his chin in a simple nod, making eye contact with the Shade. Vaiden nodded back, approaching Alumpia to sew his wound. Gabriel trusted in Vaiden's abilities not only to protect himself, but the mission too. They could not allow the rebels to assassinate Altamost, not when other avenues would unite and heal the kingdom.

***

They stayed north of Highland Road, eventually finding the base of the mountain passes for easier travel. It was cool through the rocky terrain of the mountains' feet, but not cold enough to discomfort the soldiers or slow their travel.

Gabriel spent most of the journey beside Vaiden, Kanaris, or Duke Heiron. Although he knew of the duke's ambitions, Heiron wasn't a bad man. He did care about the kingdom and its people. He understood the importance of ridding their land of the Corrupted and restoring the people's faith in one another.

The war and blight had torn the kingdom apart, causing distrust and paranoia. Everything Vaiden had shared with them about Casimere concerned every leader of their kingdom. Leeth's words were written in stone. They could not be repealed, but Altamost had convinced not only the army, but the nobles his intentions were golden.

Gabriel's jaw clenched. Nothing about the king's ambitions were clear, but they did not benefit the kingdom—maybe Altamost and his friends, but not the land and its people.

Dallia's involvement confused him. As the Leader of the Faith and a symbol of power, her responsibilities were to safeguard magic and its practitioners, instill education in the young, and remain neutral to the politics of the world. She should not have been in the king's ear and certainly not sitting on his lap.

Maybe she was in control? The thought chilled Gabriel to his core. Only High Priest Knoran had accomplished ensnaring a king. It was why Leeth wrote his laws in stone—to heed the future an unbreakable warning. No one of the faith and magic should control the kingdom, nor should the monarch control the faith. It was balanced when each remained in their place. Rothnar the Daunting may not have been a perfect king, but at least he had understood this simple truth.

"Rothnar died of poison," Vaiden said.

"I thought he died of injuries during his last battle against the vampires?" Duke Heiron turned in his saddle to face the Shade.

"Yes, injuries expert practitioners couldn't heal." He rolled his eyes.

"Do you think Altamost was behind that too?" Despite the seriousness of his allegation, the duke chuckled. "I don't see a coward like Altamost gracing a war camp with his limping presence."

The Shade inhaled sharply. "His limp has nothing to do with his cowardice or his ability to lead this kingdom. It was a terrible injury a child suffered and shouldn't be the focus of your quips. There's other, more attractive attributes of the man to find derogatory."

"So did he poison Rothnar?" Kanaris asked.

"Of course not," Vaiden snorted. "You think he got on a horse and rode to the eastern border from his estate safe in the hills of Brevene?"

"Then how was he poisoned?" Heiron inquired. "Someone from camp?"

"The vampires dipped their blades in poison," Gabriel answered. "My wife was able to save many with elixirs, but they were in short supply by the end of the war."

"The king didn't get medicine?"

"They were out by the time he had arrived."

Duke Heiron turned back in his saddle, shaking his head. "A valiant king as Rothnar the Daunting was taken down because healers didn't have elixir. This is something our reserve should stockpile. Perhaps Mysogus and the fanes spread across the kingdom could prioritize."

"Many High Elves do not practice alchemy," Vaiden said.

"Perhaps that should change," mused the duke. "Or perhaps others could develop the elixirs to protect our people from wounds practitioners cannot heal. We do rely on magic too much. Simple infirmary practices should be revisited and taught."

Gabriel agreed, but he wondered to whom Heiron was campaigning. Vaiden? The soldiers walking behind them? Had he not won them over yet? Or perhaps he wanted to impress Gabriel, whose strong bonds with the neighboring kingdoms would win him respect from their leaders? Whatever the reason, the duke was making a list of priorities for the kingdom when he was in charge—or maybe for White Star, if he failed to gain the crown.

"It is interesting when people only think to change things because someone important dies," Vaiden said. "Doesn't matter how many soldiers suffered the same fate, it's only important because a king had died that way."

Something sad shined in Heiron's eyes. "Indeed," he quietly replied.

"There's the scouts," Kanaris announced, forcing everyone to gaze at the small band of rebels resting off the road. Perry climbed to his feet, his steps quaking the ground under each boot. His scowling face described what he thought of their journey and the tasks ahead. Gabriel sympathized, though he'd rather travel to Casimere than Kiji Village. Not that the trail ahead was particularly treacherous, but he knew what lay in the village and the mountainous task given to him and Kanaris.

"The crossroad nears," Duke Heiron said.

"Aye." Perry rested his hands on his hips, his fingers playing with the hilt of his sword—a nervous gesture perhaps. "Road's clear. Doesn't look like anyone wants to go visit the Shades."

"Nor would anyone generally," Gabriel said, halting his horse. "There's a reason why it is called the Forsaken Road."

"We'll take a break here." The duke whirled his horse around to face the men. "The rebels and Kanaris will usher the ambassador to Kiji Village. You all have your tunics. Remember, you are the ambassador's escorts. His safety is your priority. White Star, we head south. In days, we will be on the outskirts of Casimere. In less than a week, it will be ours and the kingdom will be saved."

Though the men were tired of the journey, longing shined in their eyes—something mightier than a giant's stature and stronger than its grip. They were taking back their kingdom. They would save it. Gabriel hoped they were right. He hoped they could find a way to convince the Shades to leave, to cleanse the kingdom of the Corrupted and the king who'd abandoned the duties of the crown.

Everything—the fate of Eskandor—depended on their abilities to work together. They may not like each other, they may not trust each other, but each and every soldier part of this rebellion all had one thing in common. They fought for each other, their children, and the future. Gabriel respected that. Above all else, nothing mattered more to him than his family.

***

"This is where I leave you," Gabriel said, leaning forward in his saddle. Vaiden had abandoned his horse to the rebels traveling north to Kiji Village. They needed to look authentic as the escorts of the ambassador. Though it wasn't uncommon for them to travel by foot, if it was indeed an urgent message from the crown, horses were necessary.

"I'm a big boy. I can take care of myself." The Shade grabbed Gabriel's wrist, pulling him slightly down. "If anything goes sideways in Kiji," he said quietly, "you sacrifice everyone to get out of there."

"And the same, if the worst happens in Casimere."

Vaiden let him go. "I've already made it out of there once with every soldier hunting me. Second time will be a piece of cake."

"Of course, I have all the faith in you," he snorted, sitting tall in the saddle. "May Wara protect you."

"May Surnuna light your path."

"What do Earthlings say, leaving their friends?" he asked, directing his horse to the road north.

"'See you later, alligator,'" Vaiden replied, walking the other direction. "And someone else would reply, 'in a while, crocodile.'"

Gabriel shook his head, his nose wrinkling. "Earth is so strange."

Vaiden laughed, following the trail south with White Star soldiers and Perry's scouts. He would be fine, Gabriel thought. He could take care of himself. No one was more capable of that than Shades. By the time they were ten, they had to live off the land in a wildly dangerous forest, where everything either wanted to kill them for their meat or to protect themselves from one of their own kind. It was a brutal world. At least they had received the message.

Gabriel turned his attention to Kanaris and the rebels dressed in blue tunics, pretending to be his guards. He donned his golden cloak, looking ever the part in this charade. His part wasn't a lie, he told himself. He was the ambassador and the Shades did need to eliminate the Corrupted. The mechanics of freeing them from the village was most definitely a lie, but a necessary one. The blight needed to end. They could never win without the Shades.

He hoped Caroline received his message. She could convince Mysogus to send aid and help the Shades defeat the Corrupted. The blood mage and its army of dead could not continue. Eskandor—nay, the world—depended on them.

40

Despite Tatiana explaining to Zarah she could handle herself, Zarah rode with her to the office. Tatiana didn't know how she would explain to anyone why the vampire needed to be there. She didn't work in civil or wills law. Legally, unless Zarah was charged with something in criminal law, she had no business being in Tatiana's office. They were friends though. Perhaps they could spin another reason.

Zarah chatted with Darling, complimenting her newest display of flowers sitting on her workstation, the testament of a new admirer. They gossiped, showing each other screenshots on their phones of outfits they wanted to buy or vacations they wanted to take. Zarah claimed she would treat all their friends to a weekend getaway—to some luxury resort for them to relax and enjoy the ocean.

"Sugar, I don't even need an excuse. Take me. I'm yours," Darling laughed.

"Do you think we could pry Josie away from renovating the house?"

"Please, yes," Caden said, appearing at their side. He held a file out to Darling and she snatched it out of his hand. "Careful. You almost gave me a papercut."

Her lips curled back in a fierce grin. "You better be glad I didn't take a whole finger."

He smirked, leaning his elbow on the counter. "Aw, did you not like the flowers?" He gestured at them. "I thought they would brighten up the place."

"And start rumors," she scowled. "Sometimes I think you want Josie to be mad at me."

He chuckled, a sound that made Tatiana's toes curl. "Can I not appreciate all the staff for their hard work? It's been a long week, especially with these hefty case loads."

"So it's for *all* the staff?" Tatiana crossed her arms, eying her friend.

"If he wanted to treat the staff, he could have bought them all a round of drinks," she argued. "I'm tired of these pranks, Caden."

"It's not a prank," he said. "It's a thank you, Darling. So thank you for all your hard work."

"Go to hell," she growled.

He backed away with his hands held up in surrender, but the grin on his face was nothing short of trouble. It was commonplace for them to pick on each other, but evidently he'd struck a nerve with her. Tatiana wanted to ask what was going on, but Logan finally emerged from the conference room, waving her in.

"Stay here," Tatiana whispered to Zarah. The vampire responded by grabbing her wrist, forcing Tatiana to meet her bright eyes. "Don't make a scene. Use your vampire hearing if you need to, but I can handle this."

"Whose office is next door?" she asked too quietly for anyone else to hear.

"It's a storage closet."

"Perfect."

"How are you going to elude suspicion by going into a closet?"

"I'll need to take a personal call."

"There's plenty of other places more suitable for a call."

"Let me worry about that."

Zarah let go, and Tatiana hurried to the conference room, hearing Zarah ask Darling why Caden was being such a prick. Tatiana held back her laughter when she reached the door, Logan ushering her inside.

A couple of young serpents sat in chairs, testing out the faux leather. They stood when she stepped inside. Both had softer, more rounded features than most of their kind. Female serpents didn't generally look as menacing as their male counterparts, but it didn't mean they all looked harmless. Both of them had the complexion of a smooth green snake more than anything resembling a dragon. The shorter one had dark eyes while the other had brighter yellow eyes.

"This is Arkella and her cousin, Embelk," Logan announced.

Arkella, the shorter one, offered her hand to Tatiana. It wasn't custom to shake hands, but she took it, seeing no reason to refuse. "Nice to meet you," Arkella said, flicking her tongue between her sharp teeth. "I hope you can help."

Tatiana gestured at the chairs. They all took a seat, rolling up to the long table, taking up the majority of the narrow room. "Mr. Reece tells me someone contacted you with a threatening message."

"Well." Arkella clasped her hands to her slender chest. "It wasn't exactly threatening, but it alluded that they knew about Koreen, about what truly happened to him, and it alleged that I knew something about that."

Tatiana nodded, recognizing her uses of words like "alluded" and "alleged." She had chosen this language purposely. Perhaps because she was going to speak to an attorney and wanted to sound smart, or she wanted to make Tatiana feel she knew nothing and was being victimized. "Do you know what happened to Koreen?"

"Everyone knows about that night at the den," she replied, not meeting Tatiana's gaze. "I—I was there."

"Why were you were there?"

She nodded, still not meeting her eyes. "We were dating and I wanted him to leave the den to be with me."

"Why would he need to leave the den to be with you?"

Arkella bowed her head. Within seconds her shoulders began to shake. "Because I loved him," she cried. "I didn't care what the Grand Den or the Slaseezors said. I wanted to be with him and that's all that matters."

"What did the Grand Den and the Slaseezors say?"

Her cousin rubbed her back in soothing circles. Arkella clutched her other hand. "They wouldn't allow it," she sniffled. "My parents told me our families were not compatible, but it didn't make sense. They wanted to join with a family from Arda. It was important to them to have some of the old blood mixed with ours here on Earth. Koreen was the perfect candidate. I remember Mama saying so."

Tatiana exchanged a glance with Logan. His brows furrowed together listening to the serpent's words. It didn't make sense to them either. From everything they had heard, Arkella's family believed they were above Koreen and his family.

"I can't believe he went through with it," Arkella continued, sobbing. "He told me he loved me. He'd wanted to join the den so in the future he would have access to the Grand Den."

"Why was it important for him to have access to the Grand Den?" Tatiana asked.

Logan held out a tissue box and she grabbed one, wiping her eyes with it. "I am a member of the Grand Den," she exhaled. "He would have to rise to my level for coupling."

"Our granny said they make exceptions every now and then," Embelk explained. "Our family petitioned for him to be accepted, but the Grand Den said he had to join the faith first."

"His mother was friends with Rocahn," Arkella sniffled, her shaking finally settled. "The Slaseezors were looking out for him because his family returned to Arda."

"Do you know why they moved back?"

"He claimed they missed the simplicity of that world," she said. "He was worried about the rumors of the kingdom murdering those returning from Earth, but he did receive a letter from his father, saying they had settled in their family's old estate. It didn't seem like the kingdom had a problem with their return."

Something tight in Tatiana's chest eased. She was glad these rumors weren't completely true. If she couldn't win Mr. Slaseezor's case, perhaps the judge would deport him back to Arda and he could find his extended family there and be safe. It wasn't the goal though. The judge could ignore any suggestions of deportation and have him executed. The fight for Mr. Slaseezor's freedom was also a fight for his life. Only the words "not guilty" and "move to acquit" would save him from that fate.

"Miss Arkella." Tatiana laid her hand on the table between them. "I'm glad you have come forward. I know it is painful to talk about these subjects, but can I ask, why did you come to me?"

"I saw your post," she said, finally meeting her gaze. "I knew you were representing Mr. Slaseezor and I wanted to come forward earlier, but—"

"Our family didn't want to involve themselves," Embelk interceded.

"My cousin has been very supportive." Arkella squeezed her hand, smiling at her. "She gave me the courage to be here today."

"Do you know who sent you the threatening message?" Tatiana asked.

"It had to be someone from the Slaseezor's den."

"Why the den?" Logan asked.

"I found out what my parents told me wasn't true." Her voice shook with each word. "They didn't want me to believe I wasn't good enough for Koreen. That it was a mutual decision by both families that we couldn't be together, but it wasn't true. My family loved Koreen. They had accepted him, but Rocahn..."

She stared at something unseen, her green skin ashening. "Her demands were unreasonable. I mean, we knew that Koreen was desirable. We knew that meant the contract would have many demands by the den, but Rocahn went too far. She asked for too much."

"What does that mean? What did she want?"

"It was money at first," Arkella said, "but then for the den to ascend on the waiting list so she could have special access to the Grand Den's gardens, and other things that seem frivolous now. My parents only have so much reach. They could not give her everything she wanted."

"Do you know what happened between your parents and the Slaseezors?" Tatiana asked, knowing Rocahn had lied about everything. Why would she do that? Was rejection from Arkella's family worse than losing her husband?

Arkella shook her head, but Embelk replied, "My granny said they tried to bargain with her, but Rocahn wouldn't see reason."

"Was Mr. Slaseezor at this meeting?"

"I don't think Mr. Slaseezor knew anything about the demands," Arkella answered. "He was so busy with the den and the charity and getting everything ready for the ceremony. Koreen talked about how busy he was. He helped Mr. Slaseezor around the den. He said it was an honor to help him, learning about the faith and our people's culture on Arda."

Her face crumpled, but she held back the tears, blinking both layers of her eyelids. "The last time I saw Koreen before the ceremony, we got into an argument," she sniffled. "I said if they wouldn't let us couple then we could run away together. The U.S.A. has no laws against it. We are legal adults here and we could get married like you humans do, but he refused. He wanted to do it the right way within the faith."

She covered her face with both hands, her shoulders shaking again. "I told him—I screamed at him that he thought the faith was more important than me—than us. He tried to say something back to me, but I ran off. I knew he was scared, but I didn't know it was that bad."

"What do you mean?" Tatiana asked, scooting as closely as the table and chair allowed. "What scared him?"

Embelk passed her another tissue and she cleaned her face. "Rocahn," she sniffled. "She was so controlling of Koreen. I thought it was because his candidacy was so desired, but I don't know. She liked the attention. She liked controlling him. He could barely sneak out to meet me at the park in the end." Her eyes saddened at those last few words. "I went to the ceremony to show my support for him. I wanted him to know that I would wait for him to join the Grand Den and not need the Slaseezor's permission in coupling."

As if they had the same thought, Logan beat Tatiana to the next question. "Why wouldn't he need the Slaseezor's permission if he joined the Grand Den?"

"Because the Grand Den would take possession of him," she replied. "Rocahn didn't want him to join, but that's not why he was scared of her. He said once she was dangerous or that she knew dangerous people. I don't know. I've met Rocahn. She's difficult, but I would never call her mean, but I guess, people are never who they appear to be from the outside, right?"

Gary Martin had looked like a dream to Tatiana once upon a time. He'd been a prince who had swept her off her feet. They were supposed to ride into the sunset together, but he had different plans. He had been in love with someone else—a sadist, who had wanted to steal the blue fire and kill Tatiana.

Here kitty, kitty, whispered through her ears. She inhaled sharply, counting back from ten. What she had seen of Gary was only a mirage, an oasis to blind her from the truth. Had Rocahn blinded her from the truth too? She had certainly lied and withheld critical information. Why?

"Do you have any reason to believe Rocahn would hurt Koreen?" Tatiana asked.

Arkella shook her head. "He was too valuable to her because his coupling candidacy was so desirable. I mean she did like him too, doted on him like one of their own. She said he was the missing piece of their den."

Tatiana nodded, allowing a small pause before her next question. "Do you have any reason to suspect Mr. Slaseezor would want to hurt Koreen?"

Arkella shook her head. "Mr. Slaseezor was like family to Koreen. He treated him well, taught him so much about the faith. I remember seeing Mr. Slaseezor's face when he...when he stabbed him. He couldn't believe it. He tried to help Koreen, but the–the blow, it-it was to the heart."

Her face crumpled again and she buried it into her cousin's shoulder. Embelk held her, rubbing soothing circles on her back. The poor girl, Tatiana thought. She didn't deserve to go through grief so young.

Logan and Tatiana excused themselves, allowing Arkella a moment to compose herself. They lingered at the doorway, exchanging glances until Arkella finally emerged. "Ms. Smith, is Mr. Slaseezor really going to be charged with Koreen's murder?" she asked.

"He is." She nodded. "The information you've shared has been very helpful. If I need to call on you for more information or to testify, how can I reach you?"

"You can text me." She grabbed something from the purse hanging across her chest and handed it to her. Tatiana was surprised to find a well formatted business card. "My cell is on the back. I mostly respond to texts, but if you can't reach me that way, my socials are the next best place to find me."

"Thank you, Arkella," she said, laying her hand gently on the girl's shoulder. "It was very brave of you to come forward. I know Koreen would be proud of you."

A sad smile spread with her lips. "I know," she barely whispered before her cousin grabbed her arm and ushered her toward the elevator. Tatiana let them go before another thought crossed her mind. She rushed to the elevator, stopping them shy of it.

"Have you heard of a serpent named Zabetha?" she asked.

The girls exchanged a look. "My granny said someone named that was murdered by the Underground a few days ago," Embelk answered. "Why?"

"I want you girls to stay safe," she replied. "Stick together and don't go outside at night."

"Do you think the same people who murdered this Zabetha also murdered Koreen?" Arkella asked. "Could they be the ones who contacted me?"

"It's possible," Tatiana returned, though she knew the latter wasn't true. "But look out for one another."

The girls nodded, finally entering the elevator. As the doors closed, Arkella's sad eyes pleaded for Tatiana to solve this case. She turned back to Floor Two, her eyes sweeping over Command Central, finding Zarah typing on her phone down a hallway. Logan gestured for them to retreat into her office.

She wanted to ask if Zarah had heard any of their conversation with Arkella, but she knew that would only invite questions if she conversed with Zarah before her paralegal. She retreated to her office, Logan closing the door behind them.

"What background information do we have on Rocahn?" she asked, marching to her desk for the files.

"Just the standard report," he said. "There wasn't much to go on, if I remember."

She quickly scanned the report, noting he was right about how little information there seemed to be about this serpent. The more she stared at the thin file, the more suspicious it became. "I want you to do another search."

"Why?" Logan asked. "Wouldn't that only waste time?"

She raised a brow at him. He wasn't someone that questioned her orders, but he was right. There was little time to go back to the drawing board, but she'd missed the weak personal background check. It needed to be done properly. "I want you to go to public records and see if Rocahn changed her name before she married Mr. Slaseezor."

Logan's brows scrunched together, but quickly he had a thought. "You think she's lying about who she is."

"Arkella said that Koreen thought she was dangerous or that she associated with dangerous people," Tatiana replied. "That could mean she was in a gang or the Underground. She might have ties to the mob families, or she might owe one of the mob families."

"What do you mean?"

"She needed money, Arkella said. Her demands kept becoming more and more unreasonable. That means Rocahn is greedy, but we show no fraud on their charity. My best guess is that her past is coming back to haunt her."

"So the theory is she changed her name to escape debt, but how does that tie with the blood ritual and killing Koreen?"

"My theory is she knew Koreen was her best way into the Grand Den, but then she found out Arkella's family was petitioning for him to join the Grand Den without going through the waitlist."

"So she lost her bargaining piece." Logan's eyes searched for something unseen. "What did she need so badly in the Grand Den that she couldn't wait for?"

"Arkella said something about access to the gardens. I know that Rocahn has her own garden at the den and that she's had trouble keeping Ardan plants alive."

"Is that worth Koreen's life?"

Tatiana shook her head. "I wouldn't think so, but if we are to create doubt that Mr. Slaseezor had anything to do with Koreen's death, his wife seems to be the best candidate for the job. We've caught her in many lies and by omitting the truth, she's cast a lot of suspicion on herself."

"Are you going to talk to her again?"

"I'll try."

"I don't want you to go alone." He swallowed hard, his thumb rubbing a small circle into the palm of his other hand. "Koreen thought she was dangerous and he's dead. There's a rumor of another suspicious death at that den."

"Yes, I was there when they received news about that murder." She hadn't realized Logan didn't know about Zabetha—that none of the office had and she had asked Arkella about her by name. It was why she didn't like lying. She couldn't keep up the charade. Her father had said she was too honest to be a lawyer. Maybe he was right, but this case would be a lot easier if everyone told the truth and saved a good man from being executed for something he didn't knowingly do.

"Please don't go alone," he said again. "Wait for me to come or grab Caden, but don't go alone."

His first instinct was for her to bring a man, someone to protect her, but her first pick was the vampire texting in the hallway. "I will," she answered, deflating whatever weight he'd held on his shoulders. "Please work quickly on getting those personal records."

He rushed out the door nearly running into Zarah. She smiled sweetly at him, waving him away like it wasn't a big deal and that she hadn't been eavesdropping from beyond the door.

"I think I found us the perfect resort," she announced loud enough for Command Central to hear before she closed the door behind her. "Do you think they bought that?"

"I think if you tease Darling about a getaway, you better make good on it."

Zarah seemed to think about it. "It would be fun and the perfect treat after this case."

Tatiana sat in her chair, leaning back with her hands behind her head. "How much of the meeting with Arkella did you hear?"

"Most of it," she said. "I have my contacts running Rocahn's name for any information in the Underground or any of their associates."

"Arkella really loved Koreen."

"Zabetha said they wanted to run away together, or at least, that Arkella did."

"I wonder if Mr. Slaseezor knew anything about the demands for Koreen's coupling."

"Probably not. Men rarely know anything."

"I'll ask him."

"Can you see him today?"

Tatiana shook her head. "It's too late for visitors, unless it's an emergency. The officers get to decide what classifies as an emergency so this would more than likely not meet those requirements."

"Even if it means freeing him?"

"We're not there yet."

"His wife is highly suspicious." Zarah put her hands on her hips, pacing the width of the office. "I agree she must have ties to someone in the underbelly and owes them, but it is interesting she wanted access to the Grand Den's gardens, such a strange request."

Tatiana nodded, leaning forward so her elbows rested on the desk. "She loves plants. Maybe that's just a harmless want."

"The Grand Den has some of the only plants allowed by the U.S. government to cross from Arda. Rocahn could make a fortune on the black market by taking some of them or their seedlings."

"True." Tatiana hadn't thought of that angle. Maybe Rocahn had visions of becoming wealthy, but if so, why did she choose to run a non-profit charity at the den? Not every religious institute did. It couldn't just be for the tax benefits. The Slaseezors didn't make that much money.

Maybe the non-profit was some type of front to hide the money they did make from her garden? That was possible, but Zarah was correct in thinking the desirable plants from Arda would make Rocahn a fortune. That would be harder to hide in their low income neighborhood.

"What's that?" Zarah leaned over her desk, lifting Tatiana's chin gently with a hand. "Why are you pouting?"

She pushed away. "Every day it seems like we uncover more and more questions about this case, but hardly answer any of them. At least we know what happened with Arkella, but there's still questions."

"Do you think the girl lied?"

"She's in too much grief to lie. What's important to her is the truth about her and Koreen."

"Do you think Rocahn had something to do with his death?"

"Either directly or indirectly. She's hiding something and has evaded my calls and messages. She doesn't want me to talk to the Grand Den because they would have confirmed everything Arkella told us."

"Should we protect the girl?" Zarah asked.

"I asked if she'd heard about Zabetha," Tatiana said. "Someone in the family had already learned of her death."

"Her family will keep her safe."

"I hope they do."

"If something happens to her then we know Rocahn definitely has something to do with Koreen's death."

"Or the Grand Den."

"The Grand Den seemed to be cooperative with Koreen and Arkella coupling. I don't see them having any reason to hurt him. It would have been easier to refuse the coupling or say they would never let him into the Grand Den rather than allow all this controversy."

Maybe, Tatiana thought, but the question list expanded and time was running out. "I need to speak with Rocahn. Can I count on you to be my escort?"

A smile spread across Zarah's face. "Any time."

Tatiana climbed out of her chair and shuffled to the door. "You know, I wasn't joking about that retreat. Darling will mark it down."

"Then let's just go after this case is done."

The door swung open. Logan breathlessly held his phone out to her. "There's a problem at the SDC. You need to go now!"

41

The northwest region of Eskandor belonged to the ancient Kiji Forest. While most of the kingdom was inhabited, the forest remained one of the most untouched landscapes of their time. Trees wider than houses grew more enormous the further north they traveled, up the steep terrain until the vast forest leveled into a great valley.

Gabriel's breath caught gazing at the beauty of the forest, knowing treachery lurked in every shadow. The Wildlands were dangerous too, but Kiji was a different kind of danger, that had nothing to do with the evil of magic and everything to do with the unpredictability of nature. The kingdom's most vicious animals lurked amongst the trees, in its canopy, and deep within the soil.

Vaiden had spent five years of his life in this forest, surviving with nothing but the tools he'd made with his own hands. Gabriel could not imagine it. He had relied on the weaknesses of civilization in Abrita Shores, but nothing weak lived in nature—nothing easily manipulated or robbed. Everything took effort and risk, even the basics, like water and shelter.

Kanaris rode on his right, his stare searching the brush between the trees. At a lower elevation than White Star, Kiji was lush and untouched by winter. The disguised rebels behind them had grown quiet while their horses marched up Forsaken Road headed for the only village on its path.

Sweat slid between Gabriel's shoulder blades, making him want to wiggle in his saddle, but he remained focused on the road ahead. Who knew what might jump out of the shadows: big cats, giant horse-sized bugs, or arachnids as large as dogs. Whatever dared to attack them, they had to be ready.

"I've never been," Kanaris barely whispered, "to Kiji."

"I have only been myself a few times," Gabriel answered. "Only on official business."

"Does this uneasy feeling ever ease?"

"No."

Golden beams shot through the clouds, lighting the road like Surnuna marked the path, confirming they were headed the right direction. He hoped she blessed their friends south with the same encouragement. They all needed it after this long war.

In the quiet, his thoughts drifted to his wife, safe within the confines of Mysogus—or at least he hoped she was safe. The letter might have been a gamble, but he knew Caroline had allies within the magical school. Perhaps they would protect her—perhaps they knew nothing of Dallia's wrongdoings in Casimere, whatever that may be.

He hoped Caroline was able to rally the practitioners, make them understand hiding behind their wards and high walls would only help the Corrupted win this blight. Not that he wanted magical warfare, but they could not linger while the nest in Haven grew. The blood mage had made a stand at Fort Khali, unveiling its power for all to see. It wanted every surviving soldier to run to the reaches of the kingdom and tell everyone of what they had witnessed. They'd lost. They would lose without Mysogus's help—and most certainly without the Shades.

His gaze searched the distance. Nestled in the heart of the valley sat Kiji Village where the Shades had been ordered to remain until their king changed his mind. Altamost had claimed there was a greater plan involving the Shades, but he would not divulge the specifics of this plan or a timeline. It was foolish to keep it a secret and obviously irresponsible to keep the Shades confined to Kiji when the Corrupted plagued their kingdom.

Gabriel didn't understand Altamost, who had once claimed to be the distant cousin of King Duncan—the crown's most respected bearer. Duncan had prioritized ridding the kingdom of Corrupted. His journals were well preserved for every monarch after him to study. Had Altamost bothered to read his late cousin's words? Or had he cast them aside and believed he didn't need help?

Everyone did, Gabriel thought. Even the bravest, strongest, and most intelligent among them needed help. Gabriel didn't believe he was any of these things, but he was humble enough to know he couldn't fix this kingdom alone. Duke Heiron and Kanaris seemed to understand this fact too.

He hadn't decided how he aligned with the rebels, but Gabriel knew the duke and his cousin also had different goals. Kanaris wanted to avenge the fallen of Haven—to right the wrongs Altamost had committed to their village, to give them peace, and destroy the nest plaguing their lands. Heiron hoped to gain power and recognition. Maybe he would bid for the crown. It didn't mean he would win, but the people of the kingdom would note who put them first. After this war, they needed unity and trust.

Was Heiron the sort of man to lead them out of this mess? Gabriel wasn't sure. Part of him thought the duke was taking charge of the situation and showing leadership. The other part of him believed Heiron planned to exploit the kingdom at its most vulnerable stage to grasp power. He was already campaigning, but he'd joined them for this journey, shouldering the risks of rebellion.

"Do you trust your cousin?" Gabriel asked aloud.

Kanaris raised a thick brow at him. "Heiron?"

"Is he the kind of man who will put his ego aside to do what is right for the people?"

"He has lived his whole life in the service of others."

"That doesn't mean he hasn't used that opportunity to better himself."

"No, I suppose it doesn't," the rebel leader chuckled. "At a young age, he believed he was destined for greatness, but things changed the older we grew."

"Oh?" Gabriel scanned the forest to his left, looking for anything out of place. "What changed?"

"War with the vampires. It changed many soldiers."

"How did *he* change?"

"He lost a lot of men on those hills, seeing the carnage made him wish he was one of the fallen," Kanaris explained. "I remember reading his letters and wondering if I would ever see him again."

"Rothnar gave him White Star."

"It took him a long time to adjust to his position as the duke, especially because he didn't believe he deserved it."

Gabriel turned in his saddle, eying the rebel leader. "He boasts about his victories, celebrating them as if they had happened yesterday."

"Aye, he does, like anyone who wears a mask to hide the sorrow beneath." Kanaris let the weight of his dark eyes settle on the ambassador. This blight had aged him like none before, those eyes said.

Grief did that. It drained the soul of joy and left the body and mind a broken shell. Gabriel wanted to tell him revenge wouldn't heal him. It wouldn't end the pain or bring that joy back. That light was gone forever. Peace could only be found in acceptance, but he knew Kanaris wasn't ready for that. None of the rebels were. Even if Altamost was removed from the throne, could they accept the war was over?

"What does Heiron truly want?" Gabriel asked instead. "The crown? Power? Does he think it will heal his wounds?"

"He wants to be of service," Kanaris answered.

"Don't play games with me. I've heard his speeches. He doesn't make them for morale."

"Or are you choosing to believe it's more than just words?"

Gabriel fought from rolling his eyes. "I've been around for a long time. I know a campaign when I see one."

They rode in silence, taking in the quiet forest around them. The rebels remained poised, ready for anything that may strike from the trees. The quiet forced Gabriel to focus on his pulse racing in his ears. It was much too quiet. He didn't like it, especially without Vaiden at his side. The Shade had become a security blanket over their years together. Without him, Gabriel felt naked to the world.

These past decades without him had tested Gabriel in ways he hadn't expected. Like his father used to say when he was a boy, cornered he was a bear with claws of steel. In the open, exposed to the elements, only a coward remained. Gabriel's jaw locked, shoving his late father's words back. He was dead. He had no power.

His chest tightened, hands growing clammy around the reigns. He swallowed hard, biting back the panic bubbling in his throat. It was too damn quiet. For a forest filled with life, where were the songs of birds and insects?

Metal scraped sheaths, making him jump in his saddle. The rebels had pulled their weapons, aiming them at the trees. Shadows moved between the brush, easily mistaken for tricks of the eyes. Gabriel held his horse steady while the disguised rebels surrounded him and Kanaris. Their loyalty remained to their leader, but they had to play the part of the ambassador's escorts.

The figures stepped closer, the light spilling over their black tunics and blank expressions. Gabriel lifted his hand, palm up, high above his head.

"Lower your weapons," he said to the rebels. They hesitated, eying the archers. Gabriel whirled around his horse, realizing quickly they were surrounded. "Lower your weapons, I say. These are the Shades. We are in their lands."

The rebels slowly lowered their swords. None of them sheathed their weapons though. They had met one Shade already and he alone had threatened to kill their leader with a flick of his wrist. What could a forest full of Shades do?

"I am Gabriel Steel, envoy for King Altamost, come to bring His Majesty's order to your commander," he announced. "Let us pass."

The archers made no move to release their arrows or lower their bows. They stood unblinking at the rebels, poised, ready to strike. Another Shade with dark blonde hair stepped forward, his sword sheathed. He wore the same black tunic as his brethren with the same empty expression, but Gabriel recognized him as the captain of this unit.

"Ambassador Steel," the Shade said flatly, "this way."

He turned his back on the group, marching down Forsaken Road. The other Shades moved in tandem, perfectly synchronized with the rebels as they followed their captain. Eventually their archers relaxed, but kept their arrows notched as they marched along the road.

"Put your weapons away," Kanaris ordered. The men reluctantly listened. Each of their faces twisted in caution at the eerie display of the Shades.

Gabriel's blood chilled with the same uneasiness. He'd fought side-by-side with Vaiden almost his entire life, he should have been used to their off putting presence. As he studied the lifelessness of the Shades, he realized Vaiden wasn't and had never been like them. Perhaps because he was particularly trained in mirroring or he'd never served in the all Shade battalions?

His skills in stealth had set him apart, making him a match for the Forty-Second instead. Gabriel had never thought about how strange that situation was. Shades were meant for killing the Corrupted, and although Vaiden had killed countless in his life, his duties had separated him from the true purpose of his kind.

Now the bind, Gabriel thought. It had unlocked emotions in him, letting him feel like any other elf, but preserved his immunity to their magic. What would these other Shades think of that? Would they care or would they believe Vaiden was a danger to their kind and to nature?

Gabriel pushed such thoughts away. No one on Arda knew about the bind beyond him. He would keep that secret. Not even the threat of torture and death would make him betray the moon to his sun.

***

Kiji Village wasn't meant to house a battalion of Shades. It only had a few huts with thatched roofs for lodging, the commander's office, and a blacksmithing station, which was open to the air. A roped off section along the tree line served as the stables for their horses. Tents had been pitched in the heart of the field for the Shades reassigned there. Not enough, Gabriel knew, for the amount of Shades enlisted in their ranks. He wondered if the rest slept in the forest or on bedrolls in the field.

It was a grand valley, filled with blessings of Jana, to be squandered on beings who would notice nothing of its beauty or remark about the stark contrasts between the dark forest and the green grass. Gabriel observed the Shades, chopping firewood, collecting supplies, and crafting weapons. They stayed busy. No one complained or talked beyond necessary orders. The field was filled with people, but it might have been the quietest populace in the world. Some might have found it peaceful, but as Gabriel studied the rebels, he knew he wasn't the only one unsettled by their silence.

With their task completed, the unit who had escorted them to the village returned to their posts down Forsaken Road. Gabriel eyed the commander's office, knowing the greatest challenge was ahead. He had to convince the Shade command that Altamost had ordered for them to cleanse the kingdom of the Corrupted. It should have been easy, given their purpose was to kill the Corrupted, but Gabriel's stomach fluttered with doubt.

Shades were smarter than the average elf. One wrong detail in the seal, no matter how small, could spark suspicion in them. They would act fast, giving no quarter to Gabriel or the rebels. Anyone impersonating an envoy of the king would face immediate consequences. Away from society, Vaiden claimed, the Shades would execute them. Gabriel didn't doubt him, but he would fight.

"Backed against a corner," Gabriel whispered, his fingers tightened around the satchel strap across his chest. It contained the document Duke Heiron had forged with the king's seal. Gabriel had read it, instructing adjustments for the duke. After hours of debating language, they had finally completed the final draft. An intelligent man would never attempt to trick the Shades, but Gabriel had no choice.

"A bear with claws of steel," he exhaled with his head bowed. When he raised it, he held himself high with the rank of respect he'd grown accustomed to carrying. "Captain, with me," he said to Kanaris, marching toward the commander's office. The rebel leader's thick frame blocked the sun, cooling Gabriel's brow. A sweaty mess was a nervous mess, Vaiden would say. Only the nervous had something to hide.

The commanding officer of Kiji Village was a captain by rank, but given the special task of being the head of a settlement, the position had been elevated to commander. She stood by her desk, wearing the same black tunic as every Shade. Her dark eyes lifted to meet Gabriel's gaze then shifted to Kanaris when they entered. She didn't say hello or any kind of introduction, standing completely unmoved like the trees of Kiji Forest.

Sitting at her desk was a general, who belonged in Casimere, instructing the king on the Corrupted; instead, he was seated in Kiji, reading scrolls. Gabriel's heart hammered against his chest. One of those scrolls might have word from Altamost, stating the ambassador had switched sides. If the general had already read it, then it was over. Shades would protect the kingdom from any enemy, even their own.

How thorough was the king, Gabriel was left asking. He might send word to his allies of Gabriel's defect, but he wondered if the king would have thought to write the Shades. Given Gabriel's favoritism of Vaiden, it seemed likely, but the ambassador didn't normally speak with the Shade command. His rapport was with leaders beyond their borders.

Kanaris nudged him, forcing him to glance at the rebel leader, who tilted his head, eyes motioning behind them. Two other Shades remained at the door, watching the ambassador and his supposed captain. Four against two, Gabriel thought, but these were no ordinary soldiers. Each of them were perfect killers without mercy or restraint—four Vaidens.

The ambassador swallowed again, gathering his courage. They were not Vaiden, a unique case. They were soldiers, not assassins, but he would not underestimate their abilities. They had survived and conquered Kiji Forest, ended countless Corrupted, and fought vast enemies of the kingdom. No one unskilled or weak could have accomplished such feats.

"I am Ambassador Steel," he announced, his voice steady. "I've come with word from Casimere." He opened the satchel, fetching the scroll and placing it on the desk. "The kingdom calls for its protectors."

The general didn't bother meeting his gaze. He grabbed the scroll and broke the seal, studying the words on the parchment as he unrolled it. The longer he remained silent, the tighter Gabriel's insides knotted. This had to work. It didn't matter if the Shades found out the truth later. The Corrupted needed to be cleansed or they had lost the war. Altamost be damned. They could not lose—Gabriel's child and every child of Eskandor deserved a future unburdened by fear.

Gabriel didn't dare glance at Kanaris, not with the commander watching his every move. He stood confidently, like this was another procedure he'd done a thousand times for the crown. A frown naturally weighed on his face while the general read the document. No matter the chaotic panic internally, he needed to appear as any envoy who had traveled to Kiji—tired, bored, and wanting to return to civilization.

He hoped that Kanaris understood this task too. It wasn't difficult to be tired. The journey had been long—longer given the sleepless nights, spying apparitions in the darkness. Every muscle tensed, every instinct on high alert—it would make any soldier tire.

War clawed at them, dragging them through the mud, hollowing them into desperation for peace. Fear ground them to dust, sewing distrust and paranoia into the fabric of their souls. They couldn't eat for the carnage they had inflicted and witnessed on the battlefield. They couldn't sleep for the nightmares forcing them to relive their battles—to stare into the faces of those they'd killed and lost.

Gabriel had gazed into countless lifeless stares, stripped of their light, left with nothingness. Death was peace, ender of pain and struggle, but only to those dead—unless regret could imbed into the soul and pass through to Paradise.

Gabriel inhaled sharply, allowing the boredom of his face to shift in impatience. The ambassador's time was invaluable. He had other business to attend on the crown's behalf. To delay him was disrespectful, wasteful of the kingdom's time, and criminal during dire circumstances.

The circumstances were indeed dire, he thought. The longer the Shades remained idle, the stronger the Corrupted grew.

The general finally lifted his gaze from the scroll, blinking brown eyes at the ambassador. All Shades had dark eyes, emptied of life and empathy. Gabriel fought from shifting his stare from that emptiness, but he yielded, wondering how he could have spent a lifetime with Vaiden and had never truly looked into his eyes.

It was natural to look away, Gabriel thought, clenching his jaw. The Shades were used to it. Wara, they probably didn't even notice how uncomfortable their lifeless eyes were—how only the dead had stares that empty. It was why no one could hold their gaze. No one liked to look into the face of Death.

"Ambassador Steel," the general said. "The king wishes for the Shades to leave Kiji Village and return to our duties."

"The Corrupted are out of control." He nodded. "It is in the kingdom's best interest for the Shades to cleanse our lands of their evil."

The general rose from his seat. "Then why, I must ask, has General Glades not accompanied you?"

Gabriel blinked, trying to mask his surprise at such a question. Why would Glades need to be involved? Why him particularly? "The general apologizes for his absence, of course," he replied. "He is busy helping protect Casimere."

"Casimere?"

Relief spread through Gabriel's body, warm as a summer day. They didn't know about Fort Khali. If they didn't know about the fall of the fort, likely the king had never sent them word further. "Fort Khali was destroyed by the Corrupted over a month ago," he explained. "General Glades has since retreated to Casimere at the king's side."

The general nodded, processing the news with little regard. "Let us address the soldiers." He motioned to the door.

A smile crept on Gabriel's lips as he aimed for the exit. Kanaris eyed him, his stature a little more relaxed. They could win this, he thought. The plan would work. Hope blossomed in his chest, sweet as the fresh air. For a moment, he truly believed Surnuna watched over them.

His smile faltered, finding their men down on their knees. Shades stood at their back with blades drawn, ready to strike down each man. Archers made themselves known at the edge of the forest, arrows notched for anyone brave enough to run.

Kanaris drew his blade, but more Shades were there, swords pointed at the bigger man. They didn't have to say anything. A battalion of the most lethal elves surrounded them. No man could win this fight. Kanaris dropped his sword, kicking it away with his boot.

Cool steel pressed to Gabriel's throat, paralyzing him in place. The commander slowly crept forward, keeping her blade pointed at his neck. Her empty expression watched his every move. He knew she wouldn't hesitate to end his life. Shades were merciless. No amount of bargaining would gain their favor.

The general stepped toward their men, all watching their leader and Gabriel with uncertainty or anger shining in their faces. The Shade observed them, studying their appearances before he turned his attention to Kanaris. Gabriel's heart dropped to his stomach. Why hadn't he thought that the rebel leader might be recognized? Perhaps because he had no idea what Kanaris had looked like before they had met in White Star, but maybe others had supplied Casimere and the Shades with a sketch.

Surnuna, Gabriel prayed, but his voice weakened in his own mind. It wasn't Surnuna he needed to beg. Her sister, the Goddess of Strength and Courage, the mightiest warrior, the scream that froze an army—Wara created the Shades. She made them invulnerable to elven magic and weaknesses, like emotions and attachments. They followed every order, never complained, and always completed the mission. They were the perfect soldiers—and Altamost controlled them.

"I will give you the option to explain," the general said with his hands behind his back. His blank stare bore into Gabriel, sharper than any blade. "For the recording of history."

The commander lowered her short sword from his throat, pressing it against his chest. Gabriel's eyes darted from her back to the general. They would allow him to speak—a traitor from their perspective.

"May I ask questions?" Gabriel inquired.

"If you are to ask how I know the king did not send that order," he said, "it was not the seal or the wording, but how it was signed. The king only signs as the crown, never with his name."

Damn. A small detail Duke Heiron or Gabriel could have never known. "You know the Corrupted need to be stopped," Gabriel began. "You know the king is wrong to hold you here."

"What is right and wrong is not for us to determine. We are assigned to Kiji Village. Here we shall stay until another order is made by the crown."

How could he argue with someone who did not have a conscience? He had argued often with Vaiden throughout the years, finding the Shade's thoughts to be more logical than emotional. He could not win pulling on the heart strings of Shades. They had none. Perhaps Vaiden had only challenged him so Gabriel could one day debate the general of all Shades. No argument was more pressing or dire than the future of their kingdom. If this was going to be the last debate he had, he wouldn't go down without a fight.

"So the crown is your master," Gabriel said, standing tall, summoning the strength of a bear, allowing his words to be its claws. "Is the crown more respectable and more powerful than your goddess?"

"The goddesses are above all mortals."

"You wait for an order from a king, a mere mortal, but dismiss your true calling, for which you were born to serve, a calling made by Wara herself," he explained. "Purpose."

The general tilted his head, but remained quiet.

"Did Wara not create Shades to fight the Corrupted? To destroy their evil? To keep our world safe and the magic sacred?" Gabriel asked. "You may believe it is orders that keep you here, but what are the orders of a king compared to the orders of a goddess? Shall you explain to Wara why you stood idly by while the Corrupted destroyed the world her sisters built? Why you denied your purpose? Why you defied your nature?"

The Shades' dark eyes aimed at him, a thousand arrows ready to strike him down. The need to fulfill their purpose hummed around him, like the buzzing of winged insects. They knew the evil that brewed within the kingdom. Only they were built to cleanse it.

"You said the goddesses are above all mortals," Gabriel said. "Wara is above the king. Her orders are above his. She commands you to destroy the Corrupted. Why are you here?"

The general looked away, his eyes studying something unseen. Gabriel didn't dare breathe, didn't allow hope to fill his heart again while he waited for the general's answer. The commander hadn't moved. She kept her blade pressed against his chest, ready for the general's order to execute him.

The rebels waited too. Each of their stares pleading Gabriel's words were enough to change the Shade's mind. It had to be enough. Without the Shades, they lost.

Kanaris dipped his chin at the ambassador, a sign of respect. If they died, at least they wouldn't watch the world burn. Gabriel's thoughts shifted to his wife, alone in Mysogus. Vaiden was right. He should have been with her.

His arms longed for the solidness of her body. His touch craved her softness, the silkiness of her hair, and her arms wrapped around his back. If he died, he wanted to die in her arms, embraced in each other's warmth, bathed in her sweet scent. That was his Paradise.

"Withdraw," the general finally said. The commander stepped back, sheathing her weapon. The other Shades followed suit, moving in perfect synchronicity. Gabriel's lungs caved with the need for air. His body desperately clung to the wall he'd built in his mind to hold back hope. He inhaled and it breached. Its warmth soothed every sore muscle, especially his beating heart.

"We leave on the morrow," the general announced. "To Casimere."

Doubt squeezed hope with an icy hand. "Why Casimere?"

"The king must answer why we must follow his orders over the commands of our goddess," he explained. "Commander, you have the village. Make the necessary preparations."

She nodded at the general, springing toward the camp. The other Shades followed her, purpose moving with their every step. The general returned to the commander's office, stating he had much to do.

Kanaris came to Gabriel's side, nudging him slightly. "Who knew the Shades would be sentimental about their goddess?" The rebel leader crossed his arms, relaxed while he watched the Shades move around the village.

Gabriel wanted to boast, to pretend he hadn't been afraid, but he hid his shaking hands behind his back. In the open village under the sunlight of Surnuna's glory, he had been exposed and he hadn't faltered. His father was wrong. Only the brave could look Death in the face and fight.

42

The only thing that signified Forsaken Road as a road was the dirt path streaked through dead brush. It was a downhill march, zigzagging around rocky terrain. Vaiden didn't care for it. Neither did Duke Heiron's horse, which caused him to walk amongst the men while another soldier led the chestnut mare carefully down the windy road.

He needed the exercise, Vaiden thought. It would let him understand the soldier's perspective. Not that the duke hadn't lived as a soldier once. He'd risen in station and eventually served as a general before King Rothnar anointed him Duke of White Star. It had been long ago though. The duke had forgotten the tribulations of being a lower station. It was great for the calves, but torture on the feet.

The men didn't complain nearly as much as Vaiden's old comrades in the Forty-Second, but they had a far greater purpose than being the crown's personal kill squad. White Star's soldiers believed they were going to save the kingdom.

They didn't want to murder the king as much as Kanaris's rebels, but they hadn't survived Haven. They'd only heard the stories. It burned Vaiden's core to know what transpired at the fisherman village. The Corrupted had surrounded it, cut off resources from getting in, and closed off the people from escaping—a perfect capture of a village. It was shocking and horrifying what these Corrupted had accomplished.

Part of Vaiden wanted to finish them—to end the blight, but he knew Gabriel could handle the Shades. If he didn't, he wouldn't let his friend step one foot toward Kiji Village. If anyone could convince the Shades to abandon the king's order, it was Gabriel Steel.

"Worried about your friend?" Duke Heiron asked.

"I'm not worried. Gabriel can handle himself."

"I worry about my cousin every day," the duke said. "The weight of the world is on his shoulders. He feels like he must do whatever it takes to avenge the fallen of Haven. I don't disagree, but first I counseled him on realistic expectations. The king is the highest station of Eskandor. People fight for kings, even after they've been slain. I'm not sure if the rebels understand this still.

"It's why Gabriel's idea of using the council is important," Heiron continued. "By legitimizing his removal through proper channels, we can show Eskandor that our rebellion was justified, not to destroy the monarchy, but to make sure the people have a proper ruler, whose thoughts are to ensure their wellbeing."

"Not that you don't want that crown for yourself." Vaiden gave the duke a bored expression, letting his eyes show how obvious Heiron's ambition was.

"I do desire to lead people," he replied with a warm smile, "but I don't have to be the king. I enjoy governing White Star, but I will be wherever I'm needed."

"So if the council appointed one of their own to the throne, that wouldn't upset you?" Vaiden asked. "Even after all this hardship fighting the Corrupted and the crown?"

"The council knows best."

"Bullshit," Vaiden spat. "The council knows what their pockets want. Maybe a few care about the balance of the faith and crown. Some of them might actually want to better the people, but they have the same faults as everyone else."

"You mean greed."

The Shade shrugged. "Call it whatever you want. When they vote, one of them will be influencing the others to give him or her that vote and give up their power to someone else. It's all a big manipulation."

"Are you always so cynical?" the duke asked. "But I see what you mean. You have to desire the position and the desire blinds you if you *should* take it."

Vaiden sized up Heiron again. Maybe he wasn't an ambitious politician who wanted power and praise. He seemed intelligent and willing to help his people. He'd taken a position in the worst environment because a king said he'd wanted him there. Most would have declined it and stayed closer to the throne, like the nobles, but Heiron took the position and served out his duties to the best of his abilities. It was better than most who'd fancied power.

Did that make him a good candidate for the crown? Vaiden didn't know. It wasn't his job to decide these things, but he had spent a good amount of time with three kings. Rothnar had been a paranoid mess—a great military mind, but no nurturer of the people. He had such a big ego he denounced a goddess and banned worship of her. King Chorlee was also a military man, but he was soft spoken, a listener, who may have taken too long to make decisions. Who knew if he'd been a good king in the long run.

That left Altamost. Vaiden had many opinions about the current king. Some of them he'd learned about the cunning politician during their many decades together sharing rooms in Casimere. Altamost liked being in the ears of nobles and receiving praise from his superiors. For all Rothnar's paranoia, he'd never thought to approach someone like Altamost with caution. Maybe because he didn't feel physically threatened by him, but Vaiden knew that was a mistake.

Mind and body were of equal power. When someone was strong in both, they were nearly unstoppable, but that was a rare feat. Vaiden only knew of one person he'd consider both highly intelligent and physically strong—and he was a vampire millennia old.

"What qualities do you think make a good monarch?" Duke Heiron asked.

"Really?" Vaiden raised a brow at him. "You want my opinion?"

"You have been around the throne. You've had many leaders. Why not know the opinion of a Shade? Are they not the most honest of us?"

"One, you need to be a person who understands you are not the best of the best. You are not the smartest, or strongest, or the most charismatic person who has ever graced the land with your feet. You are a man with many faults and weaknesses, some of which you don't even know exist," Vaiden explained. "You must surround yourself with people who are smarter than you, who are in the business of making the kingdom the best it can be because it is their duty and *only* their duty.

"If you choose people who are in the business of making the kingdom great for themselves, they will deceive you and manipulate you to get what they want for their own greed, as we have already discussed," Vaiden answered. "Next, find someone dedicated to the military because they truly believe it is the greatest honor to serve their kingdom. Rothnar trusted the Shades because he knew they had no bias one way or the other and they would do their duty, but Shades aren't in the business of helping people because they don't care.

They should only be used for the Corrupted and keeping people safe on the roads."

"I have always believed in King Duncan's philosophy when it came to the Shades and the faith," Heiron said. "Keeping that balance is what keeps the Corrupted controlled. We should all heed his wisdom."

Vaiden fought from rolling his eyes. He did respect King Duncan, who had thought deeply about the issues regarding Eskandor's Corrupted and why practitioners of the faith crossed that line in the sand for dark magic. King Duncan had been a man with his own bias though. He was the reason why most wrote off necromancers from the start and didn't give them a chance to prove what they wanted in life. This attitude had caused many necromancers to be murdered or to turn to the dark parts of their power and become the very thing they all feared—a vicious cycle, but one that could have been avoided with the right education.

"Never think the kings of old knew everything they were doing and knew exactly how the future would be impacted," Vaiden replied. "Even Duncan failed to grasp why and how a Corrupted ensnared and killed his own son. He had terrible policies on trade too."

"He managed to open the kingdom back up to trade though," Heiron argued.

"Yes, but he made bad deals and cost the kingdom endless amounts of debt. It took over three hundred years to repair the damage he'd caused in trade. Rothnar complained about it often."

"I didn't know about that."

Vaiden spotted one of their archers creeping along the tree line. He might have pointed him out, but he saw no reason as he was an ally. The Shade instead gave him direct eye contact, letting him know he wasn't as hidden as he thought he was. The archer responded by sinking further into the shadows. At least he learned quickly.

"The monarchy is the servant of the people," Duke Heiron said. "It should be a selfless calling, just like the Leader of the Faith."

"You think the faithful are selfless?"

"No, but it takes great sacrifice to ascend to that station," he replied. "They put themselves last in the pursuit of knowledge and understanding of the goddesses, in educating the young, and preserving the sanctity of Myosgus."

"All of which are the definitions of elevating oneself to the leader of a cult," Vaiden argued. "The greatest lie they tell High Elves is that the faith is all they need. It will provide. It will guide them. It will protect them. No, only they can find what they want, need, and help themselves."

"Very Shade-like of you to say."

"If we can take care of ourselves at ten years old, why can't the rest of you?"

The duke stared at Vaiden as if he was trying to solve a mathematical equation. Eventually, the silence between them grew as Heiron turned back to the road. His eyes drank in their surroundings, the bleak gray of the mountain base where winter lingered and would eventually erupt into spring the further south they grew.

"Where did you grow up, Shade?" he asked.

"Is that really a question?"

"Before Kiji," he said. "You must have lived somewhere."

"Between Alumpius's shrine and White Star," he replied, purposely leaving out High Tower to avoid answering any questions about it.

"Aha! That's how you know how to infiltrate my city!" He grinned as if he'd caught Vaiden with his hand in the cookie jar. "You have lived there."

"You should be concerned that other people who have lived there could invade it so easily."

The duke settled. "Well, I already gave orders for the walls to be checked for any holes, just so you know. The remaining guards and soldiers will be watching over the gate and the mountain, ensuring the safety of our people within."

"Do you trust your second-in-command?"

"She's a fine woman, my wife, years of service to the military, the faithful, and the people."

"Was she a bard?"

Heiron made a face, twisting to look at the Shade.

"I'm trying to figure out what connects all these things. Bards and cooks are what come to mind first. I expect she's not one of Layetta's ladies."

The duke laughed, throwing his head back. "She was an envoy from Mysogus. Most of her term was with the soldiers at Fort Khali many decades ago. I'm not sure what she would think of someone claiming she was a Lady of Layetta. It might make her day."

Layetta was the Goddess of Fertility and lesser known as the Goddess of Pleasure. The Ladies of Layetta widely lived in Brevene, close to their goddess's shrine or at the fane where they upheld their goddess's commandments, one of which was spreading sexual pleasure.

On Earth, they would have called them prostitutes, but these ladies didn't take payment, nor were they regarded as anything derogatory. It was truly thought to be an honor to lay with them. They were one of the few groups of elves that didn't have any ill will toward Shades. Many of them believed it was their privilege to pleasure the guardians of the kingdom. One had been Vaiden's first. Gabriel had saved himself for his wife.

"Do you think Altamost will yield Casimere?" Heiron asked.

"He'll have no choice."

"Maybe your suspicions of Dallia are true and it will wake him up once she is captured."

"If he was in some spell, it would have broken around me."

"It didn't?"

"No, he remained the same." Vaiden squinted at the bright sun, finally peeking out from behind the clouds. The sunlight was warm and welcomed after his stint in the cold north. He had no desire of returning to that place ever again. Soft greenery tangled with the dried dead, blending so the pop of color wasn't too powerful, like in the middle of an ombre. The whistle of birds were the first signs of wildlife he'd experienced in weeks.

"Perhaps we will learn more once we take Casimere," the duke said.

"How does that work exactly?" Vaiden asked. "The scouts sneak in and somehow open a gate without any of the guards and soldiers noticing? It seems unrealistic to me."

"How would you do it?"

"You're asking so you don't have a plan."

"Perry knows the plan, but I'm asking for your opinion."

"Take the Crystal Keep before opening the city."

Heiron scoffed. "Impossible."

"Maybe not." Vaiden shrugged. "It would be easier to hold the king hostage, have him give the orders, and walk in rather than have a battle that would kill dozens of soldiers and a handful of innocent people in the lower rings. Climbing the levels would only kill more people and soldiers until it's a mess of bodies before being overrun by the sheer forces of Casimere. They have practitioners too so eventually they would bring out the big guns and drive you back or kill you dead. Either way, it is a recipe for disaster."

Duke Heiron's face drained of color. He stared at the Shade, stopped dead in his tracks. The soldiers behind them stopped too, studying the Shade and their leader curiously. Vaiden crossed his arms, waiting patiently. He fought from smirking at the shock shining in Heiron's eyes.

"It seems adjustments should be made to the plan," the duke said, briskly continuing his march.

***

"I don't like it," Perry said, rubbing his jaw.

Vaiden and the scouts squatted on the outskirts of the woods facing the eastern gate of Casimere. Like his last visit, the gatehouse was locked up tight. No one was entering or exiting. He watched the guards atop the wall, only visible by the torches they carried. More than last time, he thought. Altamost had not increased security measures for the rebels or the Corrupted. Did Vaiden slipping away cause the king anxiety while he lay awake at night?

It made a smile tug on Vaiden's lips, but it was short lived. More guards meant more eyes and more problems for their little band of scouts.

Four others joined Perry and the Shade on the edge of the woods: an archer wearing a green cloak, the practitioner named Alumpia, who had stitched Vaiden's brow, and two sisters from a shady guild Perry had acquired from Abrita Shores.

"I don't like it," Perry said again, growling with each word. "Changing a plan last second only gets us lot caught. We should follow the original plan."

"The plan only *you* know." Vaiden raised a brow at him. "I kindly shared mine aloud."

"You want us to climb that wall." The scout leader shook his head. "I don't know if you've checked, that wall is bloody flat. There's nowhere to grab, no less keep your feet."

"Maybe the majority of the wall is like that, but they used a different stone around the gatehouses," Vaiden explained. "It's rougher and harder to shape."

Alumpia moved up to his left. Her eyes shone with the power of Opretta. In his nocturnal sight they sparkled like perfect spinel gemstones. She'd pulled her dark curls into a ponytail to keep it from distorting her vision. It was something

363

Vaiden didn't understand about many action shows, especially those involving law enforcement. No one with long hair liked to have it down when they were working, especially in a fight. It was a liability, easily solved by simply gathering it away from the face. Vaiden's hair wasn't long enough to bother him, but any longer, he'd chop it off rather than deal with it.

He was surprised by her willingness to be near him. High Elves generally wouldn't get too close, given his presence rendered them magicless. Caroline hadn't minded, except when he'd been mortally wounded and she couldn't use her gifts to heal him.

"How long will it take to climb the wall?" she asked. Finally someone asking the real questions.

"A few minutes if we're fast," he answered.

"Maybe for a tall bloke like yourself," Perry scoffed.

"It should be easy," one of the sisters said.

"As long as we time the guards right," the other echoed.

It was truly the task—the timing. If they were too slow, one of the guards could discover them and shoot them down. If they were too fast, they'd be in the fight of their lives atop that wall.

Not that the Shade was thrilled to climb another fucking wall. He hated the idea, but it was the best way into the city. Maybe not the safest route, but no route would be. It was Eskandor's capital city—the pride and joy of Leeth the Rightful and his brother King Jarviski. It had withstood countless wars—its wall impenetrable to foreigners, but not to its own. One more time, Vaiden thought, his nocturnal sight surveying the guards again.

The clearing was at least one hundred yards—a long distance in the open, especially when executing an infiltration. The darkness would cover them until they grew closer to the wall. The torches would illuminate their approach. It was the only part of the plan Vaiden truly worried would get them discovered. If so, they were never getting up that wall.

"I don't like it," Perry said again, this time barely a whisper.

"Then go back to camp," Vaiden bristled, tired of his complaining. "Duke Heiron and White Star's finest are spread between two neighboring farms. After a week waiting there, I'm sure they could use a clown."

"I don't know what that means, but I'm sure it's some kind of insult."

He glanced at Perry's harsh features, a deep V wrinkled between his eyebrows at the top of his nose. He glowered at the Shade, his leathery skin reddening.

Vaiden's nostrils flared, tired of the fisherman's attitude. "Do you want to get this done or not?" he asked. "I don't have time to deal with cowards."

"Piss on you," Perry spat, adjusting his position to sprint. "I hope you take an arrow to the arse."

A smile played with the Shade's lips as he returned his gaze to the wall. "Aw, you say such sweet nothings to me."

The scout leader growled. Gabriel was wrong. They were getting along *famously*.

They watched the guards again, torchlight gliding across the top of the wall like fireflies. Vaiden let himself grow quiet and empty. His eyes focused on the light, counting mentally in his head. He didn't know the scouts well enough to know how fast they could move, but he could gauge it in the clearing.

"Now," he breathed, his feet pushing off the lush soil. He kept his sights on the wall, his legs bounding, but footfalls fell silently on the grass as he sprinted through the clearing.

He felt, more than saw, the scouts at his sides. The archer trailed, but he was carrying the most gear. They moved as a unit, sweeping in like a school of fish, moving with one mind toward the eastern gate. Vaiden's pulse raced in his ears, his heart pumping enthusiastically. He generally hated running, but in the open field, his muscles burning in that good way, cleaving through the clean air of Arda—it was what fueled lionesses in the pride lands.

They slowed forty yards out, crouch-walking breathlessly—no longer lionesses, but jaguars slinking through long grass. They had no cover to hide their presence, but the darkness surrounded them, masking their approach in the moonless sky. The wall radiated with light, the closer they traversed. Vaiden blinked off his nocturnal sight, letting his old-fashioned vision adjust to the environment around them.

He halted as one of the fireflies veered off its normal path. The scouts stopped along with him. He could feel their eyes, unasked questions pricking his skin sharp as needles. They couldn't speak this close to the wall in the silence of the night. It would be like standing on a stage in an empty theater and yelling through a megaphone of their arrival. Not every elf had expanded hearing, but he would bet his Viper a few of those guards atop the wall did. It was generally what earned them the job for night shift.

Vaiden's own expanded hearing picked up the scurry of rodents in the field, the bubbling stream north, and the heavy boots of the guards atop the wall. The firefly finally moved on, returning to his regular route.

The Shade moved, the scouts following his lead like living shadows. Maybe Perry wasn't the brightest bulb, but he'd buried his anger to protect the others while they moved toward the wall illuminated by strategically placed torches. They didn't cover the entire wall, lighting parts around the gatehouses, not only to invite in travelers, but to also unmask mischievous rogues.

Vaiden pressed his back against the wall in the corner where it met the different stone of the gatehouse. He bent his knees, gesturing at Alumpia, before interlocking his fingers with his hands placed between his legs. She didn't question him, stepping on his hands while he lifted her up as far as his reach would allow. Next was Perry. He was heavier, but the fisherman put his pride aside and took the assist. Vaiden gave him points for that. On the other side of the gatehouse the archer would be helping the sisters do the same.

The Shade looked up the side of the gatehouse, watching Alumpia and Perry climb expertly. He grabbed the rough stone and pulled himself up, finding foot placements and new hand placements along the way. Light passed above them, reminding them of time. They had to breach the wall between fireflies. Not an easy task, hanging by their fingertips.

They were over halfway there, making great time, when Perry's foot slipped. He stifled a gasp, flattening himself against the wall, blindly trying to find a ridge for his foot. Alumpia followed suit, obviously hearing the scuffing of his boot. Vaiden peered up the wall, watching the torchlight. His expanded hearing searched for any changes in the guards' pattern. One veered, but only slightly.

Maybe they didn't have the special hearing or only those at the main gatehouse did. Vaiden climbed, reaching up while Perry and Alumpia remained silent and still, except for the fisherman's shaking arms. He grabbed Perry's boot, giving the rebel a platform to push off. Perry didn't question it. Vaiden stilled, locking his grip, muscles tensing, taking all of Perry's weight for him to make the next grab.

They continued their climb until Alumpia reached the top. One of the sisters should have breached at the same time she did. Vaiden listened while he climbed. His fingers cramped, making him wonder how he could have climbed a mountain side like this in his youth. Perry waited for a guard to pass before he climbed over the balustrade. He wasn't as graceful as the practitioner, but the fisherman managed well enough.

Then it was Vaiden's turn. With his cowl pulled over his face, wearing all black, he was nearly invisible in the shadow of the wall. Gray was actually a better choice for stealth, but Shades wore black. Over the balustrade, he could see the next guard down the wall, still marching the opposite direction. To his left the next guard stopped to peer over the wall, looking out toward the bubbling stream. Maybe he had heard something.

Vaiden crouch-walked, soundlessly toward the inner wall, spying Perry and Alumpia retreating down the other side. The archer shot across the wall to his side of the gatehouse, catching the gaze of a guard.

Shit. Vaiden climbed over the side of the balustrade, far enough down to be hidden, but he could see the archer.

"Intruder!" cried the guard. "Stop!"

The Shade debated on helping the archer, who hesitated to join the sisters down the wall, but if he did, he would give them all up. Instead he put up his hands, sinking to his knees, just like Vaiden had instructed for them to do if any of them were caught. They would hold him for questioning on the morrow.

Vaiden looked down, nodding at Perry and Alumpia. They continued their descent. Vaiden thought it was more difficult to go down than up. Blindly finding foot holes sucked. The Shade clenched his jaw, his muscles tensed from all the climbing, being pushed over these last several months on Arda. He mentally added rock climbing to a list of exercises for his new workout.

At the base of the wall, his eyes searched the darkness for where the others rendezvoused. He found them huddled around the stables. With the market closed, it was empty. Vendors weren't allowed to stay overnight, a law Rothnar had enacted and Altamost had upheld.

When he joined them, one of the sisters opened her mouth to speak, but Vaiden put up a single finger against his lips, signaling for them to remain quiet. The sister closed her mouth, but her lips twisted in annoyance. The Shade pointed down the wall. Even with the archer captured, the mission continued. They could not rescue him from the guards, who would hold him at the gatehouse until one of the blue tunics could climb down from the castle for questioning.

In the back of Vaiden's head, he knew the guards were smart enough to know the archer wouldn't have made the attempt alone. They would be sweeping the area. Vaiden and the scouts needed to be far away by then.

Alumpia took the front, crouch-walking in her blue tunic, which appeared gray in his nocturnal sight. Perry had her back with the sisters between him and the Shade. They moved ghostly through the windy pathways between the stables, the blacksmithing station, and other permanent merchant booths. The right-most archway that led to the second ring was unguarded.

Some things never change, Vaiden thought.

Music played in a tavern, lit by the fire of a hearth and lanterns in the windows. Altamost may have increased security on the wall, but he'd allowed the citizens to continue their merry ways. Anything else might drive attention to his need to have total control of Casimere and its people. A disgruntled people were angry people. The angrier they became, the more likely they were to riot. Altamost would be faced with hard decisions then—keeping up the charade or disciplining the rioters through force. While it would be interesting to know what he would choose, Vaiden would rather stop his reign to prevent more disasters, like Haven.

The streets were bare, only a straggler here and there. They remained hidden, not wanting to alert any wandering eyes. More music reverberated through another tavern, the beat of this song was more lively. People danced through the bright windows.

"We need to go back for him," he heard one of the sisters say. "We can't just leave—"

"There's no helping him," Vaiden cut in, earning a glare from her.

"You don't know him," she scowled.

"We either save your friend or this kingdom. Choose."

She blinked dark eyes at him, processing his words. Her sister grabbed her arm, pulling her down the shadowed alley. Perry took a step toward them, but Alumpia stopped him, shaking her head.

"She's just worried," the practitioner whispered, "but he'll be fine."

"We need to go," Vaiden said, tracking the torchlight of a guard making rounds. He hadn't received word of trespassers, but the sound of heavy footsteps approached the second ring. They were coming and the scouts were behind schedule. Every second wasted was a second they could be caught and the mission failed.

43

The Preternatural Incident Task Force, or PITF, had been called to the Supernatural Detention Center. Tatiana argued with the police's incident commander and their team leader that she needed to know the status of her client, but it was clear they had no intention of telling her. The only information they had released was that a new prisoner had started trouble, injuring one of the officers. They had locked down the place, but it managed to break through its cell door.

She didn't know what the "it" was. PITF wouldn't inform her of that either. Sergeant Pérez and his team were still inside the building, aiding PITF with information by phone and video. Tatiana hadn't known they could access the surveillance cameras from the outside, but she watched the feed hoping to catch a glimpse of Mr. Slaseezor's cell.

A couple of other attorneys showed up and not long after them so did the press. Uniform officers kept them behind police tape that they'd quickly thrown up at the edge of the parking lot. Even nearly fifty yards away, Tatiana could hear them shouting questions or recording updates for their stations. While she agreed the public deserved to know when they were in danger, it was not apparent that was the case. This was an isolated incident, contained in the SDC—as long as PITF could keep it contained.

"What's going on?" one of the other attorneys demanded at her side.

"One of the preternaturals broke out of their cell, but that's all the information they would share with me," Tatiana replied.

"Let me try," another said, puffing out his chest. Tatiana fought from rolling her eyes, but instead frowned at the man. One of the PITF members eyed them, looking offended for her. "Who is the team leader?"

"That would be me," a tall broad-shouldered man with a shaved head answered. His dark skin appeared richer in the navy blue tactical gear. By the way he handled himself, Tatiana would have said military, but she wasn't sure when it came to PITF because technically they were paramilitary for the level of weaponry and strategy they used, but at the same time they were not because they didn't fall under one of the six branches of military. The only other trained police force with higher jurisdiction to handle situations involving the supernatural were the Marshals.

"Lindsey Jenkins." He offered his hand to the PITF team leader, who took it for a firm handshake. "I represent Mr. Akeen. I would like to know his status and—"

"The area is secure, Brax," another PITF member interrupted.

Brax wasn't his given name, but a code name the team leader earned. He turned to the monitors. "Sergeant Pérez, my team is ready to move in," he said into the headset's microphone. "Initiate Protocol Step Three."

"What does that mean?" Mr. Jenkins asked. "Is my client safe or not?"

Brax ignored him. "Move out," he ordered through the microphone.

Tatiana watched the eight members of the team waiting by the front doors to breach. They did so effortlessly thanks to the officers within. She knew there were special protocols to perform during a takeover of the SDC because vampires could glamour people into performing tasks that seemed helpful but were designed to spring a trap. If the protocols were not met in the right order then PITF knew a vampire was involved. That required a whole new level of protocols to take down one.

By the way PITF moved through the protocols, Tatiana didn't think a vampire was involved. That left elves, felines, and serpents. She hoped Mr. Slaseezor wasn't involved. Although he wasn't a new prisoner at the facility, she didn't know what PITF's definition of "new" was. He had been added before the weekend. Some might consider that new, but not in Tatiana's experience. Supernaturals only had a week in holding before their trials. If found guilty they either were sent to a preternatural prison, deported to Arda (if originally from there), or executed—they were rarely sent to prison.

While the injustice burned through her, she returned to her position near the entrance of the opened surveillance van to watch the monitors. The PITF members working outside of it did not seem to care if she watched as long as she didn't hamper their procedures. The other attorney came to her side while

Mr. Jenkins argued with the team leader—or rather argued at him. Brax stayed focused on his team's task, somehow tuning out Mr. Jenkins's questions.

"Do you know what the protocols mean?" the other attorney asked.

She shook her head. "Afraid not, Mr. Kinsley."

He deflated like a balloon, his narrow shoulders drooping. Sweat beaded across his forehead while he gazed at the SDC. He was older than her by the silver streaks in his dark hair. She knew him as one of the attorneys from the Public Defender's Office.

"I know a vampire isn't involved though," she added. "The protocols were met properly before they went in."

"You've witnessed a vampire take over the SDC?"

"No," she said, "but I've read about the many cases of it. One happened down in San Francisco, you know."

"That one was a lesser, trying to free a court member."

"Their master had ordered him to do it by any means necessary," Tatiana explained. "When the protocols weren't met properly PITF shifted gears and tricked the lesser into giving up the officers within, saying it was routine for them to come out before PITF went in. The vampires fell for it."

"Didn't they glamour the officers though?"

"Only to release the vampire in holding and to speak to PITF, but the vampire in charge of the glamouring didn't order the officers specifically about the protocols and how to perform them properly."

"Do you think other vampires will learn the protocols now?"

"I'm not sure how they will learn the correct order unless they do a mission just to learn the order, but the information will be lost once the vampire who broke into the SDC is executed."

"Maybe they'll use one of us," he chuckled. His hands were stuffed into his pants pockets while his eyes darted around the grounds. The smell of sweat clung to the air around him like a dirty cloud.

"It's possible," she replied, "but if one of us willingly told someone the protocols we would lose our license."

"They would just say the vampire glamoured them."

"Glamouring stops working after the vampire is dead."

"True, but they could probably use a phone to tell the other vampires before the one is executed."

She blinked at Mr. Kinsley, studying his average features. He chewed on his bottom lip, his torso rocking slightly. His dark eyes wandered aimlessly or searched for something, but what? Not that she didn't agree that if vampires wanted PITF's protocol information, they would find a way, but he seemed quite certain of how they would do it.

"Is your client a vampire?" she asked.

He blinked at her, his eyes wide and his skin suddenly milky. "You know I cannot disclose—"

"When was your client admitted to the SDC?"

"Last night."

"Shit." Tatiana raced to the team leader, pushing Mr. Jenkins aside.

"Hey!" he gasped.

"It's a vampire," she said to Brax. "It's tricking you, making the officers do the protocols in order to learn them properly."

His brow furrowed but he said nothing.

"It is going to sacrifice itself to tell the information to its attorney at the given moment and that attorney is going to share the information with the master of the court," she explained.

"Sacrificial lamb," Mr. Jenkins mused. "Vampires will do *anything* to preserve their power and court."

Tatiana glanced at her fellow defense attorney. He was dressed in an expensive suit, too hot to wear in this weather, but for the sake of professionalism he'd worn it, maybe because he thought he'd be in the office all day. His comment about vampires' sense of self-preservation struck her as odd for someone willing to defend them. Maybe he didn't take vampire clients though. She didn't know where he worked or for whom.

The team leader's eyes darted between the two attorneys. "The target is not a vampire," he said, returning his attention to the monitors. "Greenlight, Bravo."

"Paranoid, Ms. Smith," Mr. Jenkins chuckled behind her. "Maybe you weren't ready to return to work after all."

She wanted to give him a piece of her mind, but he moved away with his smartphone up to his ear. Her stare drifted to Mr. Kinsley who hadn't moved from his position. He'd crossed his arms, staring daggers into her.

Great, she thought. One fellow attorney thought she was losing it while she'd completely insulted another's integrity. She spread her hands wide, trying to convey her apologies to Mr. Kinsley. He glowered at her, returning his attention to the monitors while the team leader gave more orders to his people.

"Snipers ready," he said, making Tatiana wonder where they could be positioned. His order to the snipers also meant the target wasn't in the basement. It had broken through to the upper floors. A shot struck the air, loud as a rocket and gone just as quickly. Her pulse pounded in her ears while she studied the building, wondering if it hit the intended target. More gunfire sounded deeper within the building.

Brax shifted on his feet with his hands on his hips, listening to his team through the headphones while he watched the monitors. She saw someone move in one of the screens, but the quality of the cameras was obstructed by a haze. They had thrown smoke bombs. She wondered how that would affect the preternatural. She gathered the smell of the smoke would hinder all of them, especially serpent-kind. A flash grenade would disorient elves from the sudden explosiveness of it. They also relied on their vision, much like humans and felines.

"Good work, team," Brax said into the microphone. "Secure the scene. We are Code Four."

Code Four universally meant everything was under control and it was safe. At least, she knew police officers who had said as much.

"You three." The team leader pointed at each lawyer, his eyes narrowing. "Come with me."

Tatiana hesitated, casting a glance at Mr. Kinsley, whose hardened expression had sobered, pressing his lips into a thin line and furrowing his brow. His thumb massaged the palm of his other hand. Mr. Jenkins apologized to the person on the other end of his call and promptly followed Brax. He hustled, trying to keep pace with the PITF officer's long strides.

Mr. Kinsley gestured, silently saying "after you" to Tatiana. She offered him a small smile and proceeded after the other men. When she entered the doors to the SDC, she realized he wanted to be last in case the subject wasn't truly dead. She would be his meat shield to distract the subject for him to retreat toward safety, or perhaps she was being cynical and he had been polite.

Sergeant Pérez and his officers stood by the metal detectors, wearing bullet proof vests. A few of them held shotguns or rested their hands on their pistols. Tatiana didn't blame them. The idea that a supernatural would tear them apart to be free would make anyone want to have a gun in their hands. In the back of her head, she knew it could slow down some supernaturals, but if they wanted to escape, it would be a fight to the death. This time the supernatural had died and the officers appeared fine.

Officer Sampson smiled at her, threading his fingers through his short hair. She wanted to ask him what had happened, but she followed her fellow attorneys to the security station. Mr. Jenkins had brought a briefcase so he had to put it through the machine for scanning while Mr. Kinsley and Tatiana took turns through the metal detector. She realized as she stepped through, she had left her phone in her car. Not that she would need it, but the idea she couldn't call Zarah for backup chilled her blood.

There were plenty of officers, she thought. Even from the car, Zarah had to know PITF had secured the scene. They wouldn't have let the attorneys inside otherwise.

Tatiana exhaled, assuming the position for the female officer to pat her down. Beside her, Mr. Kinsley frowned at his officer's thoroughness.

"My buddy in human law never has to do this," he grumbled.

She stifled a quip and smiled instead at her fellow defense attorney. He scoffed as the officer finished his pat down and gave the all clear.

"The subject is upstairs," Brax announced while Mr. Jenkins began his pat down. "You may visit with your clients downstairs, but do not attempt to contaminate our scene. Any evidence you believe to have found alert a member of the SDC or one of my team. Do not touch it yourself. Are we clear?"

They nodded. Mr. Jenkins grunted in understanding. "I leave you in the hands of Sergeant Pérez and his officers." He nodded at the captain, whose lips curled up with appreciation. When police of different jurisdictions trusted each other with important responsibilities, it was a sign of respect and that Brax believed in the competence of the SDC's officers to handle the remaining supernatural in holding.

"This way," the sergeant ordered like the attorneys did not know the way to the basement. The elevator ride was quiet and crowded with all the attorneys huddled between Pérez and a couple of his officers. Sampson stood on Tatiana's left, staring straight ahead. He had his game face on, like the threat wasn't over.

"How is the injured officer?" Tatiana asked him.

"Jim will be fine," he answered with a neutral tone. "It wasn't bad."

She didn't know how he was injured, but she was glad it wasn't too serious. "That's good to hear."

"When the elevator doors open, let the officers exit first," the sergeant said. "Do not touch anything or take any photos with your phones."

Tatiana wanted to tell him she didn't have her phone, but she saw Mr. Jenkins promptly turned his off and stuffed it inside his jacket pocket. He swallowed hard, his Adam's apple visibly bobbing. She studied his manicured physique, wondering if this was his first ride down to the basement. Before she could ask, the doors opened, followed by the officers moving to the hall. The sergeant gestured for them to exit. Mr. Jenkins pushed forward, his jaw clenched, then Tatiana and Mr. Kinsley trailed behind him. They walked in that line with the sergeant and one officer leading the way while Sampson took up the rear.

The hall appeared normal. No signs of a struggle, nothing broken, and the lighting remained bright as ever. She wasn't sure what she had expected or what the police were wanting to protect, but there was no evidence to see—until they reached the cells.

Mr. Kinsley audibly gasped behind her at the sight of claw marks splitting the concrete wall. The last cell door appeared blasted open from the inside, the heavy metal bent from the impact. Blood splattered against the opposing wall, where she suspected the officer had been injured. Mr. Jenkins's summer tan paled, surveying the damage to the concrete floors where more claw marks were being observed by a member of PITF.

Another PITF officer stood by the broken door armed with an automatic rifle held in a relaxed position. "The area is secure," she said. "You may proceed."

Sergeant Pérez nodded at him, coming to a halt. He gazed at the attorneys with a raised brow, his dark eyes sweeping over them as if measuring their courage. Mr. Kinsley stood on Tatiana's right, pulling at his collar like it was too tight. Sweat beaded down his brows, forcing him to wipe it away with the back of his hand.

"Whose client was in the last cell?" he asked, voice trembling.

The sergeant frowned at him, the weight of his eyes saying more than his expression about what he thought about the lawyer from the Public Defender's office. Mr. Kinsley was a nice man, perhaps too weak kneed for working with supernatural kind, but at least he made an effort. Even the big time players in the region didn't want to tackle preternatural law. They thought it was too complicated or too risky for their track numbers. At one time Tatiana valued her wins and losses, being one of the most successful attorneys in the city, but recently—after six months ago—she was glad to be alive.

Pérez clicked his tongue. "Mr. Jenkins, your client has been neutralized upstairs. The coroner is on her way," he explained. "Before the de—"

"If he's dead then why did you bring me down here?" Mr. Jenkins scowled, his hand white knuckling around his briefcase handle. "I have other *paying* clients."

Tatiana's head whipped around. How could he be so callous? His client was dead.

"Like I was saying, Mr. Jenkins, the detectives will be here shortly," he said. "I thought you would like to see the crime scene before they arrive."

The attorney's nose wrinkled. "Why?"

The sergeant moved to Cell Three where Tatiana's client resided beyond the door. He gestured at claw marks punctured through the metal like the supernatural had tried to break it apart with its bare hands. "Your client had a clear motive for wanting to be down in this basement."

Here kitty, kitty, whispered through Tatiana's mind. Her pulse thudded in her ears as she studied the damage between the two cell doors. No feline was capable of such brute strength and Brax claimed it was not a vampire. That only left—

"He was a serpent." The words left her lips soft as a whisper. "He got arrested to initiate a hit on my client."

Pérez nodded. "That is our theory too."

"He was strung out." Mr. Jenkins waved it away. "Who knows how many chemicals were in his system?"

"The coroner will find out," the sergeant said. "In the meantime, this is an ongoing investigation. We will presume that every inmate in these cells is in danger."

Tatiana knew that meant stricter regulations, but she wasn't sure what they could do to make their clients more secure. Only their attorneys were allowed to visit them. They remained secluded in cells with reinforced concrete ten feet deep. Perhaps they'd learned their doors weren't as strong as they had originally anticipated. It meant someone would have to design even heavier, stronger doors for the SDC.

"You will both get ten minutes with your clients," Pérez announced. "Make them count."

She wanted to argue with the time, but the detectives would arrive soon. They would lock up the crime scene and not allow anyone entrance until it was processed. The sergeant was giving them the only time they had to speak with their clients.

Officer Sampson opened Cell Three and she stepped inside. Mr. Slaseezor was chained at the table as he had every time she'd entered his cell. His dragon expression sobered, looking less intimidating and more worried.

"Ms. Smith," he said. "There was a lot of gunfire in the hall."

She nodded, taking the seat across from him, foregoing all the formalities. "I don't have much time," she replied. "The gunfire was to stop a serpent that was in the cell next to you."

"What? Why?"

"He was sent to kill you."

"But—"

"Does your wife have ties to serpents in gangs or the mob?"

His brow furrowed. "Why would you ask me that?"

"Does Rocahn have ties to serpents who would want to hurt her or you?"

He shook his head. "She left the east coast decades ago. No trouble from the serpents there."

"Mr. Slaseezor, I don't have a lot of time and even less until you go in front of a judge," she said. "You need to tell me everything you know about your wife's past. Does she deal in the black market? I saw the exotic plants growing in the den. I know they could be legal, but if she's growing illegal ones—"

"My wife has nothing to do with such things," he hissed. "You need to focus on people who would want to hurt Koreen. My wife adored him. Why would she kill him?"

"I know about Arkella and Koreen," Tatiana replied, witnessing the confusion etching across his face. "I also think your wife kept many things secret from you about their coupling."

He shook his head, a loud exasperating sound escaping his sharp teeth. "You're wrong."

"Arkella's family wanted Koreen to couple with their daughter. They needed him to join the Grand Den to do that. They had even made a petition, but Rocahn made too many demands."

"You're wrong!" he spat, baring his teeth at her, leaning across the table. "My wife made no such demands. No one wanted to couple Koreen."

"Did he tell you that or did Rocahn?"

His dragon head tilted, golden eyes searching for something unseen.

"I know one of Rocahn's demands was access to the Grand Den's garden. It was an odd request, but given your wife's love of plants, I thought she needed something from it."

Mr. Slaseezor calmed, settling back against his chair. "Like what?" he asked.

"She had told me she was having trouble keeping the Ardan plants alive," she explained. "I know the Grand Den has special fertilizer that uses elven magic to keep their plants thriving. Is there something she's wanted to grow and couldn't?"

"Is that why you believe she's part of the black market?"

"You can make a lot of money on Ardan foliage there."

Mr. Slaseezor looked down at his chained hands. "She's always been interested in plants. Told me she loved to make gardens with her grandparents back east. I suppose it would be a perk for our den to ascend by the Grand Den's orders so we could have access to its gardens. Why does this mean she wants the plants for the black market?"

It was a good question. "Arkella said her first demand was money. You don't generally ask for money in coupling do you, Mr. Slaseezor?"

He remained quiet for a couple of seconds, hardly breathing.

"Mr. Slaseezor?" she demanded. "Like I said, I don't have much time. I need you to answer my questions. Your freedom depends on it."

"You humans always use our freedom against us." His head whipped up to meet her stare. "We are only allowed so much, not because it is our right but because it is the limits you are comfortable with."

She exhaled, her shoulders slumping. He wasn't wrong. The human governments controlled how much freedom supernatural kind was allowed and wasn't. Other countries would hunt them down and kill them. Some had granted them citizenship, but it wasn't the same as their human civilians.

"Mr. Slaseezor, I understand this is difficult, but you need to remember." She placed her hand between them on the table. "I'm on *your* side above all else. I'm *your* attorney. I'm here to fight for *you*."

"Even against my own wife?"

She tried to convey sympathy with her eyes, but he looked away, snarling. Then another thought crossed her mind. "Zabetha was murdered."

His head whipped around again, eyes wide as he stared at her. "Zabetha? How?"

"I know a note was delivered to your den while I was there, stating she was killed," Tatiana said, choosing her words carefully. She didn't say *all* she knew. It was splitting hairs, but she couldn't blurt out she was there when Zabetha was murdered. The officers in the hall could be listening. "Rocahn said the Underground killed her, but from my contacts, the Underground doesn't send notes." Another lie, but only because she knew Zarah hadn't sent the note and her contacts hadn't sent one either.

Mr. Slaseezor's gaze swept across the wall behind her until they finally landed on her again. "Then who killed her?"

"I don't know, but it is highly suspicious, considering Zabetha had been following Koreen before he was dead. She told me she did it on Rocahn's orders. Why would she want to spy on Koreen?"

"We were taking care of him for his family. Maybe Rocahn wanted to make sure he wasn't up to no good."

"Would you have had him followed?"

He shook his head. "The women care for the young ones."

"Is it standard practice for the young ones to be followed?"

"The ones part of a coupling do generally have escorts."

"But Koreen and Arkella's coupling wasn't finalized."

He looked away again. This time something resembling hurt shone in his eyes. "I did not know Rocahn had met with Arkella's family about them coupling, but I had been busy with the charity and getting the ceremony ready for Koreen. Perhaps she didn't want to bother me with such things."

"The Grand Den had accepted an exception for Koreen," Tatiana explained, making his head rise again. "All he needed to do was join the faith and the Grand Den would ascend him to their ranks for coupling with Arkella."

"Cutting us out?" Mr. Slaseezor's mouth hung agape, his pupils constricting into the smallest of slits. "It is a great insult for Koreen's family to be left with nothing for his coupling."

"But Koreen's family is on Arda."

"Yes, but our den..." His words stopped while his tongue tasted the air, his eyes darting around the room, searching for something unseen. A long minute he sat there silently. His dragon head remained tilted upward, staring at nothing.

Tatiana placed her hand on the table between them again. "Mr. Slaseezor, time is running out."

"My wife has asked many questions about plants on Arda," he said in almost a whisper, like he knew the officers outside could be listening. "Especially the ones from our lands and the ones from the north."

"What is north?"

"It had belonged to the vampires long ago," he answered. "Their plants are harder to grow here on Earth, much like the pink trees in the elf kingdom. They need magic from the soil."

"I see, does the Grand Den have any plants from the old vampire lands?"

"They would never bring them to Earth. It is forbidden."

"Why?"

"A lot of their plants are poisonous or dangerous in many ways. It is said the last emperor used vines to kill many of our kind. It is one of the few plants our skin doesn't protect us from, or our natural immunity to most poisons."

"What vines could hurt your kind?"

He paused, gazing into Tatiana's eyes with realization of what, she had no idea until the words left his lips. "Nightbloom."

The words chilled her blood, the cords of the knot in her stomach pulling tighter. She had never heard of the vine, but something deep inside her roared to life, preaching caution in a grave voice she desperately wanted to hear in person.

Before she could ask anymore questions, the door to the cell swung open. "Time is up," Officer Sampson announced. "Come, Ms. Smith. The detectives will not wait."

She followed his orders, not wanting any trouble for her client. Mr. Slaseezor stared up at her, pleading silently for her to be wrong about his wife. Tatiana hoped she was. She hoped someone else was behind Koreen's death, but it seemed unlikely, especially considering his own surprise when she had told him of the Grand Den's petition to accept Koreen into their ranks. Rocahn had kept that from him—had kept information secret that his favorite pupil would ascend to the Grand Den and leave them with an empty nest. It wasn't sadness in Mr. Slaseezor's eyes. It was betrayal—a hurt Tatiana knew intimately.

44

They had squatted in the darkness for over two hours while the guards of the city searched for more intruders. Vaiden did not like sitting in one place, but the scouts had made it a point that if they had continued changing positions, the chances of them being caught were substantial. He didn't like it, but he knew it would be irresponsible to expect the scouts to maneuver through the city like him, a former guard.

Perry cursed softly, kneeling in the soil beside him. Vaiden eyed the uncomfortable fisherman, but quickly returned his attention to the guards down the street. They were ending their search any moment, he thought.

"Bad knee?" the Shade asked.

"Aye, twisted it something strange years ago. Hasn't been right since," Perry answered quietly. "Healers said nothing can be done about it. Too much time lost."

"Have you thought about rebreaking it then having it fixed?"

"Why would I do that?"

"The magic will revert the damage, restoring it whole."

"You know that for a fact?"

Vaiden nodded, remembering several times he'd broken bones. "It's a pain in the ass, but it works."

"You are a Shade," Alumpia whispered. "Who healed you?"

"A vampire."

He felt the scouts still behind him—their eyes tracing his backside. It might have been strange for any elf in those days to speak of vampires, especially elves not part of the Last Empire War. He suspected none of them were old enough to have served in that hell, but no one truly needed to experience a war. It did nothing but bring about death and corruption.

Corruption they were now tasked to destroy.

"You make nice with the vampires?" Perry asked, venom lacing his words.

"No," Vaiden replied flatly.

"Then why would one heal you?"

"He's a family friend."

"So your family makes nice with vampires?"

Vaiden eyed the fisherman again, his eyes empty and blank. Perry's face was twisted with disgust. He wasn't old enough to have such contempt for vampire-kind. He had probably never met one.

"What do you know of vampires?" one of the sisters questioned. "Maybe some are good just like some of us are bad?"

The Shade shook his head, hiding the edges of a smile as he watched the guards move on. She wasn't wrong. Not all the vampires were evil like their last emperor. Some of the more decent ones had survived the war only to be slain by their neighbors or cast through the doors to Earth. Zarah had been one of the saved. A good one, he thought—someone he trusted to look after Tatiana until he returned. She would. She owed him.

"Move out," he said, crouch-walking into the dark streets of the second ring. They followed the shadows, evading torchlight and lanterns hanging from window sills. The alleys through the residential sector of the ring brought them to the courtyard between Alvez's home and others. Vaiden thought it would be a great place to hide for a few hours, but as he studied the locked cellar doors, he knew the only way inside was through the front doors.

Soldiers patrolled the front of the building. Two blue tunic guards stood at the entrance, watching their brethren closely. By their sentry posture, clearly they were posted to guard the councilman's home. A thread of anxiety pierced through Vaiden's stomach while he studied the soldiers, looping to and from the home. They weren't leaving any time soon.

"What now?" Alumpia asked at his back.

He motioned for her to go back to the courtyard with the others. She listened, giving her back to him. Strange, he thought, following her through the side yard. Had he ever met a High Elf that would gladly give their back to a Shade? He couldn't think of an instance outside of Caroline and Lewej, but they were friends. Coastal was his mother.

"Well?" Perry inquired impatiently, one knee buried into the grass.

"They're watching the house," he answered. "We'll have to move on."

"Even you said the best chance to get inside the castle was at morning shift change."

"I did, but the plan's changed."

"By Opretta, the plan keeps changing," the fisherman gritted. "We should have stuck to the original plan."

"The original plan would have gotten every single one of you killed."

Perry's jaw clenched, his brows knitting together. "You don't know that."

"I know this city and how it operates."

The scout leader opened his mouth, ready to spew more venom, when Alumpia cut in. "Where do we go now?" she asked.

Vaiden didn't bother answering her. He ducked under tree limbs headed toward the outer wall. The path forward would be trickier, but not impossible. He didn't like giving away so many secrets in one mission, but whatever ended this civil war to ultimately defeat the Corrupted was worth it. After all, he'd return to Earth, leaving behind the wreckage of this world to others. What did he care if the scouts learned the secret routes of Casimere?

Shouting filled the alleys between houses, echoed by laughter and cheering. The taverns' patrons had finally decided to go home. They stumbled across the cobbled paths, leaning on each other, some of them singing. Their loud, brash voices were the perfect cover for the scouts to race across the shadowed alleys along the outer wall straight through the third ring, headed for the fourth.

Alumpia stayed at Vaiden's back, while the shorter teammates struggled to keep up. The Shade could slow his pace, but he didn't know how long the drunken masses would stay outside. They needed to climb one more wall into the gardens.

Perry gave Vaiden an unpleasant expression when the Shade gestured up the wall, but the scouts said nothing and followed him up and over. It was an easier climb, given the perfect layout of the bricks for grabbing, as if the architects had never envisioned enemies to scale the inner walls.

They landed in the graveyard. Back again, Vaiden thought, a wave of exhaustion sweeping through him. At least no guards would be hunting him, but he observed the fourth ring above them, searching for fireflies. Torches lined the wall in fixed placements so the guards didn't have to carry them, making it difficult to track the soldiers. Smart, he thought. Perhaps something those on the outer wall could note, but Vaiden would prefer no lights so his nocturnal sight could depict shapes and movements. He knew Rothnar placed torches along the walls to offend such gifts. It made the Shade rely on his regular vision or else he'd be blinded by the light.

"How are we going to get past all the soldiers?" one of the sisters asked. "There's too many."

"We're not," the Shade said.

"What do you mean?"

He didn't answer her and instead hurried across the grass for cover behind the central monument. The statue depicted King Jarviski armor-clad atop his horse, bestowing his sword to the sky, the vision of strength and leadership. Vaiden reduced the masterpiece to a shield, safeguarding him from the eyes of soldiers on the wall. The scouts quickly rushed to his side, Alumpia taking up his left with the sisters between her and Perry.

"Where are we going?" he asked. "We need to know the plan."

"Oh, so now you want plans to be shared aloud," Vaiden scoffed.

"This isn't funny. There's a whole army up there."

"I'm aware." Vaiden sprinted to the next massive statue occupying the fallen heroes tour. He wasn't sure who this particular warrior was, but her massive statue with a flowing cape would keep them covered.

They continued to snake their way from left to right behind the statues and monuments of the fallen until eventually Vaiden steered them to the gate. It was risky. The open pathways between the gardens could get them caught if a soldier looked down from the wall at the appropriate time. He gathered the soldiers atop the fourth ring wall were more relaxed than the guards overlooking the city's outer walls. As the last defense to the palace, they would rely on warnings from the other rings before getting excited. Their mistake, Vaiden thought, shooting across the open path to the next garden.

Alumpia followed quickly, never questioning. He supposed the moonless sky helped keep them hidden, but the gardens did have lights guiding the paths between gates. Light was the enemy of stealth. The sisters hesitated, their stares observing the wall, but eventually they took their chances. Perry mouthed a swear before sprinting behind them.

Crouch-walking through Jana's garden was easier since the plants obstructed definitive shapes. They stayed low, wanting to avoid detection. Jana's garden wasn't as large as Moren's graveyard. In the daytime, it was a fixture of beauty and life, celebrating harvest and family, but in the darkness, the limbs and brush created shadows of unknown creatures lurking in nothingness. In the heart of the garden, the furthest point from light, Vaiden's nocturnal sight clicked on, navigating them through the pitch blackness.

When they approached the next gate, he turned to the scouts, who fanned out so he could see them all. Perry remained unhappy. His jaw clenched and lips spread thin. Vaiden ignored him, keeping his voice a whisper.

"We go to Surnuna's center," he said.

"It's lit at night," one of the sisters returned.

He nodded. "We'll have to be fast."

"What's at the center?" the other sister asked.

"There's a hidden door at the base of her statue. It leads to tunnels beneath the castle."

Their eyes widened. The sisters exchanged looks, surprised, but a slight smile also crept on their faces. They liked knowing such secrets. He briefly wondered what kind of work they did for their guild in Abrita Shores. Maybe they had learned all the secret paths into the duke's manor, like Gabriel had in his youth.

"How do we trigger the door?" Alumpia inquired, focused.

"Push in the sun off her left foot, the door will open," he explained. "It's located on the backside of the statue."

"How do you know about it?" Perry asked.

"It was once my job to know every entrance and exit to protect the king." Vaiden peered out the gate, his gaze sweeping over the pathway and the wall full of soldiers. "Let's go."

"Surnuna guide us," Alumpia whispered, "and Wara protect us."

The sisters raced across the pathway first, holding open the gates for Perry and Alumpia to join them. Vaiden took up the rear, watching the wall, searching for the fires flickering in the distance to rage with the power of practitioners throwing fireballs. He'd witnessed that particular defense only once during Rothnar's reign. To call it effective, would be an understatement, in both stopping intruders, but also destroying the gardens. Rothnar would have sacrificed anything for his own safety—even the sacred gardens built millennia ago to praise the goddesses.

Surnuna's garden was the largest. Her statue, a miniature of the one believed to be atop *Duna A'anar*, dwarfed the other statues in the city. Casimere was the shining light of Surnuna, a city built on her philosophies of power and life, giving to the less fortunate, rising above to guide those far below, evolving and growing outward, and paving paths for the young ones. She was the Goddess of Life—of power and the sun.

At night, her power wavered. Moren shrouded them in her darkness, aiding their efforts to deceive wandering eyes. Vaiden didn't generally think the goddesses would care about their creations' plights. He'd known nobles and kings alike to believe the goddesses were on their sides, or that their actions were sanctioned in the holiest of ways as proof from their interpretation of the goddesses's words. They only believed those things to subside their guilt or further their mental illnesses.

Engineered water paths led to the shrine at the center of the garden. Their waters funneled to the statue creating a fountain much like the one in Altamost's throne room. This piece managed to be even more intricate, displaying columns of waterfalls two stories high. At night these mechanisms were turned off. Too bad, Vaiden thought. Though he didn't like getting wet, the sound would have been a great distraction for their approach.

The scouts followed Vaiden toward the front of the center, shadowed by the low wall. He perched on his feet, squatting while facing the statue. Surnuna looked down at them, her judgmental eyes wondering if this was how they wanted to squander the life she'd given them. The distance was twenty feet to the button—completely illuminated and a target for any soldier watching the gardens on the wall.

Vaiden looked at the scouts, all willing to sacrifice themselves for their cause. Their concentrated expressions showed why they had been chosen for this task. Though the path had been filled with hurdles and improvisation, they had managed to come this far. The night was still young, he thought. The journey through the tunnels would be sightless and uncomfortable in the confined spaces with limited air. He doubted any of them were truly up for such claustrophobia, but it was the best chance they had to infiltrate the castle and hold Altamost ransom.

Ransom, his jaw clenched, not dead, acting as a puppet to allow Duke Heiron's army within Casimere, standing down the city's forces, and willingly giving up his crown. Doubt weighed in the back of Vaiden's mind, but he pushed it away. This was the only chance they had or the Corrupted would band together and destroy what was left of their kingdom.

He pointed at one of the sisters, gesturing for her to make the run for the button. She nodded, locking eyes with the carved resemblance of a sun where Surnuna's left foot pointed. From a crouched position, she pushed off the ground, sprinting as fast as her legs could carry her into the light. Like a baseball player, she tagged the sun and sprinted forward back into the safety of the darkness.

Vaiden waited, listening for movement on the wall—for a call of alarm or an order to investigate. He held up his hand, keeping the others from rushing to the statue. From their position, they could not see if the door was open. He looked to the other sister, who he had pegged as the fastest in their company. She returned his stare and nodded, getting into position. Her lips parted as she inhaled deeply, setting her sights on the target, like her sister had.

Her boots struck the ground like a feather caressing its surface. Vaiden was in awe at her nimbleness, the light-footedness of her sprint, and how she shaped to the statue, like an extra layer of skin, moving fluidly toward the door. If he hadn't seen her in action, he would have believed it was a trick of his eyes.

Vaiden's gaze shifted to her sister, waiting from the furthest point of the center. She crouched low, her eyes darting from the wall to where her sister had disappeared behind the statue. She had a better view than the others, but she made no move to communicate if it was open.

"What's the hold up?" Perry whispered.

The sister shifted on her feet, biting her lip. Her round eyes searched the wall then the statue. Vaiden didn't like it—this delay.

"She can't get it open?" Alumpia questioned.

"Or someone sealed it," Perry replied.

The Shade fought from rolling his eyes. He had gotten them this far and Perry didn't have any faith in him. It shouldn't have bothered Vaiden. It didn't, he thought at the vast emptiness in his core. The mistrust of others was expected, but doubt rang in his ears, clenching his jaw.

"I don't like this," Alumpia barely whispered. "It's too open."

"The girls already made a run at it," Perry said. "We can do it."

Alumpia's unconvinced stare landed Vaiden for confirmation, but he said nothing, turning back to the sister he could see. She hadn't moved, but her hesitation gave him pause. If her sister needed aid, why didn't she help or gesture for assistance? What was she waiting for?

A rumble shook the air. It might have been thunder, if not for the response from soldiers on the wall. Now the scout from Abrita Shores had shifted her stance, searching the skies. For what in the blackness?

"Look there!" a soldier shouted.

Vaiden couldn't see where the soldier was pointing or at what he was pointing. It didn't matter. It was a distraction enough. The Shade ran across the center, perhaps not as fluid as the girl from Abrita Shores, but he didn't need all the grace and finesse of a gazelle to accomplish this task. He reached the backside of the statue, finding the girl facing her sister, sitting and waiting. She was making "come here" gestures, but her sister wouldn't move. The more she sat still, the more her sister's arms became animated. Footsteps let him know Perry and Alumpia didn't wait for a signal.

"Gardens!" shouted from the wall.

Fuck.

The door, no bigger than that of a kid's playhouse, was open. The girl turned to him with wide eyes, her mouth hanging agape. He glared at her, but gave her his back, motioning for Alumpia and Perry to go inside. They listened, quickly squeezing through. Her sister finally joined the rest of them as Vaiden slipped inside the tunnels and slammed the door shut. He held it, putting all his weight against it while the sisters outside pushed.

Muffled voices shouted, letting him know the soldiers had arrived. The struggles against the door stopped, locking it in place. They fled, but how far would they get before they were caught? Vaiden doubted they'd make it to the next garden.

"By Layetta!" Perry grabbed Vaiden's shoulder, forcing him to face the scout leader. "Why did you do that? You left them for the guards!"

"I had to," he returned. "The soldiers on the wall spotted you two going for the statue. They had to find someone."

"You blame us?" Perry's nostrils flared. "This was your plan! You take responsibility for it."

"I am!" Vaiden pushed away from the fisherman, but Perry grabbed his arm. The Shade looked down at him, letting emptiness fill his stare black as the night. Perry let go, grimacing.

"You're willing to sacrifice all of us, aren't you?" he asked, averting his gaze.

"Yes."

"Piss on you!"

"If you think for a second that those girls are more important than this kingdom, tell me now." Vaiden paused, watching Perry's anger falter as he searched for something unseen on the old stone flooring, illuminated by the luminescent bugs clinging to the ceiling. "I didn't trust them any way."

"What does that mean?"

"They were too eager to find the tunnels, but then when things got serious, one of them hesitated, like she grew a conscience," he explained. "They were going to leave us behind."

"You don't know that."

"It was odd," Alumpia said, stealing their attention. "They've never hesitated like that before."

"Thank you." Vaiden bowed slightly at the waist, like he might royalty.

"You don't know them," Perry growled.

"I don't have to know them to know they would have left our asses behind."

"What alerted the soldiers?" Alumpia asked. "Some kind of explosion?"

"Maybe that prick Heiron got tired of waiting on us?" Perry crossed his arms.

"It changes nothing," Vaiden said, marching past the scouts. "We still have a job to do."

"The castle will know something's up now," Perry said. "They'll have everyone on high alert. They'll suspect why we were in the gardens and figure it out."

Vaiden turned on his heel, walking backward toward the darkness in the tunnels. The bugs stayed close to the fountain where water dripped, but the deeper into the tunnels the fewer bugs they would find. "Well, it's a good thing you have me," he announced, "I know where they'll hide the king."

45

When Tatiana emerged from the SDC, the reporters waved their arms, trying to catch her attention while shouting questions into the ether. The heat weighed on her like a spotlight following her every step. She squinted at the sun, wondering when the rain would move in. The weather people claimed soon, but she found "soon" never to be enough.

Before she could retreat to her vehicle and fill in Zarah on what she had learned, Brax stopped her. He gestured for her to follow him behind their surveillance van, out of sight from the media. The detectives had arrived on scene with their forensic teams. The incident commander spoke to the detectives, detailing the events inside the SDC. Tatiana suspected Brax would also be questioned.

She didn't know if it was standard for PITF to answer questions before their finalized reports, but she knew the Marshals didn't have to talk to the locals until afterward. It was a sneaky rule so they could get their stories straight, especially when innocent lives were lost in the wake of the destruction they had left behind to end a target.

"End." She shook her head. They obliterated bodies, leaving hardly anything to identify their targets. Tatiana knew of several instances where dental records wouldn't suffice. A loved one once had to identify their killed spouse by a scar on their hand, luckily that finger had remained intact. It boiled Tatiana's blood to know the Marshals had free reign to do whatever they wanted to take down a supernatural. They got the job done, but—based on the overwhelming evidence of abuse and violence—at what cost to justice?

Politicians and attorneys on the federal level argued for restrictions and monitoring of the Marshals, but so far the fear of supernatural kind was winning. Only the Marshals remained as the boogeyman against the preternaturals, keeping them behaved and controlled. If that was true, how had Lizabeth LaBelle almost governed the entire vampire community in Misplaced Stream? And how had Jen slipped through the cracks?

Now, now, kitty, whispered in her ear. Tatiana took a deep breath, inhaling the hot California air, wishing she lived closer to the coast and the water. She wanted to peel off her clothes and sink into the cool ocean, leave everything behind and float away. It wouldn't help Mr. Slaseezor though or bring justice to whoever had killed Koreen and Zabetha.

"How can I help you?" she asked Brax once they were alone behind the van.

"Why did you think a vampire had taken control of the SDC?" he inquired, resting his hands on his hips. "It was very specific."

She threaded her fingers through her damp hair, wishing she'd pulled it into a ponytail. "I'd heard how vampires in San Francisco had taken over one of their SDCs and when my colleague asked me questions about it and our situation, it seemed to fit."

His dark eyes studied her face. "You think a master vampire will order one of their lessers to learn our protocols?"

"Eventually they will want to know them." She nodded. "Whatever they can to protect each other, even if that means sacrificing a lesser and their attorney."

He shifted on his heels, suddenly uncomfortable in his vest. Sweat streamed down the impeccable bone structure of his cheeks and sharp jaw. Despite his dark complexion, he appeared almost pale. Maybe it was the heat and she was reading into it too much? She had already embarrassed herself and another attorney by throwing accusations.

"If that is all—"

"What if I told you we have intel that such an event might occur here in Misplaced Stream?" Brax questioned.

She fought from looking shocked. While the idea of vampires using their powers to trick people was old news, PITF rarely shared information, especially not with attorneys. "Why are you telling me this?" she asked.

"You have a good reputation among the officers," he said, completely neutral. "I just wanted to warn you."

"To warn me against taking vampire clients?" Now it was her turn to put her hands on her hips. Usually she wouldn't, considering it made everyone look like a teenager complaining, but the pose came naturally with the officious tone of her voice.

He shrugged, as if it wasn't intimidating an officer of the court to reject a client. "I wanted to extend a professional courtesy."

She opened her mouth to educate him on the law, but she decided he was looking out for her. Why *her* though? "Will you tell the other attorneys this too?"

He shifted again, frowning.

"Are you only telling me because I am a woman?"

His expression softened. "We all read what happened six months ago, Ms. Smith."

Bile crawled up her throat but she pushed it down. "So you don't think I can protect myself?"

"I think you look for the good in people. It's your job to protect them and maybe sometimes it blinds you from who they really are."

"My personal life and my work are separate," she gritted, hands balling into fists at her side. "And my clients are innocent until proven guilty. They should be treated no differently than anyone else."

"You saw the damage to that cell," Brax said, anger lacing his words. "They are not the same as *us*."

She wanted to roll up her blazer sleeves and show him *they* were not the same, but she couldn't. No one in the government or its authorities knew she was supernatural. It would do her no favors to reveal that information to him. He might shoot her on the spot, saying she'd tried to attack him.

The realization was like a punch to her gut. Police, like Brax and the many uniform officers she'd befriended through the years, would look at her differently. Hardly any preternaturals were used in the police. The high ups hadn't figured out a solution or didn't want to make one for human and supernatural forces to team up. She knew at the federal level they had created units, by using preternatural powers to help stop other preternaturals, but they wouldn't let anyone classified as supernatural serve on local streets. It would be too easy for the supernatural to abuse human suspects—not that any rules had stopped human cops from abusing their authority over anyone.

"Did I hear bias in your words, sir?" Tatiana asked instead. "How can you do your job objectively if you already believe the supernatural to be monsters?"

"I didn't say they were."

"You implied it."

"*You* implied it." He frowned. "Take the information how you want, Ms. Smith. Warn other attorneys if you believe it is credible, but protect yourself. The Ardans banned vampires from their world for a reason."

He brushed past her, aiming for the incident commander, before she could respond. Maybe it wasn't all supernatural kind with whom he had issues. Maybe it was only the vampires. Tatiana only knew the prejudice continued and she didn't believe it was any closer to solving.

***

"What happened?" Zarah asked inside the car. The air conditioning was welcoming after standing in the hot sun. Tatiana explained the situation, focusing on the serpent who had broken out of his cell to potentially kill her client.

"It must be the same people who killed Zabetha," Zarah said. "They are willing to sacrifice themselves to silence your client."

"If Rocahn or people wanting to hurt her are behind this, how has she remained untouched?"

"Oh, she's definitely involved."

"Mr. Slaseezor said she was interested in plants found in the vampire kingdom, particularly a vine called nightbloom."

Zarah's eyes widened as she stilled, not even breathing. She remained that way for a long minute, processing Tatiana's words. "He said what?" she finally asked.

"What exactly is nightbloom?"

"It's a deadly vine, probably the deadliest of all species on Arda," she explained. "Emperor Zerth decorated the palace in it as a deterrent against others because it couldn't hurt us, but for other races, it would be agony until they died. The emperor enjoyed others suffering."

"He used it against visitors from other kingdoms?"

She nodded, looking at her hands. "Especially the serpents because they are immune to most poisonous vegetation. Nightbloom lived in the northern reaches of our kingdom in the Shadowed Mountains. It only takes a scratch, the fever will start after another hour, and for most it is death within a few days. Some might hold out for a week, but as far as I know there's no cure—not even magic."

"Jesus," gasped Tatiana. "Why would anyone, especially a serpent like Rocahn, want anything to do with that vine?"

"I don't know." Zarah put the car into gear and drove away from the SDC's parking lot. "Is there any way to tip off the police to the possibility of this plant at the den?"

"I only received this information through my client."

"But nightbloom is extremely dangerous. It could kill anyone who touches it."

Tatiana shifted in her seat. Technically, she had already broken confidentiality principles by speaking with Zarah about the case, what was a tip off to the police? The safety of the public did override confidentiality principles.

"I could do it," Zarah offered.

"We need evidence that the vine exists before we inform the police," she replied. "I already embarrassed myself once today without sufficient information to back it up."

"What do you mean?"

Tatiana waved it away, not wanting to relive the confusion about the attack in the SDC. "Let's go to the den," she said instead, pulling her hair into a high ponytail. "Rocahn is screening my calls, but she can't ignore me if I'm standing in front of her."

"Text your firm," Zarah replied. "Let them know you are there just in case something happens."

"You think something will happen?"

"I think this serpent is untrustworthy and unpredictable."

Tatiana found her phone in the glovebox. Caden and a few others had sent messages, wanting updates about the SDC. She eyed the texts, but focused on one from Logan. He had managed to uncover Rocahn's full background from the east coast, claiming it was colorful. She replied to his text, letting him know she was going to the den to question Rocahn and to let others in the firm know her location too.

I brought backup, she added at the end of the message, knowing he'd worry for her to go alone.

Keep me posted, he replied.

She smiled at his message. He was caring and good—but so had Gary in the beginning. She exhaled, slouching in her seat with her elbow propped on the car door. The city scenery filled up her vision—a blurry mess of gray and blue shades with hints of greenery to brighten it up.

"What's the matter?" Zarah asked. "Did something come up?"

"No," Tatiana replied quickly, but then had a thought. "Well, yes, Logan received the rest of Rocahn's background from the east coast."

"What does it say?" She drove carefully around traffic, not quite speeding, but faster than most might through the city avenues.

Tatiana opened the PDF, skimming the information she already knew from their previous background check. "Rocahn Slaseezor, previously named Salee, was a *daehekans* at another den in New Jersey, but according to this, it burnt down. The investigation concluded arson, but never established who was responsible."

"She burnt it down then?"

"Maybe not." Tatiana continued to read the report. "Salee had run-ins with the police before that. Evidently she was the victim of loan sharks and had taken a beating. There's no pictures, but this police officer claimed they had broken her arm and ribs."

"Serpent bones are hard to break," Zarah said. "They are very flexible."

"So someone with experience breaking serpent bones did the damage."

"Another serpent perhaps?"

Tatiana finished reading the report. "What if she owed this loan shark a bunch of money? They beat her up when she didn't pay up, but when she didn't comply, they burnt down her den."

"Seems plausible."

"Then she moved out here, changed her name and married quickly, assuming the loan sharks wouldn't find her."

"Now they have?" The car stopped at a red light. "Why would these thugs kill Zabetha or Koreen?"

"Koreen was an asset. His coupling with Arkella could have made Rocahn a ton of money."

"But then Arkella's family backed out of the deal, learning Koreen could join the Grand Den through a petition for exception."

"Zabetha was Rocahn's friend," Tatiana said. "Maybe the loan sharks killed her to send a message?"

They rolled with traffic to the next red light. Zarah's lips pursed, thinking. The sun sank toward the horizon—another day ending quickly. Too quickly, Tatiana thought. Mr. Slaseezor's case would be in front of a judge before she knew it. They needed to solve this, to find some kind of evidence that exonerated him.

"So who killed Koreen?" Zarah asked. "Why would the loan sharks bother with a cover up? Just to blackmail Rocahn?"

"She claims to love her husband and she told me she would do anything for him."

"Except tell the truth?"

Tatiana studied the streets where people clumped together, waiting for the signal to cross the avenue. "Maybe killing Koreen was a mistake. The loan sharks knew he was close to the Slaseezors, but they didn't know he was Rocahn's investment."

"So they killed Koreen, framing her husband, then later killed her friend to make a point?" Zarah shook her head. "I've worked in enforcement. That's sloppy work and too...*much*. You break bones to make a point and threaten loved ones, but when the mark doesn't comply with the given timeline, you kill them. Business concluded."

Tatiana wanted to ask how many people she had killed doing such business, but she decided quickly she didn't want to know. Like Vaiden, Zarah worked for the Underground. Before that she had worked for Lizabeth LaBelle, performing similar jobs. How many bodies lay beneath her feet? How many of them were cold cases or missing persons reports the police had forgotten about?

One day, Tatiana knew she would be faced with representing one of her friends. She hoped to win, but she didn't know how she might feel defending someone who was, without a doubt, guilty. It made her internal scales tip a direction she didn't like, knowing she had to pick between their lives and justice.

"In your expert opinion, have the loan sharks given her too many warnings?" Tatiana asked.

"Absolutely," Zarah snorted. "They followed her all the way from the east coast to give her more warnings? Their boss is either in love with her and wants her back in one piece or they are really bad at their job."

"How plausible is it that they are just really bad at their jobs?"

"I wouldn't travel all the way across the country to kill the *wrong* people."

"So yes?"

"I think we're missing something."

"That seems to be a given in this case," Tatiana said, sinking back in her seat. "But maybe Rocahn will finally cooperate and tell the truth."

"Maybe, but if you need to get it out of her, I'm always an option."

"No."

Zarah shrugged, smiling slightly. Torturing people didn't bother her, *killing* people didn't bother her. How had Tatiana befriended such a person? What did that say about her that she was willing to be friends with a murderer? Not just Zarah, but Vaiden too? Two *successful* murderers. What was Tatiana thinking? Why was she playing with fire? If she was caught with knowledge of their business in the Underground, not only would she lose her license, but she could be prosecuted as an accessory to that wrongdoing. Were their friendships worth everything?

Tatiana shoved down such questions. She could ponder morality at a later date. Zarah may have a sketchy past, but she was helping her solve this case. She didn't have to. She chose to. If anything that was an example of her selflessness. Real evil couldn't think beyond themselves.

No protestors stood outside of the den. The news cycle had pushed on and their attention with it. Good, Tatiana thought. The serpents deserved to worship in peace.

She thought that meant no one would stand guard, but the usual subjects barred Zarah entrance into the den again. The vampire stared them down—or rather up, given they towered over her—with a look that chilled even Tatiana's blood. They stood fast though, not budging on their orders.

"Rocahn is in?" Tatiana asked.

"She never left the den," one of the guards replied. "She hasn't this whole week."

"Good, I have a lot of questions for her."

46

"Surnuna, I can't see a bloody thing," Perry growled.

"I think you mean, '*Moren*, I can't see a thing,'" Vaiden corrected.

"Piss on you."

"No thanks. I'm not into golden showers."

Alumpia exhaled heavily between them. Her hand grasped Vaiden's belt, keeping the remaining scouts from getting lost. Vaiden thanked Wara for his nocturnal sight or the task of navigating through the tunnels would have been near impossible.

Beneath Surnuna's statue the path had been wide enough for them to fit comfortably, but the further they traveled under the fourth ring to the castle, the smaller the tunnels became until the cramped space forced them to crouch-walk, sometimes barely fitting through the narrow passages. Vaiden knew a few directions would have them belly crawling, but he avoided those for his own comfort.

"How many times have you used this route?" Alumpia asked.

"Many," Vaiden replied. "Rothnar liked to do surprise drills to ensure if an emergency took place, he could get out in record time."

"Don't you mean 'we could get out'?" Perry questioned in a mocking tone.

Vaiden shook his head, quickly realizing they couldn't see him. "Rothnar only cared about himself. If anyone got left behind in these tunnels and couldn't find their way out alone, he'd let them die down here."

"You're kidding?"

"I never kid."

"Where exactly will this passage lead us?" Alumpia asked.

"You'll see."

Perry mumbled behind her, something Vaiden couldn't quite make out. He decided not to ask. The scout leader became grumpier the more of his scouts Vaiden left behind. *Better leave that one alone*, he thought; though, another voice in his head whispered darkly, *do it*.

The smell of dirt suffocated them throughout their slow march forward. Vaiden didn't like small spaces or the idea that these old tunnels could collapse, burying them alive to an early grave where no one would be able to recover them. It was the risk of the mission.

Movies on Earth liked to show rogues scaling the walls of a castle or coming through the back door—as if that was so easy. They would trot through the castle they'd never before visited, searching for a member of their team or to assassinate the tyrant living within those halls, sometimes both. They would always go undetected until they arrived within sight of the tyrant and still they would miss their shot, or an epic fight would begin between the main rogue and the tyrant.

Vaiden found these movies quite unrealistic. Servants littered the halls of a castle. Guards could be found around every corridor. There was no way for someone who didn't belong there to go unnoticed. Castles were generally designed to be a maze too. For if they were infiltrated, it would be difficult for any enemy to navigate them.

What annoyed him more was that the tyrant would fight the rogue alone. Where were his guards? No one that important would risk their life in fruitless swordplay and guards who didn't do their jobs would be executed on the morrow for treason. At least, that was Vaiden's experience.

He had saved King Rothnar from many assassination attempts, most of them performed by one of their own. A few had been carried out by professionals nobles had hired because they detested Rothnar's vision for the kingdom. Vaiden hadn't necessarily disagreed with them, but he had kept his oath as the king's personal guard. No one would assassinate his king.

No one had. Poison had killed The Daunting as Gabriel had explained to Duke Heiron. It wasn't Vaiden's fault. Rothnar had sent him to the Empire to stop the war. Vaiden had been successful. His fellow guards had failed to protect their king.

Not that Vaiden mourned Rothnar's death, but after this mess with Altamost, Eskandor needed a strong ruler. One that pulled the kingdom back together and thought deeply of their choices. Altamost had claimed to be the second coming of King Duncan, but he had only proved to be the opposite.

"What do you think of Duke Heiron?" Vaiden asked.

"Why do you want to know?" Perry countered.

"Because the man potentially could be our next king."

"I thought the council would vote between themselves to replace Altamost," Alumpia said. "That's why we are going to hold the king."

"If no one gets the majority vote or if the council decides neither of them is suitable for the throne, they can look for outside candidates," Vaiden explained. "It has only happened once in our kingdom's history with the crowning of Duncan."

"That was only because Leeth's bloodline died out," Perry said.

"The point is Duncan wasn't on the council," Vaiden replied. "He worked as a representative of the crown, making sure the lords and ladies of the major cities did as instructed by their king."

"You mean *queen*," Alumpia corrected. "Queen Ulneera was the last of Leeth's blood."

"You're right. My apologies."

"What scholars," Perry scoffed.

"I wouldn't consider myself a scholar by any means," Vaiden said. "I know a real one, a mentor of mine, but it's not exactly fair, he's lived most of history."

"How old is he?" Alumpia asked.

"To be determined."

"What do you mean?"

"Is that light ahead?" Perry asked, desperation aching in his voice.

Vaiden squinted at the distance where a star twinkled in the blackness . "Luminescent bug," he said, "but it does mean we're getting closer. The bugs are attracted to water."

"Don't tell me we're gonna emerge from another fountain," Perry grumbled. "I'm tired of your damn games, Shade."

Alumpia's hand tugged on Vaiden's belt, dropping her weight like an anchor. "That's enough," she gritted. "He's gotten us this far."

"Only half of us made it."

"The others knew the risk."

"You're only defending him because you have a soft spot for his kind."

Vaiden studied the two scouts. Perry stared straight ahead, his brow etched together forming a little V at the top of his nose. He frowned, believing his glare penetrated the darkness—that somehow Alumpia could feel it. With her head turned, Vaiden couldn't see her face, but her posture was defensive, like she fought from letting go of his belt to smack Perry in the face. He almost wanted to dare her. *Do it.*

"Elridge is in Kiji," she announced, venom lacing her words, hiding something else deep in her voice. "I would be there with him if it wasn't for the damned rules."

"Only Shades can stay in the village," Vaiden said.

She whirled around, blinking in the darkness. "He is." Her bottom lip quivered. "This is the longest we've been apart since I trained at Mysogus."

"He's a Shade," Perry spat. "He hasn't missed you."

Her face crumpled, squeezing her eyes tight. She inhaled deeply, her fingers tightening around his belt. "You don't understand."

"You're right. I don't," he said. "Why waste your time on someone who will never care about you and who will never be capable of love?"

"I can love for the both of us."

Perry shook his head, biting back more words. Vaiden bet this wasn't the first time they had played out this conversation. Part of him wanted to tell her, Perry was right. Elridge would never be capable of giving her what she desired, but he hesitated. Tatiana had given him the gift of feelings—a plague on his sanity, but he knew he didn't want to return to being a regular Shade. Emotions unlocked a new perspective for him.

"He's the reason you learned to sew," Vaiden said instead.

"I traveled to the human settlements to learn their infirmary methods. They are more extensive than our own since humans don't rely on magic." She shifted on her feet, ready to continue forward down the tunnel. "We lived in Lorro. It's outside of Opretta's fane where I attended service. Elridge had been assigned there since he'd left Kiji. That's when I met him. We've been together ever since."

"Why waste your time on a Shade?" Vaiden asked, moving forward. She moved with him, no longer anchoring them in place. "You know we cannot own property or carry a title."

"That's not important to me," she replied. "He was always there for me, a constant in my life. He protected our village from the Corrupted and repelled those at the fane from pressing into darker magic."

"Opretta did make many of them, but I imagine your friends at the fane were wary of him."

"Most High Elves are of Shades," she said, "but he was created that way. How can I judge him for that?"

"The same way you can judge necromancers for what they are," Perry growled. "The same way we can all judge Altamost for what he's done."

"What did Shades do to *you*?" Vaiden asked.

"Nothing."

"Then why do you hate us? You're not a practitioner."

"I don't hate *them*," Perry said. "I just don't like *you*."

"You're breaking my heart with such talk," Vaiden sighed. "Here I am thinking we are the bestest of friends."

The fisherman scowled, muttering to himself.

"You are different from other Shades I have met," Alumpia said.

"I haven't lived the average Shade life." More stars littered the darkness ahead of them. They were getting closer to the exit, to fresh air, and closer to completing their objective. "But Perry isn't wrong. Elridge can't love you."

"See?" Vaiden didn't have to see Perry's face to imagine his cocky grin.

"But we Shades do recognize people for how they affect our lives."

"What do you mean?" Perry asked, suspicion lacing his words.

"I have a mother. I recognize her for the important role she played in bringing me to life," he explained. "Gabriel Steel was my partner in the Forty-Second. He protected me. I protected him. I recognize him as my friend."

"So Elridge can recognize me as something important too?" Alumpia asked.

"You said he has always been there for you and protected you."

"She meant the fane."

"And *me* personally," Alumpia argued.

"It was his duty."

"It doesn't matter," Vaiden intervened. "He's marked you as someone important, or he wouldn't be a constant in your life."

"Thank you," she said the words softly. They warmed his heart, bringing a smile to his face. Perhaps Elridge would never love her, but she claimed she could love for the both of them. He had friends who had shouldered that for him. They were still around. Maybe Alumpia could go the distance with her Shade. It wouldn't be easy for someone with magic to constantly be around someone who prevented its usage, but they could work it out. Anything was possible.

Part of Vaiden wanted to tell Alumpia to look up metaphysical binds, but that thought quickly evaporated. She was a High Elf, not a human like Tatiana. Her magic had zero effect on Elridge. Vaiden didn't know much about binds and how they worked, but he doubted a third party could ensnare two elves without binding all three of them together. Maybe he was wrong, but the magic he did know required the practitioner. It was a pity, but perhaps Alumpia could embody that love for them both.

The bugs illuminated the exit, creating a frame for the door. Vaiden held up his hand, quieting the excited noises emulating from Perry. He switched on his expanded hearing, listening for anyone close to the secret entrance. After a long minute, he determined the room was empty, like it had been from when he'd served in the castle.

His fingers found the sun insignia right of the door and he pushed the button. The door sighed, dust clouding around its edges, letting him know it was open. He yanked on it, creating space for Alumpia then Perry to exit the tunnels. Vaiden followed them out, pulling the door closed behind him. Hands tugged him up, helping him stand. He stared into Alumpia's smiling face.

Perry wrinkled his nose at the pungent smells. "Where in Aegan's black heart are we?"

"A bathroom." Vaiden limped his way to the door frame. His left leg tingled with dead weight from crouching so long in the tunnels. It would end soon he hoped, cracking the door slightly to survey the conjoining bedroom. The bright candlelight at the door obstructed his vision. "I'm sure it's advanced technology to you, village boy."

"What's technology?"

"Nothing," he hissed, his leg burning slightly, but it wasn't dead weight anymore, allowing him to put more pressure on it.

"I feel a presence," Alumpia said.

Vaiden gently closed the door, glancing over his shoulder at her. She stood the furthest from him in the room. Her hands held an invisible ball, but he knew she searched through the air metaphysically, using her magic to feel life forces outside of the room. It was advanced magic for a healer.

"What's your specialty at the fane?" he asked.

"My research focused around illusions at first, but so many in my group chose the same. I decided to switch to divination, studying magical auras."

"What do you feel?"

"Something powerful, but it is stationary." Her brows furrowed, eyes narrowing on the invisible ball between her hands. "I can't see who it is, like something is masking them from my sight."

"How close is it?" Perry inquired.

"It's in the other room."

Vaiden eyed the door. "How powerful is it?"

"I—I don't know. I felt it for a moment, but whatever masked the power is strong."

He drew his short sword. His other hand grabbed the handle, casting a look at Perry. The fisherman responded by drawing his own sword, nodding when ready. Alumpia let go of her invisible ball, her eyes studying the space between her and Vaiden. Smart, he thought. She'd know how far to be away from him to use her magic.

Vaiden pressed through the door, evading to the left side for any quick attacks. None followed while the others entered. Perry had his sword up, escorting Alumpia to the other side of the room. She lifted her hands creating a small ward to protect them.

The candelabra lining the room burned his eyes with their beacons of light, forcing his nocturnal sight to disengage. He blinked into the well lit room, finding a four post bed fit for a king, but this was not the king's room, he knew. It was made for the queen.

The slither of metal, coiling like a snake at the base of the bed, drew his attention. His eyes caressed the producer of this sound—chains gliding up the satin sheets to the ankles resting on it.

"Who do we have here?" a familiar voice beckoned. The slender frame of Dallia sat up, her luscious hair spilling over her bare shoulders. She wore a lacey red nightdress that left little illusion to her body underneath.

"Grand Priestess," Alumpia gasped, her ward faltering.

"By Surnuna's good graces, why is she tied up?" Perry asked. "You said she was influencing the king."

Vaiden stepped forward, spying the manacles around her wrists. "I don't kink shame," he said, each step forward cautiously taken. Not that he feared her magic, but something was off.

Her head whirled to him, her honey-colored eyes settling on his sword. "You've come to assassinate me." A snarl twisted with her lips. Orange light blazed around her figure, like a halo born of the sun's power. She thrust her hands as far as the chains allowed, releasing the magic. Vaiden jumped through the blaze, before it could touch him it turned to mist, billowing away from him like steam.

"Don't come any closer," Dallia growled, harsh lines etching across her face. He didn't listen until he was at the foot of the bed and her expression softened. She blinked, her face filling with confusion as her eyes darted across the room, studying the others before landing on the bed and the chains. "What?" she asked, her voice alarmed. "What is this?"

Vaiden glanced at Alumpia, who watched the exchange with similar confusion. "Grand Priestess," she said. "What's the last thing you remember?"

"A–a—" She pulled on the chains. "I—why am I bound? Where am I?"

Alumpia rushed forward, taking her hand. "Grand Priestess, this is important." Her voice softened, comforting the confused woman. "What is the *last* thing you remember?"

She blinked, round eyes searching the reaches of her mind. "The Magnificent Harvest. I came to Casimere to bless it for the good of the kingdom. It was my first appearance in the capital."

"You are still in Casimere," Vaiden said, sheathing his weapon.

"What's going on?" Perry asked. "Why doesn't she remember?"

"She's under some kind of spell," Alumpia replied. "It only broke because Vaiden is a Shade."

"This happened before," he said, drawing Dallia's attention. "In the throne room."

Her brows drew as she studied his face. "I think—I think I remember you, but it's like a dream. It was bright and hazy."

He remembered how she looked at her hands wondering why magic had failed her, but that was not what had happened. The real her had broken free of the spell because he'd gotten too close.

"Does the king know about this?" Perry asked.

"I'm sure he does," Vaiden gritted. "He's the one who has her chained here."

"The king?" Dallia looked at the others in the room. "I don't understand."

Alumpia rubbed her hand in small circles, trying to soothe her. "Grand Priestess, it appears you have been a prisoner here for over a year," she explained. "We don't know how this happened, but I promise we will figure it out."

Perry sheathed his sword. "Let's get these chains off her."

"Wait!" Dallia threw her hands up, recoiling from them as much as the chains allowed. "If I have been under a spell that long as you claim, that means someone powerful enough to ensnare me used dark magic. Magic I could not defeat. If the Shade doesn't stay by my side, I will return under the spell until the caster of it is killed."

"She's right." Vaiden crossed his arms. "I can't stay beside her forever."

"We'll find out who did this to you, milady." Alumpia took her hand again. "We won't let you stay this way."

"How are we going to do that and do what we came here for?" Perry asked.

"They will reveal themselves to us," Alumpia answered.

"I have a better idea," Dallia said, gazing up at Vaiden. "Kill me, Shade."

He took a step back unintentionally. "Why?"

"Because the only magic that could do this to me was the darkest of magics," she replied, voice trembling, fat tears sliding down her cheeks. "I'm tainted. You know that. The longer I'm under this spell, the closer I am to complete corruption. I cannot allow my power to be used for evil."

His chest tightened, looking at the complete hopelessness in her face. Gabriel claimed she was a good fit for Grand Priestess, that her ascension had brought the kingdom together for a short time. What had Altamost done to her—and why?

Gabriel's words whispered through his mind, haunting him like a ghost. *"You said Dallia is influencing the king, but you're not sure with magic. I know he fancied her when she toured the kingdom. It didn't appear she reciprocated his feelings."*

Vaiden's eyes drifted to Dallia's lacy gown, the pit of his stomach blackening. He knew why Altamost had done this to her. Layetta would have her justice.

"Please, Shade," the priestess begged. "Please, don't let them use me anymore. I don't want to become the Corrupted."

He sat on the bed, offering his hand to her. She accepted it. His hand swallowed her delicate one. Her skin was soft, but where the shackles dug into her wrist had blistered into an irritated mess.

"Vaiden, this isn't right," Alumpia said. "We can find the person responsible and free her."

"The damage has been done," Dallia cried. "I am forever tainted."

"I don't believe that," Vaiden returned, lifting her hand so she could see with her own eyes what he meant. "Your nails are clean and your eyes are clear. Corruption hasn't started."

She pulled her hand from his, cupping it to her chest. "It doesn't matter. It will fester and grow."

"After we conclude our business here and kill whoever did this to you, go to your fane, live in nature, breathe the fresh air, bathe in the river, and don't cross that *line*." His eyes hollowed as his lips said those last two words. She swallowed hard, her gaze averting away from him, fresh tears falling from her eyes. "If you live a life without dark magic, it will retreat, but don't let yourself fall into temptation and give it room to grow."

"Alumpius." She smiled at him. "I haven't heard her words in so long."

"My mother is Coastal Coster, her last High Priestess," he said, standing. "She lives on with those who haven't forgotten."

"I haven't forgotten," she barely whispered, her mouth curving upward as she gazed at him.

"Then stay strong, priestess. This is not your end."

Vaiden hated leaving her, letting the spell change her into whatever plaything Altamost had conjured. He didn't know how the king managed it, but he would bet his Viper another practitioner was involved. There were many on staff in the castle. One of them had taken the scarlet paths and they would die for it.

47

Sunbeams sliced through the slats in the wall, revealing floating dust particles. Vaiden's hand raised, touching them but not feeling them on his cool fingertips. Elves believed it was proof of magic living in the air, but Earth's science had revealed the nasty truth—something that made Vaiden frown, resting his hand back on his lap.

Science destroyed ignorance, but he thought it erased mystery too. He had rather believed the reason he couldn't feel the dust particles against his skin was because of his shadeness; instead, he knew they all swam in a bath of skin cells and dirt. *Gross.*

He inhaled, despite this knowledge, scenting the old oak wood surrounding them. His gaze shifted down to the dark curls resting on his left arm and the woman attached to it. Alumpia curled around him, her swallow breath warming his side. She smelled faintly of cinnamon, the only nice thing that disturbed the dusty storage loft. Beyond her, Perry snored softly, sitting with his head wedged against a beam, keeping him upright.

Vaiden envied their ability to sleep anywhere. He had trained to stay awake for an amount of time in Kiji. His limit was four days, something that had come in handy during war and journeying far distances, but accompanying others, especially Gabriel, had taught him not everyone had his stamina.

Voices drew Vaiden to the opening in the wall across from him, sliding Alumpia to the floor. She stirred, but he ignored her, gazing down from the covered loft to far below where guards patrolled the viewing room. Between the row of guards, wearing a cap that dragged the floor, King Altamost chatted with General Glades. A dark smile widened across Vaiden's face.

"Gotcha," he whispered, purpose rolling through his limbs, blackening his core. Curious, he thought. Why would purpose want him to take down the king? He wasn't a Corrupted, but the humming of purpose didn't subside. Maybe it was what Dallia had revealed to them. Maybe it was learning how the king had abandoned his people. It didn't matter truly, but whatever he had learned had sparked purpose within him.

Down with the king, it trembled with rage.

No, Vaiden shook his head. This wasn't purpose. This was vengeance.

"Perry," Alumpia whispered, nudging the scout leader. "The king."

His eyes blinked open, bloodshot and glazed. "What?"

"The king," she urged.

He shot across to the wall, peering through a crack. "By all that Surnuna holds dear," he whispered, a rumble of excitement edging his voice. "He's here."

Vaiden scoffed. "Told you so."

"I owe you a drink, Shade."

"More likely an apology."

"What are they saying?" Alumpia asked.

"I don't know." Perry frowned, pushing his ear against the wall. "It's too much echo up here."

"That's because King Jarviski had the important rooms in the castle built to thwart acoustics," Vaiden explained. "Your puny hearing will only pick up the echoes distorted by the airy archways."

"But you have expanded hearing," Alumpia said. "You might be able to hear their conversation."

"How do you know he has expanded hearing?"

"All Shades do," they replied in unison.

Vaiden returned his gaze to the individuals in the east viewing room. It was a large, pearl white room where nobles and family representatives could meet and greet the king, discuss issues around the kingdom, and ask for favors. Hand-carved vines creeped along the rounded archways, twisting up the vaulted ceiling, painted gold in respect of Surnuna's domain. Rothnar had hated this room and had boarded it up to appease his paranoia. Maybe he had a right to be paranoid, Vaiden thought. Many people had tried to kill the late king, all of them unsuccessful thanks to the Shade.

His regular hearing picked up the wind and faint echoes of their voices like someone trying to record a speech in a windstorm. When his hearing expanded through the room, his jaw clenched as every hiss in the air and cadence of the voice balanced. He inhaled sharply, shaking his head.

A warm hand rubbed soothing circles on his back. Vaiden eyed Alumpia beside him, her closeness confusing him. When had they become friends? He would have asked, but a crescendo of voices grabbed his attention.

A few nobles, he recognized, joined the king in the viewing room. Altamost sat on a padded high back chair, observing the others from a slight dais. It wasn't the throne room where the king's status would be a symbol to all emboldened to him. In this room, speaking amongst the common, he was lowered to their level to invite conversation and for the people not to be looked down upon. Vaiden wondered if that was also a reason Rothnar had hated this room. He hadn't liked to be seen as equal or mortal.

"What news have you heard, Your Majesty?" one of the nobles asked.

"Nothing of great consequence," Altamost replied. "There was an explosion at the gate. A few brats from Abrita Shores wanted to test our walls."

"They were able to climb over them?" another inquired, audibly gasping with dramatic flare.

"One was caught on the wall," Glades said. "He was the one who created the explosion, a bit of magic powder and a torch. The wall is fine. No one was hurt."

"But there were more?"

"Two others." The general nodded. "They were caught snooping in Surnuna's garden. We have confirmed they are with a guild down in Abrita Shores and wanted by the lord."

"Were they trying to get in the castle?" the dramatic one asked. "My king, are we in danger?"

"No, no," Altamost chuckled, waving his hand. "The good general is being cautious. I have full confidence in our soldiers. My own guards have searched the castle. Everything is in order."

Vaiden scoffed, drawing looks from his companions. "Altamost believes he is safe and everything is fine, despite finding three infiltrators."

"Is he just appeasing the nobles?" Alumpia asked.

"Hard to say."

"What did he say about our people?" Perry inquired.

"They were caught."

"Not what he did with them?"

"No one asked."

Perry scowled, grumbling something incoherent to himself. Vaiden glanced at him, his jaw locked, eyes focused on the viewing room through the crack. His hands balled into fists at his side, kneeling on his bad knee.

"They don't suspect more enemies?" Alumpia asked.

"They searched the castle and moved Altamost here as precaution, so my guess is they are being thorough since they know the girls are from Abrita Shores, known sympathizers of the rebels."

"If they know Abrita Shores aligns with us then why haven't they removed the duke?"

Vaiden studied Alumpia's questioning face. Her eyes had a magical glow in the darkness, or perhaps they were so bright it appeared that way. "I scouted the duke's manor when I was in Abrita Shores sometime back for the crown. There was no proof of his switch in loyalties, but enough whispers and gossip confirmed it."

"But he's still in power?"

"Whispers and gossip aren't proof enough for the crown, only paranoia."

"Incoming," Perry said. They moved back to the wall, gazing through the openings between the slats. Tor glided through the room unhampered by the wounds Vaiden had inflicted upon him. At his back, two other blue tunics studied the faces around the king.

"The council is secure," Tor announced. "Our men have questioned the last of the servants. We believe there is no threat to the castle or Your Majesty."

"Bravo!" The king smiled, motioning to the nobles with his hands spread wide. "See? Nothing of consequence. Our guards were well prepared for this task."

"We never doubted you, Your Majesty," a noble said. "Now can we discuss this business surrounding Council Kazquer?"

Vaiden's chest tightened, rippling through his torso like waves tearing through his flesh. It was strange that guards were posted at their house, watching it, but if there was an attack on the castle, it wouldn't be odd for guards to be stationed outside of council members' homes. Problem was, the guards had been posted long before Vaiden and the scouts had infiltrated the city.

"The letters were disturbing," Altamost said. "What can we expect from council members who are not acting in the best interest of the crown?"

"The crown?" Vaiden shook his head. The council worked for the king, sure, but they were tasked with advising him for the good of the kingdom, not the crown.

"What's happening?" Alumpia asked.

"It is shocking," the nobleman said. "Kazquer seemed to be a loyal servant, but hiding that boy—"

"His son," another interrupted. "Hardly suspicious, I would say."

"The same soldier that came to this city with that Shade, who—I remind you—attacked our king in his own throne room," the noble countered.

"That hardly makes him guilty of the crime. He wasn't there."

"True," the king said, returning their attention to him. "I have taken into account the fact the young captain was not present during the attack. Tor has explained Captain Kazquer wanted to accompany the Shade to the castle, but he was denied at the gate. Perhaps the captain could have kept our former friend from doing the terrible acts he displayed, but we will never know."

It took Vaiden a long second to realize that "our former friend" was him. He had never been friendly to Altamost, but he had only known indifference back in the days before the bind. Altamost had called him one of his favorites. Vaiden didn't know what that meant even when the king had exiled him to Earth and then had threatened to execute him more recently.

"But Callum did hide his son after learning the news about our Shade friend," Altamost said. "I do find *that* suspicious, especially after our guards found the letters from Gabriel Steel, confirming a coup."

"I cannot believe the council would plan such a thing." The dramatic noble sighed loudly, hand over heart. "It pains me to imagine what Your Majesty is going through. How could your most trusted advisers believe you are an incapable leader? Look how safe we've been through this war against, not only the Corrupted, but these rebel peasants too."

"They have discovered correspondence between the council and Gabriel about removing the king from the throne," Vaiden explained to his companions.

"Shit." Perry removed his gaze from the crack. "Have they executed any of the council?"

"They haven't said, but I think the investigation is ongoing. They'll want all the evidence first."

"Does that mean they need the ambassador?" Alumpia asked.

Vaiden shrugged.

"What do we do now?" She turned her whole body toward him, brows raised with questions. "There's a lot of guards down there, more than we can see from here. We can't fight all of them."

"Sure we can." Perry climbed to his feet. He was short enough not to bonk his head on the slanted ceiling. "We'll take them by surprise."

"They'll have us surrounded with more guards before we get twenty paces from the king."

"Forty," Vaiden corrected.

Alumpia frowned at him. "That's not helpful."

"We need a distraction." Perry crossed his arms, licking his lips. "Too bad we don't have an archer." His focus on Vaiden blazed like molten lava. The Shade crouching on the floor remained unmoved. He couldn't have saved the archer. There was no going back, only forward.

"Come up with something fast," Vaiden said, allowing the emptiness to fill his voice like pure darkness. "When they allow Altamost out of this room, it becomes increasing more difficult to get to him."

"What about illusions?" Perry asked, his stare softening Alumpia between them. "Could you make one big enough to clear the room?"

"Maybe, but where?" She spread her hands wide. "I can't be close to Vaiden or my magic won't work."

"Then you'll have to rely on Perry for protection."

"You say it like I'm not good enough." The fisherman bared his teeth. "I can protect her."

"No, you need to help Vaiden with the guards. I have wards in case I get into trouble."

"Will you be able to keep up the wards and the illusion at the same time?" Vaiden asked.

"Probably not."

"Then you'll have to be hidden." He stood, hunching to avoid hitting his head. "Could you cast the illusion from here?"

She looked out to the viewing room below. "I don't know." She chewed on her lip. "This is quite far, but I could cast an illusion on the ceiling. Like a thunderstorm to grab their attention and to mask your approach. It'll be high enough that your shadeness shouldn't bother the magic."

"Sounds like a plan."

"How do you get down there?"

"I know a way."

Perry rolled his eyes. "Of course you do."

Vaiden discarded his cowl, knowing it could easily get snagged on the golden leaves twisting through the room. Perry followed his lead, only carrying what was necessary and tightening his belts and buckles. Alumpia offered him a dagger, runes carved into the blade. He waved it away, claiming he had his own. She held the blade out to Vaiden. Tempting, he thought, envisioning the blade with his collection. He didn't know if he had any with runes, but it would be useless to him if it was made with elven magic.

"You might need it," he said. She nodded, sliding it back into the sheath tied at her waist. "How long can you hold the illusion?"

"A short while," she answered. "I know that's vague."

"It'll do." He motioned for Perry to leave. The fisherman cracked the wooden door open, peeking into the hall. When clear, he moved silently through, leaving it ajar for Vaiden.

Warm hands grasped Vaiden's wrist, pulling him backward. His brows knitted together as he cast silent questions Alumpia's direction. She wet her lips, her bright eyes round and soft, filled with something Vaiden didn't understand. "Be careful," her voice trembled, her fingers tightening around his wrist. "Wara give you strength."

"I might be a Shade, but I'm not your boyfriend." He ripped his arm from her grasp, his eyes blackening into void. "Do the job. It doesn't matter if I die or we all die. Do what's needed to ensure the Corrupted don't win this blight."

He didn't wait for her reply and joined Perry in the hall. The fisherman signaled they were all clear, allowing Vaiden to take the lead. The soft look in Alumpia's eyes haunted his every step. He knew she must have looked at Elridge that way too, wishing he could reciprocate her feelings. Vaiden had the ability, thanks to the bind, but an ache deepened in his heart, knowing what he wanted he could never have—not because of what he was, but what he had done. A mountain of bodies, he remembered, not all of them deserving of their fate.

He stifled the thought, burying it into the back of his mind. They had work to do. He couldn't think about Earth—that was the reward for winning the blight, for ensuring Altamost lost the crown. Vaiden would leave it all behind and return home where his beloved Viper had better still be parked. No, that was not what he wanted, not what he had yearned to return to after all these months.

A guard rounded the corner immediately spotting them in the bright open hall. Vaiden acted, throwing a blade into his neck. His cry for help muffled in bloody gurgles as he fell to the ground. Vaiden slid on his knees, catching the guard before he could impact the hard stone floor. The sound would only draw unneeded attention. The guard's wide eyes stared at the ceiling, seeing nothing of its beauty, only blankness. Another body for the pile.

Perry helped drag the guard away, hiding him behind a thick curtain. If the wind blew through the hall right, it would reveal him, but they had no time to secure him in a closet. Alumpia would start her illusion soon enough. They couldn't delay.

"You're blade?" Perry asked in a whisper.

Vaiden shook his head, carrying on. Though he hated leaving behind a weapon, keeping it lodged in the dead man's neck would ensure his blood didn't pool on the ground, avoiding further suspicion. It was why no one should remove an object that stabbed them. Another thing that bothered him while watching action movies. Let the doctors deal with it appropriately or expect further damage, blood loss, and probably death. *Idiots.*

Rumbles of thunder shuddered the hall, catching the attention of the guards outside of the viewing room. They opened the doors, sweeping winds stealing their breaths while Perry and Vaiden hammered blades into their backs. Another body for the pile. They pushed them inside the room, closing the doors behind them.

Flashes of lightning stole glimpses of the room engulfed in blackness. Perry moved on his right, picking up speed, slicing through guards in their path. More bodies for the pile. Vaiden shook his head, letting the emptiness spread through him, letting the calm indifference blanket his mind and allowing every slash and stab of his blade be nothing but motions in the air. He was a Shade. It was his purpose to kill the Corrupted, but the crown had transformed him into a weapon. Their decision.

Warm blood engulfed Vaiden's hands as he ripped his blade from a guard's gut, his cries silenced by the booming thunder. Lightning flashed, a path to Tor revealed. Vaiden pressed forward, abandoning his dagger for the short sword. As his main guard, Tor knew the intimate details of Altamost's wickedness, making him complicit in it. He took oaths to protect the king, Eskandor, and the sacred bonds and laws of the goddesses. Dallia was the Leader of the Faith, the bridge between the goddesses and mortals, Keeper of the Faithful, and Protector of Sanctuary. Where was her protection? Tor had failed in his duties, an embarrassment to all who had taken the oath before him.

The storm above raged through Vaiden as he swung his sword, slicing open Tor's back. He fell to his knees, pressing his hand to the wound. The Shade circled him, letting the flashes of lightning shine surprise on Tor's face when he saw the blood caked on his fingers and when the lightning flashed again, he gazed up spotting the shadowy presence of the one who had gotten away. The shock vanquished into fear, filling his eyes with coming tears. No. Karma never forgot a bitch.

Do it, whispered through Vaiden's mind, heat pouring through his veins, itching with the need for vengeance. No, Vaiden thought. *Justice*. He plunged his sword into Tor's heart, twisting until the pain in his face finally relaxed. The intimacy of it allowed Vaiden to watch every light leave his eyes and fade into nothingness, empty as the Shade's eyes, but gone the soul, hopefully straight to Aegan's realm for an eternity of anguish. *Good riddens*.

He pulled his sword out, the impact of metal slinging it from his hand. Glades's battle ax cut the air above him, making Vaiden painfully aware of how obvious he was in the bright open room. Alumpia's illusion had bought them time, but their cover was blown.

Glades wore his red tunic, the respectful position of a general. Fort Khali had crumbled while he retreated, letting his men die instead of leading them away safely. He wasn't fit to wear the uniform, the fucking coward. As his ax for Vaiden's head, the general's snarl deepened with his own purpose. Since their days in the Forty-Second, he'd always hated the Shade. Vaiden evaded, staying low, bouncing on heels with every attack. Glades was a big man, thick in muscle with the strength of a bull, but slow and stupid.

Vaiden unsheathed his hunting knife, ducking under another attack. The blade grazed Glades's calf, earning a growl as he whirled around. The ax whispered past the Shade, sparking against the stone floor. He plunged the knife into Glades's side, using his momentum to slice through his meat. The general fell to a knee, his ax clattering to the floor. Vaiden scooped it up, turning it over in his hand, testing the weight.

"Curse you, Shade," Glades coughed, blood dripping down his chin. An endless anger darkened his eyes. No, he wouldn't show fear, not like Tor. His hatred was too strong. "You traitor! You unnatural bast—"

The ax struck down fast as a missile with the weight of a pile of bricks, cleanly severing the general's head from his shoulders. Vaiden cast the weapon aside, lifting his gaze to find the nobles huddled around the king. Their mouths hung agape, eyes wide with fear that they would be next.

"That was brilliant!" Alumpia's voice sang through the air. The Shade smiled, wiping his cheek with the back of his hand, ignoring the blood drying on them.

"Hiya Alty," he said. "Miss me?"

Altamost pushed the others aside, pressing forward, but not too close. "You are a Shade. *A Shade!*" He screamed like a juvenile not getting their way. "You do not have the *ability* to hurt me."

"Oh, that's where you're wrong," Vaiden said, eying Perry, moving toward the king. "Shades only do what is necessary. There's never been a reason to act on the crown until now."

"And what reason is that?"

"Trust." Vaiden unsheathed his longsword, pointing it at his companion. "Don't do it."

"What's going on?" Alumpia said closer, letting Vaiden know she'd come down to their level.

"Piss on you!" Perry spat. "He won't even protect his own people. He rather we die and become monstrosities!"

"You don't know what you're talking about," Altamost said.

"Shut up!" They growled in unison. Vaiden kept his body pivoted so Altamost was between him and Perry. He wouldn't lose sight of the king. "We agreed to do it the right way."

"No, you and that worthless ambassador did. I am here for Haven, for the lost souls who cannot speak, who *he* left to die!" To emphasize the "he," Perry pointed his sword at the king. "He let those monsters burn Haven down. I held my sister's body in my arms, what was left of her, and her girls. My nieces! Twins! They wore braids that day. They—" His breath shuddered, tears glittering in his eyes.

"Twins?" Vaiden blinked, remembering that Kanaris's granddaughters were also twins. Twins were rare for elves, especially in one village. That would mean Perry's sister was Kanaris's daughter-in-law. It was why Kanaris tolerated him. They shared the same pain.

"They're gone because of this prick!" He stepped forward, forcing the king back into the nobles' arms. They would soon run out of space or be forced to flee. There were too many of them to keep corralled. If any of them escaped, they would sound the alert.

"I agree he deserves a world of hurt," Vaiden said. "If you do this, no matter the evil he's done, history will only remember him as your victim."

"Piss on history!"

"Think, Perry! Do you really want to continue this civil war even when he's dead? What is the point with all this fighting and death, if the kingdom falls apart? Is that what your sister would have wanted?"

Perry's jaw locked, the tension reddening his face, flaring with his nostrils. His eyes darkened with hatred, staring at his enemy, inches from cutting him down. Vaiden could see him imagining it, his fingers twitching around the hilt of his sword. The temptation was too good, too real. He had the king in his sights. The only thing standing between him and his revenge was a decision.

"I don't care." Perry lunged, but Vaiden intercepted his strike, sending his sword skyward. The fisherman rebounded quickly, throwing all his strength in each swing. The Shade parried, surprised by the shorter man's vigor. He had no form, just brutal straight power as he slammed their swords together.

"Perry stop!" Alumpia shouted.

Perry wasn't the guards or Glades. He was a grieving man, fighting for the family he'd lost. Vaiden couldn't kill him for that, but he could injure him. He parried the next attack, forcing the fisherman to stumble backward. Vaiden took his shot, his boot slamming into Perry's knee angling outward. A bone crushing snap crumbled him to the ground. His leg lay at an awkward angle while Perry held it, his screams echoing off the vaulted ceiling.

"Sorry," the Shade exhaled, sheathing his sword. Alumpia pushed him aside, glaring as she tended to her friend.

"You've made a mistake, Vaiden," Altamost announced, drawing his attention. The nobles held onto their king, shaking behind him. He impressively remained calm, standing tall without the need of his cane. The Shade's brows furrowed together. The king had walked without a limp. How had he missed that?

"My friends have finally arrived." Altamost gestured behind Vaiden. Standing across from him at the edge of the viewing room surrounded by cloaked figures, the blood mage lifted its staff in a salute.

48

A different serpent led Tatiana to Rocahn. She was a young one, barely five foot tall, and sheepish, hardly making eye contact with Tatiana when they spoke. Throughout the den, the serpent led with her head bowed, watching her feet beneath the long robe. She steered them down windy halls to a room Tatiana had never before entered. Rocahn was nowhere to be found.

"She will be along shortly," the serpent barely whispered before she rushed out the door, closing it behind her, leaving Tatiana alone in the dimly lit room. Only a table sat in the middle of it where a wooden box displayed. Snakes and dragons had been hand carved into the box with a small chisel and an expert hand. She thought about snooping to see what was inside, but she didn't want to begin this confrontation with Rocahn by insulting the den's privacy.

Her smartphone buzzed in her pants pocket, making her retrieve it. The tracking app Zarah had installed on her phone illuminated on the screen, letting her know it was active. She stared at the message atop it. It was a text from Logan. She turned it off, sliding the phone back into her pocket. Whatever it was would have to wait until after this meeting.

Tatiana's pulse throbbed in her ears. What was taking so long, she thought. Rocahn knew she wanted to talk. She might also know about the incident at the SDC. Zarah advised to lead with that, throwing Rocahn off the scent of why Tatiana returned to the den.

She exhaled, leaning against the farthest wall from the door. Zarah and Vaiden had taught her to be wary of exits. Some of her cop friends were the same. They made sure their back wasn't open to a door incase of a surprise attack. Tatiana wasn't sure how likely it would be for someone to ambush a police officer or a contractor of the Underground, but better to be safe than sorry.

After a few more minutes surrounded in the deafening silence and suffocating by the heavy heat, Tatiana shed her blazer, airing out her blouse. Sweat slid down her back, dampening her underarms and bra line. Her eyes darted to the ceiling in search of fans or air vents, but found none. The room had no windows or any other obvious signs of ventilation. Was it a hot box? Did they want to sweat her out?

Tatiana could wait. It didn't matter the conditions. Mr. Slaseezor deserved his freedom.

Finally the door opened, revealing two male serpents. They slid into the room, eying Tatiana with narrowed gazes. Rocahn followed them inside, wearing a black robe, embroidered with depictions of Shoresleen.

"Ms. Smith, forgive the security," Rocahn said. "After Zabetha's death, I decided it was best to stay safe."

Tatiana nodded, wondering why she needed guards to follow her in the comfort of her own den, but she decided perhaps she didn't trust the other members attending worship. Maybe it was earned after the attack at the SDC. "I have come to tell you that your husband is fine," she began. "There was an incident in holding, another prisoner escaped, but he was apprehended shortly."

"You mean he was killed by the police." Rocahn frowned. "I watch the news, Ms. Smith."

When had they returned to formalities? "Mrs. Slaseezor, I have spoken to your husband about information I've learned over the last couple of days and I have to say." She paused for dramatic effect, glancing at the two guards staring daggers into her skin. "You haven't been honest with me."

Rocahn opened her mouth to reply, but Tatiana raised her hand. "I don't know why," she said. "Your husband is running out of time and the more I investigate his case, the more lies I catch you in. Going forward, can we both agree to tell the truth? I cannot win this case without it."

"What have you learned?" Rocahn asked, stepping toward the right side of the room with her hands hidden behind her back. She did not defend her lies, Tatiana noted. Perhaps they could finally meet halfway.

"Koreen and Arkella were approved for coupling. You met with her parents to determine terms, but your demands for him were too steep." A hiss slipped between the serpent's lips but she waved her hands for Tatiana to continue. "I also learned more about your past from the east coast."

"Why does that matter?"

"Because your list of demands for Koreen was suspicious."

"Do you not trust me, Ms. Smith?"

Tatiana folded her arms over her blazer. "How can I trust you if you keep lying, *Salee*?"

She visibly winced, grimacing from the sound of her original name.

"I know you had run-ins with loan sharks when you previously headed a den. It was burned down, possibly arson," Tatiana explained. "If these people are threatening you, we can deal with it and get the police involved, if needed."

"No police," Rocahn growled. "They only want a reason to hurt us. We will not give it to them."

"Rocahn." Tatiana stepped toward her, opening her arms wide, showing she wasn't a threat. The guards shifted in her peripheral vision, sweeping between them. "I won't hurt her," she said, but the men frowned at her, using their wide frames as walls.

"What else did you learn?" Rocahn asked. "Arkella likes attention. She'll say anything. What did she tell you? That Koreen was afraid of me? The rich always look down on the poor, declaring that we're violent like animals, all the while gatekeeping resources for themselves. They're the *real* animals."

Tatiana raised a brow. "I didn't say I spoke to Arkella."

"Of course you did," she laughed dryly. "That girl needed every excuse to be involved. What else did she tell you? How much she loved Koreen and wanted to run away with him?"

Tatiana stayed poised, staring into the menacing faces of Rocahn's guards. Their loose robes distorted their wide frames, making it difficult to identify any weapon shapes. Generally, she wouldn't have questioned if they were armed, but a cold hand slid down her back, making every hair on her body stand on end.

Here, kitty, kitty, it purred.

She swallowed hard, wiping sweat from her forehead with the back of her hand. It was a small room with off-white walls, but it was enough to make her think of another room that she'd been held in. Her heart pounded against her chest.

No, no, no, panicked breathed through her mind. *Not here*. She couldn't show weakness, not in front of Rocahn, not when she had her cornered with her lies.

"Is it hot in here?" the serpent asked, stepping around her guards. Her eyes studied Tatiana while she approached the box at the center of the room. Tatiana turned with her, forgetting to never give her back to anyone—one of Vaiden's rules. And why? She shook her head, the room seemed to spin beneath her feet, making her stumble.

"It's fine," she lied.

The ends of Rocahn's lips curled, amused by her reply. "I read about you in the *Streaming Enquirer* before we first met," she said. "You've gone through a lot over this past year from getting engaged, to losing your fiancé in a horrible shooting, to being kidnapped and held, then learning that your sweetheart wasn't dead and it was all a charade to lure you into the arms of a serial killer."

Jen's laughter poured over Tatiana's skin like hot oil. "And?" she managed to ask.

"And, here you are," Rocahn motioned at her. "Looking for faults in people you once trusted."

"You have proved not to be trustworthy, Mrs. Slaseezor."

"I have done *everything* to protect my husband."

"You might think that, but you are only hurting his defense by keeping critical information hidden. Did you ever think that someone unhappy about Arkella and Koreen's coupling might be who framed your husband for this crime?"

Rocahn said nothing. Her fingers caressed the side of the wooden box, sharp nails following the pattern of snakes slithering down the side of it. Her stare emptied, the muscles in her face relaxing as she gazed at the box. Heat welled inside Tatiana glaring at this woman, who claimed she would do anything to free her husband. She had done nothing but waste time, endangering his freedom. Why, Tatiana was left asking once again. Why would she keep lying? To protect him, she had said, from what?

"What happened on the east coast?" Tatiana inquired.

"You read what happened."

"That your den burned down. The police assumed the loan sharks had something to do with it, though they had no evidence to support that claim."

A sigh escaped Rocahn's lips. "The police are so unreliable, even in this city."

Tatiana stepped toward the center of the room, ignoring the cold fingers gripping her shoulders. Jen's ghost could take a hike. She was working. "I want to understand," she said softly.

The serpent's fingers delicately opened the wooden box. A perfume filled the room with an intoxicating scent, drawing Tatiana closer. It was sweet, clean, and relaxing—like it could make all her problems vanish. Her shoulders lightened without burden as she gazed into the wooden box, finding a vibrant flower, an ombre of purple where its center was the darkest violet before transitioning into the palest lavender on its petal tips. It was a beautiful bloom that reminded her of gardenias, though a vine twisted around it violently, protecting it from anyone emboldened by its beauty.

Beauty was pain, she thought of that perfect flower. No one could touch it without feeling the wrath of the vine's long thorns, painted scarlet, as if someone had already tangled in the vine and left fresh blood behind as evidence.

"I loved Koreen," Rocahn said. "He was dear to our den. He was going to help us ascend, but he became greedy. They always do—the young ones. They have little patience and they never see the bigger picture. My husband gave away so much of his time to him, teaching him about the faith and about Arda for Koreen to turn his back on us for the Grand Den.

"Zabetha told me everything, how Koreen would meet Arkella in secret, how she wanted them to run away together, how he had met with her parents and leaders of the Grand Den about an exception." A quiet growl vibrated deep within Rocahn's throat. "We gave him everything after his family left for Arda. He was spoiled with love and when he found someone else to love, he planned to leave us behind, just like his family had left him."

"It must have been hard to learn," Tatiana said, not quite understanding what any of this had to do with the east coast.

"I was raised differently. I was raised with respect." She frowned. "You did not turn your back on the den who sheltered, clothed, and fed you. These young ones are so disrespectful. They want to forsake our culture and live like humans, but they are not like your kind. They have little understanding of what makes them special."

"America has always had problems with cultures clashing." Tatiana nodded.

"In the east, we have our systems to keep the young ones close, but California promotes this false sense of equality. We will never be equal to humans, and even humans don't think of each other as equals. So if they do not, how can we ever be equal to them?"

"I battle these questions in the courtroom all the time. The only thing we can do is to keep fighting."

"We shouldn't be equal because we are not the same," Rocahn spat. "We are serpents. Our kind was chosen by Shoresleen. Yours was not."

"Mrs. Slaseezor." Tatiana raised her hands as if to surrender. They were off subject. She needed to steer them back to what was important. "I need to know the truth. Do you know who wanted to hurt Koreen and your husband?"

Her gaze didn't shift from the bloom inside the box. "When I found out Koreen made a deal with the Grand Den and aimed to leave us behind, I was so angry that I decided to break a promise I had made to myself."

"And what was that?"

"I left the east because business there became to..." She paused searching for the right word. "Savage," she decided. "Our den was very liked—too liked. The Grand Den in our city had taken note of how their members came to us in times of worship. They decided to make a deal with me. I would only allow certain members and send the rest their way. In return, I would have access to some of their resources.

"I always loved gardening." She smiled. "My family had these wonderful gardens. It's why I studied horticulture. I wanted to make the most beautiful gardens for all to envy. When the Grand Den gave me access to their gardens, I discovered the beauty of plants from Arda. They are more difficult to work with, but I loved the challenge of it.

"After some time it was clear that my den would not lose popularity and it angered the Grand Den." The smile vanished from her face, her eyes darkening with anger. "Prominent families had invested in my den. They gave us extra security and made business dealings, including coupling, to solidify our friendships. We were a very profitable den, something I became too comfortable with.

"I knew some of the families were mob. I could look away from the unsavory things they did, as long as we received our shares. Of course, it didn't take long for the mob families to betray each other, and we were caught in the crossfire."

"The police report claimed you owed debts to loan sharks," Tatiana interrupted.

Rocahn shook her head, closing her eyes for a moment. "Necessary lies," she said. "We had to protect ourselves, but even with all the security we had, they managed to get to us."

"They hurt you?"

She opened her eyes, staring at something invisible in the distance. "I learned later the Grand Den made deals with some of the mob families and had them turn on us. When I went to confront them about this, they claimed I had no right to enter the Grand Den anymore. I was barred from its resources. If they found any of their property in my den, they would report I was smuggling plants from Arda and that I was selling them illegally." She bowed her head. "The latter was true. It was an easy way to make a profit since the plants are so desirable. Anything exotic makes the rich open their checkbooks."

"Did the Grand Den burned down your den?" Tatiana asked.

"I'm not sure if it was them or one of the mob families, but I fled the east, changing my name for a fresh start."

"What does this have to do with Koreen?"

"I wanted advice on how to handle his situation," Rocahn answered. "I had friends still in the east. They learned how I was married and had begun a new den. They wanted to support me and moved here."

"Are they behind what happened to Koreen and your husband?"

She shook her head. "They protect me."

Scaly hands grabbed Tatiana, forcing her to drop her blazer. She struggled, but they held her in place. Her wide eyes found Rocahn's empty expression. "Let me go!"

"I thought you would find a different avenue to get my husband released," she explained. "I thought the famous Tatiana Smith would save him without needing to reveal anything about my past, without pointing fingers at me, but it's clear that what happened with your fiancé and that serial killer has changed you, has made you useless."

"That's not how legal battles work!" Tatiana threw herself, hoping to break the serpents' grips, but they held on. "I can't help your husband with no direction to defend him. I have to give the court someone to blame or they will find your husband guilty. They'll execute him!"

"In human law, you could argue someone switched the blades. That he had no reason to kill Koreen, but you had to investigate further. You had to turn over stones that didn't need to be discovered."

"What are you saying, Rocahn?" Tatiana asked, stepping on one of the serpent's feet. He didn't even flinch. "That *you* are behind Koreen's death?"

She bared her teeth, growling again. "Koreen would have left us with nothing. His coupling would have ascended us. We would have access to the Grand Den."

"And you needed the Grand Den for its resources and its gardens."

"The den is broke."

"That's not true."

"Our donations dwindle month after month. We only have enough resources for our original members, but with every new member we must ration. I had a plan to get us money, but I needed access to the Grand Den. Koreen was supposed to get us in the door, but he betrayed us."

"That's why you killed him?" Heat radiated through Tatiana's middle hotter than the afternoon sun. "For money!"

"Everyone is an investment. He was an unneeded mouth to fill, but we took him in out of the kindness of our hearts. How could he just leave us with nothing?"

"True kindness expects nothing in return."

"Kind people don't become burdens to others." Rocahn motioned for them to come closer. Tatiana dug her shoes into the floor, but it was smooth. The serpents effortlessly dragged her across it even when her legs gave out, forcing them to lift all her weight.

"What are you doing?" she asked, hating the tremble in her voice. She fought so long to be strong, for everyone to see only the top preternatural attorney in the city and not think of her as Jen and Gary's victim.

Rocahn carefully clutched the center of the bloom between her middle and thumb claws, lifting it to expose the vine. "This is the only plant I have left from my original Arda garden," she explained. "I have run out of resources to keep it alive, but it will serve me one last time, like it had my friends back in the east."

Tatiana stared at the vine's red thorns, the violent threat of them. A grave voice whispered for her to run while Jen laughed in the background. "Nightbloom," slipped between her lips barely a whisper.

"You've heard of it?" Rocahn inquired, surprise widening her eyes. "I'm sorry for the pain it will cause you, but it's necessary to remove you."

"Why?" Tatiana asked.

"You know too much, but your death will spark new outrage and prove my husband's innocence," she replied without a hint of emotion. "We already pinned Zabetha's death on the Underground. Why not let them take the fall for your death as well?"

"You killed Zabetha?"

"Don't act surprised. I know she met with you, little liar." Rocahn clutched Tatiana's left hand pulling it toward the vine. "How did you survive that night?"

"People know I'm here, Salee!" She recoiled, throwing herself against the clutches of the serpents. Rocahn hissed at her struggle, or perhaps at the use of her real name again. "You won't be able to pin it on the Underground. They'll come here."

"And I'll say you left," she growled. "I have plenty of witnesses to back me up."

"But not the most important one."

Rocahn's brows furrowed together, a question blooming between her eyes.

"There's a lady outside," one of the serpents said, flicking out his tongue between his lips. "But we'll deal with her."

"There's plenty of thorns," Rocahn agreed, pulling her arm closer to the vine. "A pity you didn't come alone. How selfish."

"Selfish!" Tatiana bared her teeth, refusing to let her fear win. No, molten lava coiled in her middle, spreading through her body into her arms and legs. "You framed your own husband for murder! You killed an innocent man who just wanted to marry the woman he loved, and you're planning to kill me and my friend to silence us!"

Rocahn pulled the vine, whisking it toward Tatiana's arm, but she stopped short, her eyes falling on the electric blue lines snaking for her hand. "What—" She recoiled, hissing and throwing the vine aside. It fell safely on the table. The serpents who held her cried out, letting go.

Tatiana climbed to her feet, scrambling for the door.

"Get her!" Rocahn ordered.

She didn't look back, not even when their hot breaths were on her neck. Her legs pounded the floor, evading other members of the den. They retreated into doorways, their eyes widening with confusion.

"Zarah!" she shouted, hoping the vampire's hearing would pick up the panic in her voice.

The den was a maze, but all the running she'd done in the past six months endowed her with strong legs, keeping a solid lead over the serpents in their loose robes. They weren't meant for running. Neither were Tatiana's loafers, but she thanked her complaining feet that she hadn't worn heels.

"Zarah!" she shouted again, rounding a corner into—a dead end. Her heart sank, whirling around to find the two serpents snarling at her. They had shed their outer robes, wearing only baggy trousers. Each serpent was thick in muscle. They moved with purpose, with knowledge and experience of how their six foot frames intimidated people.

She took a deep breath, arms held wide. Though she hadn't perfected bringing the blue fire to the surface, the threat of it was enough to make these serpents hesitate. Their nostrils flared, watching her, debating whether or not they could take her. There were two of them and only one of her. She could deep fry them so thoroughly only ashes remained. Their choice, she thought, reaching deep inside that buried pit at her core.

Gunfire ripped through the air, splitting through the left side of the hall. She dove to the ground, covering her head as bullets zinged above. When it quietened, only ringing remained. It subsided quickly, replaced by her trembling breath. She removed her arms, spying the serpents dead on the floor. Their bodies looked mauled, gaping wounds oozed, washing the floor with their blood.

"Tatiana!" she heard, but it sounded distant. "Ana!"

She pushed against the floor with her hands, her arms shaking as she shifted onto her butt. More shouting caught her attention, but she couldn't make out their words. Her vision blurred with tears, wetting her cheeks, a sob strangling her throat. She couldn't break—but the dam splintered and a flood of tears followed.

A figure stepped into the hall, dark and blurry.

"It's OK," Zarah said, her strong arms pulling Tatiana against her. Another sob ripped from her lips and she clutched her friend, crying into her shoulder. "I've got you. You're safe."

Tatiana shook her head, words lost in her throat. It was a lie. She would never be safe again.

49

Purpose burst through the chains holding it back deep inside the void at Vaiden's core. He stumbled from the blow as it raced through his veins, burning like acid, fueling him with renewed strength and focus.

Atlamost had created the blight. He had enabled these Corrupted to spread their evil through the kingdom. Why? Vaiden shook his head, turning his back on the blood mage and its entourage.

The Shade held his arms wide. "Don't tell me you did all this so you can walk unaided, Alty."

The king smiled, stepping away from the nobles, whose eyes darted from the Corrupted back to him, trying to solve the problem like a math equation. The dramatic one covered his gasp with both hands, being the first to understand the situation.

"Not only," Altamost said, waving his hand dismissively. "Your little coup will be another failure of this war, like your friend Gabriel and the rebels, and anyone who thinks they can take my crown."

"Why risk the entire kingdom?"

"The *entire* kingdom wasn't at risk!" fumed the king. "I kept all the major cities safe. Yes, Fort Khali had to be destroyed, but it was purposeful."

"What could be the purpose of killing all those soldiers who were loyal to you?"

"Their sacrifice will not be in vain, but my friend needed to test their strength, to give the people something more to fear when all this nonsense with the rebels is over." Altamost grabbed his cane forgotten against his chair. He unsheathed the hidden sword, pointing it like an extension of his hand at Vaiden. "You asked me once why I sent the Shades to Kiji. Can you guess why?"

"I expect a bunch of Shades strolling along the roads would have dampened your new friends' fun."

The king laughed, throwing his head back. "Such a sense of humor, Vaiden."

"If you didn't want the Shades around, why bring me back?"

"You were supposed to eliminate that oaf Kanaris, but Gabriel! Oh, I knew he was a mistake to keep around, but no, he's the ambassador. Everyone loves him. I had to keep him around until an accident could be arranged for him, but *you* remedied that situation, Shade. You gave me cause to mark him a traitor and look! I'm not wrong, am I?"

"Gabriel's loyalty remains to the kingdom."

"I am the only one who can determine that," he growled, heat clawing up his neck.

"Why did you order the Shades to Kiji?" Vaiden asked, keeping them on subject.

"A new order was to be issued," Altamost said, walking to the left of his chair like it was a stage and he was the actor keeping the audience's attention. "Down with the old ways. No more Leeth or Duncan. One where freedom of power isn't bound by birth, but awakened with knowledge and enlightenment."

"You sound like an Aegan salesman."

"Aegan wasn't wrong, Vaiden. She is a goddess, the same as the rest of them. Why should she be discriminated against as evil and wrong and cast aside for being abnormal? You Shades are celebrated for your unnatural abilities. Why should any of Aegan's faithful be treated unequal?"

"Because what they want is pure evil."

"Curing disease and the broken? How is that evil? I will lead this new era, curing all our ailments. The healers have lied to us all. I lived in pain because of those lies. Aegan and her faithful have shared the truth with me. We can take away all the pain."

"They forget to mention the part where you sell a piece of your soul to Aegan and she sucks the life from you."

"If she was the only evil one then why does Grita or even Opretta's magic make someone Corrupted?"

"Because it's all dark magic and it corrupts."

"That's what you have been led to believe."

"Is that why you hold Dallia hostage? To reeducate her?" Vaiden asked, keeping him in sight, ignoring the Corrupted at his back. If they attacked, he would know, but their magic could do nothing to him. He also bet they wouldn't attack while Altamost continued to talk, buying time for Duke Heiron's soldiers to storm the gates. It wasn't the plan. The gates were supposed to be open for them, but they would know something was wrong when the city didn't open by noon. Heiron planned to finish what he started, no matter if the gates were open or not.

"Dallia is the Leader of the Faith. Our marriage will make the kingdom come together, stronger than ever."

"Who will you be marrying? The real Dallia or the one you had invented?"

The king's face twisted like he'd smelled something foul. "You Shades have been bred with such closed minds, such discrimination."

"Only against the Corrupted."

"You are the only kind of elves in our kingdom that are truly an anomaly, the ones given too much power, and we have allowed it for far too long."

"What does that mean?" Alumpia asked, her magic funneling through her hands to repair Perry's broken knee. "The Shades keep our kingdom safe."

"Misguided child." The king shook his head. "After Fort Khali's destruction and the elimination of the rebels, my army would have marched north to Kiji and cleansed our kingdom of their filth."

Gasps sliced through the air, straight through Vaiden's chest. "You planned to kill the Shades?"

"Oh no, I *still* mean to." His face morphed into something alien and dangerous, almost like his skin wasn't comfortable covering his face. "When I'm through with you and your pathetic coup, I will butcher your kind, cleave them into tiny pieces, and burn all of Kiji to dust." His face relaxed, dipping into a more natural smile, but the rage in his eyes revealed a monster. "And thus, a new era will begin. One of Aegan's faithful while the rest bow in servitude."

"You're not a High Elf."

"I am transcended."

"What—"

Altamost plunged his sword into a noble's belly, the surprise echoed by his friends' screams. The king removed his weapon, the blood sliding off the blade and circling him, pulsating with renewed power. Red magic glowed around him as the noble's blood sank into his skin, snaking down to his arms like electric eels.

Behind you, purpose said, making Vaiden glance at the magic coiling around the blood mage. Perry and Vaiden had killed many guards, wrapping it the perfect gift. *Fuck.* Another halo of power circled the dead, cooler than the red, sampling the bodies left behind. Green magic engulfed this Corrupted, revealing itself as the necromancer. *Double fuck.*

"Perry, get up," Alumpia said, smacking his cheek. "Get up!"

He roused, springing to his feet. Alumpia caught him, her gaze pleading at Vaiden. "Tell me you know another way out of this room."

"Of course I do," he said, retreating to their side while keeping the Corrupted and the king in his sights. "Out that window."

"We'll die from the fall."

"No, you won't. Trust me."

"*I* don't trust you," Perry slurred.

The dead rose, unnatural screams tearing through their mouths. Their animated bodies moving slowly, dragging their feet and bowels toward the rebels. Vaiden could fight the blood mage and the king, but there were too many other enemies. They had to live to fight another day.

He opened his mouth to tell Alumpia to jump when the doors of the viewing room burst open. The Corrupted moved back, giving space to the new arrivals. Gabriel had his sword drawn, white steel ringing in the air. Blood caped his face, telling the story of a battle raging outside the room. Beside him stood Kanaris, his rebels, and a fellow that Vaiden recognized immediately, not by his face, but by his black tunic.

"Your Majesty," Gabriel said, surging forward. "I heard you've been looking for me."

"Oh, thank the goddesses you arrived, the Corrupted have—" Altamost put up his hands in surrender, the blood magic evaporating in the air. For all his talk, he retreated stumbling into his chair, playing the part of a feeble, traumatized man.

"Sit!" the ambassador commanded, the point of his blade pushing against the king's chest. "And don't move."

The Shades' general surveyed the room, drawing his sword. "Eliminate the Corrupted," he ordered, a unit of Shades sprawling into the room. They charged the necromancer and its flock, cutting them down with ease. The blood mage and two other Corrupted took to the air, climbing up the vaulted ceiling high above the Shades in safety. Arrows flew, bouncing off their wards. The blood mage pummeled the ceiling with magic, breaking it open.

"Watch out!" Alumpia shouted as pieces fell to the battle below. The fragments as big as a car, stopping midair. Cerulean halos glowed around them as figures cloaked in blue discarded them into the remaining Corrupted on the ground.

"They came." Alumpia grinned. "Mysogus is here!"

"Thank Surnuna," Perry exhaled.

"You mean Grita," Vaiden corrected, studying the open window frame.

"What are you doing?" Alumpia asked.

"I'm not letting that blood mage get away." He grabbed the hand-carved vines, pulling himself up, scaling the open window until he was on the roof. Smoke billowed in the city, his expanded hearing picking up screams and clashing metal. The high breeze took his breath away, filling his mouth with the taste of copper.

Ahead he could see the Corrupted racing across the roof. He ran, letting his feet adjust to the different textures of the roof from rough stone to smooth marble, avoiding the rounded glass domes. The blood mage used its magic to create platforms for it and its friends, hopping down the slanted roofs cautiously. Vaiden slid on his side, letting himself become narrow and tight like a Bobsled, using the ridges of the roof to create natural lanes, like a great marbled slide.

He reached for his hunting knife, unsheathing it to strike one of the Corrupted. The magical platform faltered and it fell to the roof ahead of him. He unwound, digging his fingertips into the marble to slow him down. The Corrupted slashed at him with its blackened claws, snarling its diseased mouth while they slid side-by-side. It grazed his arm, but that allowed him to grab its wrist, pulling it closer and burying his blade into its skull.

Vaiden peered down his body, spying the end of the roof and the next Corrupted within reach. The platform disappeared under the Corrupted's feet and it fell, Vaiden leaped off the edge of the roof, catching it in the air and positioning it under him, spying the courtyard below. He pivoted their bodies over the fountain, knowing only one of them could survive the fall. The Corrupted slapped at him, screaming until impact.

Vaiden pushed off at the critical point, splattering its body on the fountain side while he plunged into the water, stabbing him like a million needles. He swam for the surface, inhaling deeply, blinking away the water from his eyes.

Something heavy splashed into the pool behind him as he pulled himself up. The other body, he thought, lumbering over the side of the fountain. The blood mage crossed the courtyard overhead effortlessly on its platforms, the staff naked in its grasp. Though the Shades had arrived, he knew the power of that staff could bring down the entire city. It had to be stopped.

Being on the ground proved difficult with the ongoing battle. He reached for his short sword quickly realizing he'd lost it in the fight with Glades. The longsword would have to do. He unsheathed it, drawing his sights from the sky to beyond the courtyard where soldiers battled the dead and monstrosities. They weren't his fight, not with his brethren on the premises. His legs carried him through the fray, letting his hearing and instincts navigate the fight while his eyes searched for the blood mage. It wore red, the glow of its power streaking the air like a contrail.

He sliced down the dead, not stopping for a second. The rebels were in the thick of the fight with Casimere's soldiers guarding their backs. Archers loosed a wave of arrows striking down the dead, clearing a path. Shades pressed forward, chopping through monstrosities, while practitioners protected the soldiers afar with their wards.

The blood mage traversed through the air, searching for somewhere safe to land. It couldn't stay up there forever. Archers eventually spotted it, trying to strike it down. Its wards held while it navigated toward the lower rings. Vaiden knew they could lose it in the city where there were plenty of places to hide, but crossing into the fourth ring to the third, he found squadrons of Shades protecting the citizens of the city. Duke Heiron and a unit of his men were among them, fighting off monstrosities.

Green magic haloed several Corrupted who were caught in the middle, letting Vaiden know the blood mage had collected several necromancers for the attack on this city. They were cut off, staring down Shades and certain death. Vaiden ran for the duke, cutting through a few Corrupted of his own.

"Joining the fight, are you?" Heiron's armor shone in the sunlight, a fierce grin on his face, despite the carnage surrounding them.

"I was already here!" Vaiden sprinted through them, the Shades parting like the sea for Moses.

"Where are you going?" the duke asked. He pointed his sword skyward in reply, hot on the blood mage's trail. After expending so much magic, it would need to land soon. Vaiden searched ahead wondering which of the buildings it might land on. He'd have to climb the building; though deep in his core, he knew, no matter how fast he climbed, he could never stop it from calling the meteors. He had to try though. They could not lose Casimere.

With his sword sheathed, he crossed the bridge over the gardens, watching the blood mage's platforms end at a tavern. Finally, he thought, quickly realizing it was the tallest building in the center ring. Of course.

The wind whirled around him, storm clouds circling the sky above the tavern. Lightning cracked the sky in a flash of blood red. It had begun. Vaiden pressed into the building, throwing open the door. Patrons stared at him, hiding behind their tables. A vibration grew, clinking glasses.

"What's happening?" someone asked behind the bar. "Who's attacking?"

Vaiden ignored them, racing to the stairs. The building quaked, making him slip on a step. He quickly recovered, taking them two at a time, climbing until he found the ladder to the roof. He pushed open the trap door, hauling himself up into the darkness encasing the city. The blood mage stood in the center, the staff raised above its head, a tornado of blood magic shooting into the sky, glowing violently with its power.

"No!" Vaiden watched helplessly as fireballs rained from the sky. The blood mage let go of the staff, letting it float in place, its shrouded face sneering at the Shade. He unsheathed his sword. "Oh, let's go."

It opened its robe, producing a flail with three long spikes at the end of its chain. All Vaiden had to do was get within distance of the staff and its magic would fail. The blood mage stood in the way, holding the flail with the chain dragging the ground, waiting for his first move.

The first meteors struck, wrecking the outer wall by the fourth ring and crashing into towers of the castle, quaking the city into silence. Vaiden lunged, swiping at the blood mage, who dodged with unnatural ease, like it was made of liquid shifting in the robe.

Fire ripped through Vaiden's thigh where the flail's spikes sliced through his trousers. The blood mage whirled around, whipping the spikes for his head. He evaded, the whisper of the blades splitting his hair. The blood mage seemed to smile within the darkness of its hood, tilting its head with its arms spread wide. It liked the challenge, but it was in the way between him and his goal.

Vaiden charged again, side-stepping barely missing the flail, slashing, but only hitting air.

The blood mage moved fluidly, like a dance, its attacks precise, once clipping Vaiden in the shoulder, but managing to keep between the staff and the Shade, manipulating his steps backward and forward, gaining no ground in the end. Vaiden's jaw locked. It was playing with him. Problem was Vaiden was learning. He side-stepped again, the opposite way, switching sword hands and stepped into his swing, forcing the sword forward like a baseball bat. It slipped from his fingers, spinning end-over-end aiming for the staff. The blood mage raised its hand to intercept, but it was too slow.

A blood-curdling scream pierced the air as the sword splintered the staff, nullifying its power. The tornado of red magic evaporated, the last of its meteors breaking up in the atmosphere as sunlight penetrated through the clouds. Surnuna banished away the darkness.

Vaiden turned on his heel, grabbing the hunting knife from his boot. The blood mage screamed again, the force of a banshee slamming into him. Its cloaked body writhed, pained as if losing a limb. That pain quickly morphed into rage as it swung the flail mindlessly at the Shade. Vaiden dodged, keeping low, allowing the blood mage to control the space on the rooftop. He led it forward, letting it chase him while the spikes sailed through the air, hitting only the breeze.

It blindly raged, swinging the flail until it ran out of rooftop. Its foot slipped off the edge, dropping the flail to keep balance on the edge, but Vaiden was there, ramming his boot into its back. It fell, a sick thump splattering against the cobblestones below.

A weight shifted off Vaiden's shoulders, purpose shrinking back into the void at his core. He inhaled deeply, breathing in the clean air of Eskandor, basking in the warmth of the sunlight, knowing sleep would come easy to him that night. The blight was over.

**

"Be still," Alumpia growled, sewing up the wounds clawed through Vaiden's shoulder. They sat on Leeth's fountain, listening to the soothing sounds of the water. The third ring was emptied of the enemy, their bodies brought to the gallows for burning. A few of the buildings were damaged by the battle, but nothing as serious as the outer wall in the fourth ring or the turret between the eastern and southern gatehouses.

Vaiden grimaced as she plunged the needle through his skin, glad for an expert hand, even if she was pissed at him for breaking Perry's knee. The scout leader stood across from them, unhampered by any injury, learning how the rebels had managed to enter the city with the gates closed.

The Shades had come, bringing their battalions to the city to answer some kind of question Gabriel had asked. Vaiden believed it. If anyone could influence a whole class of people to question their priorities, it was the Nuisance of Abrita Shores. The guards atop the wall hadn't known what to think with the sudden appearance of the Shades or that a general had ordered them to open the gates—*all* of the gates.

"Just in time too," one of the rebels said. "The Corrupted had come up from the sewers, already there before any of us. The king must have cleared them a path so they could take over the city."

"So they just opened the gates?" Perry asked.

"More Corrupted and the dead ambushed the Shades, but we had their backs." The rebel beamed. "Mysogus showed up next. Glad to have them when those meteors started falling."

"Did the practitioners find Dallia?" Vaiden asked.

"Yes," Alumpia answered. "She is tainted by blood magic so she cannot return to Mysogus with them, but they will escort her to Jana's fane where she plans to cleanse herself."

"Good," he said and meant it. "She deserves peace."

"Do you think she can clean the blood magic away?"

"If a vampire can cleanse the evil of High Tower from its halls, then she can wipe away the dark magic from her soul, but it is the other scars that will take longer to heal."

"Of the king taking over her body and mind?"

"And what he did to her during that time."

"There." Alumpia moved his shirt back into place. "Finished."

Vaiden relaxed, moving so he could see her face. Her eyes swept through the third ring, admiring her friends and the locals taking care of them with food and entertainment. It was a lively place where many had died hours before. Memorials of flowers spread through the rings where soldiers, rebel and Casimere alike, had fallen. Their bodies would be taken to Moren's graveyard, preserved for the families by magic, and then buried either there with Moren or taken with their families when they returned home.

Alumpia shot up, a gasp escaping her lips. Vaiden was about to ask her a question when she bolted, sprinting toward a man clad in black. "Elridge!" She threw her arms around his neck, making him stumble. He wrapped his arms around her tinier frame with familiarity, holding her close though his face shadowed with indifference.

A smile drew on Vaiden's face as he averted his gaze, catching Alvez joining Perry and the rebels. The recently freed archer and sisters from Abrita Shores offered him a pint of ale in celebration.

"My son seems fond of the rebels already," Callum said, standing by the Shade. "He said you claim Perry will help him find the rest of his men from Fort Khali resurrected by necromancy. After searching the dead, Alvez says four remain."

"Perry and his scouts will look after him like one of their own," Vaiden answered, remembering the surprise on Perry's face when the Shade had recommended him. "He knows a thing or two about needing closure."

"We all do, especially after this war," the councilman said.

"How is the voting going?"

"Altamost has broken the sacred laws of Leeth and many more oaths he had taken before the goddesses. He will be executed on the morrow for all the citizens of Casimere to watch."

"Who will replace him?"

"The council agreed it should be Ambassador Steel." Vaiden's head whipped up, staring at the councilman. "He declined, stating that he will be retiring from service. He's starting a family, I hear."

Vaiden found Kanaris and his cousin, Duke Heiron, parading down from the fourth ring. "Who else will the council consider?"

"There's a list, but it will be no small task to replace the leader of our kingdom."

"What about Heiron?"

"He's on there. Does he get your vote?"

Vaiden climbed to his feet, easily dwarfing Callum. "Council Kazquer, I have no vote. I'm just a Shade."

"A Shade who may have saved this city, if not the whole kingdom."

"It's all in a day's work."

Callum chuckled, shaking his head. "I'm glad to have met you," he said, retreating to his son and the rebels.

***

A teary-eyed Caroline finally let go of Vaiden, pushing him toward her husband while she composed herself. Gabriel patted Vaiden's shoulder. "Are you sure you want to go back?" he asked.

"I'm sure. You have no idea how good I have it there."

They stood before one of the doors that connected their world to Earth. A practitioner had awakened it. Its magic wasn't from the elf, but from the world itself, or at least that was the running theory. The transparent waves of sapphire and magenta swirls called him home between the ancient roots of a massive tree tangled with the stone of the archway outside of Brevene, where Gabriel and Caroline planned to build their new home.

Gabriel's jaw clenched, holding back tears. "Moon."

Vaiden hugged him, sighing against his shoulder. "Sun."

They stood there until Gabriel stopped shaking, surrounded by wildflowers and singing birds, a moment they had known would happen after they won the war. It was done. Vaiden earned to return home—his home. It didn't make it any easier, not as his chest tightened with the idea of leaving behind his best friends.

Gabriel pushed away, wiping his face with both hands. His sky blue eyes met the Shade's darker ones with a smirk, hiding the pain he had stored since Vaiden had first crossed through the doors fifty years ago. "See you later, alligator."

A wide grin spread across Vaiden's face, letting it reach his eyes with new light. "In a while, crocodile."

50

Tatiana stood by Sergeant Pérez while Officer Sampson removed the chains from Mr. Slaseezor. He slowly stood, rubbing where the manacles had been placed over his wrists.

"Thank you," he said to the officer, somehow meaning it. After all he had been through, Tatiana was surprised by his kindness. He crossed the threshold of the cell door, a sigh escaping his lips, his tongue lipping between them to taste the air.

"You are free to go, Mr. Slaseezor," the sergeant said. "The State of California thanks you for your cooperation during your time here, but from me and our staff, we hope to never see you again."

The serpent nodded at Pérez before following Officer Sampson down the hall. Tatiana patted his back as they walked along, reassuring Mr. Slaseezor this was no trick. Once they rode the elevator to the surface, he was free.

It dinged, the doors sliding open, revealing the officers within and their newest prisoner. Rocahn—or Salee—gawked at her husband. Sergeant Pérez and Officer Sampson stood guard between Mr. Slaseezor and his wife while the other officers pushed her into the hall.

"I'm sorry!" she cried while they dragged her to the cell her husband had occupied for a week. "You must understand! I did it for us! Please forgive me!"

Mr. Slaseezor kept his head down the entire time, never making eye contact with her, never saying a word. Officer Sampson took them up the elevator while the sergeant stayed behind to help secure the prisoner.

"Thank you, Ms. Smith," Mr. Slaseezor said in the quiet of the elevator ride. "You never gave up on me and thanks to you, we know the truth about what happened to Koreen."

She smiled at him, his dragon eye staring down at her, a sadness glittering in it. "It was my privilege and honor."

"You will always be welcome at my den."

The doors slid open, the bright lights of the main hall blinding them temporarily. Officer Sampson stepped out first, holding the doors open, a friendly grin spread on his face while Mr. Slaseezor then Tatiana exited the elevator. She realized they may not witness many of the supernatural leaving this facility alive, but when an innocent was released from prison, it was a relief that not all accused were guilty. Some were kind people, trying to make a difference in their small way, shadowed by circumstances beyond their control.

Tatiana escorted Mr. Slaseezor out the front doors, where a group of supporters rallied with cheers and love in their hearts. There were serpents from his den, others from the community, and some people he'd never met, holding signs of joy, praising his release. Mr. Slaseezor's eyes widened at the group of faces before him, baffled by their support, especially the young ones.

Reporters stood at the edge of the steps, snapping pictures of their descent as Mr. Slaseezor thanked the people. His den had supplied a car for him and Tatiana helped him to it, knowing she'd already instructed the press that she would speak to them alone. The supporters and police helped create a barrier between them and the press, allowing him to slip into his car peacefully. She watched him drive away, happy for the case to be over and that a good man would return home.

When the support group thinned, returning to their vehicles, the press moved forward freely, thrusting their microphones into her face.

"We are pleased to have discovered the truth," Tatiana said. "Rocahn Slaseezor framed her husband for murder when she is, in fact, responsible for the tragic events that led to Koreen Tolhsee's death, confessing to switching the blades. My client and Mr. Tolhsee can now rest easy knowing that justice will be served."

"Tatiana, can you tell us what happened at the den?" a reporter asked. "Why did Mrs. Slaseezor try to kill you? How did the police know you were in danger and what is next for your client?"

"Mr. Slaseezor will return to his den and continue to teach the community about their faith," she explained. "As you all know, there was an attack on the SDC a couple of days ago where a serpent had broken out of his cell. The police in their quick, but thorough investigation found that this prisoner had been hired by Mrs. Slaseezor to kill her husband in order to keep her secrets safe.

"What happened at the den was a desperate decision by Mrs. Slaseezor to silence me before I could reveal her lies. PITF moved quickly on their orders to arrest the serpents involved in the attack on the SDC, including the neutralizing of two serpents inside the den. I thank PITF and the many officers of our great city, whose speedy call to action, who not only saved my life, but Mr. Slaseezor's as well."

"How are you doing, Ms. Smith?" George Zeilberg asked from the crowd. "Six months ago you were held by Jennifer Verniski and Gary Martin, and now this. How are you holding up?"

She frowned at him, expecting the call of the siren or for Jen's voice to echo through her mind, but they did not come. The reporters waited for her answer, their microphones and smartphones waving in the air. She squared her shoulders, one of her best business smiles sliding across her face almost too naturally.

"I'm doing great," she said. "I thank you all for your support over these months, but if you really want to help, check out Pearson and Associates website where we are advocating for survivors of trauma and speaking out against violence in our community. Thank you."

The police escorted her to her car where Zarah waited inside. "How'd it go?" she asked.

"Better than expected."

"Was George an ass?"

"Of course."

"You want me to remind him of his place?"

Tatiana made a face, putting her car into gear. "What I really want is a hot bath."

"Or how about that retreat I promise?" A wicked grin spread across Zarah's face.

"You didn't!"

"Four tickets to paradise," she said. "You, me, and the girls—this weekend."

"You're amazing."

They pulled out of the parking lot, raindrops dotting the windshield.

***

Tatiana wrestled with her purse. Her fingers twisted through its pockets for her apartment keys to no avail. Purses were gateways to a different dimension. Sometimes she could find what she needed in a timely fashion. Sometimes she had to dump the whole thing to discover hidden treasures. Her fingers slid over the familiar rough edges she knew to be the keys. She grasped them as if they would slide into the void and be forgotten forever. It had been a long day.

A week ago she had been in the sun, relaxing on the beach with her favorite ladies, away from the city and every reporter who wanted to know her traumas. After pictures were leaked of George following Tatiana around the city and even to her home, her firm threatened to press charges, claiming George wasn't on assignment and was stalking her. The *Streaming Enquirer* held strong until a social media movement about privacy forced them to suspend him for unprofessional conduct, impending an investigation. He had backed off, but Tatiana knew it was temporary.

The lock clicked open and she swung the apartment door open. As she stumbled through the doorway, her purse strap slipped off her shoulder, making it awkward to carry the briefcase and the files under her arm. She exhaled heavily, throwing them all to the floor of the entryway. A new case, a new mess, but she wasn't in the mood that night.

"Hey," a voice called deeper in the apartment.

Heat poured over her like a waterfall of lava, she embraced it and forced the blue flames to her hands as she faced the intruder. They did not run or act surprised by the display of power, which only raised more alarms than eased her. A silhouette emerged into the dim lights of the hallway from the kitchen so she could see them more clearly.

Her heart pounded so savagely against her chest she thought it might crack through. The flames extinguished quickly from her hands, making them naked and harmless.

A shaky breath escaped her lips as she said, "Vaiden."

He chuckled, a sound that radiated through her body with dark promises. She leaned heavily against the sideboard stepping over the case files on the floor.

"Come here," he beckoned.

She threw off her heels and ran full speed at him. "Vaiden!" She sprang into his arms. He laughed into her hair, holding her body tightly against his. She nuzzled against his neck and breathed in the earthy tones of his scent, finding safety at last. They held each other for a moment until Tatiana finally moved back to see his face.

"When did you get back?" she asked.

"Just now." He smiled and it reached his eyes, so the tiny eclipses of his irises lit up.

"Does anyone else know you're here? Coastal will want—"

"No." He laid a single finger over her lips, slowly caressing it over them and down her chin. His eyes followed the movement, and then flicked up to meet her stare. "I only want you."

She pushed away, raising a brow at him. "No, you only want to watch your show."

"You know it."

The Nine Goddesses

Surnuna *[sir nu nuh]* The Sun, Goddess of Life, Light of All Paths

Grita *[gree tah]* The Teacher, Goddess of Craft and Sorcery, Creator of High Elves

Layetta *[lay eh tuh]* The Heart, Fertility Goddess, Goddess of Pleasure

Aegan *[a gan]* Goddess of Disease and Famine, Creator of Blood Magic, Mistress of Evil

Wara *[war uh]* The Protector, Goddess of Strength and Courage, Creator of the Shades

Alumpius *[ah lum pus]* Goddess of Wisdom, Bringer of Voice and Devotion *banned from worship by King Rothnar the Daunting

Moren *[mor in]* The Moon, Goddess of Death, Mother of Vampires, Creator of Necromancy

Jana *[ja nuh]* The Mother, Goddess of Harvest and Riches, Protector of Children

Opretta *[oh pret tuh]* Goddess of The Arts, Creator of Illusionary and Divination Magic, Bringer of Mystery, Joy, and Curiosity

About Elves

The oldest living race on Arda, elves live in the kingdom of Eskandor. They are eternal, meaning they live unnaturally long lives and do not seem to age through that time. They worship the nine goddesses and have erected shrines and statues of them throughout their kingdom. They believe when they die they will live on in Paradise. Anyone who violates the goddesses' words will be cast to Aegan's banishing realm, living in agony for eternity.

Novices are elves born with little-to-no magic. Those sensitive to magic cannot harness it, but do retain the ability to feel auras and sense when magic has been or is being used. They are the most common kind of elves found on both worlds.

High Elves are the most magical elves. They spend their lives studying magic and serving the goddesses. Once their magic potential is realized, they are accepted into Mysogus, the School of Magic, also known as Sanctuary. Each High Elf will devote their studies to one type of magic, typically under their assigned goddess. Most High Elves are born under the sign of Grita, Jana, Opretta, Aegan, or Moren. Born necromancers will not be allowed to live and train at Sanctuary. They will live and learn their craft at Moren's fane.

The Corrupted are High Elves tainted by dark magic. They are commonly elves born under the sign of Aegan or Moren, but any magic can be abused and fester into corruption. The obvious signs of corruption are the blackening of the nails and changes to the eyes. The Corrupted can come in different levels of power. Necromancers that cross into corruption are those who use their gifts to create abominations, raise the dead, and control vampires. Blood mages are practitioners who are Corrupted through blood magic. Like the name implies, it uses blood as fuel for its power. Soul suckers are the highest form of Corrupted. They feast on the lifeforces of others to prolong their lives, generally when faced with certain death.

Shades are void and immune to elven magic and are considered anomalies. As protectors of the kingdom, they serve Wara to cleanse the land of the Corrupted. Scripture states the goddess stripped them of emotions that may distract them from their duties; therefore, Shades are hollow, apathetic beings. Before their tenth birthday, Shades are taken to Kiji Village for training where they will spend five years in the surrounding forest. The survivors will earn their place in the all Shade battalions to fight the Corrupted.

The faithful are elves devoted to worshipping and spreading the word of the goddesses. Most are High Elves, traveling between the fanes to educate those living in rural areas of the kingdom.

The Ladies of Layetta are a group of women dedicated to spreading the love and word of their goddess, especially through sexual pleasure. Most of the faction lives close to Brevene, near Layetta's shrine and fane. They uphold Layetta's commandments and are often called upon if someone violates them, especially in the form of rape, where if the offender is found guilty, they will be burned and stoned to death. It is one of the greatest honors of those born under the sign of Layetta to become one of her ladies.

About Serpents

Originally from Arda, serpents live in the swampland kingdom southeast of Eskandor. They are cold-blooded creatures with a natural immunity to most poisons. As the largest population on Arda, serpents are known for their traditions, obedience, and love of sweet drinks.

They worship Shoresleen, the sky serpent, whose visage is similar to a dragon. Yanam is the religion's Heaven where Shoresleen awaits them with glory. The Morenlands are where the unworthy of Shoresleen shall wander aimlessly forever. Every night serpents gather in a den, a house of worship, where they praise Shoresleen for selecting them as the "chosen ones." A *daehekans* is the head of the den and leader of the family.

The Grand Den is the mightiest den in the kingdom. It is the place of worship for the royal family and their subjects. On Earth, there are many Grand Dens, one per major city with a large serpent population. Lower dens on both worlds follow the teachings of the Grand Den, wishing to ascend to its level. The Grand Den can elevate one den over another, making it more desirable to worshippers. The Grand Den can also bestow the *daehekans* and their family with special privileges only found in the Grand Den, such as access to their ancient gardens or archive of information passed through the generations.

To join a den, a family had to sacrifice one member to Shoresleen. A blood ritual would be performed by the *daehekans*, where a ceremonial blade would be plunged into the heart of the serpent, killing it thusly. Although, the sacrificial part of the ritual was outlawed in the kingdom centuries ago, serpents still use the ceremonial part as an initiation into a den.

Serpents have many traditions, one of which is arranged marriages. The selecting period, when families evaluate if their offspring are compatible and lucrative for both families, is called coupling. Serpents will not begin coupling until their mid-twenties, but most families start negotiations long before then—though no interactions between the offspring will be allowed before the required age of coupling as it would be improper and is punishable by shunning of the offending families.

A coupling lasts for one week. During this time the offspring will live together, share interests, and have sex. If the offspring find they are incompatible, the marriage will not move forward. Both families must agree the coupling is a success for the marrying of the offspring.

Like most class societies, serpents do not believe in marrying below stature. A member of the Grand Den will not marry a member of a lower den. The lower den member will have to ascend to be considered for coupling. Petitions of exception can be made to join the Grand Den for individuals and families of the religion, who wish to ascend without their den. These exceptions are highly vetted, but not impossible to achieve with the right connections.

About Vampires

Originally from Arda, the vampires lived in the region of the Shadowed Mountains. They are eternal, meaning they live unnaturally long lives and do not seem to age through that time. For millennia, they prospered alongside humans as factions until war led them into uniting as a nation. Many humans were force-turned during this time to build their army.

Their empire would last six hundred years until Emperor Zerth raged war against the other kingdoms. After devastating losses through the world, a council of the different nations decided the vampires were too dangerous to let live. Those who survived the war were hunted down and executed or given the option of passing through the "doors" found around the world. During those days these "doors" were believed to lead to Aegan's banishing realm. In more recent years, it was discovered they led to Earth.

The vampire kingdom is now referred to by Ardans as the Last Empire.

Traditionally, vampires live in groups called courts—something they regressed to when moving to Earth. A court is made up of lessers, greaters, and masters.

Lessers are the lowest tier of the vampire hierarchy, often referred to as "baby vampires." They possess elevated senses, like hearing and smell, night vision, regeneration, and increased speed and strength to that of humans. Some lessers can glamour, the ability to manipulate the mind, thoughts, and memories of others. The "call of a lesser" is a silent plea for a lesser to join a court. It can only be heard by a master. Lessers are the "working class" of the court.

Greaters are significantly more capable vampires, displaying signs of "master potential." These signs include: potent glamour, excessive speed and strength, and magical gifts. While magical abilities are not realized as a greater, it is one of the rarer signs to the path of becoming a master. It is a greaters responsibility to assist the master of the court with protecting, managing, and providing for the lessers.

Masters are the most powerful of vampires. When a vampire reaches master potential, it produces the venom to create more vampires. Masters can have many abilities that set them apart from lower tiers, especially with telekinesis and magical users. Not all masters gain this type of power, but all do gain the ability to communicate with their lessers through telepathic-like abilities.

An understudy is a newly realized master, who shadows a veteran master to learn how to lead a court. Most understudies begin their education as greaters. Fully realized, an understudy will have the ability to put theory into action. It is a crucial point in a master's life and will generally steer how they operate their court.

The turned are people who became vampires through bites of a master. It is the most common way for a person to become a vampire. The force-turned are those who were unlawfully turned against their will.

The natural-born are those born as vampires. It is exceptionally rare to find one.

Renfields, or flies, are humans that do the bidding of vampires in hopes to become one of them. Most of these individuals work for the Underground, the illegal operation of the preternatural community. They are named after the infamous character in Bram Stoker's *Dracula*.

A chosen child (or parent) is a vampire not turned or born to another but through phenomenon develops a bond stronger than any other vampire connection. There is no clear explanation for what causes the "phenomenon" or why it happens.

There are two vampire languages. The "old language" has been abandoned since the Last Empire and is no longer recognized or remembered. The newer vampire language is a simplified version of the old one, making the pronunciation and spelling of the words much different.

Vampires pray and make offerings to Moren, who created the undead and necromancy. She is considered the vampires' mother. The Moren Ways refer to instructions the goddess left for her creations. It is considered an archaic blueprint for courts. During the reign of the Last Empire, worship of Moren was forbidden.

Part of the vampire religion is the Undying. It is a ceremony performed to consensually kill a vampire. Originally, these ceremonies were performed by necromancers, using their magic to prevent the vampire from feeling pain and slipping off to death peacefully. Trust in necromancers thinned over time as they used their powers to control the undead rather than aid them. Currently, the Undying is only performed on vampires convicted of murder, have turned ravenous, or who's mental compacity has declined significantly due to living unnaturally long lives.

About the Author

Melissa Plunkett is a writer of all things fantasy and science fiction. She lives in Arkansas where she plots to take over the world with prose...or maybe just share interesting worlds with anyone that dare dive into an adventure.

To discover more of Melissa's stories:
Website: mdpthatsme.wixsite.com/melissaplunkett
Instagram: instagram.com/mdpthatsme
Twitter: twitter.com/mdpthatsme
TikTok: tiktok.com/@mdpthatsme

www.ingramcontent.com/pod-product-compliance
Lightning Source LLC
Chambersburg PA
CBHW020458260626
47156CB00006B/1777